THE SEVERED AND THE HUNTED

HEXSPHERE CHRONICLES BOOK 1

BECCA C. SMITH

Published by Red Frog Publishing a division of Red Frog Media

Visit our website at www.redfrogpublishing.com

First published in 2023

ISBN 9781949877588

Printed in the United States of America

CHAPTER 1
ELLA
5 years ago

Tick.

Tock.

Tick.

Tock.

Testing day was finally here.

Ella Buckley swung her legs nervously off the waiting room chair's ledge, her feet not quite reaching the floor. The cushion was made of vinyl, and the bottom of her thighs stuck to the surface. She chastised herself for wearing shorts, but it was the middle of summer and she had no idea the Caster Intelligence Unit office would have such uncomfortable sticky chairs. Dread coursed through her at the thought of jumping off her seat when her name was called. She'd either feel ripping pain, or it would sound like she'd farted. Both options made her stomach churn.

All this aside though, Ella didn't want to leave the chair.

Because once she did, her life would be over.

She scanned the room for the hundredth time, making sure she didn't make eye contact with any of the other kids, but a quick head count told Ella there were fifteen of them there. No adults. No parents.

No one to save you.

Saying good-bye to her parents before she entered this room had made her heart thunder in her chest because the three of them knew it could be the last time they ever saw each other.

Trying to distract herself, Ella focused on the room itself. CIU definitely didn't care about décor, that was for sure, with the tan-painted walls, six rows of the stupid black-and-chrome chairs with every two rows facing each other, TV monitors in each corner playing CIU recruitment videos on repeat, and a couple of paintings that were random colors. It felt more like an office building than a CIU testing room.

Ella had dreaded the day she turned twelve for this very moment. From the fidgety almost bored temperaments of the other kids in the room, she knew with certainty that no one was like her.

No one was a Dis-con.

The most feared and hunted humans on the planet.

Being a Dis-con meant Ella was immune to all spells, and since spells pretty much ran the world, that made her dangerous.

And CIU was about to find out.

Which meant . . .

Actually, she wasn't sure what it meant. No one had any idea what happened to Dis-cons once they were discovered by CIU. And it wasn't as if she could hide from CIU. They were everywhere, in every country and every major city. And testing at the age of twelve was a worldwide law. If anyone failed, they were never heard from again.

Taken.

The running theory being that it was either experimentation or death. Those seemed to be the only two options people ever thought were viable.

Ella shook her head, thinking through it logically. If it was death, then why not test everyone as a baby? As horribly morbid as it sounded, if a baby was tested and found to be a Dis-con, then CIU could end them there instead of letting the Dis-con have a chance of growing up.

No. It had to be experimentation.

Ella gulped self-consciously.

She hoped, anyway.

And twelve was the number CIU could stomach.

The CIU recruitment video stopped on the monitors, and a new video began. Ella groaned internally as she had seen this video hundreds of times before and there were just as many variations of it everywhere in the world. A visual representation of their motto for dealing with Dis-cons, the three Rs: Recognize, Run, and Reach out.

The first frame of the video was a close-up shot of a man with a jagged scar down the left side of his face, eyes menacing, lips snarling.

The narrator's voice was gritty and deep. "All throughout history, Dis-cons have shown what they're capable of."

A woman walked through a raging fire completely untouched, blade in hand, the fire parting, repelled by her body itself.

"Immune to all spells, a Dis-con can walk through any security system, any army, or any protective detail."

Ella had always thought the narrator's voice in that particular bit laid it on thick. It wasn't as if she had any goals of raiding another country or murdering a government official.

The video began playing a series of scenes after that. One of the pope in his bed as a Dis-con held her blade high, the cardinals around the pope casting spells that left the Dis-con untouched. With the swish of her blade, the scene cut to another Dis-con sneaking in through a window with a spelled alarm that didn't go off. He moved toward a sleeping woman in her bed, blade in hand, another swoosh and the carnage went on, ending with their motto—*Recognize, Run, and Reach out*—in bright flashing letters.

Ella was used to seeing footage and hearing stories like that. From Dis-con serial killers to assassins to super soldiers, the world stayed afraid of Dis-cons because of that kind of propaganda. Not that a lot of it wasn't true. There was a list of Dis-cons that was constantly being referenced to prove the point of how dangerous they were.

But Ella didn't feel dangerous.

And she certainly didn't want to hurt anyone.

Only Trackers had a worse reputation than Dis-cons. Terrorists that killed Dis-cons on sight, no matter what age.

And at least CIU publicly denounced them.

When Ella was ten, the news showed footage of a young boy of seven being smashed by a swing set that a Tracker flung at him with a telekinesis spell. She had puked every hour for the entire day and vowed never to go to another playground again. Her mom had held her all night since Ella couldn't think about sleeping after witnessing something like that.

The more Ella thought it through though, the more she believed CIU didn't kill.

Only Trackers were cruel enough for that.

She hoped so, anyway.

Ella's hands began to sweat the more she thought about it. She let her eyes wander around the room again, hoping to distract herself from the impending doom that awaited her behind the black metal door to her left.

"Ella Buckley. Please proceed through the door," a woman's voice announced through a speaker somewhere over Ella's head.

A loud clunk, then the black door swung open on its own.

Ella had seen five kids go through that door since she got there, and four had come back.

The fifth sauntered in with a slight pep in her walk.

What would these kids think when Ella didn't come back?

Shaking her head from morbid thoughts, Ella slid off the chair. No horrible leg ripping or fart sounds. One good thing at least.

The young girl eyed Ella as they passed each other. She gave Ella a friendly smile, as if to tell her that she had nothing to worry about, that the whole thing had been easy.

Easy for a normal person.

Not for a Dis-con.

Wiping her hands on her shorts, Ella walked through the doorway and into a hallway with stark white walls. The black metal door gently closed behind her.

"Follow the arrows, please." The woman's voice sounded from another invisible speaker above.

Ella's gaze lowered to the floor, where red arrow decals lay on top of gray square tiles. They stretched ahead about a hundred feet, then disappeared around the corner.

Gulp.

Walking forward, Ella kept a slow pace.

She had a plan.

As a Dis-con, Ella shouldn't have been able to perform any spells.

But she could. Well . . . she really wouldn't call it spell-casting since she didn't actually use her voice, but when someone was performing a spell, it was as if Ella could physically feel it. Like living air pressure pressing up against her, but since she was a Dis-con, it didn't affect her like it was intended to. Almost like two magnets set the wrong way so they'd repel each other. But on occasion, Ella had been able to control that pressure and use it as a type of telekinesis by pushing objects away from her.

She had no idea what it meant.

It was supposed to be impossible.

The very nature of being "disconnected" from spell-casting meant a Dis-con shouldn't be able to do anything when it came to spells.

But Ella could.

Her plan was to get the CIU tester to cast a spell, recite a telekinesis spell she'd memorized, and push against their incantation.

Turning the corner, she jolted to a halt at seeing an open door a few feet ahead of her.

A dead end.

Her destination.

Taking a deep breath, Ella walked through the doorway and into a small square room with blue walls, the same gray tiling on the floor, and a large mirror facing her. A woman with loosely waved hair and wire-framed glasses sat behind a metal table with a pad of paper and pen in front of her. Her tight thin lips barely smiled at Ella as she motioned for her to sit in the metal chair across from her.

Don't mess up.

Don't mess up.

After Ella situated herself, the woman said, "I'm Agent Ackerman. I'll be your Dis-con tester today. I have a few questions for you before we start."

"Okay," Ella squeaked. Yes, squeaked.

Agent Ackerman tried once again to smile, but it didn't look natural for her. Ella wished she'd stop.

"What is your full name?" she asked.

"Ella Eleanor Buckley."

"Do you know why Dis-cons are dangerous?"

"Because there's no defense against them."

Though Trackers killed Dis-cons just fine and they didn't always use spells, Ella wanted to argue.

"And why is that?"

"Because they are immune to spells."

Dis-cons also couldn't cast anything, so . . .

"Have you ever performed a spell?"

Lie.

"Yes."

"Has anyone ever cast a spell on you?"

Be convincing.

"Yes."

"Do you have a speech impediment that would affect your spell-casting?"

Ella's parents had worked with her for years trying to get her to perfect a stutter, but it was much harder than just repeating the first letter of random words over and over. CIU knew that Dis-cons used this tactic to hide the fact that they couldn't spell-cast, so they knew exactly what to listen for if a Dis-con claimed they had an impediment. And Dis-cons had to memorize every spell imaginable so they could fake a reaction, like Ella had had to do, so for her to add a speech impediment on top of that was too much. She never could get it right. When her and her parents realized she could push against spells, they instantly switched their focus to that. It would be solid proof for CIU.

A drop of sweat rolled down Ella's forehead, and she gently wiped it away with her hand.

Agent Ackerman either didn't notice or, more likely, didn't care. "I'm going to cast a spell on you, okay?"

This was it.

Ella prayed it was something she recognized.

But even if it wasn't, Ella had to push against it. She didn't know if she'd get another chance, and she certainly couldn't cast on her own.

Agent Ackerman's voice was gentle and soft.

At least it wasn't a Torment-hex. Those tended to be short and staccato. Not that Ella really thought CIU would torture children, but still. She had no idea what to expect.

A thrill washed through her.

She knew this one.

An eye-twitching spell.

Agent Ackerman was almost done.

Should she just twitch her eyes and not push against it?

But what if she asked her to perform a spell after? Even if she twitched her eyes, she'd still need to prove herself.

The heaviness of the air around Agent Ackerman's spell pushed itself toward Ella.

Now or never.

Ella said the words of a telekinesis spell right as Agent Ackerman finished casting, then pushed as hard as she could against the air of the spell around her, sending the CIU agent's pen flying at the mirror behind her.

Flexing every eye muscle possible, Ella faked her eyes twitching like she'd been hit by three casters.

"Whoa." Agent Ackerman reacted by leaning her head back. "I didn't mean to overcast like that." She quickly cast the counter spell, and Ella listened very carefully for any sign of trickery. Ella wouldn't put it past CIU to try to catch a Dis-con faking a reaction by mispronouncing a counter spell. But Ella heard every word correctly, and when Agent Ackerman finished incanting, Ella stopped twitching.

Agent Ackerman bent down to the ground and picked up her pen, then nodded to Ella. "I didn't tell you to cast anything."

She was going to puke.

"I figured you'd want me to. You didn't want me to?" Ella asked as innocently as she could.

To Ella's relief, Agent Ackerman shrugged. "You saved us both some time." She forced another awkward smile at Ella. "You may go."

Ella didn't move.

She froze in place.

Agent Ackerman tilted her head sideways, her smile finally turning into a genuinely amused one. "You can leave now, Ella. You passed."

The words didn't sound real in Ella's ears.

The agent now seemed to notice the sweat on Ella's forehead. "You might want to cast an anti-sweating spell."

That did it.

Ella leapt to her feet, then forced an awkward laugh. "No,

that's okay. I like sweating."

Before Agent Ackerman could react, Ella wheeled around and hurried out the door, following the backward arrows toward the door she had come in through. The black metal door swung open automatically as she neared it, the next kid heading toward her for his test. While she passed him by with a smile, a tear fell down Ella's cheek.

She did it.

She passed.

And puking still wasn't off the table.

Present Day

Ella really hoped no one could see her.

Sitting under the bleachers in the gymnasium was her spot. She had no idea the varsity basketball team was going to be practicing this early in the morning. School hadn't even started yet! Under the bleachers was her small little oasis away from pretty much everyone at Tristan High. Keeping her secret of being a Dis-con was a daily struggle. Passing the CIU test at twelve kept suspicion off her for the most part, but everyone knew that Dis-cons found ways to fool the test, including CIU. And worse, there were still the Trackers, which would mean instant death if they found her out.

The smooth rubbery texture of the floor had almost become comfortable at this point. Ella kept thinking she'd stuff a pillow in her backpack from home, but how awkward would that be if anyone ever caught her pulling it out? Besides, if she shifted around enough, it wasn't so bad. The trick to not being found was coming at a time when the bleachers were closed, which wasn't that hard considering the school only really opened them for games and assemblies. No one thought to look under the bleachers when they were closed. It was a tight fit, but cozy. Being right up against the wall at least gave Ella some kind of back support, but she didn't have enough room to stretch her legs out. She couldn't complain though; sitting cross-legged was more comfortable to her anyway.

The squeaks and thuds of sneakers and basketballs reminded Ella she wasn't alone.

No one saw her, thank goodness, but she tucked herself in closer to the wall just in case. The last thing Ella needed was to be called out for stalking the basketball team. It definitely would look kind of pervy for her to be hiding in the bleachers during practice, especially since it was Ella's first year at Tristan High, so no one really knew who she was. Moving to a new school her senior year hadn't been ideal. It wasn't as if she had any friends at her old school, but still, to start over for the last year of high school? It was just cruel. She'd arrived in September right as the school year started at least.

Shaking away thoughts of things she had no control over, Ella pulled out her prized possession from her backpack: Veil. It was the newest game console from Hex Solutions, and it was Ella's lifeline. In public, she was completely alone since her parents had a rule that she couldn't make any friends for fear of them finding out what she was, but at home, she'd been playing MMORPGs (Massively Multiplayer Online Role-Playing Games) since she was thirteen, so she had a handful of really great online friends. Of course, they knew almost nothing about her since she had to hide behind whichever avatar she'd created. But still, they were people she could talk to, play with, joke with, and just *be* . . . and it was glorious.

And Veil was the first *portable* gaming console, which meant Ella could play anywhere now. Including under the bleachers of her high school.

Flipping the on switch, Ella marveled at the fact that Veil didn't require spell-casting to activate. So many games and events Ella could never be a part of simply because it required a spell-activation or the actual game itself was incanted. Ella wondered how many other Dis-cons played console games for the same reasons as her. To at least have the illusion of friends.

After detaching the foldable headset embedded on the top of the oval-shaped console, Ella placed the headband on the crown of her head, lowering the two bars on either side until they lined up with her eyes.

On the screen of the device was the game Ella had been playing for the last two years, *Hexsphere*, a blinking start button under the title. The new expansion came out a couple of weeks ago, so everyone at school was buzzing about it—more arenas, dungeons, and player versus player battle grounds. With so many students playing, Ella often wondered if she was playing with anyone she'd recognize in person, but it was safer for her not knowing. Her parents would flip out anyway if game friends and real people ever overlapped. The game was already on its third expansion, and Ella was one of the first to sign up when it came out. Her parents agreed to pay the monthly subscription, it being a compromise for not having real-life friends.

When she hit start, the cramped bleachers and distant basketball players dissolved in front of her and her new surroundings built into place in full three-dimensional virtual reality. Ella stood at the starting point of the game, a nondescript industrial room with the most recent character she played shifting back and forth on her feet, ready to play. Underneath the character was her name, level, and class: FearlessGirl22, Level 40, Class Dis-con. FearlessGirl22 didn't look anything like Ella, with her short bright blue hair, crop T-shirt, and ripped blue jeans as opposed to Ella's real-life style of a floral princess-sleeved top, black jeans, and wavy black hair.

Tucking a strand of her hair behind her ear, Ella accidentally shifted Veil enough to disturb the imagery of the game, seeing a flash of the basketball players racing across the court oblivious to the girl under the bleachers. After she situated the headpiece properly once again, the game screen snapped back into view.

Hexsphere comprised of "evil" classes, Trackers or Dis-cons, and "good" classes, Skeins or Agents. Ella didn't bother with the "good" classes. She had one Tracker, just to try and figure out tactics to maybe use against them one day, but she pretty much stuck to playing Dis-cons.

On each side of the screen was the list of her other characters and their varying levels. The left side was labeled with *Trackers* and *Dis-cons*, the right side labeled *Skeins* and *Agents* (which was currently blank). FearlessGirl22 was the highest level on the Tracker/Dis-con side. Ella hovered over her highest level Tracker character, MindlessTwit85, which was a level 39. Clicking on the character brought her into the center of the frame, replacing FearlessGirl22. Where FearlessGirl22 looked well thought out and put together in terms of avatars, MindlessTwit85 wore all black, with blonde stringy hair and dark circles under her eyes.

"Not today, evil one," Ella mumbled under her breath.

She scrolled back to FearlessGirl22 and clicked *Select*, which replaced MindlessTwit85.

A quick black screen, then Ella stood at the house she'd created in-game for FearlessGirl22. She'd used almost every gold piece she'd ever earned playing to get it exactly the way she wanted. Standing right outside, Ella admired the dark stained horizontal slatted wood sides and the redwood shingles on the roof, all perfectly imperfect, giving it a kind of cozy patchwork design. Large windows lined the outside walls, meeting in the middle at a wooden door with the cutout of a round stained glass window depicting a cherry blossom tree with rich pink petals and black branches and trunk.

This home felt more like home than her real one, simply because her parents made Ella move every two years to be safe. Sometimes she wished she could be homeschooled. At least then they could stay in one place. But there were random tests for homeschooled kids, knowing it'd be the easiest to hide a Dis-con.

Her parents did everything to protect her, but she could see it as clear as day: they weren't happy.

At all.

The guilt was almost too much at times.

A prompt flashed in front of her: *Would you like to start your mission?*

"Not yet." Ella couldn't help talking out loud when she played. The immersive gameplay made it difficult to remember sometimes that it wasn't real.

Internally, she thought, *Just let me see my boy first.*

Walking up to the door, Ella made her character open the door and step inside.

The interior was simple, all one open floor plan with a set of stairs to the left that led to the master bedroom. Moving FearlessGirl22 with the console into the kitchen, there, in all his glory, she found . . .

Ash Torres.

He was too pretty for his own good. Was she a stalker? Maybe.

Creating an avatar of the boy she liked in a virtual reality video game might border on creepy, but really, Ella just liked looking at him and not because he was cute (because he was definitely that), but because he had a presence about him that she couldn't describe, a quiet confidence that she envied and an air of kindness that seemed to sparkle from his eyes.

Of course, Ella had never spoken to Ash—not the real one, anyway.

Because, yeah, that would be insanity. Creating a "game" Ash was far more reasonable and pretty much the only way Ella would ever be able to interact with him in her lifetime.

Not only because she was a Dis-con, but also because Ella liked Ash unreasonably, and she knew she would say something idiotic if given the chance.

These were facts.

Really, her *only* option was to continue to hang out with an avatar of him in the game. At least it was private. Home bases were a part of the game, and online players could only enter other players' domains if invited. And Ella had no intention of ever inviting anyone to her house. It was her sanctuary.

Another memo popped up over FearlessGirl22's head. *Alarm reminder: First class of the day starts in ten minutes.*

Ella groaned. Probably not enough time to finish a mission, but maybe she could get started on one?

Or maybe she could just have pretend breakfast with Ash and stare at his beautiful eyes.

Call her creepy. She didn't care. Ella would never be able to be with anyone anyway, so at least she could enjoy her game life.

A virtual life was better than no life.

Ella's heart fluttered.

Uh-oh.

One annoying side effect of being a Dis-con was that Ella's heart felt like it was skipping beats whenever someone incanted a spell at her or near her if it was powerful enough. It made sense since her body was essentially a physical deterrent to spell-casting, but it was such a jarring feeling when she was suddenly aware of her heartbeat and it wasn't beating properly.

Pulling off the headset, Ella stuffed Veil into her backpack, listening carefully for anyone casting a spell in the vicinity. For her heart to be skipping like this, the spell had to be a big one. Maybe someone was going to play some elaborate practical joke on the entire basketball team. It wouldn't be the first time. Only a few weeks ago, an unknown prankster cast a spell that made all the balls fly up to the ceiling. It took a Skein from the school district to get them all down.

On instinct, Ella stood in a panic, her head almost hitting one of the folded rafters. She barely had enough room to sidle out from the bleachers, but her gut told her she needed to, her ears finally picking up the faint sounds of the caster incanting the spell.

Ella cleared the bleachers. Her back faced the double metal doors that served as the entrance and exit to that wing of the gym.

The basketball players were oblivious as they continued to play.

The voice grew louder, but Ella couldn't see anyone anywhere.

Hairs raised on her arms as the voice grew even louder: staccato and harsh. Only destructive spells sounded like that.

Ella's head spun, and she grew faint as her heartbeats skipped uncontrollably. She heard the blood pumping irregularly in her ears: *ga-glump, ga-ga glump, ga-ga-ga glump*.

This had never happened to Ella before.

She'd never been around a spell that powerful.

The invisible force of it bumped up behind her and beside her at once, the pressure of it pushing her forward toward the players on the court.

Ella watched in horror as all ten players dropped to the ground with loud thuds.

No more squeaking sneakers.

Basketballs dribbled on their own until they rolled away.

Then, just as suddenly, the pressure stopped.

Ella's heart began to regulate itself.

She searched everywhere, trying to find the person that had cast the spell, but nothing. It was as if the voice had come from the air itself.

Bile reached the top of Ella's throat. The players lay on the ground, their skin blistering as if someone had poured boiling water all over their bodies.

No screams.

No movement.

Terror filled Ella.

Were they dead or just unconscious?

Her first instinct was to run and help, find out if they were okay . . .

But then it would be obvious to everyone that she was a Discon since the spell hadn't affected her. Or they'd blame her and think she was the one that had cast the spell.

Ella's fear froze her.

And then the screams started.

Relief was the first thing Ella felt, relief that they were alive, but it was quickly replaced by horror at their shrieking. She pushed aside all her fear and raced to their sides to check and see what she could do to help them.

The blisters weren't as bad close up, but they still looked incredibly painful, and they were all covered from head to toe. Lizzie Trent was the worst as her blisters were filled with a watery puss that oozed out of the thin skin of the pustules. But Ralph Vereen, who lay next to Lizzie, was a close second with a few puss-filled blisters of his own.

Ella had a hard time keeping her breakfast in her stomach at this point.

The smell.

She'd never experienced anything like it. The only thing that came to mind was rotted food at the bottom of a garbage can.

Lizzie grabbed Ella's forearm and paused, as if waiting for something to happen.

Waiting for it to blister?

She hoped not.

Because it wasn't going to happen.

Finally, Lizzie croaked, "Ambulance . . ." then dropped her hand back down to her side.

She probably hated Ella for not coming up with that one on her own.

Ella didn't know what she had planned to do to help in the first place, but calling an ambulance was a big "duh." She quickly dialed the National Emergency Line.

"NEL. State your emergency," the operator said in an almost casual tone.

"I heard someone cast a spell, and the entire basketball team is covered in blisters or burns, I can't tell which. We're in the gymnasium at Tristan High," Ella sputtered, breathless.

The woman's voice immediately tightened. "We'll send Emergency Hex Technicians and a Caster Intelligence Unit immediately. In the meantime, do not touch the victims. If it's a contagion spell, we don't want it to spread. And keep anyone else from touching the victims as well. Do you understand?"

Ella looked down at her forearm where Lizzie had touched her, but there was nothing.

Only she knew that it didn't mean it *wasn't* a contagion spell since she was a Dis-con.

Ella answered, "I understand."

"Good. Both units should be there within ten minutes. Can you hold people off until then?" The operator talked slowly, making sure Ella understood every command.

"Yes. I can do that," she answered.

The operator hung up the phone, and Ella waited for the circus that was sure to come.

Standing amongst the writhing basketball players, she was completely helpless. None of them were sitting up or standing. They just kept moaning and screaming in pain.

Ella addressed the group of players, "Help is coming . . . I'm so sorry. I don't know what else I can do."

She'd never felt so useless in her life.

And finally the screams had drawn the attention Ella dreaded.

High school students rushed inside the gymnasium, faces worried, then shocked, then terrified at what they witnessed.

At that moment, Ella's worst fear came to fruition.

All eyes turned toward her.

And every single one of them stared at her with the surety that she was the monster who'd cast this.

Ella was in serious trouble now.

CHAPTER 2
WREN

Wren Martis had to get the burns off her hands and arms quickly.

That went . . . well.

As well as could be expected.

A blister popped on her arm, and Wren had to fight back the urge to scream from the intense pain. One side effect of casting a spell that strong: there was always some kind of blowback.

But Wren had hit her target.

Lizzie Trent—or whatever her real name was.

Lizzie was a Tracker.

The Tracker that had decapitated her Dis-con mother and laughed while she did it.

Wren had been thirteen years old, only four years ago. It felt like an eternity.

It was nice to have any name if Wren was being honest. Before finding Lizzie at the school, Wren had only referred to her as Evil Incarnate. Giving an actual name to the murderous she-witch after four years of searching only made Wren's mission feel more real, more focused. But Trackers never used their real names. Lizzie Trent was only her most recent alias. And Lizzie might have been pretending to be Wren's age, but she knew she was in her twenties at least.

The plague spell wasn't enough to kill Lizzie—it wasn't meant to—but Wren would get there eventually. She wanted Lizzie to suffer first. Death was too easy.

Lizzie would die eventually though, or Wren would die trying.

Looking around to make sure no one was in sight, Wren recited a healing spell. The rush of cold relief flooded through her arms. Within seconds, Wren's hands and arms were clean. At casual glance, even a Skein, CIU or otherwise, wouldn't be able to know she had cast that plague spell. Skeins were the highest rank of spell-casters out there, and Wren knew CIU never hired anyone less than that. And being that they had offices in every country and city around the world, that was quite a feat.

But CIU would be spell-locking the school down with a sealing-dome as soon as they arrived per protocol on an attack like this, and their rules dictated that they'd have to cast a signature-reveal spell on each and every person in the school. A spell that would show if a caster's spell signature matched the attack spell, which under normal circumstances would worry Wren. But she had invented a spell that could actually *change* her spell signature—something no one had ever thought was possible.

But Wren was full of impossibles.

She'd never put the spell to the test before though. Today was the day. Her backup plan if the spell failed was to break free from

CIU by any means necessary if she had to. It wasn't an ideal option, but it was an option. It was worth it to see if her spell worked.

And the plague spell might not have gone to plan, but Wren knew one thing now for sure:

Ella Buckley was a Dis-con.

Wren wanted to be angry at Ella for blocking the true effects of her spell (because let's face it, Ella's presence in the gym shattered the spell to bits so that all the players got hit and not just Lizzie like she had planned), but now that Wren knew Ella was a Dis-con, she'd protect her at all costs.

Like she'd promised herself.

Like she'd promised her mother's decapitated head and body as they were dragged away by Lizzie.

Glancing out the window, Wren watched as the Caster Intelligence Unit cars and the Emergency Hex Technician trucks arrived in the parking lot. Only a few CIU agents headed for the gym with the EHTs, but the remaining dozen or so began incanting.

The floor shook slightly under Wren's feet as the CIU's sealing-dome locked into place. A large opaque protective barrier now draped over the entire school and a good portion of the surrounding lawn. It was used to isolate crime scenes as well as potentially trap the perpetrator inside, like Wren. After incanting, the CIU agents began setting up an exit station next to a door-sized opening to the dome. The only way in and out.

Peeling her eyes away from the window, then craning her neck down both ends of the hallway to make sure no one was around, she began to cast her homemade spell that would change her spell signature. Wren's words weaved around her, transforming the very essence of who she was. She could almost see the quantum waves twist and layer around her, like displaced air.

Wren finished incanting and hoped the spell would work.

Slowly, she walked toward the main hallway and pretended to be curious about the CIU and EHTs' sudden arrival in case any students walked by. The EHTs would be healing the players soon, and the CIU agents that went into the gym would be performing a re-creation spell, several times most likely. But Wren wasn't going to show up on any re-creation spell. She'd made sure of that. She'd created her own hiding spell as well, and it was better than anything on the market and, if she was being honest, well beyond Skein level.

No.

Wren's main worry was for Ella.

She hoped Ella ran.

She hoped they didn't find her.

Because if CIU discovered she was a Dis-con?

If Lizzie did?

Wren would need to keep Ella safe.

Focus: today's mission.

Attacking Lizzie had only been the first part. Wren had known that CIU would lock down the school and send everyone home after the attack. She counted on it.

Wren had been following Lizzie outside of school for weeks now, but the Tracker kept her cover well, not doing anything out of the ordinary, and Wren had never been able to figure out where Lizzie lived. She'd somehow always elude Wren at night. Wren had even cast a spell to break into the school directory, but of course, there was no address listed.

So Wren had cast the plague spell for two reasons. One: to create enough of a connection with Lizzie to perform a tracking spell (connections were vital to making them work). And two:

Wren needed to spook Lizzie enough to make contact with a higher rung in the ladder of the Trackers. If she was lucky, maybe she'd find out another member of the Trackers' elite: the Order of Eleven. A council of eleven of the top-tier Trackers. They had an odd number so that there were never any ties in votes for whatever nefarious thing they were voting on, and most of the members were hidden, very rich, and usually a higher-up in some kind of government position. They had money, so their network was huge. Wren had figured out who eight of them were; the other three were still a mystery.

Wren's plan for Lizzie though was to go home and combine two of her most powerful spells: tracking and quantum phasing.

And Lizzie wasn't the only Tracker at Tristan High either. Rachel Fen was for sure and possibly Shara Ralter. Like Lizzie, Rachel wasn't her real name or, most likely, Shara's. But apparently, Lizzie and Rachel had been using those names for a few years now, and Wren had yet to find out what their true names were. Trackers were like that. Cowards and hypocrites that hid behind aliases. Proudly killing Dis-cons with laughter and glee while at the same time hiding themselves in glamour spells while they did it.

Wren still needed to confirm that Shara was a Tracker though. She was pretty sure she was, but Wren would never kill anyone that didn't deserve it, so she had to be positive first. Wren hadn't technically killed anyone yet. She wanted Lizzie to be her first. But if Ella was in danger, she'd kill whichever Tracker she needed to.

Shara kept to herself mostly, but she had been spying on Ella for a while now. It was what alerted Wren to the possibility that Ella might be a Dis-con. Wren supposed she could have done her own experimentation on Ella by casting a spell on her to see if it worked, but even the slightest possibility that Ella could have been a Dis-con dissuaded her from doing that. What if someone would have seen? Wren would never expose a Dis-con. Ever. She'd die first.

Things hadn't happened the way Wren wanted today—why of all days was Ella in the gym when she cast her attack on Lizzie?—but it was nice to know for certain what Ella truly was.

The hallways were still empty as Wren walked toward her locker. Tristan High was set up as two big indoor hallways stacked on top of each other with classrooms and lockers on either side. Since it was two levels, there were two sets of staircases located at each end of the halls, and the building itself held about a couple thousand students, roughly five hundred in each graduating class.

The rubber soles of Wren's shoes squeaked every few steps as she walked across the cheap linoleum floor laid out in blue squares. Some squares were chipped and curling in a few places, and Wren didn't care to admit how many times she'd tripped on the curled edge of a particular linoleum square in front of Hex Lab. Counting down the metal lockers on her right side, she was still a ways away from her own.

The silence was eerie.

Probably because Wren knew she was the cause of it.

Glancing at the empty hallway, she realized that even if the screams hadn't drawn everyone to the gym, the arrival of CIU and the giant sealing-dome locking them all in definitely would have.

Wren looked around for Ella to see if she had made it out as well, but she worried Ella somehow got stuck in there.

Lizzie might suspect Ella, but Wren wouldn't know until she saw the Tracker again. The impact of Wren's plague spell was significantly reduced because of Ella, but those bursting pustules on Lizzie's body brought a smile to Wren's face. From the blowback blisters alone, Wren knew she had created something really painful.

Wren kicked a stray pencil on the ground in frustration. She hadn't wanted anyone but Lizzie to get hurt. She knew there was nothing she could do about it now, but it still made her stomach turn at the thought.

"Hey, Wren, did you finish the homework for Hex Lab?" A voice sounded behind her.

Moira Kurt walked up to her, backpack levitating closely behind. She was a junior, but her spell skills were off the charts—almost as good as Wren's. Almost. Moira was the only person Wren talked to at school just because . . . well . . . because Moira kind of forced her to. Wren was pretty sure that once Moira recognized someone at her spell level, she saw someone who understood her. Plus, Wren liked her. She seemed as if she was a genuinely good person and eager to learn, which Wren had a lot of respect for. Wren wasn't as open about her skill level because she wanted to blend in and not draw unnecessary attention to herself, but Moira was more observant than the others and had figured it out.

Dressed in a loose red polka-dot crop T-shirt and fitted black jeans, Moira always looked put together. Sometimes, Wren was a bit jealous considering she pretty much wore the same thing every day: black T-shirt and beat-up jeans. There were more important things than clothes and looking good though, and dressing like she did helped her blend in better anyway.

Moira's long hair fell over her eyes, and she tucked it behind her ear, then glanced at Wren expectantly.

Oh yeah. Moira had asked her a question.

"I did finish my homework, but I kind of half-assed it," Wren answered.

The last thing she wanted to think about was second period,

especially since she knew school wasn't happening today, but Moira seemed oblivious.

Students that had arrived via the parking lot when CIU cast the sealing-dome spell passed them by, practically running toward the gym, and Wren wondered how Moira didn't notice that anything was out of the ordinary.

Pulling out a two-inch-high miniaturized dollhouse from her backpack, Moira showed it to Wren. "It was my mom's dollhouse when she was a kid. I found it in the attack. You think Mr. Finley will like it?" Her face scrunched with worry.

Seriously. Wren just couldn't right now.

As impressed as she was with Moira's work (the interior details alone were perfection), Wren didn't care about Hex Lab and shrinking spells, though she did have her assignment in her locker. She'd shrunk her dad's broken-down truck he had parked in the backyard. He worked night shifts, so he wouldn't notice its absence while he was sleeping during the day, and the neighbors were probably happy the eyesore was gone.

Wren hated that truck.

Her mother was murdered in that truck, which was why her father wouldn't let go of it. It was like he felt that his wife was a part of it somehow.

A rage boiled in Wren's veins.

Lizzie needed to die.

She'd witnessed the murder with her own eyes, though Lizzie, like every other Tracker, thought she was perfectly disguised with a powerful glamour spell. But Wren had seen through the blank face Lizzie thought she was displaying, using a counter spell of her own. Because Wren had been preparing for that day since she found out her mother was a Dis-con. She had just hoped it would never come. And Wren had tried to protect her mother, but being a Dis-con, her mother was un-protectable by spells.

Lizzie Trent had murdered her with no remorse. No regret. Only sheer happiness. Her giggle as she decapitated Wren's mother, then dragged the head and body away like it was butchered meat—it was etched in her memory forever.

And Wren planned on laughing the exact same way when she finally ended Lizzie's life.

She tried to shake her head clear of the memory, but her pulse raced out of control. Wren glanced at the students heading for the gym. "Moira, are you serious right now? You haven't noticed the giant sealing-dome outside and everyone running to the gym?"

Moira's eyes widened, and she raced to the window next to them. Staring at the opaque dome and the flashing lights of the CIU cars through the window, her eyes widened even more. "Holy. What the heck happened?"

"I don't know. I was on my way to my locker when I felt the dome seal into place," Wren lied.

"You think it was Trackers? That we might have had a Dis-con in school?" Moira's face had gone pale.

Wren didn't like being compared to Trackers, and she also didn't like that she couldn't read Moira's expression. Was Moira afraid of the Trackers or the possibility of a Dis-con? Wren couldn't be friends with a Dis-con hater. If she found out that was the case, Wren would cut Moira off completely. But instead of asking Moira, Wren played it cool and shrugged. "I don't think so. It looks like CIU is setting up a testing station at the exit, which means they'll be casting a signature-reveal spell."

Moira nodded in understanding. "So it was some kind of attack spell. Yeah, definitely not a Dis-con." She glanced up at

Wren, then toward the students headed for the gym. "I'm going to go check it out. Meet you near the exit?"

"Yeah, sure. I'm going to get my stuff from my locker."

Moira left towards the gym, and Wren kept her distance from the remaining straggling students around her, talking to no one. Wren had established her loner persona pretty well at this school. Though she'd only been there a few months, her memory spell made everyone believe she'd been there for three years.

Except for Lizzie and Rachel.

The one surgery all Trackers underwent was the attaching of quantum repellent gear to their temporal lobes, which essentially meant no memory spell would work on them.

But that had been a part of Wren's plan to remove suspicion from herself when moving to the school they were stationed at. Wren needed them to believe she hadn't wanted to move there so they wouldn't suspect her.

The public might not know about these surgeries, but Wren did.

Full-on brain surgery. Cracking open the skull, finding the right section of brain, and placing the miniaturized gear there with the sole purpose of affecting that area so they couldn't be attacked by certain spells. It wasn't a little ironic that they were essentially making themselves Dis-cons, when their only purpose in life was to wipe out Dis-cons. But unlike Dis-cons, their spell-casting ability was unaffected by the repellent gear and most of their Trackers were Skein level. Dis-cons with powers—it was basically what they were striving for if they sat and thought about it for a second.

To be safe from *their* spells though, Wren had devised a counter spell for anyone who performed a mass memory spell on her, so she knew for a fact that Lizzie and Rachel had arrived a couple months before she did, though everyone else thought they'd known them since grade school.

Here was the timeline Wren knew so far: Ella had arrived at the beginning of the school year in September; Lizzie and Rachel arrived two months after her in the beginning of November, Shara quickly after them in mid-November, and Wren a month and a half later in January right after holiday break.

Being that it was the end of March, that clocked Wren as having been at Tristan High for three months now.

But why? Why had Lizzie and Rachel arrived two months after Ella? It didn't seem like Ella was even on their radar from what Wren had noticed. What possible assignment could have brought them to Tristan High?

It didn't matter.

Her mission was what mattered.

But she still needed to lie low.

And lying low had become a full-time job since her mother was killed.

She had moved three times in the last four years.

The first time to Philadelphia because she thought she'd found a lead on Lizzie's (back then, Evil Incarnate) whereabouts, but it was a dead end.

Larry (her Tracker babysitter she wasn't supposed to know about, assigned to keep an eye on her after Lizzie murdered her mom) had traveled with her, though he still thought he was being stealthy.

Her and her father stayed in Philly for almost two years before she found another lead in Columbus, Ohio, but that turned out to be nothing as well. And yet again, Larry followed.

The last place was Portland, Oregon, when the news reported

the decapitation of a Dis-con. Wren had stared at the footage for hours and had convinced herself that the killer was Evil Incarnate. Since the face of the Tracker was glamoured blank, it was impossible to tell who it really was, but she made her dad move there regardless. Again, Larry followed.

But after working for months on counter spells to dodge Larry and going to the site of the murder with a holographic video of the Tracker killing their victim, Wren was able to reveal that the Tracker wasn't Lizzie.

It was actually a lucky break finding Lizzie in the first place. Wren had followed Larry one night after school when he had thought Wren was safe at home like she had done many times before. The idiot led her right to Evil Incarnate. Wren still remembered how her heart had raced when seeing the face of her mother's killer. She had thought it would never beat normally again.

At that meeting, Wren had found out she was at Tristan High and her alias was Lizzie Trent.

Wren had known it would be tricky to arrive at the school without suspicion.

The daughter of a Dis-con suddenly showing up at the high school they were stationed at would be pretty suspicious. Even though Trackers were arrogant and could never conceive that anyone would be able to break their signature blank-face glamour spell they cast while murdering Dis-cons, Wren still wanted to make sure that neither Lizzie nor Rachel paid her any attention.

So she enacted her plan.

When she found out Lizzie's location was Los Angeles back in Portland, Wren made sure Larry followed her home to "witness" a confrontation on the phone with her father. Her dad had shut down after her mother's murder, leaving Wren utterly alone to deal with her death, so she was never able to get him to do anything in person, but he was always willing to be a silent lump of coal on the other end of a phone call. Wren pulled out all the stops, fake crying about having to leave her home in Oregon and how she'd already moved so many times in the last four years and didn't want to live in Los Angeles. Then whining at the unfairness that her father's work had insisted he transfer. Wren had heatedly yelled into the phone that she would cast a memory spell on the school in LA to make them think she'd been there three years already so she'd fit in and not be the "new" girl.

The phone call served two purposes: one, to convince Larry the move was real (she was seriously wondering how he fell for her excuses every single time) and two, to tell her dad they needed to move and he needed to apply for the transfer.

As soon as she arrived at Tristan High, she cast the memory spell to sell her story, knowing full well it wouldn't work on Lizzie and Rachel. Though just for an experiment, Wren had added something extra to her memory spell, just to see if she could break past the quantum repellent gear on Lizzie's and Rachel's temporal lobes. But from everything she'd witnessed so far though she was positive it hadn't work on them.

So her ruse had worked.

The recon she'd already done on Lizzie and Rachel proved to her that they only viewed her as a secondary assignment. Larry strangely hadn't followed her on this move. Too many Trackers in one school? Wren didn't know. But Lizzie and Rachel seemed to have taken over Larry's *job*. Simply keeping an eye on a kid whose mom they killed. Wren's blood boiled thinking of how amused Lizzie had been when she recognized Wren. How she almost wished Wren knew it had been her, just to see Wren's face.

Lizzie would see Wren's face all right.

When Wren was slicing Lizzie's head off her shoulders.

Taking a deep breath, Wren focused on the fact that Ella was a confirmed Dis-con. She wanted to talk to Ella directly to see if her extra flourish she had added to the memory spell had had any effect on *her*. If it had, that would be huge. It would mean the effort Wren had been putting into spell-casting since her mother died was working. Because spells that would work on Dis-cons could not only possibly protect them, but also might potentially work on Trackers in the future.

Wren didn't want to get ahead of herself though.

Concentrate.

CIU was shutting down the school, and Wren had just laid out the entire varsity basketball team.

Wren's heart sped up again.

She needed to calm down.

She couldn't look guilty.

CIU agents would be coming in at any moment to wrangle everyone toward the exit and testing.

Taking in deep breaths, Wren tried to steady the internal imbalance of her body.

Wren hated it when she got like that. When her emotions were so strong her motor functions didn't align properly with her brain. Breathe. Left foot forward. Right foot forward. Breathe. Left foot forward. Right foot forward. Breathe.

Her heart began to slow down to normal.

She arrived at her locker, spelling the lock open. The school didn't like that and had restrictions against it, but Wren didn't really care at the moment. Opening the metal door, she examined the contents inside: schoolbooks, backpack stuffed on top, and . . .

the miniaturized truck parked in front of the books. She stared at it for a few seconds, her pulse starting to pound again. Taking it in her hand, Wren squeezed her fingers around it until she could feel the sharp metal edges and corners breaking her skin.

Her mother had died in that truck.

In this now tiny toylike piece of metal.

Wren decided then and there she would never re-enlarge it. Maybe removing the only thing her father seemed to care about from sight would provoke him into saying or doing anything. Part of her longed for it. She couldn't remember the last time he'd said more than a sentence to her. It didn't seem to affect his work though, and thankfully, there were offices in every major city, so transferring was easy when Wren wanted to move them. Like a machine, he left every evening for his night shift, then came home every morning and went to bed. Every day. Every single day.

The only upside to his zombie behavior was that he let Wren decide where they lived and how they lived. He never argued, he never said anything, simply packed everything up and moved to wherever she said they had to move. He obviously knew on some level what Wren's mission was, but he couldn't wake up enough to care.

Maybe he was hoping she died too.

After pulling down the backpack, Wren stuffed the miniaturized truck inside without glancing at it again, then placed all her books inside as well. She noticed the blood on her hand from the dozens of cuts the tiny truck had caused and incanted a healing spell. Wiping the rest of the blood on the inside of her backpack, she cast a quick levitation spell so she no longer had to carry the heavy load. The mundaneness of the actions helped her calm down again.

Closing her locker, Wren turned toward the exit.

The halls were empty. At this point, everyone was crowded around or near the gym or waiting in line to be tested at the exit. Their backs were visible from both locations, and she was still a good two hundred feet away.

Wren disassociated from it, even though she was the one who'd caused it.

But she knew everyone would be fine. Wren was the one who had cast the spell, so she knew extensively the damage it did. It would have done a lot more damage if it hadn't scattered, but even at full power, it wouldn't have killed Lizzie. It would have hurt her a lot more than it did though. On that, today was a disappointment. Wren didn't care how crazy that sounded. If it meant she was insane, then so be it.

Lizzie deserved to die.

This was a fact.

But above that, *all* the Trackers had to be destroyed.

And Wren needed to be the one to do it.

CHAPTER 3
ELLA

Ella's entire body had tightened into a giant knot of tension when she heard the thump of the sealing-dome a few moments before. She'd recognized the sound instantly not from personal experience, but from her game *Hexsphere.* She noted to herself that the creators of the game had nailed it on the sound effects.

Impatiently staring at the door, Ella actually wanted CIU to walk through at this point.

It had to be better than the mob of glaring students looking as if they wanted to tear her to pieces. She decided to speak before they swarmed over and mauled her. "Obviously, you know CIU is here from the sealing-dome. The varsity basketball team has been attacked, and they may be contagious, so I was advised to have everyone stand back!"

The word *contagious* seemed to have the proper effect, whether they trusted her or not.

Rachel Fen, though, didn't appear to want to take orders from Ella.

Big surprise.

"How do we know you didn't do this? That you're not killing them now?" Rachel stepped forward.

Rachel Fen was a mean girl through-and-through. Ella still didn't understand how Rachel and Lizzie had gotten so popular so fast, especially since they were so mean. Rachel and Lizzie were new to Tristan High, even newer than Ella was. They had only started school a couple months after her, but everyone acted as if they had grown up with the two girls. They had been instantly popular, probably because of their good looks and perfect bodies. Ella had been lucky so far to not register on Rachel's attack radar, but now, standing over the writhing varsity basketball team, she was pretty sure Rachel was taking notice.

Not good.

Why hadn't she run again?

Stupidity?

Fair.

But no.

Potential Rachel Fen torture or not, Ella had stayed because these students might have died if she hadn't done something. Ella might've been forced into public isolation for being a Dis-con, but it didn't mean she shouldn't care.

The victims' screams transitioned into moans. That was something at least. Some of them were attempting to sit up, Lizzie being one of them.

Trying to sound confident but not really succeeding at all, Ella said to Rachel and the crowd, "CIU will be coming through those doors any second, and you know they'll cast a signature-reveal spell on me, if you're suspicious. And their Skeins will perform a re-creation spell, so stay back." Ella wasn't exactly happy about that, but it was the truth. Luckily, even as a Dis-con, she didn't have to worry about the signature-reveal spell not working on her. The spell would simply come up blank, which translated to a non-match. It had happened to her once in the tenth grade when Jenny Filnicky had used a spell to cheat on her history exam. Mr. Trainer cast a signature-reveal spell on every single one of the students. When he'd reached Ella, he performed the spell, then waved her aside. No match, so he moved on. Ella had almost yelped in relief but managed to keep a neutral expression.

Swallowing hard in fear, Ella instantly thought about how her parents were going to be furious when they found out she'd put herself in this position.

But she couldn't think about that now.

Most everyone there looked relieved that CIU was there and on its way. The fact that CIU was pretty much everywhere in the world was terrifying for Ella, but for most people, she could only assume it made them feel safe and protected.

Rachel eyed her with some doubt though, so Ella added, "Whatever this is, it really might be contagious."

Lizzie spoke, and her voice cracked from screaming. "Please, Rachel, stay back. You don't want this." Lizzie's and Rachel's eyes met, and Ella swore they communicated some kind of message to each other.

Apparently it must have been for Rachel to back off, because she took a step back. It surprised Ella to see Rachel's furrowed brows crinkle in genuine concern for Lizzie's well-being, but Rachel's eyes were still trained on Ella.

Lizzie's warning was also enough for the other students, and they moved back a few feet, closer to the exit but not leaving entirely. The voyeur instinct in them all waited to see what CIU would do.

Ella noticed Rachel mumbling something to herself. Was she casting a spell? Concentrating, Ella focused on Rachel's mouth and the words spilling out of it until she barely made out a slight displacement of air. Definitely casting something. But what? No flutters, so it wasn't directed at her, thank goodness. If Rachel wanted revenge thinking Ella was guilty, now was the time to do it before any adults or CIU walked in.

But nothing.

Whatever spell Rachel had cast didn't reach her, so it must have been something for herself. Or for the other students? Why was this worrying Ella so much?

Because she was standing over Rachel's best friend, and from her intense glare, Ella knew she blamed her.

To Ella's relief, Mr. Velenti and Ms. Busby raced inside the gymnasium, obviously alerted by the noise and commotion. Mr. Velenti was the vice principal and pretty much the enemy of all students, and Ms. Busby was the principal: hard personality, but fair.

Ms. Busby's eyes met Ella's. "What's this about? What's happening? Where's CIU? There's a giant sealing-dome over the entire school!" Her attention then focused on the monstrous blister on Lizzie's face, and her hand went to her mouth. "Ella, what happened?"

"Some kind of virus spell," Ella responded quickly. "Listen, I don't know what's taking CIU so long—"

She didn't have to finish her sentence as four CIU agents entered the room, along with five Emergency Hex Technicians.

The EHTs immediately went to work on the basketball team, using protection spells to quarantine the victims, then healing spells to rid them of the burns and blisters.

Ella's heart began to flutter again, but it was a lot less intense than before.

Finally, she walked away from the varsity team. An EHT quickly cast a quarantine spell on her, and Ella pretended to stagger from the jolt of the spell as she saw the basketball players do.

Ella had her act down to a science at this point. She'd had to memorize so many spells and the physical reactions they caused, just so she could fake it if people cast spells on her. At least the heart flutters gave her a slight heads-up. Not that this had happened a lot in her life. Another good reason to not be the center of attention . . . like today.

She was so screwed.

Ella's reaction satisfied the paramedic though, and he moved on to another victim.

The CIU agent in charge approached Ella as the other agents cast a roping spell to hold the students and the two adults back.

"Agent Alvarez," the agent introduced herself. She was rigid in her stance, all business. Pretty but stern, hair pulled back in a tight bun, fitted suit that flattered her curves. "Hold still." Agent Alvarez cast the signature-reveal spell on Ella, then nodded her head. "You're clear." She said it loud enough for the crowd to hear, though Ella could tell from Rachel's evil eye squint that Ella was still suspect number one. Alvarez nodded toward the basketball team. "Were you the one who found the victims?"

"Um, yes." Such confidence. She wouldn't suspect Ella had something to do with this at all.

But Alvarez's face softened a bit as if she'd dealt with nervous witnesses her whole life. "What's your name?"

"Ella Buckley," Ella uttered, a definite shake to her voice. Annoying.

"No need to be nervous. I know how terrifying this must've been for you, seeing your classmates attacked like this, but I need you to focus and remember everything you heard and saw. Agent Gilroy will perform a re-creation spell, but as I'm sure you know, there's no sound since we don't want the spell to be repeated, so I need you to be our ears. When did you find the students?" Agent Alvarez spoke clearly and calmly, which put Ella a little more at ease.

Ella wasn't sure what to say though. She might have to lie. Because if she didn't, they'd figure out she was immune and a Dis-con.

Ella decided a half-truth was the way to go. Even with a re-creation spell, her place in the bleachers was close enough to the door that she might be able to fake that she'd come in through the hallway outside if it came to that.

After taking a deep breath, Ella said, "I heard a voice. A whisper, actually." It had been the fluttering of her heart that had alerted her, but the voice came soon after, so it wasn't much of a lie. "It must have been the tail end of the spell, because when I raced over here, I wasn't affected by it at all." Nice. She didn't have to mention her location. Well done.

But would Alvarez buy it?

The CIU agent that Alvarez had referred to as Agent Gilroy began to incant. Ella had watched enough crime shows to identify a re-creation spell, so there was no need to pretend to have a reaction. Of course in the shows, the spells were mostly cast in Varian, the alternate language used to verbally recite spells without actually casting anything. And sometimes, the writers would make up the words completely while making them sound close enough to the real spell for anyone to recognize it.

Before everyone's eyes, a ghostlike hologram appeared all around them. The transparent basketball players played their game, moving through the current players on the floor and the EHTs.

It was fascinating and surreal, but most of all, it was terrifying.

Ella tried so hard not to stare at the bleachers, but she had to know if she'd been seen by anyone in the re-creation spell.

Her shoulders relaxed as Agent Gilroy's spell focused only on the players. The outer rim of the gymnasium was fuzzy, thank goodness. Now that she thought about it, re-creation spells were like that. The spell itself fed off of the energy used for the attacking spell and the matter it created. Ella guessed the fact that she was practically anti-magic herself obviously helped her at that moment.

Ella's entire body tensed watching the players get hit by the spell in the re-creation. Like a cloud of disease and suffering, the incantation's power hit the students all at once. Their holographic mouths opened in silent horror as burns and blisters formed on their skin until they all fell to the floor, unable to stand from the pain.

Seconds later, Ella's translucent form ran up to Lizzie and Ralph. Lizzie grabbed Ella's arm, then Ella called the NEL and the crowd of onlookers arrived.

Agent Gilroy stopped the spell, and his attention focused on Ella. He was tall and handsome in a government agent kind of way and couldn't have been more than twenty-five. He carried himself with confidence, and his eyes glinted with a kind of cockiness that Ella wasn't sure she liked. "It obviously wasn't a contagion spell since a victim touched you. You were lucky you weren't hit with the spell."

Good news: he didn't suspect Ella of being a Dis-con.

Bad news: because of Ella, they were forming their investigation on false observations.

The spell *could* have been a contagion.

The EHTs had decontaminated Ella and the basketball team when they first arrived, but if Ella hadn't been a Dis-con and it *was* contagious? The disease would have spread to her no question.

And there was no way to know that now and no way to tell CIU without admitting what she was.

Agent Alvarez appeared to pick up on Ella's discomfort and said, "You aren't under suspicion. The signature-reveal spell cleared you. You can relax." They looked over at the basketball team. The EHTs' healing spells were working, and most of the burns and blisters were already healed. "And even if it hadn't, this kind of spell requires a massive amount of energy, and there would've been some blowback for the caster. He or she would have burns or blisters themselves. They'd have healed them by now, of course, but we can see from the re-creation spell that you were clean."

That was an added relief.

Ella had never witnessed blowback before, only in movies or television or occasionally the news. They didn't really teach spells that were powerful enough to cause blowback in school or to the general public either, so seeing it in person was rare.

Probably a good idea considering people like Rachel Fen and Lizzie Trent existed.

They'd either be the targets or the ones experimenting.

Ella hoped the agents didn't want to investigate further as to why she wasn't affected by the spell. It had been a long time since Ella had been this close to someone in a position to destroy her life if they found out she was a Dis-con. She thought she'd be used to the terror that ran through her veins all day every day. The fact that the fear was worse than she'd ever felt it before was enough for her knees to shake.

When they almost buckled, Agent Gilroy caught Ella by the elbow to steady her. "Easy now."

She wanted to push him away but found that she needed him for support. All the adrenaline finally dipped, and her body was collapsing from the crash. "Maybe I should sit down."

"Good idea." Agent Gilroy led her over to a couple of foldout chairs that were roped off from everyone else, and she sat. The students' and teachers' eyes bounced back and forth between Ella and the quickly healing basketball team. She was surprised that there was still so much hostility in the students' eyes. They'd just seen her cleared. Why would they suspect her anymore?

After she steadied herself, Agent Gilroy sat next to her, his expression friendly. "I'm Malcolm, by the way."

"Ella." Yeah. Duh.

But Agent Gilroy didn't seem to notice as he continued, "We'll be taking the basketball team to the hospital for further observation. Sometimes spells have a delayed time attack. Maybe you should come too?"

"But you said I wasn't affected." Ella's throat began to close from panic.

There were definite tests at the hospital that would prove she was a Dis-con. It was one of the reasons she avoided them entirely. Ella turned her ankle once when she was ten and had to bite through the unbearable pain every time she walked until it eventually healed.

Injuries were fixed up pretty quickly with a simple healing spell, so she could never let anyone know when she was hurt. It was too dangerous.

"You weren't affected by the spell. I could tell immediately," he said in what she was sure was a tone designed to calm her down. "I'm a Skein. All CIU agents are. We're trained to see spell residue more clearly, and I saw it around you when the basketball player touched your arm, but it didn't cause you any damage."

Ella almost vomited.

How could there be residue on her if she was a Dis-con? Was it because of her strange ability to push on spells? It saved her at her Dis-con test when she was twelve. Had it saved her yet again?

And a Skein?

Ella suspected the CIU only hired Skeins, but in all the terror of what had happened, she hadn't thought about it. Meeting one in person made her more paranoid. Skeins were the best of the best. Their incanting capabilities were unmatched. If anyone could figure out Ella was a Dis-con, it would be a Skein. It made her instantly grateful that she was on file for passing the Dis-con test. But any more tests and Ella would be in trouble.

Another wave of panic hit her.

"My backpack!" she yelped, not able to stop the words from coming out of her mouth.

A backpack with a game inside that if anyone turned on, they would find out she had created a copy of Ash Torres as her boyfriend!

The mere thought of Ash ever seeing something so humiliating was almost more terrifying than what Ella had just witnessed in the gymnasium.

Malcolm observed her reaction and responded, "You have personals in there?"

Ella nodded her head. "My Veil is in there. My parents saved up to buy it for me. I don't want it to get stolen." A convincing lie. She hoped.

Agent Gilroy's expression softened with sympathy. "I can get it for you. Where is it? Near the left or right of the door?"

Ella froze again.

She'd admitted to having a backpack. A backpack that was under the bleachers, which put her in the actual room when the spell was incanted.

But Agent Gilroy had seen the residue of the attack spell on Ella. In his mind, it didn't seem like it had even occurred to him that she might be a Dis-con.

So maybe being in the gymnasium when it happened wasn't a big deal.

Right now, Ella was more afraid of people finding that Veil and opening up *Hexsphere* since she was positive she wasn't being accused of being a Dis-con at this point.

"It's under the bleachers," she said in a rush.

Agent Gilroy's expression was suddenly alarmed. "You were in the gymnasium when the spell was incanted?"

Oh man.

She didn't like that look.

But Ella was committed at this point.

She nodded.

Malcolm was on his feet and next to Agent Alvarez's side in seconds, whispering furiously. The both of them walked over to her, looking worried. "You're sure you were in this room when it happened?"

Most everyone's eyes were on Ella and the two agents now.

Great. More stares.

"Yes. Is that strange?" she asked as innocently as she could, though Ella knew it was *absolutely* strange.

"It means the attack was directed. Whoever did this specifically targeted the basketball team." Agent Alvarez looked like her mind was going a mile a minute.

"It's also another explanation as to why Ella didn't develop the burns when the girl grabbed her arm," Malcolm added.

Alvarez nodded, then turned to Ella with a tense smile. "Thank you, Ella. I'll need your number if we have any more questions."

"Of course," she said, though that thought made every muscle in her body tense.

Moving away from Ella, Agent Alvarez and Malcolm pulled the nearby Principal Busby aside, but Ella was still close enough to hear them.

Agent Alvarez said, "School will be cancelled today per CIU protocol, and everyone in the dome will be subject to a signature-reveal spell upon exiting."

Ms. Busby nodded in agreement, then asked, "You really think the attacker stuck around?"

Malcolm answered, "In most cases, attackers do stay near, but the tests are mainly used to help us rule out suspects."

After a brief pause, Ms. Busby straightened her blazer. "I'll organize the line to the exit and try to keep everyone calm."

"Thank you. CIU appreciates your help." Alvarez gave a curt nod to Ms. Busby. "Time to let us do our work. And I hope I don't need to remind you to keep this quiet for the standard ten-hour press silence?"

"No. You don't need to remind me. I'm only going to call the parents of the students who were attacked and Ella's. Your sealing-dome will have already attracted them anyway. If they report it, that's on them." Ms. Busby practically huffed.

Um.

"You don't need to call my parents. I'll tell them. I live really close." Ella knew it would reveal that she was eavesdropping, but the thought of her parents hearing about this from her principal? They'd be dragging Ella out of the state and to a new location by nightfall.

"That'll be fine, Ella. Go ahead and go home and get some rest." Ms. Busby didn't seem bothered at all that Ella had been listening in. In fact, only concern reflected in the principal's expression.

Agent Alvarez nodded toward the waiting crowd. "If you could remove everyone, that would be the most helpful."

Ms. Busby placed her hands on her hips, all business, turning to Mr. Velenti. "I'll cast the intercom spell from here. You go and round up the stragglers."

Mr. Velenti nodded and left the gym.

Ms. Busby cast a spell, and her voice sounded not only from her throat, but from the intercom as well. Ella could hear the echoes of it in the hallways beyond as Ms. Busby turned to the rest of the students in the gym. "Everybody get into single file and head to the sealing-dome exit. There has been an attack on the varsity basketball team, and we'll be closing down the school for the day. A signature-reveal spell will be performed on you as you leave."

Slowly, the students started to leave the gym.

Agent Alvarez and Agent Gilroy walked off, talking with fervor, and Ella knew the information she gave them had ruined their investigation. They'd be looking for the wrong kind of spell. Ella being in the gym when it happened made them think it was a directed attack. Her being a Dis-con might prevent the only people capable of tracking down the person who did this from doing so.

It hurt.

It scared her.

But what could she do?

After conferring with Agent Alvarez a few moments more, Malcolm hurried off, heading straight for Ella's hiding place. Before she could panic, he came back with a small smile and handed Ella her backpack. "You can trust me," he said.

But that wasn't what Ella worried about.

She worried about the fact that a Skein from the CIU couldn't trust *her*.

"Thanks," she said.

Holding her backpack close, Ella wondered if the psychopath who did this would ever be caught.

CHAPTER 4
WREN

Wren waited in line to exit the sealing-dome. There were at least twenty people ahead of her, the CIU agents casting the signature-reveal spells quickly and efficiently, making the line move along at a good pace. Taking deep steadying breaths helped Wren stay calm. If the spell she'd invented to change her spell signature didn't worked, she'd have to attack fast and run.

The line was loose, some students standing together, some apart, but all were gossiping about the morning's event. Wren didn't have to strain her ears very hard to hear what most of them were saying.

"I can't believe CIU let her go."

"Did you see her standing over their bodies?"

"I don't care if she passed the signature-reveal spell, she's obviously guilty."

"If they don't expel her, I'm going to have my parents call the

school. I won't feel safe with her around."

Ella.

She didn't make it out.

But she'd had time. Wren knew that for a fact.

So why hadn't Ella run? She was a Dis-con; she shouldn't have been taking those kinds of risks even after passing her Dis-con test at twelve. Wren was dying to know how she'd managed that. Another question to ask Ella if Wren could muster up the courage to confess that she knew what Ella was.

And now everyone was blaming Ella for something Wren did.

But why?

If Ella had been cleared by a signature-reveal spell, then why was everyone still so suspicious?

It made no sense.

Unless . . .

Wren cast a quick reveal spell and saw residue on specific students walking around her.

The students who were spouting paranoid rants against Ella.

Spelled.

Probably by Rachel or Lizzie.

Rage flowed through her.

Lizzie must have noticed that Ella hadn't been affected by the plague spell, so her suspicions would be up and so would Rachel's, which only made Ella more vulnerable to them both. Trackers knew that Dis-cons had ways to fool the Dis-con testing. They hunted everyone just the same, whether they'd passed the test or not. And standard protocol for Trackers would be to go after Ella to confirm whether or not she was a Dis-con. They'd be relentless.

Wren hoped her spell to change her signature worked,

because getting home was vital at this point. She needed to track Lizzie and make sure she didn't go after Ella.

Only ten people in front of her.

"Hey." Moira joined Wren in line, arms crossed, head glancing over her shoulder.

"Hey," Wren answered back, not wanting to elaborate.

Nine people.

Moira focused her attention on Wren unfolding her arms from her chest. "It was Ella Buckley that caused all this." She waved at the sealing-dome and the CIU agents ahead of them in line. "She used a plague spell on the varsity basketball team."

Eight people.

Internally, Wren grumbled. Moira had been there, so she'd been spelled too.

If she knew a counter, she'd have incanted it immediately on Moira. Hearing her speak the paranoid rant about Ella sickened her. Because it was her fault Ella was in this mess.

Wren wanted to slam her fist into a wall. Lucky there were none near her, or she might have.

She should have killed Lizzie and been done with it.

But her goal was to kill *all* Trackers, not just Evil Incarnate.

"Did CIU arrest her?"

Moira's face turned thoughtful as they moved ahead in line. "No. She's in line behind us. Look at how squirmy she is though," Moira said as if this proved her point.

"You would be too if everyone blamed you for something you didn't do." Wren knew Moira couldn't help it. Lizzie's or Rachel's spell was clawing into everyone's subconscious like a buzzard ripping into prey. Wren would need to counter it to keep Ella safe, but she didn't have much experience with spells that fed off emotions. She'd have to look through her journals in her safe when she got home.

Moira appeared to be working things out, obviously surprised at Wren's defense of Ella. "But CIU lets suspects go sometimes, don't they? When they don't have enough evidence?"

Wren eyed Ella shuffling uncomfortably twenty or so people back. The students around Ella gave her a wide berth. Whether they were spelled or not, the rumor mill did the rest. The whole school would be blaming Ella before the day was out.

Seven people.

Ella's eyes kept darting to a specific spot, and Wren's heart broke a little when she realized it was Ash Torres.

Wren recognized the signs of a girl with a crush.

Ash was a handsome guy by most standards, and even Wren had to admit his eyes were swoon-worthy. But from the flush in Ella's cheeks and the way her grip tightened on her backpack, it wasn't hard to deduce how Ella felt about him. At least not for anyone who was paying attention.

Turning back, Wren shrugged. "If they really thought she was guilty, they wouldn't let her leave this dome. Why do people think Ella did it? Didn't CIU cast a signature-reveal spell?" She tried to act as casual as possible, but her insides churned. Wren hoped logic would win out with Moira and the spell would fade.

Wren hated that she put all that attention on Ella. She'd sworn to protect Dis-cons after her mother was murdered, and now she had put one in direct danger.

"Supposedly, but even if she didn't cast the spell itself, she still could be behind the attack, maybe have some kind of accomplice. She was caught standing over them all after it happened." Moira seemed to think this was the deciding factor for guilt.

The spell was obviously rooted deeper than she'd hoped.

Six people.

Wren's heart squeezed at the thought of Ella trying to help. It was the only reason why Ella would be standing with the victims, putting herself at more risk of being discovered. Her kindness reminded Wren so much of her mother she almost lost her footing as they moved forward. She swallowed hard and took care to hide any emotion from her voice. "That only means she tried to help. I don't think that makes her guilty."

Five people.

Moira shook her head. "I couldn't see her through the crowd, but everyone that did is saying she looked guilty, like they'd interrupted her."

If Moira was this paranoid, Wren definitely needed to find a counter, or things could get out of control.

"I don't know. I feel like that's gossip, especially since she *cleared the signature-reveal spell*," Wren emphasized. "And looks like she's about to have it cast on her *again*." Wren nodded back toward Ella in line. Besides, Wren knew Ella's *look* was her terror of being discovered as a Dis-con. There were several times when Wren's mother had that expression as well. Guilt and fear were virtually the same on a person's face.

Four people.

"Maybe," Moira said. But Wren knew it was the spell that kept Moira from being convinced.

"Well, I do. Ella's an easy target because she's a loner." Wren made sure her eyes met Moira's. "Like us."

A flash of guilt appeared in Moira's expression.

Maybe she was breaking through to her?

Three people.

Moira turned her head toward the CIU agents only a few feet away. "Two people, then we're up."

Wren's knees almost buckled at Moira's words. She steadied herself by planting her feet solidly on the cement walkway to ground herself.

Moira briefly touched Wren's arm sympathetically, then smiled at her. "It'll be fine. I've had to have a signature-reveal spell before. They're really no big deal."

Wren berated herself internally for her knees betraying her. She brushed Moira's hand aside and shrugged. "Yeah, I know. I just haven't had breakfast yet. My blood sugar must be low."

Wren couldn't tell if she'd seen disappointment in Moira's eyes when she removed her hand off her arm or something else, but she didn't have time to ponder it because the CIU agent closest to her waved Wren toward him. "Over here," he added as if Wren hadn't understood his physical command.

Probably because her feet were still planted. Move!

Wren had to mentally and physically push herself to the CIU agent. His shoulders were slightly slumped, and his under eyes were swollen and darkened. A bit of blowback from casting the same spell hundreds of times. They'd have to swap these agents out soon if they wanted them to be of any use later in the day.

The agent began to incant.

Wren held her breath.

A blasting spell would do nicely if this didn't work. She readied the words in her head.

But it was over.

"Thank you," the agent said, then turned to the student behind Wren. "Next."

Wren walked out the exit until she was a good distance away, clenching her lips shut for fear of yelping with joy.

She did it.

She actually did it.

Wren wanted to immediately share her success with someone.

Not just someone, but her mom. She could picture her mother smiling at her, beaming with pride.

Wren dug her nails into the palm of her right hand to stop herself from crying.

There was no one to share with, and she needed to pull herself together.

As if hearing her thoughts, Moira walked up next to her. "I have a power bar in my backpack if you need it."

The sparkle of concern in Moira's eyes nearly took Wren's breath away. "Oh, that's really nice. Thank you."

Moira's face lit up as she rummaged through her levitating bag and pulled out a foil-wrapped energy bar before handing it to Wren. "Of course."

Wren wasn't hungry at all, but she took the bar out of politeness and to keep her cover story intact. After unwrapping the bar, Wren took a bite. Peanut butter chocolate chip, pretty good. "Thanks."

"Sure." Moira's lips curved into a small smile, shy and sweet. "Well, I should be going. See you tomorrow?"

"Yeah. See you tomorrow," Wren said, finding that the smile she gave Moira was genuine. She watched Moira leave in the opposite direction of where Wren was headed.

Wren needed to talk to Ella, find out where her head was at. She had no intention of revealing herself or her mission, but she had to know if Ella was okay and at least let her know that she was a friend. Above all else, Dis-cons were Wren's top priority.

All Wren had to do was walk slowly enough for Ella to catch

up. Wren had never cared much before, but she and Ella walked the same street to get home, though Ella's house was farther from the school than Wren's. She didn't know exactly where Ella's house was since she'd never had the need to pay attention, but with school zoning laws, it couldn't be that far from Wren's.

Slowly, Wren made her way across the grass inlay between the faculty parking lot and the outer sidewalk, keeping her side vision focused on the students exiting the sealing-dome. Once she spotted Ella, Wren slowed her pace down even more.

Crossing the street brought Wren to the suburbs of Los Angeles and the street she lived on. Craftsman style houses in varying shade of blues, grays, and yellows lined each side of Cursor Street, with smooth cement sidewalks and long slabs of green grass. An occasional tree was planted along the path in the grass area but nothing over ten feet, definitely not enough to give any shade but also not big enough to push up any destructive roots into the sidewalk or street either.

Once on the sidewalk, Wren walked ahead to give a little distance between her and Ella. She didn't want it to look like an ambush. She wanted it to seem like she had slowed down enough for Ella to catch up. Wren remembered how her mother had avoided people, so she imagined Ella would have the same instincts.

She glanced back briefly. Ella was now walking on the sidewalk a few hundred feet behind her.

Time to slow down. Without looking like she was slowing down.

Acting as casually as possible, Wren forced her legs to take smaller steps while keeping her upper body loose, as if it were normal to walk like turtle.

With a quick look back, Wren's heart sank when she noticed

that Ella had slowed down as well.

Ella knew.

She knew Wren was slowing down to talk to her.

And she didn't want to talk.

Under normal circumstances, Wren would respect this, but she desperately wanted to reassure Ella. Wren slowed down more, her steps closer together. No matter how hard she tried, she couldn't make it look natural.

Out of the corner of her eye, she noticed Ella drop her backpack and the contents spill on the sidewalk.

Wren breathed in deep.

Ella wasn't ready.

And Wren wasn't going to push her.

Maybe an opportunity would present itself at school.

Wren hurried her pace and jogged the rest of the way to her small two-story Craftsman house. She climbed the three small steps that led to a wraparound porch, unlocked the light gray door, and stepped inside.

It was still morning, but her father wouldn't be home for another hour or so. Him working nights allowed Wren a certain freedom to do the things she needed to for her mission. It also meant she rarely saw him, which was the way *he* liked it. The only time their paths crossed was the few hours after school and before his shift started. Not that a single word was ever spoken, but occasionally, Wren would watch him from afar, analyzing every movement and gesture he made, hoping that one day he would wake up and be the dad she remembered.

The more time passed, the more her hope died.

She needed to accept the fact that it was never going to happen.

Upon entering, a staircase was the main focus, leading upstairs to the bedrooms. To the left, an untouched dining room mocked Wren with its empty chairs and a layer of dust on the table, and to the right was an equally abandoned living room consisting of a large couch, recliner, and coffee table. Beyond the staircase, an open doorway led to the kitchen, pretty much the only room Wren and her father ever occupied on the few occasions they crossed paths.

Wren walked to the bay window in the living room that looked out onto the sidewalk. As she approached, Ella hurried by, glancing at her phone as if she were late to something, then practically ran past Wren's house.

Oh, Ella.

With an exasperated sigh, Wren put her feelings about Ella avoiding her aside and made her way to the door under the staircase. Opening it, she walked down the ten cement stairs that led to the basement, her sanctuary.

Her operation room.

Decor was minimal: operation board, plushy red chair, six-foot foldout table, and a couple of wooden chairs and a couch. The operation board was mounted to the wall, eight feet across and six feet high. It was big. And if Wren was being honest, she needed another one, maybe two. Everything she'd learned over the last four years she put on this board in the form of a spider diagram with three-dimensional holographic images of each person involved. It was so crowded with information and connections between people, companies, and locations, she was pretty sure she was the only one who could understand it. So much work, and she'd only scratched the surface.

But that wasn't important right now. Right now, she needed

to cast a tracking spell on Lizzie and use quantum phasing to spy on her.

Wren had invented a spell for quantum phasing, something that no one even thought was possible, like the changing of her spell signature. She had an uncanny knack for inventing impossible spells. She had no idea why her brain worked that way. She would see things form in her head like a pattern, fitting together in what felt like the most obvious way, then when she'd try it (because it certainly couldn't be *that* easy), the spells always seemed to work.

To the world, quantum phasing was purely theoretical. Even the world's best Skeins had written it off as fantasy. But Wren had figured it out. So far, she'd only used it to break into top secret military vaults. There was no defense against something that didn't exist, after all. It allowed her to phase outside of her physical body and travel to the vaults in incorporeal form without detection. And these vaults had given her access to some nasty spells like the plague one she'd used on Lizzie and inadvertently on the entire basketball team. She'd phase in, memorize the spells, then break the quantum phasing spell, her spirit form slamming back into her physical body. All she had to do then was write everything down and—voilà, an arsenal of attack spells.

Time to use it for spying.

Wren had never tried it in this way before, but she was ready. She didn't want her attack this morning to be for nothing. Pulling a slip of paper off her board labeled *Tracking,* Wren plopped down on the couch, shifting herself until she was completely relaxed and comfortable.

Deep breath.

Incanting the quantum phasing spell would be easy. She'd performed it so many times she had every word and syllable memorized. It was the tracking spell she needed a little help with, and she had to perform that first. Wren tried to stay away from tracking spells in general because they were highly unreliable, mainly because they depended on a person's connection with the one they were tracking, hence why Wren performed the spell on Lizzie this morning. She needed a stronger connection than simply her burning hatred for the murderer. She hoped it would be enough.

Wren recited the spell on the piece of paper to perfection.

A holographic webbing formed around her as the last words of the tracking spell left her mouth—a map. The names of each street lay in three-dimensional lettering across their respective locations. A bright white dot at its base represented Wren, but she had yet to find Lizzie's white dot. Maybe her connection wasn't as strong as she thought. She concentrated on Evil Incarnate, and the glowing white dot appeared. Lizzie was on Garner Street about a mile from the school.

Now for quantum phasing.

Wren recited the spell by heart, powerful and confident.

As the final word left her mouth, Wren's incorporeal form shifted out of her physical body that lay slumped on the couch, a shell with no consciousness. The form she was in now was completely invisible, but her vision was clear. And it knew exactly where to go.

Wren's spirit form flew through the walls of the basement to the outside, heading for Garner Street and Lizzie's last location. The tracking spell would dissipate in a few minutes, but she didn't have to worry too much about anyone looking in and seeing her since she'd affixed a glamour spell permanently to the windows.

Quantum phasing felt like flying did in a dream, soaring

and free, no physical ties to anything as she traveled over the Los Angeles suburbs. Each block had its own personality of architecture and social hierarchy, one block modest and small, the next with seven-bedroom mansions.

The streets below matched the webbing map of the tracking spell back in Wren's basement with perfection. Garner Street was just ahead. Wren's incorporeal form slowed down as she reached the street, searching for any sign of Lizzie outside. When that didn't work, Wren flew to each window of each house in the vicinity of where she remembered the glowing dot to be.

After the third house, she found her.

Finally.

Wren had found Lizzie's lair. (Because evil had *lairs* not houses.)

Sitting in the living room of a four-bedroom Spanish style home, Lizzie relaxed on a couch, the arched window framing her like a horror movie. Across from her on a wooden dining chair was Rachel. Odd to be sitting on a dining chair and not the plush recliner right next to her, but Wren couldn't explain the mind of a Tracker when it came to comfort.

Wren's spirit form pushed through the window and hovered above the two Trackers. The house itself was sparsely furnished, again with the little to no comfort. The couch and the recliner were the only cushions to be found.

No sign of Shara anywhere. Interesting.

From the emptiness of the house, it was obvious to Wren that Lizzie and Rachel were on some kind of finite mission for the Trackers. They hadn't expected to be there this long or they would have made this space more comfortable. Or would they have? Maybe they didn't live here? Maybe this was some kind of headquarters? They probably had their own homes far from here. So why had they shown up at Tristan High two months after Ella? Did they know she was a Dis-con? No. If they had, she'd be dead already, so that part had to be coincidence. It had to be something big if there were two of them, possibly three if Shara was indeed a Tracker.

Rachel shifted closer to Lizzie on her chair. "Are you sure you're okay?"

Lizzie shrugged. "I'm fine. We need to find out if we were compromised. That attack was directed at me. I have no idea why it fractured."

"Crappy spell-caster," Rachel answered with confidence.

Wren's ego wanted to lash out at the insult, but considering she was *quantum phasing* over their heads, she had a perverse sense of satisfaction that they had no idea how powerful she really was.

"Maybe. I can't shake the feeling that it's something more though. I thought Ella might be the spell-caster at first, but when I touched her, she had no reaction." Lizzie leaned back on the couch.

"Well, I cast a quick paranoia spell on all the students there, so the whole school should be after her head by tomorrow. We'll have to stick to our normal taunt-and-observe mode though because I don't want to blow our cover. But if she is a Dis-con, we'll need to take action." Rachel sat up as if ready to hunt Ella down.

Wren had been right. Rachel had cast a spell to make everyone suspicious of Ella. Wren wanted to leap back into her body and kill them both now.

"We'll have to test her first, but yeah, that's where my gut is taking me." Lizzie sighed as if something else weighed on her.

"You thinking we should finally give the recruitment pitch to our main objective?" Rachel watched Lizzie with studied purpose.

"Tomorrow. You have first period with her, right?" Lizzie asked.

"Yeah. Quantum spell-casting. It's been five months of observation, and so far our intel has been accurate. The girl is powerful beyond what we observed. She'll be a good recruit if we can turn her." Rachel spoke like a soldier, all business.

If Wren had breath to hold, she'd have been holding it then.

Were they talking about *her*?

Was Wren their mission?

To recruit her as a Tracker?

They had to know she'd never consider something like that after what they did to her mother.

But it couldn't be Wren. She'd arrived at Tristan High two months after they did. So who?

Lizzie got to her feet. "I'm going over to Ella's. Cast a quick spell, see if she reacts. If she doesn't, I'll take care of it."

Rachel stood as well. "All right, but if you kill her today, text me so I can head over to our objective's house and try to recruit her. Priorities, remember?"

"You'll be my first text," Lizzie said with a casual wave as if they were talking about nothing serious.

Rachel nodded. "You want me to order Thai for lunch?"

"Yeah. We'll go over the game plan when I get back, but I don't want to stay here tonight. I'm going to head home after."

"I might stay here. I don't really want to commute from my apartment tomorrow. It took a full two hours this morning. I'm going to practice my recruiting speech, especially if I might have to do it early. It's gotta be a good one." Rachel shook out her hands like she was prepping for a boxing fight.

Wren was about to jump back in her body to hurry to Ella's house before Lizzie could get there when Rachel's next words sent a chill down her spine.

"Seriously, I know killing is your favorite, but recruiting Moira Kurt is why we're here. If you don't find an opportunity to take out Ella now, we can always do it later if she's a Dis-con. Maybe show Moira how it's done."

Lizzie pouted. "Fine. But you're really being a buzzkill right now. Killing is so much fun," Lizzie said with a smile, then walked out the front door.

Wren barely had time to process everything she'd heard.

Kill Ella now?

Recruit Moira?

Too many conflicting emotions. She needed to prioritize: Ella was in danger *right now*, and Wren needed to help her.

CHAPTER 5
ELLA

Ella stared up at her house as if for the last time, and if she was being honest with herself, it might very well be when her parents found out about this morning. On the outside, it was as nice as any of the other houses on the street—two stories, dark cobalt blue paint on layered wood planks, white trim around the windows and doors, and finally a deep red painted front door with silver finishes. Ella walked up the paved stone path that a perfectly cut lawn framed, pulled out her key, and opened the door.

The inside was not as perfect.

The story of her existence.

Even though they had moved in seven months ago, there were still boxes left unpacked. Not a lot, only a few stacked by the stairs and up against some of the walls, but it was enough to keep her from feeling truly home. That was their life. Never staying in one place for too long.

Everything else in the house was clean though. Ella's dad was a stickler for cleanliness. Clutter, he wasn't so on top of, but you could eat dinner off the floors. John Buckley was a master of cleaning spells. It was a gift he turned into a business at one point in their lives. But the exposure to so many different families and the possibility that they'd figure out Ella's condition forced him to shut the business down. That and the fact that they moved around too much. A cleaning business ran on recommendations and trust. It was too difficult to restart every time they arrived in a new place.

They relied on her parents' consulting services for money. Both Nara and John Buckley were at Skein level, so their spell-casting abilities were something they could monetize. Ironic, considering they had a daughter who was a Dis-con.

But, being consultants did mean that they could work from home, which gave them the freedom to move anywhere and at any time.

Her mother yelled from the kitchen, "Ella? Is that you? What are you doing home so early? Are you sick?"

Walking past the foot of the staircase and into the living room, Ella headed to the swinging kitchen door and entered.

Both her parents were at the kitchen island, laptops out, sitting on stools, cups of coffee next to them. Most of the kitchen was white, from the cupboards to the marble countertops to the white octagon tiled flooring, the gray grout being the only contrast. But her mom had to have a splash of color wherever they moved, so there was a bright teal subway tile backsplash running above the long counter against the back wall.

Upon seeing Ella, her father gave a friendly wave, while her mom stood up and hurried over to her daughter. Pulling away, she asked, "Is everything okay, sweetheart?" Her mom placed the back of her hand on Ella's forehead. "No fever."

"I'm fine, Mom, really. The school sent everyone home. And I have something to tell you guys," Ella began tentatively.

Rip off the Band-Aid.

Her mom's face tensed immediately. "What happened?" Her voice was quiet and shook slightly.

Ella's dad stopped what he was doing on his computer, his full attention now on his daughter.

The pressure was real.

Here went nothing.

"There was an attack on the school today in the gym . . . and I was in the room when it happened." Ella knew that would be enough for her parents to connect the dots.

A long silence followed, until her dad asked, "And CIU?"

"They performed the signature-reveal spell on me and didn't think it was me, and the re-creation spell made them think that it was a directed attack since I wasn't hurt." Ella didn't want to give them any details that would stir up a desire to move again.

Her mother tapped her index finger on her chin. "They didn't suspect you of being a Dis-con?"

"The CIU agent said he saw spell residue on me, so I don't think it even occurred to him that I might be a Dis-con."

"What?" they said at the same time.

"Yeah. I can't explain it either. Must've been the type of spell, but either way, I think it saved me from any suspicion," Ella rationalized. She still didn't understand it.

Her mom shook her head. "But no spell we've ever cast on you left a residue. It's one of the reasons we knew for certain you were a Dis-con."

Her mother was in full panic mode, Ella could tell.

Ella's dad turned to his wife as if Ella wasn't in the room. "Do you think he lied? That he's tricking her to get her guard down?"

"It has to be. We need to *move*." Her mom's voice shrilled on the last word.

"Just stop," Ella interrupted, though part of her now wondered if her dad was right and CIU would be knocking on their door any minute. Regardless, trap or not, Ella had to calm the parental units down first, or they'd be in the car driving away in less than an hour. "It was the spell. Trust me. I talked to Agent Gilroy at great lengths. He's a Skein, and he doesn't suspect me at all." Ella forced a smile. "I'm positive I'll be fine."

Ella wasn't as positive as she forced herself to sound, but she hoped it was enough to convince her parents not to move again.

"We'll be the judge of that." Nodding to her husband, Ella's mom said, "Turn on the news."

"It won't be on the news yet. It only happened an hour ago," Ella answered.

Her parents nodded, knowing that the ten-hour press hold would be in effect for another nine hours or so.

"You didn't talk to anyone about this, did you? You only talked to the CIU agents and that was that?" Ella's dad prodded.

Knowing that it would be on the news eventually, Ella added, "Well, I was the one who called CIU. I kind of ran to the victims to help."

"What?" Her mom was on a serious *What?* repeat pattern.

At this point, Ella was pretty sure her mother was going to have some kind of breakdown. "I couldn't sit there and watch the kids from my school suffer. It was horrible. Some kind of plague virus spell, burns and blisters . . . I had to help."

But her parents were enraged, nostrils flaring, tensed jaws and steely eyes.

Ella knew it was out of fear for her, but her temper matched theirs. "You can't expect me to isolate myself forever! Is that what you want for me? To never have friends? To be stuck with you two for the rest of my life? I might as well kill myself!"

Knowing how unfair that was, Ella wanted to immediately apologize, but she ran away instead. Flying by the living room, she took the stairs two at a time until she reached the second floor and her bedroom, which was the first door on the right. Slamming the door behind her, Ella threw herself on the bed and cried into her pillow.

She knew what she said had been horrible, but arguing with them only solidified how much of a prisoner she was.

Slowing down her breathing and rolling over on her back so she wasn't suffocating on her tears anymore, she attempted to calm down. It took a few minutes before she could breathe without a choked sob, but she was finally able to steady her emotions.

She needed to distract herself.

Pulling Veil out of her backpack, she decided to play.

Placing the virtual reality headset on and flipping the eye-bars over her eyes, Ella turned on *Hexsphere*. Signing into her character FearlessGirl22, she barely paid attention to virtual-Ash and the house she'd created. She just wanted to play.

With the only real friends she had: game friends.

She navigated to her friend list. She had four people to choose from who she'd grown close to over the last couple years. Unfortunately, all of them were grayed out, which meant they were offline.

Sighing in disappointment, Ella had hoped Buster44 would

be online. He was one of her favorite people to play with because she always felt like such a badass when they played together. From always taking out the Trackers in new and inventive ways to solving the more complicated puzzle chambers, Buster44 always had her back.

Ella hit start. She'd be flying solo today.

The three-dimensional words floated above her head: *Would you like to start a mission?*

"Yes, please," Ella said aloud, but for game purposes made her character reach up and hit the 3D lettering.

Virtual reality games like this had saved Ella's life. She truly believed this. The full immersion experience eased Ella's thoughts of loneliness and made her feel alive. This game in particular also gave her a sense of security. If she could fight game Trackers, maybe she'd be able to fight them in real life if they ever found her. It made her feel less vulnerable, less helpless, like she'd have a sporting chance.

Her virtual house (and the beautiful Ash in it) dissipated before her character's eyes, replaced by a dark alley. Two brick buildings formed the alley itself, at least seven or eight stories high, each lined with rickety metal fire escapes up each side.

Ella's view outside the alley was of a gothic cityscape, pointed spires reaching into the sky like a city full of monstrous needles, but she knew up close, the detail of the game designers really shined. Arches framed by stone, staircases that led to nowhere, and an obscene amount of clock towers. (Someone was definitely obsessed with a good clock tower.) She liked this particular cityscape the most. Though there were many others, this one was the darkest, which for some reason made it feel more real to Ella.

Three-dimensional text popped up above Ella's character's

head. *Buster44 would like to join. Accept?*

"Heck yeah." A surge of excitement raced through her. The very person she'd wanted to play with. It felt like they were connected somehow. Of course, like all her gaming friends, she had no idea who Buster44 was in the real world. He could've been a she or live in another country for all she knew, but it didn't matter. In-game, she was FearlessGirl22 and he was Buster44, and they were comrades to the end.

Ella made her character reach up and smack the *Accept* letters.

With a popping sound effect, Buster44 materialized in front of her. He was tall compared to FearlessGirl22's smaller stature—a little over six feet if Ella were to guess. His head was shaved, and he had a scar over his right cheek and a black goatee. He wore a brown duster with black T-shirt and jeans underneath. Beautiful, but also someone you wouldn't want to mess with.

A dialogue bubble formed near his mouth. *Hey, FearlessGirl22, you ready to take down some Trackers?*

Ella pressed a button on Veil, and a virtual keyboard materialized in front of her. As she typed, a dialogue bubble popped up from her character's mouth. *Always.*

SLICE!

A Tracker blade flew at Buster44's head with frightening speed.

FearlessGirl22 grabbed a garbage can lid from the ground and swung it up toward the blade, hitting it full force and sending it scattering across the alley floor.

Two Trackers, one male, one female, leapt into the alley.

Ella switched into "whisper" mode on Veil so she could type to Buster44 privately without the Trackers seeing what they were saying.

Ella typed, *Grab the Tracker blade and throw it in my direction.*

In a text box right above the virtual keyboard, Buster44's response was quick. *On it.*

Buster44 jumped at the brick wall, then propelled himself backward toward the fallen Tracker blade.

FearlessGirl22 leapt up to the fire escape above her head, grabbing on to the rungs, then swung hard and fast. Using her momentum, she kicked both Trackers in the face. Both stumbled back a few feet.

The female Tracker cast a spell, aiming it at the fire escape FearlessGirl22 still hung on to. With a ripping crunch, the fire escape collapsed from the eighth floor down. Ella's character jumped off right in time.

Text box: *Got it. Catch!*

FearlessGirl22 landed on her feet and reached up, catching the Tracker blade's pommel perfectly in her palm. Gripping tight, she sliced at the female Tracker's neck. Her head toppled from her body, landing with a sickening thud on the ground.

The male Tracker screamed in fury, then cast another spell, aiming it at the second set of fire escapes on the other building. Crunching metal twisted and fell, swinging toward both FearlessGirl22 and Buster44.

Buster44 pushed her out of the way just in time, though he wasn't as lucky, the tail end of the metal scraping his ankle.

The male Tracker pulled out another Tracker blade from a sheath on his back and swung it at Buster44's head. FearlessGirl22 blocked it with the blade she held. Swinging, blocking, swinging, blocking, each strike almost threatening to end each opponent, the Tracker moving forward, FearlessGirl22 walking backward.

With each strike, FearlessGirl22 barely kept her balance from the force until her foot caught on a fallen piece of metal from the broken fire escape. She fell to the ground on her rump, still blocking the male Tracker's blows as he now had higher ground, pounding on her blade.

Ella's character's health bar was dangerously low. She was about to die in-game. She just hoped she could respawn fast enough to help Buster44 before the male Tracker took him out too.

Her health bar began flashing red.

FearlessGirl22 kept her blade up, still blocking each blow. At this point, the Tracker used his sword as a blunt object, hacking at FearlessGirl22's blade. As the flashing red bar was about to become empty, a bar of jagged metal swung down hard, smashing into the male Tracker's head with a loud crunch. Tossing the metal bar aside, Buster44 reached his hand down, and FearlessGirl22 took it. He lifted her to her feet, her health bar now replenishing.

A dialogue bubble formed from Buster44's mouth. *We did it. That was a close one.*

You're telling me, Ella typed, and the bubble formed above her character.

Ding, dong.

Ella's heart stopped in her throat. Was that the doorbell? *To her house*?

She typed in, *Gotta go. I'll check to see if you're playing later.*

Buster44 responded, *No worries. Catch you later.*

Ella pulled off the Veil visor and switched off the game. Swinging her door open wide, Ella raced down the hallway, then down the stairs. Her parents were already there, staring at her wide-eyed.

Her mother whispered harshly, "Is it CIU?"

Ella's dad looked through the peephole, his fists clenched. "It's a student, or at least someone who looks Ella's age."

A student?

Here?

"I'll get it," Ella volunteered bravely, though she didn't feel brave at all.

Why would a student be here at her house? How would they even know where she lived?

Grabbing the knob, Ella opened the door.

Standing in front of her was Wren Martis.

CHAPTER 6
WREN

"Hey, Ella. Just wanted to check in and see if you were okay," Wren said quickly so Ella's parents wouldn't be immediately suspicious of her motives.

Wren lucked out living so close to Ella as she was able to run to her house after uniting her incorporeal form with her corporeal one. Lizzie would have to drive, but she knew she'd be there at any moment. Of course, Wren had had no idea which house was Ella's at first, so she'd had to cast a spell that got her into the school directory online, where she looked Ella up.

"Oh," Ella stammered as her parents stood behind her like nervous pillars. "I'm fine. A little frazzled is all."

Get ready to be frazzled some more, because a Tracker is coming over any minute to test to see if you're a Dis-con. "Do you mind if I come in?" Wren asked. She knew they'd come up with an excuse, so she didn't wait for an answer and pushed her way inside to the front foyer.

"Oh, uh, we were about to spell an early lunch . . ." Ella's mother began.

Wren cut her off. "That sounds lovely. Thank you so much for inviting me." Cringe. But necessary.

A few awkward looks exchanged, then Ella's dad said, "You're welcome, and you are?"

Ella answered, "Wren Martis. She's in my quantum spell-casting class, first period."

"I didn't know you had a friend, Ella. You should have invited Wren over sooner." Ella's mom threw Ella a pointed look.

Wren didn't want to cause any more trouble for Ella than she already had, and assuming Ella's rules had been like her mother's rules, Wren was pretty sure they'd given Ella a "no friendship" clause, so Wren interjected, "This is actually the first time we've spoken, but after the craziness of this morning and Ella's heroics, I had to come over and make sure she was okay. I live down the street from here."

Visible relief crossed Ella's parents' faces, and they both nodded. It was her father that spoke though. "Let's all get something to eat."

He led the way toward the kitchen, followed by Ella's mom, Ella, then Wren. Right as Ella's father walked through the kitchen threshold, there was a knock on the door.

Lizzie.

All three of the Buckleys jumped at the sound, then a furtive exchange of glances.

"Maybe another student checking in?" Wren offered, trying to ease their obvious anxiety.

"I'll get it," Ella said, hands clenched while she moved past Wren to get to the door.

Ella's parents forced smiles at Wren, and she smiled back, then nodded her head toward Ella. "I'll go with her, see who it is." Turning her back on Nara and John Buckley, Wren quickly joined Ella's side as they approached the door.

Ella's eyes darted sideways at Wren, but she said nothing as she turned the knob, opening the door.

Lizzie Trent stood in front of them, sending a momentary flash of curiosity in Wren's direction. But then her gaze moved solely to Ella. "Hey, Ella."

"Uh, hi," Ella responded with a slight squeak in her voice.

Lizzie shifted from foot to foot as if she were nervous, but Wren saw her eyes were focused, active, a hunter. "I wanted to say, I don't think you cast the plague spell this morning. I can't say the same for the rest of the school, especially Rachel." Her eyes bored into Ella's. "Rachel *really* thinks you did it. She's probably just being protective of me, but I thought you should know."

Ella swallowed hard. "Oh. I . . ."

Wren interjected, "CIU cast a signature-reveal spell, and it came up negative though. Plus, again at the sealing-dome exit. Double proof. Right, Ella?"

"Um, yeah." Ella took in a deep breath.

This girl was flailing. It was probably more real-life interaction than she'd ever had in her entire life.

"Signature-reveal spells can be tweaked," Lizzie answered sharply.

"Can they though? I've never heard of anyone being able to do that," Wren quipped back, staring Lizzie down while trying to hold in her rage.

"That plague spell was like nothing I've ever seen, and if one was capable of casting that, they might have been able to cast something that would help them get away with it." Lizzie now stared at Wren, eyeing her intensely.

Did she know about Wren? She hadn't said anything to Rachel at their hideout. And she suspected Ella of being a Dis-con, not a Skein-level caster. Unless she was changing her theory.

"Who is this?" Nara stepped beside Wren, startling her out of her spiral of thoughts. John stood on the other side of Ella.

"I'm Lizzie. I was one of the victims this morning. I don't think your daughter is guilty, but everyone else does. I just wanted to give her a heads-up." Lizzie smiled with an evil glint in her eye, knowing full well how panicked it would make Ella's parents.

"You know what? I'm going to skip on lunch. Thanks so much though. Lizzie, let's leave the Buckleys alone. Ella's been through a lot today, as have you. I'm sure she appreciates your warning, but now's not the time, don't you think?" Wren forced as much sincerity as she could into her words. She didn't want Lizzie to perform a spell.

Lizzie paused, then sighed, eyes on Ella's mother. "I could cast an antianxiety spell on Ella if you think it'll help. I'm sorry to cause even more stress to your lives."

But Nara Buckley handled Lizzie like a practiced champ. "We'll be casting our own spells on our daughter, but we appreciate it." She turned to Ella casually. "I think the neck and shoulder relaxer will do nicely?"

"Uh, yeah, that sounds good, actually. Thanks, Mom." Ella's eyes met Lizzie's. "And thanks for suggesting it. I was too freaked out to think about it."

A flash of disappointment crossed Lizzie's expression, but she nodded. "Anytime. I hope to see you at school tomorrow?"

Ella forced a smile. "Yeah, see you then. You too, Wren."

Wren gave a small salute to Ella as she walked out the front door. It took everything in her power not to strangle Lizzie right there, but Ella's safety was priority.

As Ella began to shut the door, she yelled out to Lizzie. "And I'm glad to see you're doing okay."

Lizzie nodded and smiled. "Thanks."

With that, Ella closed the door.

Wren knew Ella wasn't safe from Lizzie's testing by any means, but at least she'd stalled her for now, and if she was lucky, for a day or two.

And so began the longest walk of Wren's life, even though it was only a few seconds. Evil Incarnate and Wren made their way to Lizzie's car, the silence between them palpable, almost as if Wren's hatred was creating a barrier of an invisible storm, ready to lash out and destroy her enemy. But instead of attacking Lizzie, Wren said, "Have a good day, Lizzie." Her stomach roiled with acid with each friendly word.

"You too." Lizzie walked to the driver's side of the car and opened the door. Before she slid inside, she said, "Keep your guard up for that attacker. We don't know when or if they'll strike again." Lizzie's tone almost seemed pointed, as if she were testing Wren's reaction.

"Of course. Thanks for looking out. You be careful too. From what I heard, you got the worst of it. I hope you weren't the actual target." Wren forced another smile, but part of her grin was real as she recognized a flicker of concern on Lizzie's face.

Because Lizzie *should* be concerned.

The next attack Wren cast would be to kill.

CHAPTER 7
ELLA

"Get away from the door." Ella's father grabbed her by the arm and pulled her away, dragging her toward the kitchen.

She shrugged him off with a huff midway, though her insides shook and she thought she might vomit right there. "I'm fine. They were just seeing if I was okay."

Ella's mother whirled on her. "I don't know what either of those two girls were doing, but an idiot could see they both had alternate agendas. We need to move. Tonight."

Both Wren and Lizzie had acted strange—Ella couldn't deny that—but alternate agendas? "I'm pretty sure they both think I cast that plague spell, *which* is good. The last thing on their minds is suspecting me of being a Dis-con." Ella crossed her arms defiantly. "And we're not moving! That would make people even more suspicious than they already are."

"I don't care if they're suspicious! Damn it, Ella! We're trying to keep you alive!" Ella's dad's voice rang with exasperation and exhaustion.

"You don't think I know that? But what kind of life is this? You two aren't happy! You're miserable! And *I'm* the reason!" Tears rushed to Ella's eyes before she could stop them.

Both her parents' demeanors slumped at her words, their brows furrowed. "Oh, Ella," her mom said. "You are our entire joy in this life. Keeping you safe is the only thing that's important to us."

Before Ella could react, both her parents' arms wrapped around her in a family hug. She let her tears run free against their chests, and they did the same. They stood like that for a long while, until finally, Ella slowly broke free.

"Can we just wait a few weeks to see how things go? I promise I'll be the first to pack if I think anyone suspects me of being a Discon." Ella tried to sound convincing.

Her parents exchanged wary glances, but both nodded. "We want reports from you every day after school."

"Of course. I'd do that anyway."

Ella's mom kissed her forehead. "We'll stay for now."

Smiling up at her mom, then her dad, Ella took a deep relieved breath. "Thank you."

Finally, her parents smiled back, a little bit of normalcy peeking through. "Now go play that game of yours. It'll take your mind off everything."

Her mother knew her well.

Not waiting for another response, Ella leapt up the stairs to her room. Maybe Buster44 was still on and she could play another round with him.

Throwing on the headset, Ella switched Veil on and entered

the game as FearlessGirl22. She needed to be a Dis-con with power, because right now, she felt powerless. Not one, but *two* people from school showing up unannounced at her house at almost the exact same time? Did they plan it together? Ella didn't think so since Wren practically shoved Lizzie out the door as soon as she arrived. Did Wren think she was protecting Ella in some way? Lizzie did come off as aggressive, but Ella could hardly blame her from what Lizzie had gone through only hours ago. Ella would be looking for someone to blame too.

The world of *Hexsphere* materialized all around her until she was at FearlessGirl22's house with the replica of Ash inside. She glanced at him briefly and wished he had showed up at her door instead of Wren and Lizzie. Scratch that. Ella would have passed out the instant she saw him if his cute adorable face was on the other side of her front door. No. Staring at the creation she'd made in her video game was as close as Ella wanted to get to Ash. Any real-life contact and her brain would explode.

Shaking thoughts of Ash from her mind, Ella brought up the virtual keyboard and typed *Buster44* into the search window.

Buster44 is in mid-battle at the Fortnight Oasis. Would you like to request to join?

Ella typed in *Yes* and waited.

It took all of two seconds for the scenery to shift and swirl around her. Now, she stood in the center of a seemingly empty ruin of a skyscraper among an entire city of apocalyptic ravaged skyscrapers. She had played on this battlefield before, but it had been a while. One thing she remembered the most was . . .

. . . flying Tracker blades from the broken floors above.

Ella made her character duck just in time while at the same time grabbing two of the blades that clattered at her feet. Last time she'd fought here, FearlessGirl22's arm had been sliced clear off, but she'd still managed to win one-handed.

Over here! Buster44's text bubble popped up to FearlessGirl22's immediate right. Swinging her character's head right, she saw Buster44 take cover behind a broken brick wall. Tightening her grip on the two Tracker blades, FearlessGirl22 ran to Buster44. As she reached the broken half wall, another Tracker blade helicoptered toward her head.

Swinging her own blade, FearlessGirl22 smacked the oncoming blade with a loud clank, causing the attacking sword to fly back where it had come from.

Ella typed, and the bubble formed at her character's mouth: *How many?*

Five. All on level two, Buster44 said.

Not one has dropped? Ella typed.

Buster44 shook his head in the negative. *Weird, right?* His text bubble floated next to him.

It *was* weird, especially for this battleground. Usually, by now at least one or two Trackers would have dropped to form a closing jaw with Trackers on both high ground and low ground. Though high ground still gave the Trackers the advantage, Ella tried to think of how to use the fact that she and Buster44 were alone on the bottom level as a way to beat them.

The debris and fallen bricks around them lifted into the air.

A levitation spell.

Ella wished she could use her real-life Dis-con ability and push on the levitation spell itself, sending all the debris up to the Trackers above them. But this was a game, and what she could do was impossible, not to mention the fact that she'd never heard of anything like it before.

Diving down behind the small cover of wall they had, FearlessGirl22 knew they'd both be crushed by the amount of junk flying their way, from rebar to chunks of cement. They'd be flattened and punctured, their game characters dying instantly. No wonder the Trackers stayed above. This must've been new programming since so many players probably knew how to escape the old way.

Buster44 didn't bother hiding, knowing their fate as well. Instead, he decided to make light of their characters' fates and danced a jig. Ella laughed, then controlled FearlessGirl22 to stand up next to him, then typed *Forward slash dance*, and her character began to dance next to him. She imagined whoever was playing Buster44 laughing with her as the they performed the silly dance the gaming programmers had made for the characters.

Right as the debris was about to hit, a wave of recklessness hit Ella, and she typed in *Forward slash push levitation spell.* She had no idea what made her type that. What was she thinking? It wouldn't do anything.

Waiting for the inevitable error message to pop up on her screen as it usually did whenever she entered a typo or a command that didn't exist, Ella's eyes grew round as the command did *exactly* what she'd asked.

As the debris was about to make contact, it reversed its course and flew back up to the five Trackers now standing on the precarious second floor. It hit them with stunning impact, impaling some with the rebar and some with shards of glass and some with stone and brick. They all toppled to the ground with loud splats and crunches.

All of them were dead.

What did you do? Buster44 was no longer dancing.

Ella yanked off her headset and switched off her game, her breath coming in ragged gulps.

What just happened?

Ella had typed in her exact power and *it existed.* It had been coded into a public game.

Which could only mean . . .

There were others like her.

A terrified thrill raced through her. Before she could let her mind travel too far into full panic mode, Ella tossed aside Veil and grabbed her laptop off the nightstand. Ella typed into the search engine box: *using forward slash push levitation spell Hexsphere.*

Waiting the infinitesimal half a second it took for the results felt like an eternity, but a wave of relief hit Ella when she read the headline: *Programmers at Hex Solutions Add a New Twist to* Hexsphere *Where Players Can Push Back on Spells.* There were a few other articles, all with the same message and some with instructions on how to type in the command. She searched for the dates of each article. Each was posted in the last week, so this was brand-new information.

Ella let out her breath. A lingering doubt itched at the back of her head though. Could it really be coincidence that game programmers came up with the *exact* power Ella had? Or was one of them like her and wanted to impress their bosses? Or did they know a Dis-con like her and recklessly decided to put it in the game, putting that Dis-con at risk? Because this was huge. And terrifying. What if CIU or Trackers themselves thought there was some validity or even knew of Dis-cons pushing back on spells? And what made Ella want to type that command in the first place? It had been so irresponsible. She was full of irresponsible today, it seemed.

Leaning back on her pillow, closing her laptop, Ella took deep calming breaths to slow her heart rate down.

Was this a good or a bad thing? She couldn't decide. But one thing was for sure: what started out as a fun release from today's events had turned into something ten times more perplexing.

Ella just hoped typing in that command wouldn't come back to bite her.

CHAPTER 3
WREN

Right foot. Left foot. Right foot. Left foot.

Wren breathed in deep.

Speaking actual words to Lizzie had sent her heart thundering in her chest. The Tracker had driven off ten minutes ago, but no matter how hard Wren tried, she couldn't get her body to calm down. She'd been going to school with Lizzie for three months now, but she'd never spoken to her. She'd never spoken to her *ever*. Wren's first real contact with Lizzie was casting the plague spell on her, and she had kind of wanted to keep it that way.

But Ella's safety came first.

Pretending to be civil to any Tracker let alone Evil Incarnate had taken every ounce of self-control Wren had in her. But she'd done it. It was over.

And it was time to calm down.

So why couldn't she calm down?

Wren focused on each step again, on the cement underneath her feet, on the grass edging on her left, on each neighbors' lawn to her right. Grounded. Left foot. Right foot. Breathe.

It didn't take long for her to reach her house.

Once Wren stepped inside, her heart rate slowed to a somewhat normal pace. She felt safer on her home turf, though she probably wasn't, but at least she had a stash of spells that were downstairs and ready to cast if she needed to. Always vigilant. Always expect an attack.

As she walked toward the downstairs door, the sound of keys rattled from the front door.

Frank Martis. Wren's father.

She glanced at the clock on the wall. Wren had forgotten completely that her father came home midmorning. Normally, she was at school.

He worked nights as a customer service representative for Ditell-tech, one of the five major holo-phone companies. He knew absolutely nothing about holo-phones or the spells required to run them, but his job was to calm customers down and take complaints. Wren was pretty sure he hated the job, though she wouldn't really know because he rarely spoke to her. But she knew he kept it because he could transfer easily from city to city. It was the only form of affection he showed her, keeping himself available to move at a moment's notice.

Frank walked in and nearly tripped bumping into Wren's still body. He took a moment to acknowledge her presence (this in itself was an anomaly), looked as if he was going to ask why she wasn't at school, thought better of it, and trudged upstairs toward his bedroom and his awaited sleep.

"I'm fine, by the way!" Wren couldn't resist yelling at his departing figure.

Her dad mumbled something under his breath but didn't break

stride, nor did he turn back to face her. He kept walking up the stairs until he was out of view.

A light click of the door closing ended the only interaction Wren was going to get from her father for the morning. It was more than she normally got. And at least he hadn't noticed the missing truck in the backyard, although a small part of her wanted to see if it might jolt him out of his self-made coma. It didn't look like that would be today.

A rush of rage suddenly flowed through Wren.

No. She wasn't going to let him get away with ignoring her this time.

She raced up the stairs after her father and swung open his bedroom door. Frank stood in a T-shirt and boxers, holding the comforter on his bed up, about to climb in.

His eyes met Wren's, and there was a flash of shock.

But still no words.

"Talk to me!" Wren screamed louder than she'd expected.

"I need to sleep." His voice was barely above a whisper.

Wren wasn't having it.

She leaned forward and grabbed her father's upper arm, forcing him to make eye contact with her. "You can sleep later! Don't you even want to know why I'm home early? Aren't you worried? Don't you care?" Wren knew the answer to all those questions was *no*, but for some reason she needed to hear him admit it.

"Wren, I need to sleep so I can work tonight. Someone has to pay the bills." His tone was soft, not accusing, simply matter-of-fact and devoid of any emotion.

He wasn't listening.

He couldn't hear her.

Unwanted tears of anger filled Wren's eyes. "So I'm just a *bill* to you?"

He moved his eyes down, focusing now on the comforter.

"Look at me!" Wren shook him.

Frank gently pried Wren's hand from his arm but refused to look at her. "I'm going to bed now. Please leave."

Wren might as well have been slapped in the face.

Her tears dried up from the indifference that began to bubble up inside her. "Fine. You don't love me anymore, so I won't love you." The words stung to say aloud, but they helped Wren gain her focus back.

Her father was a shell. She couldn't care about him anymore. And he certainly didn't care about her.

As if proving Wren's point, Frank didn't respond to her words. He simply crawled under the comforter and turned on his side so his back faced her.

Wren stood there a few seconds longer, her emotions peaking and falling in waves of anguish to total numbness. Finally, she forced her feet to move, walking out of his room and shutting the door. Wren surprised herself by not slamming it. But the numbness was taking hold as her anger began to seep out. Feeling as little as possible was the only way for her to cope.

With a deep steadying breath, Wren slowly walked down the stairs and directly down the other set of stairs that led to the basement—her safe space.

After plopping down on the plushy red chair, Wren stared at the operation board against the wall.

One thing she hadn't done yet was fully test Rachel Fen to determine which parts of her brain repellent gear had been attached to. She examined all the research she'd done on the brain, floating in holographic glory off the board. So far, she'd been able to pinpoint five places in the brain that seemed to be protected: the temporal lobe, the occipital lobe, the cerebellum, the hypothalamus, and the brain stem.

The temporal lobe was a given. Wren had actually discovered that fact in the Nigerian military vault. Trackers did it mainly because it affected memory and decision making—key factors if you were a murdering machine that needed to remember who you were hunting.

The occipital lobe was for blocking visual spells like glamours and such, but the cerebellum was an advantageous one to get gear attached to as well because it affected balance, coordination, and muscle control. An efficient killer needed to hold a Tracker blade and have the ability to use it.

The hypothalamus, which affected hormones, also regulated body temperature and maintained physiological cycles. Wren knew a few good hypothalamus spells she'd stolen from Iceland's vault that she would gladly test out on Lizzie.

But the brain stem itself was the doozy because it controlled breathing, blood pressure, heartbeat, swallowing—basically all the motor functions. China had some nasty spells that effected the brain stem. Thank goodness Lizzie's brain stem was clean.

Wren had been researching the brain almost as much as she'd been researching Trackers. The act of attaching miniaturized repellent gear to Trackers' brains was not something that most people believed was real. It sounded like a fantasy. But every single military vault she'd broken into had proof, so she researched and tested.

She'd done extensive experiments on Lizzie (and some on Rachel), but a lot of her findings had come from Larry, the Tracker that had been assigned to watch her, and four other Trackers Wren had found by following Larry after he stopped watching her for the night. She discreetly experimented on them when they were at their respective schools. Schools were the best places to find Dis-cons who had passed their Dis-con tests, so there were at least two or three Trackers in every school in the country, possibly the world.

Waiting through the eighth grade had been the biggest torture. When Lizzie killed Wren's mom, she had been posing as a high school junior. After discovering Lizzie and her alias, Wren found out she'd moved from school to school and still passed for a teenager. Wren could tell, but no one else seemed to. Her best guess at Lizzie's age was somewhere in the twenty-four to twenty-six range, which would have made her around nineteen or early twenties when she murdered Wren's mother. Young enough to want to prove herself—probably why Lizzie was so gleeful when she decapitated her.

Breathe.

Breathe.

Breathe.

It was all Wren could focus on.

Breathe.

Lizzie laughed.

Breathe.

Blood poured down what was left of her mother's neck.

Breathe.

Her mother's eyes as they stared at her in horror as the Tracker blade sliced clean through.

Breathe.

The protection spell Wren cast, failing miserably.

Breathe.

Watching the light snuff out of her mother's eyes as her head rolled out of the truck.

Breathe.

Calm down!

Stop thinking!

Breathe.

Blankness.

Breathe.

Blankness.

Breathe.

Wren's heart rate slowed, though sweat dripped down the back of her neck from the residual panic and her hands shook. She almost lost it that time. The spell that morning had obviously triggered her emotions, plus her confrontation (or non-confrontation) with her father, plus having to be civil to Evil Incarnate. It was too much. Even for her. Usually, she could keep her feelings in check, but coming so close to exacting revenge on her mother's killer must have brought up too much emotional baggage for her to cope with.

Wren had to keep it together. If she was going to take down the Trackers, she couldn't be this weak.

One more breath and she was almost completely relaxed, her hands still again.

Thinking of her mission, she knew she needed to add one more person to the spider diagram—one she never thought she'd ever have to add.

Moira Kurt.

Moira.

Wren could see it. She knew how powerful Moira was.

A class behind Wren, but so much more advanced than anyone at the school. No wonder Moira had jumped onto the Trackers' radar.

Wren couldn't explain it, but she felt like there was some other reason Rachel and Lizzie wanted Moira on their team.

Moira was most likely an innocent at this point, but would she be for long? Would Rachel and Lizzie's rousing speech about destroying Dis-cons excite her? Would it appeal to her? The thought brought bile to Wren's throat.

On one hand, Moira had been quick to blame Ella for the plague spell, but didn't that mean Moira thought Ella was a terrorist spell-caster and not a Dis-con? And on the other hand . . . it was *Moira!*

With a grunt, Wren pried herself up off the chair and strode over to the board, then opened her phone and scrolled through her pics until she found one of Moira taken at lunch. Wren didn't take many pictures for recreation or fun, but sometimes to fit in, she'd make an exception. Wren had been eating lunch with Moira one day and thought it was an appropriate time for a "friend pic," and from the smile on Moira's face, she definitely seemed happy about it.

Wren traced a finger over Moira's picture. Moira couldn't be turned. Could she? Wren didn't want to believe that someone she liked so much would consider becoming a Tracker, but fear of Dis-cons ran deep in the world, and Wren didn't know how Moira felt about it. How could she? They never got too heavy in their conversations. Wren had never allowed it.

Casting a quick spell, she pulled the picture of Moira out of the phone to create a three-dimensional hologram like the others on the operation board. Wren moved it with her hand like a floating bubble and placed it between Rachel's and Lizzie's holographic images. Wren didn't consider Moira a Tracker yet, but knowing that she was being recruited put her next to them.

Wren stared at the holograph, trying to find some kind of answers in an empty image.

She'd have to be on guard with Moira in the future.

She'd also have to find out whatever she could about the girl.

Research was Wren's best friend.

No more being blindsided. Not like she'd been when her mother was attacked.

Sighing deeply, Wren pried her eyes away from the operation board and walked to the couch where her laptop lay on a cushion.

Sitting down and flipping open the computer, Wren got to work.

Her preliminary search brought up nothing incriminating. Moira's parents had gotten divorced a year ago, resulting in her and her mom moving here to Los Angeles.

Did Trackers recruit people with broken homes? Manipulate them? Convince them that somehow a Dis-con was responsible for all their problems in life? Wren was sure it was all of the above.

But one thing was for sure: Wren didn't know Moira at all.

Wren needed to change that. For her mission. How else could she counter Rachel and Lizzie's recruiting speech?

Moira Kurt was about to become her best friend.

Starting tomorrow.

CHAPTER 9
ELLA

Ella jolted awake at the knocking on her bedroom door. It was a gentle knock, but she'd obviously been in a deep sleep.

"Yeah," she croaked. "Come in."

Her mother opened the door but stayed in the hallway. "Looks like school is happening today."

Ella stood up at her mother's words and stretched. "I figured. Any word on CIU still hanging around?"

"According to the news, they'll be conducting interviews in the next couple of days." Her mother sighed nervously.

Ella walked over to her mom and hugged her. "It'll be fine, Mom. I was already interviewed, and they cast a signature-reveal spell on me, remember? Twice. I'm safe. Trust me." Ella pulled back so her mother could see the determination in her eyes.

It must have worked, because her mom's face softened and she kissed Ella's forehead. "I do trust you. It's everyone else I don't trust. But don't worry, I'm not going to do anything. We'll see this through." She touched Ella's arm affectionately. "But I am getting our finances in order just in case."

Ella groaned. "Mom . . ."

"*Just in case.* You can't expect me to do nothing." Her mom gave her one last squeeze on the arm. "You want me to drive you to school?"

Ella had a momentary panic-flash of possibly being cornered by Wren when she'd walk past her house. "Um, yeah, that would be nice."

"Great. We'll leave after you eat. I spelled you a nice breakfast. Not healthy, but well deserved."

"Oooo, that sounds like my kind of breakfast." Ella perked up at that. If her mother said it wasn't healthy, it had to be good.

Her mother's smile lifted Ella's entire mood. She savored the moment since the pit of her stomach told her more chaos was heading her way.

But getting a ride and avoiding Wren Martis was at least one less thing to worry about.

Now all she'd have to worry about was the entire school thinking she was guilty.

And the fact that someone out there working for Hex Solutions may know about a Dis-con like her. If someone programmed it, someone knew her ability existed. Having had the entire night to ponder it, Ella was convinced of that.

And she definitely would *not* be telling her parents about it.

Ella smiled back. "I'll be down in a few."

With that, her mom left, and Ella shut the door behind her.

After quickly dressing in jeans and a princess-sleeved T-shirt, Ella stuffed Veil into her backpack. She planned on researching the game from the inside if she could. Plus, Ella would be in full avoid-everyone mode, so having the game would be a good escape when she could find a pocket or two of time.

Grabbing her backpack, Ella headed downstairs to the kitchen.

"Oh *wow*," Ella said as she took in what awaited her on the counter.

A chocolate brownie with a five-inch mound of whipped cream and chocolate sauce poured on top sat on a plate in front of her. Both her parents' eyed Ella with expectancy.

Ella's heart grew five sizes. "This looks amazing. You've never let me have sweets for breakfast before though."

"Like I said upstairs—well deserved," her mother said.

Ella's dad walked over to her and embraced her tightly. "We're so sorry we didn't even console you or make sure you were okay yesterday. We went straight to running. We made an already stressful situation for you so much worse. Can you forgive us?"

Pulling out of the hug, Ella took a swoop of whipped cream with her finger and savored its deliciousness in her mouth. "I'd say this is a good start."

The three of them laughed, and Ella's mom conjured another two brownies for herself and her husband. "We'll all be rebels today."

Ella's dad didn't need to be told twice as he dug into his brownie almost as fast as Ella did hers. After a proper pig-out, Ella felt fully jolted with sugar and was ready to face the day. In her sugar buzz, she was almost grateful for Lizzie stopping by to warn her that other students may blame her for the plague spell. It had mentally prepared her for whatever might come her way. She'd have to keep her ears out for any spell-casting so she could fake a response, but she had confidence her heart flutters would give her some warning.

Placing the now empty plates in the sink, Ella's mom smiled at her. "You ready?"

Ella nodded and realized with a little bit of confidence that she actually was. "Let's do it."

After another hug with her father, Ella and her mother hopped in the car and were at the front of the school in minutes.

Scoping out the property, her mother noted, "I only see three CIU agents near the front."

"Yeah, same. That guy there is one of the agents I talked to. His name is Malcolm Gilroy. He genuinely seemed nice." Ella watched Malcolm from afar talking to an agent she didn't recognize.

The sealing-dome had been removed, and the front entrance was packed with students.

"Are you sure you want to go today? You could stay home with us." Her mother's eyes were widened with anxiety.

Ella touched her mother's arm to calm her. "I'll be fine. I promise." Although a part of her wanted to take her mother up on that offer, a bigger part wanted to get the inquisition over with. Maybe CIU would have already caught the guy and Ella's life would be back to normal in no time. Well, normal for her, anyway.

Her mom reached out and gently squeezed Ella's hand. "Okay. Call me or come home any time during the day. I love you."

"I love you too, Mom." Ella squeezed back, then grabbed her backpack and left the car.

Slowly, she walked toward the entrance and crowd of kids piling into the school.

Ella jumped at the sound of a honk.

Turning, she shook her head. Her mom had tried to stay parked in the unloading zone to watch Ella walk into the school, but an impatient parent behind her needed her to move so they could leave. With a final wave, Ella's mom drove off.

Whispers reached Ella's ears as students walked by her:

"Pretty sure she did it."

"Can't believe she came back."

"You think CIU will arrest her first period?"

"People can fake signature-reveal spells. I saw it on that serial killer documentary."

Ella ignored the general comments and only listened for casting spells. But so far, no one was trying anything.

Ella could handle gossip, though she didn't understand why everyone was so vehement about her "guilt." They just needed someone to blame, she guessed.

Still, she had to remain vigilant. She couldn't have someone casting a random spell on her and it not working.

Pushing her way through the crowd at the front door and avoiding Agent Gilroy entirely, Ella made her way toward quantum spell-casting.

At least Ash Torres was in her first period.

His beautiful self would be a nice distraction.

CHAPTER 10
WREN

Wren made her way through the hallways of Tristan High toward first period. The buzzing of paranoid whispers about Ella surrounded her and made her stomach churn with guilt.

The spell was still intact, obviously. Wren hadn't been able to find a proper counter spell in her safe for the Ella-hate incantation Rachel had cast yesterday. She had hoped it would have faded already.

Apparently not.

Priorities though.

Four of the people Wren needed to keep an eye on were in quantum spell-casting, so she wanted the time to be productive toward her mission. She had Ella, whom she wanted to protect from Rachel and possibly Shara. Rachel because she was a Tracker, Shara because she was possibly a Tracker, and Moira, who was on Rachel and Lizzie's recruitment list.

Ella had either anticipated that Wren would want to walk her to school, or she just wanted the safety of her mother giving her a ride. Either way, Wren hadn't had the time she'd wanted to talk to Ella some more. Not that she would reveal anything to Ella, but Wren was responsible for her being in danger, and she didn't take that lightly.

Shara was a big priority today. Wren needed to know for sure if she was a Tracker or not, but Rachel was the top priority. A Tracker's standard strategy was to provoke and observe, so Wren expected Rachel to cause some kind of stir with Ella in class today. The spell from yesterday primed Ella for an emotional slaughter and a class full of students who'd cheer Rachel on. Of course, sometimes provoking a target backfired on the Trackers if the person wasn't actually a Dis-con and ended up casting a nasty Torment-hex out of anger. But if the target was a Dis-con, provoking them was the easiest way to flush them out without using spells themselves. Wren needed to stay vigilant and make sure neither Rachel *nor* Shara cast a small spell on Ella to see if she would react to it.

It was a lot.

It was overwhelming.

But Wren was ready.

Her plan: sit in the back of the classroom and watch how they interacted with Ella.

Strategies helped calm her nerves.

Moira pushed through the crowd until she was by Wren's side.

Suddenly, Wren didn't know how to act, how to talk, how to form a single expression on her face that didn't look like she was sizing Moira up. Who was this girl? Had Rachel given her the speech she had planned yet? Was Moira officially a Tracker-in-training?

"What's up with you?" Moira asked innocently.

Nope. Still nothing Wren could think of to say.

"I know you think she's innocent, but I'm kind of freaked that Ella is coming to school today. You still think she didn't do it?" The slight shift in Moira's eyes indicated to Wren that she was concerned about Wren's reaction.

Stupid spell.

Her voice came back. "I'm positive she didn't do it. Why are you on this again? I never took you for buying into gossip. It's beneath you." It sounded harsh even to her, but Wren hoped she could jolt Moira into reality with a good shaming.

Moira flinched as if Wren had hit her. "I . . . I guess . . . Rachel got in my head. Her arguments are pretty solid. You should listen to what she has to say."

Wren's chest tightened as she tried to control the rage boiling inside of her. *You mean the spell she cast on you that you're too blind to see?* Wren wanted to say, but instead, she said, "*Rachel*? Are you joking? The meanest girl school? Since when did you start talking to her?" Gain information. Asking the question instantly tamped down the anger and helped Wren focus. How long had Rachel been having private conversations with Moira?

"Not long. She needed help on her quantum spell-casting homework a little over a week ago. She's been super sweet. With me, anyway," Moira said defensively, as if this would convince Wren that Rachel was somehow a normal teenager.

"Well, she's not. Just promise me you'll be as suspicious of Rachel as you are of Ella whenever she talks to you again." Why had Wren said that? She should've shut Moira down and vowed to never talk to her again. The girl was a liability. But the thought of Moira becoming a Tracker that Wren would have to kill someday broke her in ways she couldn't explain.

"Did Rachel do something to you?" Moira's fists clenched. She looked downright protective.

Wren had to admit, it gave her a slight thrill to see Moira like that in regard to her.

"Just promise me?" Wren asked again.

Moira nodded, curiosity mixed with a bit of fear in her eyes. "I promise. And I hope you're right about Ella, because we're about to have class with her, you know."

"Oh, I know, and do I looked worried?" Wren made sure she said it in a way that left no arguments on where she stood on Ella's innocence.

"No," Moira admitted. After a moment, she tilted her head to the side as they walked, looking up at Wren thoughtfully. "Who could even think of doing something so horrible?" Moira asked. "And what if they're not done yet? What if they wanted to kill someone?"

Moira didn't know how right she was.

Wren did want to kill someone.

Moira's new friend Rachel, for one.

Wren stopped Moira in the hallway, placing her hand on her shoulder. It wasn't in Wren's nature, but she felt the urge to calm Moira down. Probably because Wren knew not only was *she* the cause for Moira's panic, but the Tracker's paranoia spell didn't help either. "Moira. Relax. I know you think Ella did this, but I know she didn't. I just know. And besides, even if I'm wrong, which I'm not, she's not stupid enough to try again the day after. It would be too obvious. She'd be arrested on the spot."

"I guess," Moira admitted. "But if she's crazy, she won't care. I'd rather not be in the same room with her."

Wren took her hand away from Moira's shoulder, and they began walking toward class once more. The problem with paranoia and fear spells was that people were naturally afraid. It rooted deep inside and only grew, a person's own narrative feeding it until it transformed into a poison. Listening to the gossiping voices around them, Wren hated Rachel and Lizzie even more, and she hadn't thought that was possible. When the seed was planted about someone, especially with a spell, it was almost impossible to convince anyone of their innocence.

"Look, you and I are practically Skeins, probably beyond Skeins if we're being honest. We can handle anything, including some crazy plague terrorist. I'll sit in the back and you sit in the front. That way, we've got the room covered if anyone tries anything." Wren cleverly came up with a plan that would allow her not to sit with Moira. Wren usually sat in the back anyway, but the way Moira was freaking out, she was almost positive Moira would have sat with her. And Wren needed to keep an eye on Ella. The mere suspicion that Shara could potentially be another Tracker, let alone knowing for sure that Rachel was one, was enough for Wren to be extra cautious.

Wren couldn't believe she had put Ella in so much danger!

Frustration built inside of her to the point that she wanted to scream.

Breathe.

Calm.

Breathe.

Calm.

"That's a good idea," Moira acknowledged Wren's plan. "But if I see Ella do anything that seems suspicious, I don't know if I'll be able to keep quiet. I know you trust her for some reason, but I'm not convinced."

Wren's instinct was to lash out, but she stopped herself. Moira was spelled. It wasn't her fault. Wren would find a way to break it. And she actually didn't mind that threat. After all, Moira possibly speaking out against Ella could provoke Shara into doing or saying something that might tip her hand. Of course, Rachel may take advantage too, instead of Shara, but Wren couldn't worry about that. All she could do was observe. "You do what you gotta do."

Reaching the quantum spell-casting classroom took only seconds. It was already filling up. The room itself was larger than most, being that it was a science class. In the front half were seven rows of desks with ten desks to a row, and in the back were four rows of long tables equipped with sinks that were used for spell labs.

Ella sat at a desk near the back.

Perfect.

Wren nodded to Moira, indicating that she'd sit next to Ella. She was lucky there was an empty seat. As Wren sat down, she couldn't help but look at Ella. She truly was beautiful, though she tried her best to blend in. Dressed in a cute floral T-shirt with princess sleeves and black jeans, Ella tucked her thick wavy black hair behind her ear. Her eyes kept looking over at Ash Torres like they had in line yesterday. Yup. Definitely into him.

Moira acknowledged Wren with a slight nod herself and headed to the front of the room, hands shaking slightly.

Wren's chest ached.

Moira.

The plague spell had definitely done a number on her, and Rachel's fear spell didn't help matters.

Wren remembered the first conversation she'd had with Moira. It was her second day of school (though her memory spell had made everyone think she'd been there three years), and she'd just given a presentation for Hex Lab about using the kinetic energy from a spinning sphere to create enough power to charge a battery. After class, Moira had raced up to Wren, asking her how she'd managed to combine two rotation spells to get her results. Not even the Hex Lab teacher, Mr. Finley, had noticed that. Wren was so shocked that Moira had not only been so observant, but also had the skill level to recognize the amount of power it took to combine two spells like that, that she'd immediately started gushing about how she did it.

Somewhere in the middle of her explanation, it occurred to Wren that she was actually talking to someone. At that moment, her brain had told her to run, that it had been a mistake. She'd gone four years without making contact with anyone. All that mattered was the mission.

But when talking to Moira, Wren's whole body had flushed with . . . energy? Happiness? Relief? She had almost cried. With her father barely acknowledging her presence and her mother gone forever, Wren had kept herself company with her vengeance and her purpose, so to finally speak to someone? And have them respond back?

Wren had rooted herself in place and savored every morsel of conversation they had that day. She had told herself that would be it, that she had enjoyed that brief respite from her mission, but she'd never speak to Moira again.

But the next day, Wren found herself initiating a conversation with Moira. *Initiating!* From then on, Wren had just accepted Moira as a cover friend. But now? Being recruited by Trackers? Wren may have to see her as an enemy.

Wren refocused on Shara and Rachel and protecting Ella.

Shara sat a few seats away, but Rachel wasn't there yet. Maybe conferring with Lizzie or her Tracker overlords? Wren didn't know. She wished she could cast a quick spying spell to check. But a Tracker would spot that right away. And from the way the air sizzled with nervous energy, everyone was on high alert after yesterday's attack. Wren was positive anyone would notice a spell being cast at this point.

Moira's eyes glanced at Wren as she sat down, slightly widened and full of fear.

There was that ache again.

What would Moira do if she found out it was Wren who had cast that plague spell?

Probably be terrified out of her mind.

Because what Wren did *was* terrifying.

But what she was going to do would be so much worse.

No Tracker was safe from Wren.

Even Moira, if she became one.

CHAPTER 11
ELLA

Why? Why was Ash Torres so cute?

Why did he look like a chiseled masterpiece just sitting there?

Something had to be wrong with him. No one could really be that perfect. Ella would think he used a glamour spell if she wasn't a Dis-con that it wouldn't work on.

She couldn't seem to stop her hands from tingling when she glanced in his direction. He sat two desks away, also in the back but in the seventh row next to the wall of windows that made up the entire side of the classroom. The view of Ash was way better than the actual view outside, which was the teachers' boring parking lot.

Ash was a nice distraction, but her brain still pondered *Hexsphere*. Her paranoia worried that gameplay was being watched by CIU or worse the Tracker organization and Ella would be flagged. Even though she knew it had been in the news and wasn't a secret on any level, it still bothered her that the command existed in the first place. No matter how many ways she thought about it, it still felt like a trap somehow.

But as far as school life went, Ella really hoped they'd find the guy that cast the plague spell so she could go back to being invisible. Though she didn't know how likely that would be considering CIU was acting on the wrong information.

Ugh.

She glanced over at Wren Martis sitting at the desk next to her in the back, third row. A pang of guilt washed through Ella. She'd deliberately avoided Wren twice now, once on her way home yesterday and again this morning when she took a ride from her mom. She didn't know why. Wren was a sweet quiet senior. Of course, she appeared as if she didn't eat or sleep much, and she always wore the same black T-shirt that looked like it hadn't been washed in a few days and jeans that had a few holes in them—and not the kind that were fashionably added before purchase. No, these holes had been earned by wearing them every day since school started.

Wren wasn't popular or unpopular. She just didn't really exist to most people. Ella hardly ever saw her interact with anyone except Moira Kurt, which was why Ella had first started noticing her, since Moira was a whiz kid that everyone paid attention to. But "not existing" was a bond Wren didn't even know she and Ella had.

Wren's eyes briefly met Ella's, and she smiled warmly.

Ella nodded politely. At least Wren wasn't mad at her, it seemed. When it looked as if Wren was about to say something, Ella turned away, ignoring her yet again. What was wrong with her? Groaning under her breath at her own behavior, Ella pulled out her quantum spell-casting book from her bag. Staring at the cheesy cover of the textbook made her smile. It was of a man speaking an incantation with visible waves flowing out of his mouth.

Ella's smile quickly faded as she prepared for another boring class.

Only a few minutes to go and their teacher Mr. Tildon still hadn't arrived. Strange for him, but there had been a terrorist attack yesterday, so maybe he'd gotten held up somehow. Rachel Fen, however, strode in like she owned the place. Lizzie had mentioned the night before that Rachel fully believed in Ella's guilt, but Ella hoped Rachel would leave her alone.

As Rachel glanced at Ella with a look of utter disgust, she whispered something in her neighbor's ear. Their eyes immediately went to Ella, and they chuckled.

Great.

Absolutely none of that could be good.

A twinge of jealousy hit Ella when Rachel's gaze turned to Ash and she smiled her oh-so-perfect smile directly at him.

And he smiled back.

Mr. Mute!

Ella's Mr. Mute.

Did they know each other? Were they friends? Or worse . . . were they dating?

Why did that idea hurt so much?

Ella didn't know Ash. He could date or like or be friends with anyone he wanted.

But Rachel Fen?

She was so mean.

Reality check.

Ella knew nothing about her crush.

She didn't think her mood could deflate more.

Ella assumed because Ash was so quiet like her, that he was

somehow the shy but sweet type.

The harsh truth was . . . Ella had made that up.

He could be a jerk for all she knew.

But sparkly eyes!

Ella had probably made that up too. After all, she mainly hung out with the avatar she'd created in her game. Maybe the sparkles came from fake-Ash and not the real one.

Their exchange ended when Rachel sat down in her seat near the front of the class.

As if on cue, the bell rang.

Still no Mr. Tildon.

The class began to chatter, taking full advantage of the teacher's absence.

Ella buried her head in her quantum spell-casting book as more and more eyes darted toward her. People were talking. And they were talking about her.

Rachel Fen stood up abruptly. "Why are we all just sitting here when there's a terrorist right there!" She pointed at Ella accusingly. "Ella Buckley was at the center of the basketball team when CIU arrived."

Moira Kurt stood up as well, though she appeared less sure of herself than Rachel. Ella wouldn't be surprised if Moira ended up being a Skein. The girl was more talented than any other person in the school, hence why she was a junior taking a senior course. Moira would be attending college-level courses by next year since this class was the only quantum spell-casting course Tristan High offered. "Ella, maybe you should go home for a few days. Put everyone's mind at ease."

Way more polite than Rachel, but it still stung.

Ella knew how mobs worked though. The longer she'd stay

away, the more solidly they'd believe in her guilt. She figured if they saw her with their own eyes, they'd see she had nothing to hide.

Other than the fact that she was a Dis-con, which would arguably scare them more.

Yeah.

"Oh, we can do better than that, Moira. Mr. Tildon isn't here, so I say we go through Ella's bag and see what she's hiding in there. CIU seemed very interested in the fact that Ella had been hiding it behind the bleachers. What were you doing in the bleachers, Ella?" Rachel seemed as if she were daring Ella to speak.

Do not engage.

"I was playing my Veil, and the team is okay because *I* called EHT," Ella answered defensively. "And CIU let me go after the signature-reveal spell came up with nothing."

Good way to stick to a plan.

This time, she promised herself to not react, no matter what Rachel said, but there was no way Rachel was getting her bag.

"Just because CIU cast a signature-reveal spell on you doesn't mean you're innocent. Maybe they let you go to spy on you. There are probably spying spells on you as we speak," Rachel said.

Spying spells?

Uh-oh.

Could they?

If Rachel was right, then CIU would find out spying spells didn't work on Ella. They'd know she was a Dis-con.

She was in serious panic mode.

Rachel took it as proof.

"Why do you look so scared? Something to hide?" Rachel sneered.

Everyone was outright staring at Ella now—everyone except

Wren Martis, whose eyes darted between Rachel Fen and strangely Shara Ralter, of all people.

Where was Mr. Tildon?

But Rachel was on a roll, and she had what she loved most: center stage.

She walked up to Ella as if she were a brave soldier facing an enemy she wanted to prove she wasn't afraid of, then reached down and grabbed Ella's Veil out of her bag before Ella could move to stop her.

"Give that back!" Ella tried to snatch it back, but Rachel stepped back, easily avoiding Ella's attempt to grab it.

"Playing a game, were we? Or were you planning your attack spell and trying it out on the basketball team?" Rachel was in control now, as if she were a lawyer at a court case.

"I'm serious, Rachel. Give it back." A slight shriek of panic laced Ella's tone.

With a puff in her chest, Rachel smiled, seeming to feel even more justified in snatching it. "I bet the spells are in this device. Masked by something so the CIU agent didn't notice. He obviously fell for your innocent act."

Rachel turned on Ella's Veil and clicked *Start* on *Hexsphere*. She cast a spell on the device, but Ella didn't recognize it.

Ella's knees nearly gave out. Rachel had incanted a holograph spell.

A holograph spell that made the entire game come to life in the classroom itself. And currently, they all stood in Ella's starting area.

The area with the house.

And the avatar of Ash.

Rachel's face beamed with glee. "Someone is obsessed. A

stalker, are we?" Rachel laughed. "You actually *created* your very own boyfriend." She flashed a smile at Ash. "What do you think? Flattered or disgusted?"

Half the class roared with laughter. Another quarter looked at Ella and avatar-Ash warily, and the last quarter tried to act as if they didn't really care or even acknowledge the hologram surrounding them.

After Rachel squeezed out every last laugh she could at Ella's expense, she turned off the Veil, and the hologram disappeared with it. She slammed it on Ella's desk. "I still think you did it, and I'm going to make sure you pay before you hurt anyone else."

"I didn't hurt anyone," Ella said softly. She was on the verge of tears, and she didn't dare look over at Ash, who was probably as embarrassed as she was. And she was positive his answer would have been *disgusted.*

"We'll see about that." Rachel gave Ella one last look of reproach, then spun around and walked back to her seat.

What a performance.

Could Ella punch Rachel now?

Could she punch herself now?

As in knock herself unconscious so she didn't have to be there anymore.

Ella refused to look at Ash.

What must he be thinking?

That she was a psycho. And she couldn't really argue with him there.

Barging into the classroom, Mr. Tildon arrived disheveled and oblivious to the tension in the room. "Sorry for the delay. Had to meet with CIU about the attack yesterday." He rushed up to the front of the room, grabbing the textbook off his desk. "Open your books to chapter six. We're going over the breakdown of telekinesis spells. Maybe have a lab or two," Mr. Tildon said, slightly out of breath. He was a burly man in his late sixties with white hair, dressed in a blue long-sleeved button-up shirt and tan slacks. He'd been teaching for forty years. Needless to say: he was over it.

Labs usually shot panic through Ella's nerves, but having a holographic display of avatar-Ash pretty much blew any kind of reaction she'd have to labs out of the water. Telekinesis spells were the easiest to fake anyway. All she'd need was a lab partner that could cast a successful telekinesis spell. She'd be able push back on it to make it look like she was succeeding as well. She'd just look like a bad caster rather than what she was. So far this year, there had been five labs, and she'd failed every single one of them. But a couple other kids in the class had failed too, so at least she hadn't been singled out.

Ella had tried (in a non-alarming kind of way) to get out of taking quantum spell-casting in the first place, knowing full well that students had to perform spells. But when Vice Principal Velenti started asking her more and more in-depth questions as to why she didn't want to take the course, Ella had backed down.

She told him she was intimidated and scared she'd fail because she wasn't very good at performing spells. He seemed to have bought it, mainly because Ella was seventeen and could only be standing in front of him if she'd passed the Dis-con test at twelve, but it was probably a risk Ella shouldn't have taken.

Glad no additional focus was put on what Rachel had just done to humiliate her, Ella flipped to chapter six with everyone else in class. There were more hammy pictures of people with their mouths open and visible waves pouring out of them, leading to a water bottle and a pair of glasses being lifted into the air. Of course, no one could actually see the quantum waves from spell-casting in real life, but the book was trying to show a visual representation of it.

"Who can tell me why the incantation has to be spoken precisely for a telekinesis spell to work? Or any spell for that matter?" Mr. Tildon asked, still oblivious to the mood of his students.

Ella glanced at the incantations written in the book with the Varian version underneath in case someone wanted to recite the spell out loud without actually casting it. She was sure she'd be able to pull off three of them, depending on how good or bad her lab partner was. That was if anyone would partner with her.

Moira Kurt raised her hand, and Mr. Tildon nodded for her to answer.

Moira glanced back at Ella, her eyebrows furrowed in concern, then turned back to Mr. Tildon. "In order for a spell to work, the words have to be spoken precisely and in the correct frequency for the quantum waves to react as the caster intends, whether that be an interaction with an object such as telekinesis or creating matter from nothing like yesterday's attack on the varsity basketball team." Her eyes roamed in Ella's direction again.

Ella really wished she'd stop doing that.

"That's correct, Ms. Kurt." Then Mr. Tildon droned on about telekinesis spells and how quantum waves used air displacement with the right incantation to lift objects. Ella found it difficult to focus on any one thing. Darting eyes kept flying her way, and she was still scared to death to look at Ash. She wanted to burn her Veil in a giant bonfire at this point. Ella couldn't even deny that she was a stalker. She'd literally created a three-dimensional avatar of a boy so she could hang out with him.

And now everyone knew about it.

Maybe Moira's advice was good and Ella should go home. Forever.

After Mr. Tildon's lecture, he called for everyone to partner up. Ella wanted to puke. She was pretty sure at this point that no one would want to be near her and she'd have to suffer the humiliation of Rachel pointing it out.

Before Ella could make an excuse and run out of class (yes, her feet were ready to go), Shara Ralter gently touched her arm. "You want to pair up with me?" she asked.

Ella almost wanted to cry it was so unexpected. "Um, yeah. Thanks."

They walked to the very back of the room, using the corner of the lab table closest to the windows. Ella noticed most of the students found spots at the four rows of tables as far away from her as possible, and even the pair near them kept their distance.

This was going to be fun.

CHAPTER 12
WREN

"I don't think we should sit this close," Moira whispered to Wren as Wren situated herself on a lab table with a clear view of Ella.

"You don't have the slightest bit of sympathy for the girl? That was pretty brutal." Wren said, wishing she had been able to step in and cast the smile off Rachel's face. But she had needed to watch Rachel *and* Shara to make sure they didn't cast anything directly at Ella. And right now, she needed to concentrate on watching every move those two made. If Shara or Rachel did anything to hurt Ella, Wren would take them down. She didn't care if her cover was blown; she'd protect Ella with her life.

Moira's face fell a bit. "Yeah. But it also shows she's a little psycho though, right? Making an avatar of someone you have a crush on?"

"If it were a celebrity, no one would've batted an eye. Who

cares if she likes a guy in our school?" Wren was over Moira's uncertainty, spell or not.

"I guess," Moira conceded, though Wren could see from the way Moira's eyes kept darting toward Ella that she still suspected her.

Focusing on the task at hand, Wren examined the small pile of objects in front of her that lay at every station. They were supposed to use them for the telekinesis spell lab: a ruler, a bottle cap, a pencil, and an empty mint tin. Small and easy for beginners. Poor Ella would fail, and Wren was terrified that Shara and Rachel would notice and use it as proof that Ella was a Dis-con. Ella had narrowly escaped Lizzie's wrath last night, and Rachel probably planned on some kind of secret attack today to test Ella.

Rachel's obvious taunting earlier had been expected; it was the typical Tracker move. But it was the fact that Shara had picked Ella as a partner that was making Wren almost sure Shara was a Tracker too. And Rachel was angled so she could keep her eyes on Ella like she was Shara's backup.

And Ella was completely oblivious.

She had no idea the danger she was in at that very second.

"Should we incant a spying spell?" Moira asked. She appeared more curious than scared now.

"That's a good idea. I have the perfect one," Wren volunteered. She had planned on doing that anyway, but since Moira had suggested it, she wouldn't have to hide her incanting. Plus, Moira would have cast the spell on Ella, and Wren already knew that wouldn't work because she was a Dis-con. She needed to cast it on Shara.

With a quick nod to Moira, Wren faced her so no one else could see her incant. As a cover, Moira opened her book to the chapter on telekinesis and spoke the proper spells, floating both the ruler and bottle cap at the same time. She barely had to look at the book because the spells were so easy for her.

Wren focused the spell to interact with her left ear and Moira's right. A secondary perk of spying was that maybe hearing Ella would help Moira tone down her suspicion and allow the paranoia spell to fade. Hopefully Ella's sweetness and innocent nature would show through enough for Moira to break out of it.

A slight jolt from the force of the spell formed an invisible thread, tying their ears to Shara's.

Wren's view was of Ella, so she couldn't see Shara's face, only the back of her head, which irked her. She wanted to examine every stare, every smirk, every possible expression that might reveal what her true intentions were.

Moira jumped when Shara spoke.

"Ignore Rachel and the others," Shara said.

It sounded as if Shara was right in front of them. Moira's smile and raise of an eyebrow indicated that she was impressed by Wren's spellwork. It was working better than Wren had hoped. All business, Wren nodded toward the floating ruler and bottle cap. Moira took the hint and moved on to the next spell in the book, incanting it quickly, causing the ruler and bottle cap to weave in the air in perfect symmetry.

Ella responded, "It's kind of hard to ignore life-sized holographic images of me being a stalker."

"Yeah, I know, but Rachel Fen has done much worse, right? Didn't she spell a guy's underwear to his locker last week? While he was wearing them? He was stuck there for hours."

Typical of a Tracker.

"I hadn't heard about that. I guess I kind of keep to myself."

Wren glanced at Moira with a raise of her eyebrow, mouthing, *"Such a good person."*

Moira sighed in . . . disappointment? Shame? Wren couldn't be sure, but it did seem like she might be rethinking her opinion of Rachel. Good.

Shara continued, "Aside from Rachel, I think everyone else is just scared of what happened yesterday."

That could potentially be another form of provoking Ella into admitting guilt.

Wren wished she could see Shara's face! She'd know if she was being sincere or not.

Ella responded, "I know. I'd think the same thing if I were them. I couldn't leave them there, you know? I had to try to help."

Which was the truth, and Ella's genuine kindness twisted Wren's gut.

Shara answered, "I know. I believe you. You would have had burn marks from the spell if you had done it. Not even a Skein could pull off that kind of destruction spell without some kind of injury."

True. And the injuries had been significant. But if Shara was a Tracker, she would've already suspected that Ella was a Dis-con and this might still be a line of questioning designed to cause Ella to slip up and reveal something unintended.

But Ella shrugged and said, "That's what the CIU agent told me."

Relief filled Wren. Knowing that one piece of information meant that CIU definitely didn't suspect her as the culprit. During their re-creation spell, they would have seen Ella almost immediately after the attack, and being both innocent and a Dis-con worked in her favor.

Shara's head motioned toward Ash. "You know, Ash isn't looking at you. I don't think he cares, if it makes you feel any better."

"You don't think he cares that an avatar of him was just plastered in everyone's faces?" Ella said sarcastically. "I don't think I can ever look at him again." Her voice was soft with humiliation.

Moira's eyes met Wren's, and there was a twinge of sympathy there. Okay, progress. She needed Moira on Ella's side. Make it as difficult as possible for Moira to listen to Rachel.

Shara replied kindly, "With everything that happened in the gym, no one will remember the hologram."

A sweet lie.

Ella laughed. "Yeah, right. This is Tristan High. They have the capacity to remember both."

"True. Well, if you need anyone to talk to, I'm around," Shara offered.

So far, Shara wasn't acting like a Tracker. Rachel's previous performance was more their style. But maybe Shara was a new level of Tracker—a calmer, more manipulative version?

"Thanks," Ella said sincerely, and Wren's heart ached for her. For her loneliness. She knew that feeling well. Ella gathered herself and took a deep breath, nodding to the pile of lab items. "We should probably get to it."

Wow. Initiating the spell lab, knowing full well she couldn't perform any of the spells? That was bold. If Shara was a Tracker, that might be enough to throw her off.

"I'm terrible with telekinesis spells," Shara lied. Wren knew it was a lie because she'd seen Shara spell her backpack every day to her locker. Since Wren started to suspect Shara as a Tracker, she'd noticed right away how many spells she used. And how many spells she tried to hide.

"Me too," Ella responded with a large sigh.

"I'm actually terrible with all spells. I don't think I've managed to make one work properly all year. Must be nerves from moving to a new place," Shara lied again.

She had to be a Tracker. This was next-level provocation. Did Shara really think Ella would confess anything to her? Wren's hands tightened on the lab table, ready to fight if she had to.

Moira's eyes widened as she glanced down at Wren's white-knuckled hands squeezing the counter. She mouthed, *"What's wrong?"*

To her, she was simply listening to a conversation with two people confessing they were terrible at spells, which from the relaxing of Moira's shoulders, had actually been a positive thing. But to Wren, Shara was up to something.

Wren whispered back, "Nothing. The listening spell gave me a bit of blowback is all." She figured it was the easiest and most believable lie.

It worked. Moira nodded as if it explained everything.

Ella responded to Shara. "I'm pretty bad too. There are a few of us in here that might as well be called Dis-cons at this point." She laughed. Smart girl. It was always better to joke about it; avoiding the mention of Dis-cons was far more suspicious. "I'll go first. Give it try," she volunteered.

Wren already knew the outcome, but she couldn't hide the smile when Ella mispronounced one of the words in the spell. Moira smiled back, thinking they were sharing a joke about how bad Ella was at spell-casting.

Shara responded, "I think you got a word wrong."

"Maybe that's my problem. I'm horrible with pronunciation," Ella explained.

Ella was setting a precedent for bad spell-casting, something Wren's mother used to do as well. Passing the Dis-con test was only the first hurdle in hiding from the world. The upkeep afterward was exhausting. Wren had never wanted to hug a person more. It pained her to think of the kind of life Ella had had to live.

Trying the spell again, Ella mispronounced a different word this time. She thudded her head on the lab table, really selling her exasperation.

"You still got a word wrong," Shara informed her.

Wren wished there was such thing as a mind-reading spell. She wanted to know what was going on in Shara's head. Was that proof to her that Ella was a Dis-con? Wren discreetly looked over at Rachel, whose eyes were glued to Ella.

This was bad.

One known Tracker and one suspected Tracker were watching Ella intently.

More danger for Ella.

Wren shifted in her chair until she completely blocked Rachel's view of Ella. Out of the corner of Wren's eye, Rachel moved her chair over, but Wren kept adjusting as if she couldn't get comfortable until Rachel finally gave up and turned her attention back to her lab.

If Ella wasn't going to be able to perform a spell, she didn't want Rachel to see. It would be bad enough with Shara witnessing it.

"Maybe if I can hear the way you say it, I can do it too," Ella suggested, though Wren didn't know how that would help.

Shara paused as if she didn't like that idea.

At this point, Moira was more interested in Wren's reactions than anything Ella and Shara were talking about. She was probably wondering why Wren appeared to care so much about a seemingly mundane conversation between two terrible spell-casters.

Shara's shoulders shrugged, and she recited one of the telekinesis spells. The bottle cap easily lifted into the air. Ella then recited the words correctly, and the ruler raised a couple of inches off the table.

Oh.

My.

God.

Wren's heart raced.

Ella.

Ella.

Ella.

She was like Wren's mom.

Wren couldn't calm down. Sweat beaded on her forehead, and a drop trickled down her face. She wiped it before Moira noticed.

Ella had used Shara's spell-casting to push against it and make it look like she was performing a levitation spell herself.

Just like Wren's mother could do.

As far as Wren knew, no other Dis-con in history had been able to do that. It was how her mom had passed the Dis-con test when she was a kid. Maybe it had been the same for Ella?

In Wren's deep dive research into the Trackers, she'd found an encrypted document that took her days to decode. In it, she discovered that her mother's strange power was almost the reason why the Trackers might have let her live, but their Order of Eleven voted to have her killed instead. Too scared of what it meant? Wren didn't know.

And now Ella had the same power?

Taking deep breaths wasn't helping Wren; it was making her

feel like she was running out of oxygen. She counted while she breathed, then held her breath for the same amount of time—a kind of restart.

It helped.

Moira eyed her curiously, then asked, "Are you all right? I think you were right. Ella's a terrible spell-caster. She'd never be able to pull off that plague spell. And she absolutely would have had burns or blisters on her hands and arms right after, but she was clean. I really should have thought of that. I just let Rachel get inside my head."

In more ways than one.

From Moira's grimace, Wren could tell she was chastising herself for not thinking things through before accusing Ella, her mind breaking the paranoia spell on her own.

Wren would be happy if she wasn't losing her mind from shock.

"Hey, I did it." Ella's voice cut through Wren's astonishment. Ella acted as if she were proud, but Wren could hear the relief in her tone. She had brilliantly steered that entire conversation with Shara, getting Shara to perform the spell so that she could tap into the quantum wave that levitated Shara's bottle cap and then pushed against it to lift the ruler.

Breathe.

Hold.

Breathe.

Let go.

Breathe.

Hold.

Breathe.

Let go.

Wren managed a smile for Moira. "I told you. I knew she was innocent," she said, desperately attempting to hide the sheer and utter surprise from her voice.

Focus.

Focus on Shara's reaction.

It was all that mattered in that moment.

Wren calmed down further when Shara continued through the list of spells, now entirely uninterested in Ella. Shara had definitely wanted to observe what Ella could do, so that still made her a suspect of something. But Wren was one hundred percent certain now that she wasn't a Tracker. A Tracker was not only trained to look for Dis-cons, but they were also trained to specifically look for what Ella had just done. So who was Shara? And why did she want to test Ella like that? Maybe she was an undercover CIU agent? Wren would keep an eye on her. CIU dismissed the idea that Dis-cons could ever tap into any spell-casting and quantum waves. They'd never seen it firsthand, so of course, it was only mythology and fiction to them. If her mom hadn't been one, Wren probably wouldn't have believed it either. She could only assume that Trackers believed because they had seen it. Plus, they were much more into unproven sciences and evolution than any other organization. And in that one case, they were right.

Thank goodness Wren had blocked Rachel's view of Ella. If she had seen that? There could have been a fight then and there.

Wren's heart beat faster.

But Lizzie. Lizzie who had killed Wren's mother for being like Ella. If she found out?

Lizzie already suspected Ella was a Dis-con, and once she had proof, it'd mean Ella's death anyway. And now that Wren knew Ella had the power to push quantum waves? Breathe. Breathe. Breathe.

This was huge.

This was huge.

Wren incanted the secondary spell that broke their connection with Shara's ears and forced another smile at Moira. "Well, at least we know for sure she's innocent now." It took all of her concentration and energy to say that as calmly as possible. Her insides boiled with terror and panic, but her body shrugged casually, almost disinterested.

Moira nodded. "She's absolutely terrible at spell-casting. And she wasn't faking it. I could tell by the amount of power that went into her levitations. It was very weak."

Damn. The fact that Moira could sense that kind of thing only reinforced why the Trackers wanted her so badly. She was definitely more powerful than Wren had suspected. But if Moira knew the "weakness" she'd sensed was because Ella had been using Shara's own spell to lift the objects, her mind would be blown. At least Moira had broken Rachel's paranoia spell and wasn't blaming Ella for the attack yesterday morning though.

Moira pressed her lips together. "But if Ella didn't do it, then who did?"

Me.

Wren shrugged back and incanted the spell that levitated the empty mint can. "Who knows? We'll have to keep our eyes out."

Looking around the classroom, Moira nodded. "I hope whoever it was got it out of their system."

"Yeah." Wren pretended to agree, but inside, she was counting down the minutes until she could strike again.

CHAPTER 13
ELLA

Ella's shoulders tensed as she continued to push on Shara's spell. The ruler was pathetic, wobbling and barely above the table, but it was up, which was all that mattered.

Shara shrugged and continued to incant, making the floating bottle cap move in a wave pattern just as the book said it would, while Ella used every ounce of her concentration to keep the ruler in the air. Shara was good. So why had she made such a point to say how bad she was? To make Ella feel better? Shara had probably noticed how terrible Ella was at spell-casting this year and didn't want to make her feel bad or self-conscious. It made Ella like Shara even more.

"So why did your family have to move?" Ella asked conversationally. Now that she'd proven she wasn't a Dis-con, she found that she wanted to know more about Shara. Ella's parents would kill her as this was dangerously close to being social and possibly making a friend, especially after having not one, but two unannounced visitors at their doorstep yesterday, but she didn't care at the moment. And she desperately wanted to be distracted from her brain, which was currently torturing her by replaying Rachel turning the classroom into Ella's own holographic hell. She'd have to delete avatar-Ash as soon as she got a chance.

Shara incanted a spell that somersaulted the bottle cap in the air—not a spell that was in the book. "My dad got a new job. He's a consultant, so we move around a lot. What about you?"

"Same." Ella said what was easy, but also true. Her parents were consultants for the very reason of being able to move at a moment's notice.

Shara glimpsed over at Ash, who frowned as he tried to levitate one of the objects to no avail. "He seems to be having the same trouble as us."

"Us? You're making that bottle cap do things that aren't even in the book," Ella said before she could stop herself.

Ella kicked herself internally. She was supposed to blend in, not bring attention to herself.

But Shara's claim that she wasn't very good at spell-casting was an obvious lie, and it began to bother her.

Shara immediately set the bottle cap down by grabbing it midair and placing it on the table. "It's a spell I learned from my dad ages ago." Her face flushed as if Ella had caught her doing something illegal.

"I didn't mean anything by it. I'm just impressed." Ella tried to make up for her blunder. "You saw how terrible I am at spells."

"I've seen worse." Shara relaxed a bit, then she eyed Ash again. "He must be frazzled because of the . . . you know . . . hologram thing. He hasn't been able to levitate anything."

Ouch. "Yeah."

Shara turned away from Ash, then gave her a sly smile. "He *is* pretty cute. I see why you made an avatar of him."

"Don't remind me." Ella groaned. "And now I've ruined his lab on top of it? I'm truly a horrible person."

Shara incanted another levitating spell, lifting the tin can into the air. It wobbled a bit, as if she were trying to prove that she wasn't as good as Ella had witnessed. Ella quickly incanted the same spell and pushed against the force of hers, lifting the ruler once more.

"You're not a horrible person at all. Rachel is. Everyone has crushes. You have nothing to be ashamed of." Shara tried to cheer Ella up.

"But does everyone create an actual avatar of their crush? And practically everyone in school plays the game, so they know how much time you spend at home base." Ella's voice rose a couple octaves at the end in embarrassment.

"I guarantee you're not the only one in this school who has made an avatar of someone they like in that game. Please, I made one of Rob Grender from *Field Patrol*. It's totally normal," Shara said in the tone of an adult comforting a teenage girl who hadn't experienced life yet. But regardless of tone, the sentiment set her at ease.

"You did?" Ella could hear her own pathetic-ness in her tone.

"Heck yeah. Games, pics, drawings, holos. You honestly think you're the only one to stare at your crush from a distance? Please. You're fine." Shara gave Ella a reassuring smile.

Shara's words blanketed Ella in a small sense of relief.

Maybe Ash wouldn't care?

Maybe he'd take it as a compliment.

Ella hoped so.

She released her hold on the ruler and let it drop to the counter. Her eyes accidentally met Wren Martis's, and she was full-on staring at her. It was such a surprise Ella quickly focused back on the fallen ruler at their table. The compulsion to look at Wren again since her expression had been so intense was strong. Why was she staring at Ella? Her paranoia was off the charts because Ella swore Wren had looked at her like she knew *exactly* what Ella was doing with Shara's spell. And if Wren knew that . . .

No.

Impossible.

No one could know what Ella did because no one had ever done it.

But *Hexsphere* . . .

The command to push back on spells.

Maybe more people than Ella had ever dreamed knew about what she could do, what possibly other Dis-cons could do.

But Wren Martis?

Ella shook her head.

She was being silly.

Wren was probably spacing out and Ella had read her expression wrong.

Only one way to check.

Ella quickly peeked over at Wren. Sure enough, she was talking with Moira and casting another levitation spell, her eyes nowhere near her.

Ella's shoulders relaxed in response.

What had she been thinking?

She was obviously frazzled by playing the game last night and typing in that command. Add that to what had happened in the gym yesterday and the possibility of being caught as a Dis-con? Then today with Rachel opening her Veil and exposing her borderline obsessive crush on Ash? No wonder her brain was on overload.

For safety's sake, Ella decided not to push on any more of Shara's spells for the rest of the lab. She'd mispronounce some more words when she incanted from now on.

Ella honestly didn't know why she had performed it as much as she did. She had been so set on proving she wasn't a Dis-con that she had put herself in danger yet again. What if Shara had sensed something with her spell? Sensed that Ella had piggybacked off of it? She couldn't afford anyone suspecting her of anything.

Shara kept peering over at Ash, and Ella's heart dropped. Shara liked him. Ella could tell by the way she looked at him. She was sure she had that same look on the daily. Shara probably wanted to pair up with Ella because of what happened with the holographic beatdown by Rachel. See if Ella was really a stalker or not—or suss out her competition.

And from Ella's stellar performance, she now knew she was no competition at all.

If Shara was really interested in Ash, then Ella had no chance. Shara was so beautiful and smart and either humble or a liar. She was going to go with humble, though she kind of wished she was a liar because then she wouldn't be so perfect.

Ella hunched, and her chest deflated.

She didn't know what she was thinking anyway. She couldn't have real-life friends.

Friends outside video games were too dangerous.

She'd already risked everything yesterday morning; she couldn't keep putting herself and her family in danger, especially when her parents were teetering on the verge of moving at any wrong sign.

Focusing only on the objects in front of her, Ella didn't look at anyone in the classroom. Just kept her head down until she could leave.

After what felt like an eternity, the bell rang and class was finally over.

Ella stuffed her book back into her bag with her Veil and hurried to the door to avoid Ash completely.

But she nearly smashed into him waiting at the doorway. Blood rushed to her face as her plan to escape was clearly foiled.

Cautiously, Ella peeked up at his face. His brows were furrowed, and he glared at her as if she had cast a Torment-hex on his kitty.

Oh boy.

At that moment, Ella could guarantee with certainty that he did not "see it as a compliment" that she'd created an avatar of him in the game.

Before she could defend herself (knowing full well there was no defense for creepiness), Ash raised his voice, angry. "Stay away from me."

She was going to puke.

She willed herself to hold it in. She didn't want to add vomiting on Ash Torres to her list of humiliating moments today.

Ella managed to spout out, "I'll delete it. I promise. And I'll stay away, of course. Although, I already pretty much stay away from you anyway . . ." Why was she still talking?

For a split second, Ash's eyes flared with a tinge of . . . guilt? Sympathy? Sadness? Ella couldn't quite pinpoint it, but it was better than rage.

Oh. Nope. There was the rage again. "Go away!"

Ella wanted to defend herself and scream that she had been trying to run out the door when he stopped her, but nothing came out of her mouth. She was too rattled by Ash's anger.

Rachel, who was right behind Ella, laughed out loud. "Way to put Ella in her place, Ash. I think he deserves a round of applause."

Ella's ears drowned in the sound of the class clapping.

"All of you! Leave me alone!" Turning abruptly at the now dying applause, Ash hurried out of the room.

Seeing Ash look at her with such anger made Ella want to crawl into a hole and hide.

Since there were no holes around, second period would have to do.

At least Ash and Rachel weren't in calculus.

Ella practically ran out of the classroom, keeping her head down, ignoring the gossiping whispers.

This was quite possibly the worst day of her life.

CHAPTER 14
WREN

Poor Ella.

That was savage.

Walking through the door, Wren filed into the suffocating and claustrophobic crowded hallway like the rest of the herd. She kept her eyes and ears open, always watching, always listening. Due to Rachel's spell, the main source of gossip was still Ella and how she'd tried to murder the basketball team yesterday, but Wren knew Ella's hologram reveal and Ash's outburst would be added pretty quickly to Ella's rising tally of gossip-worthy events.

No one paid attention to Wren. No one ever did. She wanted to keep it that way.

Moira walked up next to her. "I gotta get my assignment out of my locker. See you in class."

"Sounds good," Wren responded, and Moira took off down the hall.

The miniaturization assignment was due today, but the truck was still in Wren's backpack, so she didn't need to go back to her locker.

Wren had other things to do before class.

Rachel brushed past Wren as if she were on a mission, and Wren immediately followed. She still hadn't tested all of Rachel's defenses yet, so maybe she could manage to figure some of those out while simultaneously eavesdropping. After class today and doing her job as a Tracker to provoke a potential target, she'd have to report what happened, whether it be to Lizzie or someone above the two of them. Either way, Wren wanted to hear everything she had to say.

Hurrying through the halls toward the exit, Wren followed Rachel as discreetly as she could. Luckily, the crowds of students loitering in the hallway made it easy to blend in.

Pushing the exit door open with her lower back, Rachel picked up her pace, moving off toward the left, away from school and out of Wren's view.

Exiting the school, Wren searched for Rachel. She quickly spotted her at an almost run until she stopped next to the giant oak tree that acted as a guardian to the front of the school property. Rachel pulled out her phone.

Nowhere near for Wren to hide, but she needed to know who Rachel was talking to.

Hiding behind the outside wall of the school, Wren tried to think quickly since all Trackers had quantum repellant gear attached to their temporal lobe, which included the auditory cortex, so she wouldn't be able to listen in by casting a hearing spell to Rachel's ears.

Looking up at the oak with its twisting branches and the thousands of small green leaves, she could make out a couple of squirrels and a few birds.

Wren shrugged. Between a bird and squirrel, she decided to go with a squirrel, only because she could physically see their ears. At this point, that was the only deciding factor, because she had no idea how well squirrels or birds could hear.

After Wren cast the spell on the closest squirrel to Rachel, her voice became loud in Wren's ear.

"I told you. I saw the tail end of her casting a levitation spell in lab. I even provoked her in class. She sat there like a scared animal. If I wasn't playing this role, I'd feel sorry for her."

As the squirrel leapt to another branch, Wren had to strain to hear the person on the other end of the phone, but she was pleasantly surprised that it was possible.

"Yeah, but I can't stop thinking about how she had no reaction to the plague spell when I grabbed her arm. There has to be a reason for that."

Lizzie.

A stroke of luck brought the squirrel a few branches closer.

"I don't know what to tell you. Granted, my view was partially blocked by Wren, but from what I saw, she cast the spell and the ruler lifted. And every time I could get a peek, something else was levitated."

Wren flinched at Rachel saying her name so casually. Yes, she knew they'd taken over for Wren's previous Tracker spy, Larry, but it made her skin crawl to think about them having even a momentary thought of her. Especially Lizzie.

Lizzie's voice pierced through Wren's thoughts. "Did you make sure she cast the spell *after* her lab partner and not during?"

Wren's breath caught in her throat. Lizzie was asking if Ella was like her mother.

And she was.

"I honestly couldn't see. I'll make sure I have a complete view next time. Get your dad to pull his strings again with Mr. Tildon so we can do labs tomorrow too. Him coming in late today was perfect for what I had to do. Tell him thanks."

Dad? Who was Lizzie's dad? Someone higher up in the Tracker food chain obviously if he could get a teacher to show up late and change his lesson plans with a simple phone call. Did that mean Mr. Tildon was a Tracker? Or worked for the Trackers? Wren's mind reeled.

"You can tell him yourself. He's coming to the house tonight."

Wren noticed the way the color drained from Rachel's face at that. She was scared of Lizzie's dad. Interesting. But Rachel's verbal response sounded light as she said, "Perfect."

"Meet you at lunch." Lizzie ended the conversation.

Rachel dropped her phone in her bag, then headed back toward the school.

De-casting the listening spell on the squirrel, Wren hid until Rachel walked through the doorway to the main hallway.

Time to figure out what gear Rachel had implanted in her brain.

So far, Wren had tested Rachel's occipital and temporal lobe for quantum repellent gear. Her occipital was clean (a week ago Wren was able to mess with Rachel's vision for all of quantum spell-casting), but the temporal lobe had been a given. Her hypothalamus was clean; Wren had given her a good case of the sweats during lunch for Taco Tuesday. So all Wren needed to check was Rachel's brain stem and cerebellum today, then she'd know every area of the brain Rachel had repellent gear attached to.

Only ten students separated Wren and Rachel, plus the general crowd of students heading to their classes.

Now was her moment.

Brain stem first.

Hiding her mouth with her hand, Wren made it look as if she were coughing as she cast a simple throat-closing spell.

Rachel coughed.

Wren carefully maneuvered closer for a better view.

Coughing wasn't enough. Wren needed Rachel on her knees gasping for air to be sure.

Intensifying the spell, Wren added a few more staccato beats that she'd learned from Italy's military vault (they had a knack for brain stem spells and torture).

But nothing.

Rachel barely cleared her throat as she continued to laugh and talk with another popular kid Will Locke.

Brain stem definitely had gear on it.

Cerebellum next.

Wren had to work fast since the bell would ring in a few minutes. A simple toe-numbing spell would work. If it was successful, Rachel would trip, but it was small enough that hopefully Rachel wouldn't suspect anyone was casting a spell on her. Bending down to the drinking fountain to make sure no one suspected her of incanting a spell, Wren cast the toe-numbing spell at Rachel. The words flew out of her mouth, fast and succinct.

Rachel reached up and hugged Will, then laughed and waved as she . . . completely fell on her face from falling over her numb toes.

A few laughs from the remaining students were quickly hushed by the evil glare from Rachel as she stood up. Shaking her foot, her face scrunched in annoyance as Rachel half walked, half limped toward class.

Cerebellum clean.

Good.

Wren had a lot of bone-cracking Torment-hexes that would be perfect for Rachel Fen.

She had wanted to cast them on Lizzie, but Lizzie had repellent gear on her cerebellum.

Two Trackers at Tristan High.

And Wren knew both of their weaknesses.

She couldn't wait to use them.

The crowds were mostly dispersed at this point as students went into their classrooms, but there was still a good amount of people walking with purpose. Wren immediately turned right and headed up the stairs to the second level where Hex Lab was. The staircase was like an extended V, with two flights of ten steps each that stretched to the second floor.

Shara walked past her at a fast pace. Wren's eyes automatically followed where she was headed. Only the back of Shara was visible as she hurried through the remaining throng of students. They only had about three minutes before the last bell rang, and Shara seemed to have a purpose—that was plain as day—and it wasn't getting to class on time. Since Shara had been on Wren's potential Tracker list, she had her schedule memorized, and right now, Shara had English comp on level one.

So what was she doing on level two and in such a hurry?

Wren had to know where Shara was going.

She managed to follow Shara's movements through small peeks between shoulders, arms, and legs since apparently no one wanted to be on time for class! But finally, Shara slowed as she approached a man several classrooms down.

A man Wren recognized.

CIU Agent Malcolm Gilroy. He was the poster boy for CIU

and a scarily good Skein. Wren had done her research on the CIU—almost as much as she'd done on Trackers—because no one knew exactly what CIU did to Dis-cons if they were discovered at their Dis-con test at twelve. At this point, Wren was relatively sure they didn't execute them like Trackers did, but if not that, then what? Imprisonment? Induced comas? Experiments? Wren was still looking into it.

Shara handed him a slip of paper, and Wren shuddered as she pretended to tighten her shoelace.

That was it, then.

Shara was CIU.

And worse: a CIU Dis-con scout.

It was literally her job to find Dis-cons who had managed to fool the test administrators at the age of twelve.

It made sense now that her interest in Ella had immediately dispersed when Ella "performed" the levitation spell. The ruler flew, so she wrote Ella off as a bad spell-caster and nothing more. Shara must have felt she had to up her game after the attack yesterday. Ella's lack of spell-casting ability in class (and probably others at this school as well) had obviously hit CIU's radar months ago when Shara arrived. And today, with Ella being in the gym?

Ella was like her mom, and that had saved her.

From CIU, anyway.

Shara barely acknowledged Malcolm as she hurried past him, disappearing in the crowd toward the second staircase that would lead her down to English comp.

Tucking the small slip of paper in his front suit pocket, Malcolm walked down the hallway in the same direction as Shara.

The bell was about to ring, and Wren needed to get to class.

She walked in the opposite direction of where Malcolm was

headed, though she wished she could follow him and read that piece of paper.

So Shara Ralter was a CIU Dis-con scout. Wren needed to stay vigilant and keep her eyes on Shara. CIU was too unpredictable. There could be some believers in the CIU of Dis-cons like Ella, and if there were, who knew what they'd do to Ella if they suspected her.

And if a renowned agent like Malcom Gilroy was there?

This investigation was about to get real.

Wren had to hide herself and what she did, because she wouldn't let anyone, not even CIU, keep her from her mission.

CHAPTER 15
ELLA

Hurrying to calculus, Ella headed up to the second level of the school with only two minutes until the class bell rang.

She traversed the packed staircase, shielding her eyes from the onslaught of stares thrown her way. Like before, when she'd walked in the hallways, her senses were heightened. There was still a chance someone would secretly try to cast something on her, whether it be a truth spell, a tripping spell, or anything really. Ella didn't trust anyone, so when she arrived on the second level, she waited for her heart to flutter and listened for any casting, on the ready to fake a reaction.

Feet.

Feet were good. Ella followed her feet with her head down, eyes down, counting the doors as she went. It was the only way she could avoid everyone.

Frantic whispers about the basketball team being at the hospital yesterday for further observation reached her ears. Ella knew it had been just a precaution because Agent Gilroy told her as much. Plus, every single player was back in school today, but no one seemed to care.

Hence, the rumor mill was out and spouting worst-case scenarios.

By the time Ella got to calculus, most of the basketball team was dying and the murderer (her) had apparently left a note that there was going to be another attack.

Yeah.

She was almost grateful she'd been there and knew the real scoop from CIU.

Almost.

Part of Ella wished she was blissfully terrified with everyone else. At least then she wouldn't be suspect number one. She was still confused as to why everyone was so adamant about her guilt, especially with CIU clearing her, but what could she do?

And if no one thought she was guilty, Ash would still just be an impossible crush and a really good-looking avatar in her game.

Oof.

Not even looking up, Ella reached for the doorknob to the calculus classroom.

A hand gently touched her arm, pulling her away.

Startled, she lifted her head to see . . .

Agent Malcolm Gilroy.

His smile was reassuring. "Can I talk to you for a minute? I've cleared it with your calculus teacher."

"Um, sure." What else was she going to say?

Ella really didn't need any more eyes on her, and having a CIU agent come for follow-up questions the next day never looked good.

"Let's go somewhere more private." Agent Gilroy led the way.

Students parted for them as if they were celebrities. It was better to think of it that way than what was really going on in their heads, which was that they were parting for a criminal about to get arrested.

But as they headed down the hall, Ella's fellow classmates walked inside their designated classrooms, and soon, the corridor was empty.

"Ms. Busby said there's any empty study hall room up here." Agent Gilroy kept his tone light, conversational.

Ella really hoped he was not planning on ambushing her as soon as they walked in the room.

What if they thought Ella was the caster? Even with the signature-reveal spell, maybe her being a Dis-con had somehow skewed the results. They would expect her to attack if she was cornered.

Deep breaths. Relax.

After Agent Gilroy opened the door for her, Ella passed through the entryway to a nearly empty room. Only a few broken desks were piled in the back.

No ambush.

But also nowhere to sit.

Hopefully this would be fast.

Not that the damage wasn't already done in the court of public opinion. A meeting with CIU the day after the attack? In front of witnesses? Ella might as well have stamped *Guilty* on her forehead.

"What can I help you with, Agent Gilroy?" Ella asked cautiously, terrified that he'd figured out that she'd lied.

"Please, call me Malcolm," he said for the second time.

Ella always felt strange when people of authority asked her to use their first name. Years of hiding who she was had given her a sense of subservience that allowed her to blend into the background easier.

“Sorry . . . Malcolm.” The name sounded awkward on her tongue.

“Don’t apologize. I just want you to feel more comfortable.”

Calling him by his first name did the opposite for her, but she wasn’t about to tell him that.

Malcolm continued, “I came down to the school today to clear up a few things.”

“Okay.”

“After everyone left yesterday, I performed the re-creation spell seven more times to see every angle and detail possible, and we managed to figure out where the attacker was standing when they incanted.”

Ella prayed he wasn’t about to say that the attacker was behind her.

“And the attacker was right behind you.” Malcolm finished his sentence like a final nail in Ella’s coffin.

“Did you see who he was?” Deflect. Good one.

“No. He or she was smart enough to perform a kind of glamour spell that prevented us from seeing who they were. But you seem pretty confident when you say *he*. Are you sure it was a male voice?”

“Not really. The whispering was harsh and staccato. It could have been a girl, I guess.”

“It’s just, the spell seemed to be a focused attack based on the trajectory and severity of the wounds on the victims, Ralph and Lizzie being hit the hardest. The fact that it completely bypassed your body to get to the basketball team yet still left residue on you shows us that this attacker is at a Skein level at least, maybe higher."

And there it was.

The part of the investigation that was inevitable.

How could this high school girl not be affected by a virus spell when the caster was right behind her?

And now they were going on the assumption that this attacker was higher than a Skein.

Because of Ella.

She could never tell them that the spell didn't bypass her. Instead, it went straight through her.

Ella's chest squeezed with guilt.

But what could she do?

More people could get hurt, maybe even die. She had to tell him!

"I don't know," Ella said instead. She was a real hero.

"Would you mind if we did some testing on you?" Malcolm asked, observing her reaction at the question.

Ella couldn't show him her terror. "Sure." Did she just agree to testing?

Malcolm smiled gently. "Great." He handed her a card with his name, phone number, and the address of the local CIU office. "Come by in the next couple of days, and I'll have everything set up. The sooner the better though. Maybe we can pick up on some more of that residue I saw on you yesterday."

Ella still wasn't sure what he saw.

He continued, "I know you're seventeen, so you don't need your parents' permission, but would you like them to be there? I'd understand if you do."

Ella almost choked at the thought. This was *exactly* what her parents would use as reason to move again. And Ella didn't want to move. She decided then and there she wasn't going to tell them.

She shook her head. "No. That's okay. They have to work." Lies. They worked from home. But Malcolm didn't need to know that. "I'll come by tomorrow." What was she doing? Her instinct to please was going to get her killed. But not going could get other people killed.

Her gut screamed at her that it was time.

Time to come clean and turn herself in.

Malcolm shook her hand with a friendly smile. "I'll see you tomorrow, then." Pulling his hand away, he nodded to the door. "I saw how everyone was looking at you. Are you going to be okay?"

No. "Yeah. It'll blow over when you catch the guy . . . or girl . . . or whoever."

Malcolm seemed genuinely concerned about Ella's well-being as he nodded. "Okay. Well, call me if you think of anything new or if you just need to talk." He pulled out his phone. "Keep the card, but let me give you my direct line."

"Right." Ella tried not to gulp as she pulled out her phone, allowing a *TOP CIU AGENT* to electronically transfer his information into her address book. After her phone beeped once to indicate the task was completed, Ella smiled. "Thanks."

Even though he was probably only six or seven years older than Ella, Malcolm had a fatherly vibe to him that was comforting. She wouldn't call him in a million years because of her fear and crippling shyness, but it was really nice that he appeared to care.

And besides, she should be celebrating. She was going to CIU tomorrow to be put to death for being a Dis-con.

Ugh.

Ella knew that was probably not true, but that was the problem: no one knew what happened to Dis-cons when they were discovered by CIU, especially the ones like her who had cheated the Dis-con test years ago. Were they punished for lying? Were they executed? The fact that no one had ever heard from one again pretty much made it feel like it would be a death sentence.

But weirdly, that option felt better than moving. Moving was mentally and physically exhausting. Ella didn't think she could do it again. She didn't want to.

Malcolm opened the door for Ella and walked her back to calculus. Without another word, she entered the classroom and immediately sat down in the first desk available, which was near the front.

Ms. Forester acknowledged her with a nod as she continued her lecture. No one said anything, but she caught glimpses of the stares from the corners of her eyes. Ella refocused her brain to concentrate on Ms. Forester's words. She liked math, and learning new equations was a good way to distract herself.

A good half hour into the class, the loudspeaker beep chimed, and Ms. Forester stopped her lecture to listen with the rest of them.

Ms. Busby's voice sounded on the speaker above the classroom door. "Attention, students. We are pleased to announce that the varsity basketball team has made a full recovery from the horrendous attack yesterday morning. They were released from the hospital yesterday and sent home for some rest, but every single player is here today fully recovered. Also, the CIU wants to thank Ella Buckley for her quick thinking and bravery in risking her personal safety to aid the victims after the attack. We all owe her our gratitude and are proud that Ms. Buckley embodies the traits we honor and strive for at Tristan High. Thank you, Ms. Buckley. I will announce further updates as they come. Have a good day."

With another beep, the intercom went silent.

Ella could feel the burn of her cheeks at Ms. Busby's words. She was pretty positive Malcolm was responsible for that announcement. What a nice guy. She didn't think it would stop all suspicion and accusations, but it would definitely help. At least in the short term, the stares in class went from repulsed to curious.

The rest of the class was uneventful, and Ella took some comfort in throwing herself into Ms. Forester's lecture. Homework was assigned, the bell rang, and she was off to her next class.

Glares were now a mix of suspicion, awe, sympathy, and genuine gratitude. Definite improvement.

Now if only Ella could erase the incident where Rachel outed her crush to Ash by making the entire classroom a hologram of her stalker-y ways and consequently Ash screaming at her, Ella could almost get through the day.

Did it really matter though?

It was probably the last day of school she'd ever attend after going to CIU tomorrow. She was almost looking forward to it. No stares, no embarrassment, just disappearing into the CIU building forever. The last thing she wanted was an angry earful from the boy she liked, and if she never had to see him again, she could hang out with his avatar and not the reality of his beautiful brown eyes looking at her with disgust.

Yes. Planning her demise wasn't as horrible as she'd always thought it would be.

It was strangely a relief. Years of hiding who she was, isolating herself from anyone that could be a true friend, moving every couple years, never feeling at home—it had taken its toll.

There was always a possibility CIU wouldn't discover Ella

was a Dis-con, but it she doubted it.

So this was it.

A rush of exhilaration filled Ella. She knew it should be fear and terror, but it was elation instead. Added bonus: maybe once CIU knew, she could tell them everything about the attack. That way, they could catch this guy with all the pertinent information.

Because let's face it: Ella was not a detective. She didn't know the first thing about finding some crazy person who was probably at Skein level.

Feeling better and better about her future, or lack thereof (though deep down, she knew she was in some kind of fear-denial), Ella headed toward the crowded staircase to her next class.

Walking down the hall, Ella had to hide the look of shock and disappointment when her eyes caught Rachel Fen laughing with Ash at Ash's locker. He was half smiling back, shifting from leg to leg as if he were uncomfortable with the attention. But with Rachel's hand on his arm as she laughed again, it only solidified that Ash was on her radar and was soon to be promoted to the realm of popular kids whether he wanted it or not.

Not that Ella ever had a chance with Ash, but now it wasn't even a blip of a possibility. She guessed she was relieved in a way. It was weirdly scary to like someone. And now that the possibility of ever getting together was gone, there was suddenly no pressure.

And he had been so angry.

He could have at least been a little nicer about the fact that Ella had secretly created an avatar of him so she could hang out with him anytime she wanted.

Yeah.

She'd have been wigged out as well.

It was weird.

And he had every right to be upset.

But to immediately hook up with Rachel Fen?

Rachel Fen, who Lizzie had expressly said thought Ella was guilty.

Okay. They hadn't technically hooked up, but close enough.

Without another glance, Ella walked past them and four doors down to geography.

CHAPTER 16
WREN

Wren sat at the desk next to Moira's in Hex Lab. It was a smaller classroom: five rows of individual wooden desks with attached metal seats and seven desks to a row. Class was full, and Wren was the last to sit down right as the bell rang. She noticed that everyone had their assignment placed on their desk.

She bent down to reach into her backpack to retrieve the shrunken truck, then stopped herself. Pulling her hand back as if it had caught fire, Wren sank into her seat.

What had she been thinking?

Wren couldn't show anyone the truck.

She had altered a spell she stole from Nigeria's military vault to shrink the truck. An entirely illegal spell, well beyond what was assigned to them. In World War V, the Nigerians managed to shrink the entire invading force of Chad, ending the war with one spell. From the foundation of that miniaturization spell, Wren had reworked it for the truck.

Moira sat with her dollhouse she'd miniaturized in front of her. She smiled proudly at Wren, then mouthed, *"Where's your assignment?"*

Wren mouthed back, *"I forgot it."*

Moira's eyes rounded, and Wren would have thought she'd just told Moira her favorite show had been cancelled. "Oh!" Moira dove into her backpack, pulling out a water bottle, then tossed it to Wren.

Luckily, Wren's reflexes were sharp, and she caught the bottle easily. "What's this for?"

"Shrink it," Moira whispered. "Just do it."

Picking up on Moira's fear of coming into class empty-handed, Wren didn't think; she cast the spell that was in their textbook, and the water bottle shrunk to the size of her thumbnail. Those around her had shocked and amazed expressions on their faces. The spell wasn't easy.

For high school students.

But compared to what Wren could do? It was child's play.

Mr. Finley stood from behind his desk to walk in front of the classroom. He was a short man, a little taller than Wren (she was five feet, four inches), and chubby, with a perfectly round face and bright expressive eyes. She had to admit, he was her favorite teacher, only because his enthusiasm was so contagious. Part of Wren believed she initially shrunk her father's truck to impress Mr. Finley the more she thought about it. And now she was grateful to Moira for making her shrink the water bottle. Wren didn't think she could handle a look of disappointment from her favorite teacher.

"Okay, class, do we all have our miniaturization projects ready?

Let's put them on our desks if you haven't already. Come on, let's see these beauties." His smile was infectious, and Wren found her heart beat speeding up at the thought of him seeing what she had actually done with the truck. But if he figured out she'd altered a spell, and a shrinking one at that, he'd be forced to report it whether he wanted to or not, even without knowing about the blowback. Because there had been blowback. Wren's entire body had been like a giant sunburn.

A couple of groans from the students who weren't prepared, a couple darting glares of jealousy directed at Wren for her quick project success, but overall, the rest of the class appeared excited to show off what they had done. There was a tiny toothbrush from Rick Grazer, a shrunken doorknob from Sally Frost (Wren hoped that didn't come from anywhere important, but it also gave her ideas for breaking into places if she had to), John Krill's miniaturized couch (which was pretty impressive as well), and Emily Jordan's tiny wooden chair. Those were all she could see from her vantage point, aside from her own water bottle and Moira's dollhouse. Wren was actually very impressed.

This was too *normal.*

Wren couldn't fall into this state of being. She had to be vigilant. It was so easy to jump into the stream and go with the flow of life and school. But she'd made her attack yesterday morning. Her plague spell told Lizzie that she was onto her and that she was coming for her and the entire Tracker organization. But now thinking of it, Wren didn't want them to know it was her, not yet anyway, so maybe being "normal" worked to her advantage at this moment.

And besides, it felt good.

Wren pressed her lips together tightly, her teeth biting into the soft tissue of the inside of her mouth. Tasting the iron of her own blood brought Wren back to her center.

All Trackers must be stopped. They must be punished.

Wren nodded internally as her mind shifted back to her goal. She might die in the process of destroying the Tracker organization, but that was a risk she was willing to take. She'd dedicated her life to this, so it was only fitting that she might lose it in pursuit of her objective.

Mr. Finley pulled Wren out of her thoughts as he noticed Rick's toothbrush and picked it up, admiring the quarter-inch-sized brushing utensil. "Very good, Mr. Grazer, very good. Nothing melted, nothing lost during the transfer. Excellent work."

Rick's grin said it all. He'd be riding high for the rest of the day for sure.

Mr. Finley's eyes widened, and he let out a small giggle. "Oh, Miss Kurt, you didn't?" Standing between Wren and Moira, Mr. Finley picked up Moira's dollhouse and examined it more closely. "Damn near every piece inside is perfectly miniaturized as well, no blending or cluttering. I'm so impressed, Moira. Stunning."

"Thank you, Mr. Finley." Moira blushed.

His eyes roamed to Wren's desk. "Ah," he said. Picking up the water bottle, he nodded with approval. "Very nice, Miss Martis. Excellent work." As he placed it down on her desk, he said, "But maybe next time you won't wait until the bell has rung before you do your assignment?"

Wren's eyes flew to Mr. Finley's, shame coursing through her. Even the slight hint of disappointment in his expression was enough to cause Wren's stomach to twist. But she answered, "Yes, Mr. Finley."

"Still. The cast was perfection, as always."

With that, he moved on to the others in class.

Moira gave Wren a combination of a shrug and a thumbs-up.

Wren nodded in thanks, but the bile in her stomach continued to roil.

Stop.

She couldn't care.

Grades didn't matter.

Teachers didn't matter.

Nothing mattered except killing every last Tracker.

With a deep breath, Wren calmed her stomach and threw a few fake smiles and rounds of applause for her fellow students. Their miniaturization projects helped her focus. She'd learned it was all about what people viewed on the outside that mattered. No one wanted to dive that deep. Most people were selfish that way. They only cared about what was going on with them.

Wren was no exception, but at least she admitted it, accepted it, and acted accordingly.

The rest of the class flew by, and Wren found that she'd spent most of it calming herself down. There had been a brief announcement in the middle from the principal, telling the school to basically be nice to Ella, which was a good thing. Hopefully it'd help dissolve Rachel's paranoia spell. Wren was almost positive Agent Malcolm Gilroy had been responsible for that one. Another bit of information Wren tucked in her reservoir of CIU research.

When the bell rang, Moira was instantly by her side. "I can't believe you forgot your assignment. Even if Mr. Finley knew you cast that right before class, you're still going to get an A. Your work is amazing."

"Thanks again for helping me out." Wren handed Moira back the miniaturized bottle, and Moira tossed it in her backpack.

Wren had disconnected herself from school again, so she could care less about a good grade, but she needed Moira close. If Rachel convinced her to turn . . . Wren was going to try her hardest not to let that happen. Impulsively, Wren pulled out the truck from her backpack, handing it to Moira.

"I tweaked the spell in the book, and I didn't want to get in trouble," Wren said quickly. Why was she doing this? Breathe.

Because she needed Moira to trust her.

If it came to it, Wren would need Moira on her side, maybe even to join the fight. Trackers were already trying to recruit her, so it wasn't like she could stay neutral. Wren had to show Moira a little bit about what she could do.

Moira stared at the truck in her hand, not blinking for a second. "Wren," she whispered. "There are so many moving parts . . . This is . . . I don't know what this is."

Students shoved past them, jolting them into a slow walk.

"I know it's a lot," Wren responded. "But I worked out a reversal spell, so no one has to know. I can put it back to normal size." She had no intention of doing that, but now that Moira was so worked up, she needed to calm her down somewhat.

Moira's eyes widened beyond what Wren thought was possible. "You tweaked the spell *and* worked out a reversal spell?" She shook her head in shock. "That's beyond Skein level work. Is it legal?"

No.

"Of course. I didn't do anything I couldn't find out of a textbook," Wren lied. "I used a college level textbook instead of ours though." She smiled to sell the ruse. "I didn't think Mr. Finley would appreciate it."

"Can you show me?" Moira's gaze penetrated Wren's in a way that caused Wren to stop in her tracks.

Moira stopped as well, and they stared at each other as students walked around them.

Wren knew that look. It was the same look Wren imagined she had on her face anytime she learned of a new spell she wanted to experiment with. But by showing Moira the spell, Wren risked exposing her spell signature. Come to think of it, she'd already risked it by testing Rachel earlier and shrinking that bottle. Wren may have changed her signature yesterday for the CIU tests, but that was temporary. CIU would be able to match any of the spells she'd performed today if they were paying attention.

She couldn't risk it.

"Maybe later? I gotta get to class." Wren grabbed the truck back and stuffed it in her bag.

"Yeah, cool," Moira said with her hand still held out where the truck used to be. "Um, Wren?"

"Yeah?"

Moira opened her mouth to say something, then shook her head. "Never mind. I'll see you later. Cool spell." And she was off, down the hallway without another glance in Wren's direction.

Breathe.

What had Wren done?

What had she exposed?

Without thinking, Wren had just shown Moira Kurt a glimpse of a stolen spell from Nigeria's military vault.

Stupid.

If Moira had already accepted Rachel's invitation to be a Tracker, she'd tell her for certain.

She accepted that outcome.

Wren would be ready.

The question was, who would come for Wren first? Lizzie? Rachel?

Or Moira?

CHAPTER 17
ELLA

The rest of the day went surprisingly fast. Ella kept to herself at lunch, which she normally did anyway.

But talk of *Hexsphere* was always the highlight of Ella's time in the lunchroom. Even if she didn't join in the conversation, just listening made her feel part of something bigger than herself, less alone.

"I have a level 40 Tracker that would crush your Dis-con."

"I'd like to see you try. I just got the Joran Tracker blade that dropped in the Chicago Speakeasy Dungeon."

"Are you serious? Epics are like one in every thousand drops."

"Yeah, exactly. You've got to see this thing. I sliced a Tracker's head clean off with barely a swing."

"Okay, I'm playing with my Dis-con, then. You can help me level up."

"I was playing with my main last night and obliterated a Tracker

mid-fight with a new spell. Like his head exploded after I cast it."

"Your Skein or Agent?"

"Skein."

"Where the heck did you get that spell? I want it. Can I get it on the Auction House?"

"I don't think so, unless it's sellable. I got it on a drop when I won an arena game. I'll show you after school."

Ella was just grateful that Ms. Busby's announcement seemed to have shifted gossip off of her, at least temporarily, back to what was more normal: *Hexsphere.* And with the game's expansion being so new, Ella's peers obviously wanted to escape from the very real attack that had happened yesterday.

Shara tried to talk to her again, but Ella quickly made excuses and walked away. She successfully avoided Ash Torres and only received a few scathing looks from Rachel and her cronies. Ms. Busby's sentiment on being grateful to Ella was completely lost on her, which she kind of expected considering Lizzie's warning at her house yesterday. But overall, students kept their distance.

When Ella didn't show up to school the next day, she was sure their opinions would go straight back to blaming her for the attack, but at least she wouldn't be there for that.

Wow.

Ella was shocked at how calm she was.

It was as if she were in a walking coma, seeing everything and everyone around her but not being able to react—or not wanting to react felt more like it.

Her bag was full of books as she exited the school. It was in moments like this that she wished she wasn't a Dis-con. A quick lightening spell would've helped so much with the weight of her bag. Why was she bringing all her stuff home, anyway?

If Ella's life was ending tomorrow (figuratively or physically), she really didn't need to do any homework.

Oddly, she was pretty happy about that.

Ella jolted out of her "coma" when she thought about what her parents would do or think when she didn't come home tomorrow. The knot in her stomach returned and brought a ton of its friends to join in the squeezing of guilt.

Because Ella wasn't going to tell them she was going to CIU.

If she did, they'd try to stop her. Probably kidnap her and she'd wake up in another state, knowing her mom.

Ella's heart hurt thinking about them and the devastation they'd feel.

But maybe they'd feel relief too.

They could live normal lives, live anywhere they wanted, stay as long as they wanted, truly be happy.

Ella knew she was a burden, though they tried to convince her otherwise, and now, because of what she had agreed to do today with Malcolm (still felt weird about calling him by his first name), she didn't have to be one anymore. And the fact that the basketball team had made a full recovery, a part of her felt like it was meant to be. Maybe this was what she needed to do . . .

Let go and be herself.

For once.

Even if it meant her life as she knew it was over.

Ella was so tired. She'd never realized how much until now.

"Hey." A gruff voice sounded from behind her.

Ella was off school grounds at this point, the school a distance away, and was about to cross the street onto the green grass-lined sidewalks of suburbia. Turning, her palms immediately began to sweat as she came face-to-face with Ash Torres.

"Uh . . ." No words.

Was he going to yell at her again? He didn't look mad, at least. He looked upset for sure, but not the glary scary boy from before.

Her game avatar did Ash no justice, she realized as she stared up at him, unsure of what to say. How could anyone be that perfect? From his smoldering eyes to his sculpted face, he looked utterly gorgeous in a simple white T-shirt and jeans.

Ella decided to wait for him to speak.

"Sorry I yelled at you," he said quietly while simultaneously peering over his shoulder to see if any straggling students were watching.

They weren't.

"Sorry I created an avatar of you in my game," Ella said. Not stalker-y at all.

Ash was silent for a moment, which only caused her hands to sweat more. Seriously, did she have some kind of mutant sweat glands? Ella silently prayed he wouldn't want to shake her hand. That would be weird on principle, but she wouldn't be surprised if he asked after the day she'd had.

With the two-story high school looming behind Ash, Ella faced both her crush and the building of the last two days' torment as his backup. She was grateful Rachel didn't suddenly appear to make out with him and try to cast some Torment-hex on her, which would fail, so she'd have to fake-react, so . . .

Stop.

Silences were never good for her.

But Ash still wouldn't say anything.

"Okay, well . . . I should go home." When in a crushingly awkward moment: run away. Ella's go-to had never failed her before.

"Yeah," Ash finally said. "I just . . ."

Ella wished he would say something. She really didn't want to stand there and stare at him in awkward silence. It was a nice view, but still, her hands were going to start full-on dripping soon.

And she talked with her hands!

Was sweat going to flick off her fingers and hit Ash's perfect face?

Ella's mind melted at the horrific thought.

"Um . . ." Yes. She knew she would say something profound eventually, and finally her wish was granted.

Ash took a deep breath, then said, "I wanted to be left alone, and now because of you, everyone is focused on me."

Ella's stomach twisted in ways she didn't think were possible.

That hurt.

Because it was true.

"I think they're more focused on me," she said, hoping to somehow make the situation better.

"But you seem to handle it better than me." Then he looked her in the eyes with an intensity that practically buckled her knees. "I can't have attention on me. I *can't*."

Ella understood, though for different reasons. She was a Discon, so it was obvious why, but Ash? He was so beautiful, and the most popular girl in school (though a vile human being) seemed to like him. These were all good things in high school.

Avoiding eye contact, Ash explained a little more: "I have clinical anxiety. Staying in the background is how I cope. When Rachel . . . you know . . . showed your home base . . . I freaked. I yelled. I lost myself. I . . ." He looked like he was about to have a panic attack. Ella knew because she'd had them herself.

Out of instinct, Ella moved her head until she forced Ash to look at her. "Breathe. Big and deep." She did the same to show him how. He followed her lead and took a deep breath, then slowly let it out.

He still looked shaky, but definitely calmer. "I don't think I'll come to school for a few days. Maybe people will forget."

"Rachel likes you. She doesn't like me. She won't forget." It was her fault that he was in this mess. Though it hurt to do so, she asked, "Do you like Rachel? Because I'm sure she'd keep you out of the spotlight if you asked . . . or if you two dated or something." Rachel obviously liked Ash a lot, and she had a considerable amount of power at Tristan High. If she told people to leave Ash alone, they would.

Ash's eyes were still trained on Ella, and a physical wave of emotion hit her from the way he looked at her. It was as if he could peer into the very center of her being. It was intense, and Ella's adrenaline kicked into high gear when he said, "I'm not interested in Rachel. But I'm scared that if I reject her, she'll make my life even worse."

It suddenly occurred to Ella that she was having an actual conversation with Ash. In about twenty seconds, she was sure she'd pass out. But the fact that he'd admitted he wasn't interested in Rachel? It was enough to want to cancel her appointment with CIU.

That brought her down.

Her life was a ticking spell-bomb.

And she was tired of hiding and running.

Ella agreed with Ash. "Rachel would do that, you're right. But it probably wouldn't last long. Maybe a week or two. You could survive until then, couldn't you?"

Ash didn't look like he could, but then his eyes bored into her very being once again. "Maybe if you're there."

Knees? What knees? Ella almost fell. Luckily, she steadied herself before she looked like an idiot by collapsing on the grass. Because if she had fallen on the ground, Ash probably would have offered his hand to help her up. And since Ella's hands were the equivalent of sweat waterfalls at that point, he'd have slipped and been on his behind right next to her.

It didn't matter anyway. She wouldn't be at school tomorrow.

She'd never be there again.

She'd never see Ash again.

This one moment was a present from the universe, but nothing more.

Ella sighed. "You don't think I'm a stalker?"

Ash shook his head. "No."

How could such a simple answer create so much turmoil in her stomach? It was the way he said it. He meant it.

There was a connection there.

She had been right.

"I really should be getting home." Ella said words she didn't want to say.

Slowly, Ash nodded, then looked back at the school. He stared at the student parking lot, as if having a serious internal debate with himself. Finally, he turned back to Ella. "My car is back there. Can I give you a ride?"

Could she? One last rebellion before she was sacrificed to the CIU gods? Her entire being ached for it. To spend time with a boy she liked. Not just any boy, but Ash freaking Torres!

But fear overrode any desire, and she shook her head. "I live really close."

Ash's shoulders slumped, which made Ella's chest hurt. "Are you sure?" he asked.

Ella paused. She wasn't sure. She was sure she was being "good," something she'd had to be her entire life, but . . . "You know what? That sounds great. Thank you."

Had those words actually come out of her little rebellious mouth?

Ash's face beamed. "Great. I'm right up here."

Ella smiled and walked side by side with Ash.

What was happening?

Also, they weren't talking.

This was awkward.

The only saving grace was that Ella's hands had miraculously dried up. Small favors.

After a good three minutes (Ella counted in her head) of walking, they arrived at Ash's blue sedan. It was a two-door and looked to be about twenty years old with the dents and divots to match.

Ella reached for the passenger door, but Ash stepped in and opened it for her, waving his hand toward the plushy gray seat. "After you."

"Thanks," Ella said, hoping her face hadn't exploded red.

After she slid inside the car, Ash closed the door for her and hurried to the driver's side, getting inside himself. "Where to?" he asked.

Ella pointed to where they had just stood. "It's down Cursor Street."

"Perfect. I won't even have to cast a GPS spell." He smiled.

Ella was relieved he hadn't asked her to perform one. If she thought the walk over to his car was awkward, she could only imagine how it would have been explaining why she didn't want to cast the spell.

Pulling out of the parking lot, Ash turned on Cursor Street, and yet again . . .

Nothing.

Say something!

Why had Ella agreed to take this ride?

To seize what she had left of her life.

Speak, Ella, speak.

"How long have you lived in Los Angeles?" she asked. Good. That was a good one.

Ash's grip on the steering wheel loosened a bit. "A couple years. We move around a lot."

"Same," Ella said.

"How come?" Ash asked.

Well, how did she walk into that one? "My parents are consultants. Their job forces them to travel."

"Same." Ash took his eyes off the road for a second to glance at Ella.

Could eyes sparkle more than his? Ella didn't think so.

He concentrated back on the road. "Are we close?"

Ella shook herself out of her momentary Ash stupor. "Oh, yeah, four houses down. Actually, can you pull over here?"

"Uh, sure." Ash pulled the car over to the curb and parked.

"Sorry, it's just my parents are super strict. They'd freak out if they saw I got a ride from someone." Ella hoped she wouldn't have to explain further.

She didn't.

"I totally get it. And it would probably be worse if they knew it was a boy?" Their eyes met momentarily. Ash's lips curved into a perfect smile.

Ella's heart pounded in her chest. "Exactly."

"It'll be our secret." His voice was soft and gentle.

It was the way he looked at her in that moment that could've melted Ella where she sat.

And then he leaned in.

Leaned in!

For what?

A kiss?

Oh gawd.

"Thanks for the ride," Ella sputtered as she threw open the door and spilled out of the car. Before she shut it, she smiled shyly. "See you tomorrow."

Lie.

Because Ella knew perfectly well that she'd never see Ash again.

CHAPTER 13
WREN

Walking into her house, Wren wondered where Ella had been. She'd waited near the crosswalk to try to walk home with her, but Ella never showed.

Wren was still in shock after what she'd witnessed today in quantum spell-casting.

Goose bumps rose on Wren's arms.

Ella was like her mother, and now there was nothing on the planet that would stop Wren from protecting her. She just wished Ella would slow down enough to let her.

The rustling of drawers and doors upstairs indicated Wren's dad was getting ready for work.

She walked over to the door that led to the basement, gently opened it, and then closed it behind her. She didn't want to see her father right then. Not after the day she'd had. Part of Wren wanted to share what she'd seen Ella do, but the bigger part, the part that didn't know how he'd react, kept silent.

Wren walked down the stairs and plopped down on the red recliner, gathering her thoughts. She wanted to quantum phase to Lizzie and Rachel's hideout house right now, but decided to wait until it was dark.

She stared at her board. Not even her dad knew the details of what she did down there. There was no doubt he knew her intentions, because he never questioned their moves, and Wren had to believe a part of him wanted her to go down this path. A path he was too much of a coward to take.

The creak of the floorboards above her caused her chest to tighten.

Wren had no idea if he had noticed the truck being gone yet. It had already been a day, and he had made it quite clear yesterday that he didn't want to be bothered by her. He'd probably go to work like he normally did. Little to no contact with her, exactly how he liked it.

His footsteps walked across the living room floor directly above Wren, then stopped. She stood still, waiting. Waiting for a possible reaction from him, whether it be about the truck or the way he shut her out the other day. It wasn't likely, but Wren found that she yearned for any kind of emotion, even if it was explosive. But after a few long moments of silence, she figured he must've been in the kitchen prepping a meal for his shift.

Looking back at the board, she let her mind relax so that she could tackle her strategy from all angles.

Wren officially categorized Shara as a Dis-con scout. Still not sure how much of a danger she would be, especially to Ella, but it was good to know once and for all who Shara was.

She shook off the disappointment at not being able to talk to

Ella further. She wanted to help. Her mother used to talk about how she'd never made any friends for fear of being found out, but when she met Wren's father, she couldn't resist. And then she had Wren, and she said it had been worth the risk.

Maybe her mother would've still been alive if she had decided to walk away from Wren's dad and never pursued him. Wren wouldn't exist, but her mother would still be there.

But that didn't happen.

Maybe it was destiny.

Maybe the reason she chose to be with Wren's father was for Wren to exist to take down the Trackers once and for all so they wouldn't kill any more innocent people like her mother and Ella. She had to believe this.

A loud thud from upstairs jolted Wren out of her thoughts.

That was new.

Wren's heart raced at the possibility of her father waking up from his self-induced coma.

Pounding feet reached her ears as the door to the basement swung open.

"Wren!" her father screamed from the top of the stairs.

A thrill raced through her veins. Wren couldn't remember the last time he'd called her name out like that.

Sure, he sounded angry, but she'd take it. After yesterday's indifferent reaction to her, some emotion was exciting.

It had to be the truck.

After he stomped down the stairs one cement stair at a time, her father's eyes met hers, and from the flared nostrils and the clenched fists, he really did seem angry.

Wren couldn't explain why this made her so happy, but it did. He might've been furious, but his eyes were alive. Alive! Blood rushed to her head from the emotion of it.

"Where is it?" he screamed.

The shock of his reaction caused her to freeze. No words came out of her mouth.

"Wren!" he yelled, this time closing the gap between them, hands grabbing her arms, eyes wide. "Wren! Are they coming?"

His body language, his facial expression—Wren had been wrong.

He wasn't angry.

He was scared.

He thought Trackers took the truck.

Why would he think that? Why would he think that they'd care about a stupid old truck where they murdered a Dis-con?

But fear had no rationality.

Wren's voice was strangely hoarse as she said, "I shrunk the truck."

His grip lessened, but she desperately wanted him to grip tighter. This was the first time she'd felt connected to him since her mother died.

Relief. Confusion. Fear. And so many more emotions cycled on his face.

But now that the imminent threat was gone in his mind, the worst seemed to be happening. The glaze in his eyes began to take over once more. His arms dropped to his sides as he nodded. "We're not in danger?"

"Trackers did not take the truck," Wren confirmed.

Her dad seemed appeased by her statement. He began to turn to go back upstairs, almost fully a zombie once again.

Not going to happen.

Wren incanted a spell fast.

His whole body froze in place mid-turn as she finished incanting.

Only his face was unfrozen, and his eyes darted back and forth in terror.

At least it woke him up again.

Wren had to keep him "alive."

Now that she knew he was in there, she needed him. She needed him back.

Wren needed her father.

She didn't want to do this alone. He was the only one who understood. He was the only one who'd experienced what she experienced. He was the only one who'd lost the most beautiful person to ever exist. Her mom. His wife. They should've been bound by their grief, not torn apart by it.

He began to incant a spell that would undoubtedly release him from her muscle-locking spell. He said the words slowly, sadly. He didn't want to talk to her. He wasn't angry that Wren had trapped him. He just wanted to leave her.

Again.

But she was quicker.

Wren incanted the rest of the muscle-locking spell, this time encompassing his throat and mouth.

"Why can't you be my dad?" Wren choked out.

Her father stared at her with a sadness that crushed her.

"If I let your vocal cords free, do you promise to talk to me?" Tears streaked her cheeks. "Please, talk to me."

Wren incanted enough for him to have use of his neck. He nodded, tears flowing down his face as well.

She said the words that allowed him to speak.

He didn't seem sure how to proceed. Finally, he said, "I can't live like this anymore."

"You think I can?" Wren asked incredulously.

"I think you're stronger than me. I think you're capable of doing what needs to be done for what those monsters did to your mother." He gasped, his tears overwhelming his ability to breath. "I can barely live."

His words cut every part of her.

"I watched my mother be decapitated in front of me. I've needed you!" Wren's anger overrode her sadness.

"I know," he cried, his body surreally stiff from her spell.

Her spell.

She had been forced to paralyze her father just to talk to him.

After an agonizing silence between them, he asked, "Can you . . . can you make me forget?"

Wren wanted to scream. She wanted to rage. How dare he want to leave her? He always wanted to leave her!

Breathe.

Breathe.

Breathe.

Calming a little, she stared at her broken father. He'd been broken since the day her mom was murdered. Wren lost her father the same day she lost her mother. And she could see with perfect clarity that she was never getting him back. The pieces that had held him together were shattered, and there were too many pieces to put back together.

She couldn't speak, having no idea what to say.

Wren knew what he wanted, but she was worried she was too selfish to give it to him.

He begged, "I know you're beyond a Skein level. I know there's probably no one as powerful as you on the planet. I know you can do this. Think of how much happier we'd both be. You could change my memories and make me think that Isabelle died of natural causes, that she was never a Dis-con, that we've been living here a few years like you've made all the neighbors and your school think. I'd just be one of the people you alter." More tears streamed down his cheeks. "Please, Wren, make me the father I was before all this. Make me the man who would hug you every time I came home from work and read you bedtime stories before you went to sleep at night. Make me sad that my wife passed but able to move on. Please."

Wren fought the growing lump in her throat. She almost choked on it.

"I don't want to be alone in this," she admitted.

He could barely breathe from his stifled sob and his frozen body as he said, "But Wren, you have been alone. I've been gone this whole time."

It wasn't fair.

It wasn't right.

He was still being a terrible father.

How dare he ask this of her?

"Please," he choked.

That one word crushed her.

And she knew in that moment that though she was furious at him for asking, she would do it.

Wren nodded.

Her dad openly cried now, relief and bliss radiating from his face, the only part of him that wasn't frozen.

She walked over to the wall, her body on autopilot. She slid the board over to reach her safe. Twisting the dial until it clicked, she opened the small metal door. Inside were all her stolen spells, written in journals and on parchment paper. Thumbing through the pile, she found what she was looking for. She had stolen it from Japan's military vault, and it was the most powerful memory spell she had, used in the war between Japan and Russia in 1923. Japan had performed the spell to make every Russian citizen believe that Japan had already won and that Russia had surrendered. The rest of the world leaders knew the truth, but they didn't dare tell Russia, so happy the war had ended. To this day, the Russian ancestors believe the lie of the memory spell, even though the truth had come out fifty years later.

It would work.

Flipping to the spell in the notebook, Wren's eyes met her father's, her vision blurred from her tears. "Are you ready?"

He nodded, his face soaked with tears. "I do, you know. Love you. I didn't say it yesterday because I'm a coward. But I love you." His voice was barely a whisper.

"I love you too," she managed to say.

Taking a deep steadying breath, Wren stared at the page and recited each and every word precisely. The spell had been cast. She had three minutes to feed him the new memories.

Three minutes.

Three minutes and her father was a new man.

As Wren rewrote the last four years of their lives, a strange peace overcame her. These memories might've been fake, but maybe they'd make their lives easier, less painful. Only one of them would keep the memory of what happened to her mother alive. He'd feel her loss, but not be destroyed by it. Wren weaved in instructions to forget everything in the past four years, then she built new memories from scratch: a peaceful loving death for her mom; how they mourned her together and it brought them closer; their move there just a year after her death; memories of them laughing again; him helping her with homework; trips to flea markets, stores, and cafés—a life they never had, a life they'd never have. Finally, Wren mentioned the truck in case her neighbors thanked him for getting rid of it. She told him he'd thought he could fix up the old clunker, but decided it was too big of a project, so he sold it to a junkyard.

And with that, Wren was done.

She was alone.

Truly alone.

Her dad collapsed to the floor as she released him from the muscle-freezing spell. That happened sometimes when the memory spell was so thorough. The receiver could be unconscious for a couple of hours at least. Then they'd wake up with the new memories. She'd have to call his work and let them know he'd be a few hours late.

A quick levitation spell and her dad floated at her waist level. She pushed his body easily up the stairs and into his bedroom, laying him down on his soft mattress. He was as private as she was, so she didn't worry about co-workers or neighbors bringing up any old (real) memories.

Closing the door behind her, Wren shut the door on the only other person who understood what she'd gone through. It was a burden she carried herself anyway. Her dad was right. He'd never been strong enough. And now he'd be happy. Wren found that thought lifted her spirits some.

She'd have to keep her mission secret though. Downstairs would have to be glamoured at all times from now on, but it was a small price to pay for peace.

Wren's chest relaxed.

Peace.

Yes, that was the right word.

Determined.

Free.

Releasing her father from all that pain, anger, and terror made them both free.

CHAPTER 19
ELLA

Ash drove away, and Ella sighed. The sun was already setting on the horizon.

She walked into her house cautiously. Though Ash had parked a few houses down, it didn't mean one or both of her parents had not seen her exit his car. After having two students show up at their house yesterday, getting a ride home from a boy would definitely send them over the edge.

She was surprised they weren't packing already. But after tomorrow, they could decide to pack or not to pack, because it wouldn't matter. Without having Ella as an anchor, they could finally do whatever they wanted.

She looked both ways into the dining room and the living room. Her parents were nowhere to be found.

"You in the kitchen?" Ella called out.

Ella's mother opened the kitchen door and waved her toward her.

"Yeah, we need to talk some things out."

That didn't sound good.

Placing her backpack down on the ground, Ella walked to the kitchen like she was walking the plank.

Her mom held the door open for her, and when she entered the kitchen, her dad was sitting on a stool at the island. "How did it go at school? Any suspicions?"

"No one thinks I'm a Dis-con. Terrorist maybe, but not a Dis-con," Ella answered honestly.

Ella's mother let the door shut behind her. She reached out and hugged her. "They still think you cast that plague spell?"

Ella nodded into her mother's shoulder, then pulled out of the embrace. "That Rachel girl Lizzie mentioned yesterday was the worst." She didn't want to go into details about the hologram incident. They'd just ask more questions.

"What did she do?" her father asked, brows furrowed with concern.

"Typical mean girl stuff. I don't really want to talk about it. But the last thing on her mind is me being a Dis-con. She one thousand percent thinks I'm guilty." At least Rachel wouldn't bother her anymore after tomorrow.

Her mom kissed her head. "I'm sorry, sweetie."

Ella's dad sighed deeply. "I hate that you're going through that, but it's better than the alternative."

Was it? "Yeah," Ella answered.

Ella's heart fluttered.

"That's weird . . ."

BOOM!

The house shook violently to the left, then to the right, as if a giant hand had grabbed it by the sides and tried to tear it out by its roots. Ella and her mom almost toppled to the ground from the force, while her dad held on to the island for support.

"Was that an earthquake?" her mother asked breathlessly as the house settled.

Ella gasped. "It was a spell. My heart fluttered."

BOOM!

CREAK!

Ella's mom fell to her knees from the jolt.

Both Ella and her dad helped her back up to her feet.

"Are you okay?" Ella asked, chills racing up her arms.

This was an attack.

"The Trackers have come for you!" Her mom's hand shook as she carefully peeked out the kitchen window. "I see three of them."

Ella moved next to her mom, taking her hands to steady them, then looked herself.

There in her backyard was Rachel Fen in mid-cast.

Next to her were two of her lackeys, students from the basketball team, Ralph Vereen and Sarah Walker. Ralph had gotten hurt almost as bad as Lizzie.

"They aren't Trackers. They're from the basketball team. They're here for revenge." Ella tried to calm her parents down in arguably the weirdest way.

"Oh," her father said awkwardly. "That's better, then?"

"Aside from our house possibly getting destroyed, yes, it's better," Ella's mom answered.

BOOM!

The house shook violently again. This time, the cupboard doors flew open, and a stack of plates and bowls tumbled to the ground, smashing into pieces.

Her dad quickly spelled the shards of porcelain away so they wouldn't cut themselves.

Ella needed to call CIU. They could help before things got any worse. But how could she in front of her parents? They'd never agree to that.

Ralph Vereen's voice boomed from the backyard. "You may have fooled CIU, but we all know it was you, Ella! Don't worry. We're just going to do to you what you did to us!"

"Well, that's not going to happen." Ella's mom paced away from the window, jaw clenched in what Ella always referred to as her mother's *thinking mode.* "Unless . . ." Walking through the door to the pantry, she disappeared from view.

"What's she doing?" Ella asked her father.

He raised an eyebrow, and his lips turned into a smile. "I think she's going to erase any possibility that they would ever think you're a Dis-con."

"How can I fake a plague?" Ella's voice raised an octave.

Her mother walked out of the pantry with a small tote bag in hand. "They're out there. You're in here. All we have to do is listen to the spell they cast and use *this*"—she lifted the bag for emphasis—"to convince them. It's already getting dark. We don't have to be perfect."

"We don't have to be perfect at what? What's in that bag?"

"Makeup, prosthetics, you name it. I didn't know if we'd ever have to use it, but now's the time if any."

Ella wasn't as convinced of her mother's makeup skills considering the woman never wore a drop of it. Her panic took over, and she discreetly pulled out her phone. Her parents were so busy looking through the bag, they didn't notice. Quickly, before they could see, she hit the button with Malcolm's contact number.

The faint sound of him picking up and saying, "Ella, is that you?"

"What was that?" Ella's mom searched for the sound of Malcolm's voice.

"I think they're about to attack again. We should get ready," Ella said loud enough for Malcolm to hear.

CRASH!

The kitchen window shattered with a force that caused all three of them to hurtle to their knees. Glass rained down toward their hunched backs, but Ella's dad cast a quick spell that evaporated it mid-air before it made contact.

Go Dad.

Ella looked down at her phone. Malcolm had hung up. Good. She knew it meant he was on the way.

"Let's stay on the floor. We don't want them to see us," her father said.

Her mom pulled out a kit of makeup and brushes, followed by a small bag that had a stack of clear and opaque sheets of rubber. "John, you know what you have to do."

Ella's heart sank. She knew what that meant. He nodded, taking a deep steadying breath.

Ella's mother then to turned to her. "Let those freaks know where you're at so they can cast in this direction."

Ella nodded and yelled, "Leave me alone! I didn't cast that plague spell!"

From outside, Ella heard Ralph say, "She's directly under the window!"

Rachel incanted words that were sharp and pointed.

Ella's heart fluttered intensely. This was a big spell.

As it flew toward her, she felt the strange bubble of force push toward her.

Her father moved his body in front of Ella and her mom, taking the full force of the spell. He stifled a scream as dark black blisters began to form all over his face and body.

Ella wanted to push what was left of the invisible bubble back on her attackers, but she knew she couldn't. She didn't want her dad's pain to be in vain. Because if the people who blamed her for the plague spell got their revenge, they'd leave her alone. Her parents were right about that.

Her dad couldn't hold back his screams any longer, but her mother was already at work trying to recreate the exact blisters onto Ella. She started with her face since that would be the easiest for Rachel and the others to view.

Outside, Ralph's voice was suddenly panicked. "That sounded like a man. Are you sure we have the right house? We should get out of here!"

"It's the right house. It was probably just her dad," Rachel answered, obviously not caring who got the tail end of her spell.

"We didn't sign up for that," Sarah said.

"Yeah, let's go," Ralph agreed.

Ella's mom finished the third black blister on Ella's face and whispered, "Scream and show them your face."

Grabbing her father's hand, Ella lifted him to his feet as she stood up herself, screaming. It was almost black in the backyard by now, but Ella knew Rachel, Ralph, and Sarah could see her from the kitchen lights.

Ella's eyes met Rachel's as she faked another scream of anguish, and she was surprised by what she found there.

Confusion?

Why would Rachel be confused by hitting her target directly?

Ella didn't have time to ponder as Malcolm's voice boomed

with some kind of spell outside. "CIU! Stay where you are!"

The attacking trio ran fast and hard into Ella's neighbor's backyard. Two CIU agents Ella didn't recognize ran after.

Malcolm said, "Ella? Are you okay? Can I come in? It's Agent Gilroy!"

Ella's mom cast the spell to cure her father, all the black blisters disappearing instantly. To Ella, she said, "What did you do?"

"I thought we needed help," Ella tried to explain as her mother, not so gently, pulled off the prosthetics from Ella's face while her father used a makeup remover wipe to take off her makeup.

"If we don't get this off in time, he'll *know*." Her mother's eyes bulged in terror.

Ella knew she was right and grabbed a wipe herself and scrubbed as hard as she could at her face.

"You're good. You're good. A bit red . . . here." Her father took a wipe and scraped his face full force until his skin was also tinged in red.

"We're in the kitchen, Agent Gilroy," her mother yelled out the open window. "There's a door back here. Her mom took the bag full of makeup and prosthetics and shoved them in the island cupboard.

Straightening her clothes, Ella's mom walked to the back door and opened it.

There was Agent Malcolm Gilroy, face scrunched in concern as he looked at Ella and her father. "The red should go away in a few minutes. That happens with plague spells. Are you all right?"

"We're fine, Agent Gilroy. Thank you for coming when you did," her dad said with sincerity, though Ella knew the last person her father wanted in their kitchen was a CIU agent.

"I'm glad Ella called. I used a tracking spell to her phone, and we were able to get here in minutes. Hopefully my guys will catch your attackers. Do you know who they were? Did you recognize any of them?" he asked.

Ella thought for a moment about ratting out Rachel and the others, but she didn't want any more attention on herself. Agent Gilroy would have questions about her red face tomorrow when he found out she was a Dis-con.

"No. It was dark. We couldn't see them," Ella said.

Malcolm paused as if he didn't believe her. But after a moment, he nodded his head. "Okay, well, I'll leave you to it. You need me to cast a window-replacing spell?" he asked.

"No, we have it from here, Agent Gilroy. Thank you again, so much. We really appreciate it." Her mother laid in on thick.

"Of course." Then he smiled and nodded to Ella. "And I'll see—"

"—me at school. Yeah. I'll see you there," Ella lied and hoped he'd understand.

Malcolm paused again, then nodded once more. "See you then."

With that, he left out the back, and neither Ella nor her parents took a breath until the sound of his car was long gone.

"Well, that was a thing." Ella's mom let out a relieved sigh.

"I think we just saved you from ever being accused of being a Dis-con though." Her father couldn't hide his smile.

Ella forced a smile as well, not wanting to break the moment between the three of them. They were so happy, thinking she was safe. And seeing the scrape marks on her father's face that she knew would be there for a while twisted her stomach. He'd done that for *her*.

"Could you make those brownies again?" Ella asked to change the subject.

"You don't even have to ask," her mother said and kissed Ella's cheek.

Ella decided to push aside her shame and enjoy this moment while she could.

Because she'd never have a moment like this one again.

CHAPTER 20
WREN

Wren stood in the kitchen leaning her elbows on the marble top of the island waiting for her dad to come down. It had been a couple of hours, so the spell should have taken its hold, which meant he'd be waking up soon.

It had taken Wren the entire two hours to calm herself down and prepare herself for the new version of her dad. Or technically, the "old" version. The version he used to be before Wren's mother was killed.

With each steadying breath, she shifted her mind into her safe place. The place where she could detach, where she could focus, where she wouldn't fall apart.

The real test would be when they were face-to-face. When his eyes would no longer be dead, but alive and full of . . . normalcy.

The sounds of her father's bedroom door opening and shutting reached her ears.

Wren's heart jumped in her throat.

Calm.

Breathe.

Stop feeling.

Stop feeling.

Stop.

Disconnect.

"Hey, kiddo. I must have slept in," her dad said as he hurried down the steps.

If Wren breathed, she'd cry, so she held her breath.

His words were the nicest thing he'd said to her in years, and it wasn't even a compliment, only a term of endearment. Wren had forgotten what those felt like.

Forcing a smile, Wren responded with what breath she had in her lungs. "It looked like you needed it. I called your office and said you'd be in at seven."

Glancing quickly at his phone for the time, he shook his head with a smile Wren hadn't thought she'd ever see again. "What would I do without you?" He reached her side and scuffed the top of her head affectionately.

Wren tried to steady herself against the wave of emotion his action caused.

She needed air.

Wren breathed.

Tears threatened to well up in her eyes.

Disconnect.

She had her dad back.

Stop.

No feeling.

He called her kiddo.

No emotion.

Like he used to.

Disconnect.

Shaking her head, Wren stayed focused.

It wasn't real.

"You okay?" he asked, his eyebrows crinkled in concern. "Have a bad day at school?"

"The varsity basketball team was attacked by a virus spell yesterday. It really freaked me out." Wren watched his expression, testing her spell to gauge what his reaction might be. If he looked suspicious of her or confused in any way, she may have to repeat the spell again.

But he reached out his hand and placed it on Wren's shoulder, squeezing it gently. "Oh, honey, I'm so sorry. That's horrible. Is everyone okay? Did they catch the guy?"

She reached up and touched his hand on her shoulder awkwardly. She didn't know how to be affectionate. It had been too long. Her instinct was to grasp it, squeeze it, hold it forever, afraid the spell would break and he'd be a zombie again, but instead, she took her hand away and looked into his eyes. "Everyone's fine. The EHTs were able to fix them right away. And no, they haven't caught the guy."

Squeezing her shoulder one last time, he pulled away, then walked to the fridge, opening it wide. "Thank goodness. I know I used to pressure you about getting into sports, but I've never been happier that you said no." He pulled out his metal lunch container and placed it on the kitchen island.

Wren feigned a laugh, though it was clumsy in her throat. She wasn't used to being casual or normal at home. It didn't feel natural. "He's still out there though. I'm just scared of who he'll attack next." She wasn't. It was her. But she needed to know how he'd react.

His expression shifted to one of intense concern. "You can stay home until they find this guy. I'll call the school and say I don't feel like you're safe there. Whatever you need, Wren. I've got your back."

Wren had to hold her breath again.

What was wrong with her?

She needed to keep it together.

Casting the spell was supposed to make her life easier, not more difficult.

Wren just hadn't expected the change from zombie to overly protective father to affect her like that.

She would have slapped herself, but she needed the spell she cast on him to work.

And so far, it seemed to be.

Yes.

This calmed her.

Think rationally. Think logically. Think practically.

Wren's father would no longer be a problem.

He was now a sweet, caring, loving dad who would do anything for his daughter.

Finally, she responded to him. "No, Dad. It's fine. I'm pretty good at keeping my ear out for spell-casters. I'll be okay."

"You sure? Say the word and I'll call." He appeared determined.

Breathe.

Calm.

Disconnect.

"Yeah, I'm sure. Thanks though," Wren said.

Her dad glanced one more time at his phone. "I gotta go,

kiddo. You going to be okay alone?"

The shock of him asking that threatened to overwhelm her again, but she tamped it down. "Yeah. I'll be fine. I've got some homework to do. It'll keep my mind off of things."

He gave her a quick wave, then said, "I'll see you in the morning when I get back. Have a good night."

"Have a good night at work," Wren said, the words as foreign in her mouth as his were.

With that, he left the house.

Wren stood for a few more moments by the island, gathering her thoughts and emotions.

Breathe.

Detach.

Disconnect.

She wanted something to focus on to distract herself from these emotions roiling around in her brain and threatening to ruin everything she had worked for. Wren decided it was time to spy on Lizzie and meet her dad. Wren could only imagine what a Tracker dad would be like. Probably not pleasant considering the genuine look of fear she'd seen in Rachel's eyes at the prospect of meeting up with him.

Wren walked down the stairs to her operation room. Sitting cross-legged on the couch, she incanted the spell that separated her from her body. It was much easier the second time, now that she knew Lizzie's location. She flew easily over the suburban houses until she found the house she was looking for.

Diving her incorporeal form through the roof, she found Lizzie sitting in the living room eating some form of spelled frozen dinner. With only a few bites left, Lizzie resembled a machine—scoop, bite in, chew, swallow, repeat. Did she do anything for fun?

Was she just a focused killing machine?

The front door opened, and Wren expected Rachel walk through, but it was an older man in his fifties.

Wait.

"I'm in here, Dad," Lizzie called out.

Wait.

Wren recognized the man instantly.

Verner Grant.

One of the richest men alive and a member of the Trackers' Order of Eleven, if not the head himself. He touted himself to the public as a multibillionaire businessman. No one knew he was a Tracker, let alone a leader of them. Wren had only found out when she broke into France's military vault, where they had made reference to the Order and Verner having a seat. Apparently, they owed him a lot of money.

But Verner Grant being Lizzie Trent's father?

She guessed it wasn't *Trent*, was it?

Wren vowed to do a deep dive search on Verner Grant and his children. She had done a search before, but according to everything she had found, he had a son and daughter, Haley and Chase. But Haley was not Lizzie. She was seven.

So was Lizzie illegitimate? From a previous marriage? Some kind of secret child?

The urge to jump back into her body and start researching was so strong Wren almost gave into it, but she forced herself to stay, knowing that the conversation Lizzie and her dad were about to have might be important.

Verner sauntered into the living room as Lizzie pushed aside her now empty dish. "What's the news on Moira Kurt? Sadie talk to her yet?" Verner sat down on a chair across from her.

"Call her Rachel, Dad; otherwise, I'll forget and slip up at school. And I think she talked to Moira after school today. She hasn't come back yet from her excursion to Ella Buckley's house. She's testing to find out for sure if she's a Dis-con. She was going to take Moira with her if her talk was successful."

Wren would have puked if she'd been in her body. So Rachel, Sadie, or whatever her name was, had given Moira the rallying speech. What was her response? Did she go to Ella's? Was Ella okay? Wren could physically feel her heart pounding back in her stationary body. If she didn't calm down, the quantum phasing spell might snap, and she didn't know what the consequences would be.

Concentrate.

Listen.

Detach.

"I'll call her Rachel, but I'm not calling you Lizzie. I fought too hard with your mother to name you Madison." He grinned.

They were acting like a normal family, just joking around, while simultaneously talking about recruiting murderers and testing potential victims.

"Ha ha, yes, I know, your favorite movie, *Madison Sunset*." Lizzie rolled her eyes. Or, Wren corrected herself, *Madison*. Okay. This was information she could use.

Verner sat forward, serious. "And you two are both sure Moira's memories were wiped?"

"Yes, Dad, Rachel quizzed her and Moira doesn't remember anything."

"Good. Otherwise, I'm not sure if we'd be seeing Sadie . . .Rachel ever again. Moira is powerful." He leaned back in the chair.

Wren's mind raced. What erased memory would make Moira

want to hurt Rachel . . . Sadie?

Sadie is Rachel. Sadie is Rachel. Sadie is Rachel.

Madison is Lizzie. Madison is Lizzie. Madison is Lizzie.

Wren repeated this in her mind over and over until she knew she'd never forget. Because she'd only think of these snakes by their real names from now on. It made her mission more real. Visceral.

Sadie hurried inside the house, slamming the door behind her. "Ella isn't a Dis-con." She walked in, then jumped at seeing Verner. "Oh, Mr. Grant, hello. I'm glad I didn't miss your visit." Wren noticed Sadie's hands had a slight shake to them. Wren couldn't really blame her; the man was intimidating.

"Sadie." He nodded.

"*Rachel*, Dad, please," Madison reminded him.

Verner grumbled under his breath and stood as Sadie joined them in the living room. She stayed standing. Only Madison remained seated.

"You're sure?" Madison asked.

"I'm positive. I cast that nasty plague spell with the black blisters. Both her and her dad were covered in them," she answered triumphantly.

"You made sure it wasn't makeup or some other kind of ruse? Dis-cons do all sorts of things to hide who they are." Verner didn't seem convinced.

Sadie paused.

Uh-oh.

Because Wren knew full well that it probably *was* makeup.

"CIU showed up, and we had to run. I brought two students from school, and I couldn't have them getting caught. I don't know what they'd tell them. It took me two hours to lose CIU. That's why I'm late," Sadie explained.

"You didn't answer my dad's question. Did you make sure?" Madison stood now, eyes boring into Sadie's.

"It was dark, but yes, I saw the blisters." Sadie's voice was soft.

Verner turned his attention to his daughter. "You may have to do some more tests, just to be sure."

"Of course," Madison said with confidence. She nodded to Sadie. "What about Moira? Did she go with you? How did your conversation go?"

"She said she'd think it over. But I'm thinking it might be a yes," Sadie said.

There was a knock on Wren's front door upstairs.

Breaking the quantum phasing spell, Wren flew back into her body.

Her heart pounded.

What had she just heard?

Moira was thinking about it?

The knock sounded again.

And Wren's heart beat even harder.

No one came to her house.

Not once.

Was it CIU?

No.

CIU would have broken the door down if they had confirmation she was the attacker.

Was it her dad? Did the spell she used ruin his brain and now he didn't know who he was anymore? Or where work was? Or how to drive?

The knock sounded a third time.

Wren quickly cast a spell on her operation board for both Lizzie and Rachel, changing the names to their real ones, Madison and Sadie. Once she finished that, she headed up the stairs, still undecided if she'd answer the door.

Maybe it was just a salesman or religious person. She should ignore it. That seemed like the logical thing to do.

"Wren? Are you there?" Moira's voice was muffled through the door as Wren arrived upstairs.

Moira?

Here?

Why was she here? Wren knew Sadie had given her the speech, and Sadie seemed pretty sure Moira was in. Was she coming to recruit Wren into being a Tracker? How did she know where she lived?

Part of Wren wanted to keep still until Moira left, but strangely, she craved her company. Or at the very least, she needed to know if Moira was her enemy now.

Wren walked to the front entrance and opened the door.

Moira stood on her doorstep, head slightly dipped and eyes darting. "Hey. Sorry to show up like this." She waited for Wren to say something, but Wren just watched her carefully, ready for a sudden attack in case Moira had figured out she was the one who'd attacked Madison—potentially Moira's new ally. Moira continued, "I knew your dad was gone. I remember you said he worked nights. I just need someone to talk to." She shifted back and forth between legs, then her eyes met Wren's. "Can I come in?" she asked quietly.

"Of course," Wren said and waved her arm wide, welcoming her inside, watching her every move.

Moira's head dipped down again as she entered the house. Wren hoped to all that was holy that Moira was conflicted about Sadie's pitch and not an eager new Tracker about to attack to prove something to her new masters.

"Are you going to say something?" Moira asked as she continuously tapped her forefinger to her thumb.

A nervous habit.

A nervous habit Wren had never seen Moira do before.

"You came here," Wren answered calmly, keeping her ears open for any sudden casting she might try. Wren shut the front door while keeping her eyes on Moira. "Is everything okay?"

"I . . . uh, yeah. You probably think I'm psycho for showing up uninvited. It's just . . ." Her hand reached for the doorknob. "I should go. I'll see you at school tomorrow."

Placing her hand on top of Moira's, Wren stopped her from turning the knob. "I don't think you're psycho." Their eyes met, and Wren's face flushed from the intensity. Her hand tingled where it touched Moira's.

What was wrong with her? Moira could be her enemy! But maybe Moira wanted to talk about it. Ask Wren what to do. And maybe she could tell Moira the truth.

Pulling her hand away from the door, Moira was out of breath. Wren motioned for Moira to follow her into the kitchen, and she trailed behind Wren until they both sat on stools underneath the kitchen island.

After a few moments of silence passed between them, Wren asked, "Why did you come over? And how did you know where I live?"

Twisting circles with her finger on the marble surface, Moira made sure their eyes met. "I know where you live because I've followed you home before. I've never had the courage to knock." She finished the rest of it fast, as if scared of Wren's reaction. "And I know you've only been here a few months. Your memory spells don't work on me. I invented a counter spell against them. My parents tried to spell me once, but I didn't want to forget."

That was vague.

Moira's hands were in her lap now, fidgeting as she waited for Wren's response. "Plus, I just had a conversation with Rachel Fen—"

Words flew out of Wren's mouth before Moira could react. She went for the same muscle-locking spell she'd used on her father earlier since it was fresh on her mind.

Moira's eyes widened as she realized Wren was casting.

"Wren, stop!" Moira managed to spout out before Wren had her completely locked in place on a stool.

Wren couldn't risk Moira attacking her. But she did have hope. Hope because Sadie was sure Moira had had her memories erased, but now Moira was saying she had a counter spell for all memory-erasing spells. She didn't know what it meant, but she planned on finding out.

She cast the spell to release Moira's face and head like she had with her father. Wren needed to see Moira's reactions while she interrogated her.

"Rachel tried to convince you to be a Tracker," Wren said, analyzing every single movement Moira's face made.

Moira couldn't hide the shock in her expression. "How did you . . . ?" She shook her head. "Of course you'd know. You know everything. Yes. She did. But I would never." Wren could detect no sign of this being false, and instead of screaming at Wren to let her go, Moira simply said, "Wren, I would *never*."

Doubt ate at her.

No.

"You can trust me, Wren. I have secrets too."

Wren's instinct was to immediately distrust her, but she was right. Wren already knew Moira had lied to Sadie if Moira just admitted that memory spells didn't work on her. And the fact that Moira knew Wren had only been here a few months proved that was true. Moira had more secrets than only her spells, but the fact that she'd created a spell that protected her against memory spells as strong as the one Wren had used meant Moira was more powerful than she'd ever imagined. It also meant Moira had a reason to do it. Necessity bred invention.

Wren decided to at least listen to Moira for the moment, and she released her from the spell. Moira's body jerked forward slightly from the force.

"Tell me," Wren said.

Moira situated herself on the stool and held her hand out for Wren to sit next to her. After Wren sat down, Moira said, "I've never told anyone what I'm about to tell you, but if I can trust you, maybe you can trust me."

Wren's mother was decapitated by a Tracker that went to school with her.

Somehow, Wren didn't think anything Moira would say could come close to that.

After taking a deep breath, then swallowing hard, Moira said, "My twin sister, Luna, was a Dis-con, and she was killed by Trackers."

Um.

What?

Wren couldn't speak. She couldn't move. She listened.

"The Tracker that killed her had a glamour spell that was too advanced for me to break through. I just saw blank terrifying skin looking back at me while they killed Luna, like every other Tracker we see on the news. They bludgeoned her to death, Wren. I can still see the pool of blood under her head. Her eyes were dead and empty."

Moira took a moment to gasp for air, then she continued, "My parents were inconsolable and wanted to forget everything. They tried to cast a memory-erasing spell on me, but I fought it. I didn't want to forget about Luna. It's difficult to describe how powerfully bonded twins are. I needed to remember her. I always blamed myself for the fact that she was a Dis-con, that somehow in the womb, I'd stolen her powers. I know it sounds stupid, but I was so powerful, even as a child, it made sense.

"So right before my parents cast the memory-erasing spell on me, I managed to block some it, only because I had been working on ways to protect Luna, ways that would maybe work on Dis-cons." Tightening her jaw at the memory, Moira continued, "It was enough for me to remember her, and it took me a lot spell experimentation to finally break the rest of the memory spell. They spelled everyone else too, completely erasing her existence. I don't even have pictures of her. We were fraternal twins, so we didn't look alike. I wish we'd been identical so at least when I looked in the mirror, I could remember her."

Her eyes bored into Wren's. "I chose not to break the spell on my parents because that's what they wanted, but a part of me wanted to. Wanted them to remember. Like, how dare they erase the memory of their own child?" Moira clenched her fists. "My twin."

Moira sighed heavily, relaxing slightly. "It ended up tearing them apart anyway. I think on some level, they remembered and blamed each other. My dad left, and my mom and I moved here. New city, new people. She seemed . . . happy? Content, anyway. As angry as I was with both my parents, I didn't want to return their memories." Moira reached across the marble surface, taking one of Wren's hands in hers. "So no. I would *never* be a Tracker. Honestly, it took everything in me not to kill Rachel right there."

Wren could barely breathe.

Sitting across from her was a kindred spirit. Someone who knew exactly how she felt. Who hated Trackers as much as she did.

Someone who could help her, gladly, because she felt the same.

Finally, Wren answered, "I'm going to kill every single last one of them until their organization is destroyed and they can never hurt another Dis-con again. I thought you came here because Rachel talked you into it."

Moira's entire demeanor became charged with intensity. "She thinks the memory spell that my parents put on me worked. That I don't remember having a sister. I wanted to cast some horrible hex on her and run, but I know how dangerous Trackers are, so I said I'd think about it. But I'm going to have to give her an answer at some point." She paused, then bit her lower lip. "They killed someone you loved too, didn't they?"

"My mother. Decapitated." Wren sighed, then truly tied her fate to Moira's. "It was Lizzie Trent, but her real name is Madison. She's the Tracker who killed my mother."

An intense moment passed between them, then Moira's eyes widened. "*You* attacked the varsity basketball team?" Her eyes darted away, then returned to Wren's. "And you know it's Lizzie—Madison—because you figured out a way to break the glamour spell when she murdered your mother?"

"Yes," Wren answered. "On both accounts. Like you, I'd been working on a spell that could possibly work on Dis-cons. The addition I made to a de-glamour spell worked, and I saw Madison with perfect clarity. As for the basketball team, the plague spell was only supposed to hit Madison, but I had some interference."

Moira's eyebrows furrowed in confusion, then she squeezed her eyes shut, realizing the truth. "Ella." Her hands shook. "Oh god, she really is a Dis-con."

"Yeah."

Moira opened her eyes, shaking her head. "She refracted the spell by trying to help, so it spread across the others. That's why you were so adamant about her innocence. I'm such an idiot. Wren, Rachel went after her today. I didn't go because we saw Ella cast a levitation spell in quantum spell-casting. Oh god, we have to go help her." Moira shifted in her seat, ready to leave.

Wren reached across the space between them and clasped Moira's hand to steady her, needing to touch her. "It's okay. Ella is okay. Rachel didn't hurt her. I'll tell you everything I know. I promise."

Moira's hand tightened in Wren's, and her jaw tensed, eyes fierce. "I will protect Ella with my life like I should have with Luna."

Wren squeezed her hand back. "Dis-cons must be protected at all costs."

They were on the same page.

"What's the plan?" she asked.

CHAPTER 21
ELLA

Ella sat on her bed in her room with a stack of pillows propping her up against the bed frame. Ella and her parents were exhausted after the fiasco that had happened downstairs, so they decided to turn in early. Of course, sugar was now pumping through Ella's veins, and she wasn't tired at all.

She had been attacked.

By Rachel! Plus Ralph and Sarah? She was willing to accept they thought Ella was guilty for casting that plague spell on them, but to hurt her father like that? It was unforgiveable.

Not that Ella could really do much about it as a Dis-con—a Dis-con that was about to turn herself into CIU—but still. Maybe their guilt would be enough punishment whenever CIU figured out who actually cast that plague spell.

Speaking of CIU . . . Though Ella had done this countless times over the years, she decided to try one more time to find out anything she could about what they might do to Dis-cons. Maybe she'd find something to give her hope? She wasn't holding her breath, but she had to try.

After flipping open her laptop, Ella typed in: *What does the CIU do with Dis-cons?*

All theories. All guesses. Nothing official.

Like every other time she'd checked.

She scrolled through some of the titles of personal blogs and articles. None of them mentioned death or executions, which might not have been accurate, but did give Ella the slight bit of hope she had craved. Only one claimed to have a personal connection, simply titled: *CIU Brainwashed My Dis-con Daughter*.

She read through the blog post carefully. The man wrote in a way that indicated he was proud of the fact that his daughter was a Dis-con, not ashamed in any way. Ella wondered what that would feel like since her own parents acted like they were harboring a criminal.

CIU discovered his daughter in high school five years after she cheated her Dis-con test at age twelve. She had only been seventeen, and the man had demanded that CIU return her.

Ella's age.

That poor girl thought she'd beaten the system like Ella had, and then boom, CIU discovered her and took her away.

Ella shook the disturbing parallels away and focused back on this man's story.

After three years, he developed a facial recognition spell, which he cast on an internet search engine to recognize his daughter and how she would look at twenty in any new photo or video. Finally, he got a hit at some business building in New York in an office party photo. He flew there immediately, and when he confronted her, she acted like she'd never seen him before in her life. When he attempted to talk some sense into her, he said three CIU agents came out of nowhere and escorted him to a plane and back to his home. He claimed to be on a no-fly list and a no-state-borders list for reasons of "domestic terrorism." He'd been fighting it ever since, but according to his blog, it had already been a decade.

Ella had no way of knowing if any of the man's story was true or not. The upside would be that his Dis-con daughter was alive; the downside would be that she had no memory of him. But if she was a Dis-con, how would a memory-wiping spell work on her? That would be impossible. And how did she end up in New York at some random office? Even if they had found a way to wipe her memories without a spell, she'd still be a Dis-con and could be discovered again. But if CIU knew where she was and let her be in public, why take her in the first place?

It made no sense.

It had to be a lie.

But a tiny seed of doubt gnawed at the back of Ella's head and told her that it wasn't.

Finding nothing else that triggered a gut reaction (because, honestly, that was all she could really go on at this point), Ella clicked on the official CIU website.

She navigated to the page dedicated to Dis-cons and was greeted with a brief history of the origins of Trackers and CIU itself:

Founded in 1405 in France, Trackers swept across Europe into Asia, even crossing the oceans to the Americas, wiping out any Dis-con they came in contact with. Collateral damage meant nothing to them, as long as they eliminated their target. A behavior that they still employ today.

Their reign of terror went on as such for fifty years, until finally a man named Robert Fowsden put together a team of soldiers that he called his Caster Intelligence Unit, and so began CIU. Wherever the Trackers went, CIU went, until almost every country in the world had a base or station dedicated to CIU. It has only grown since then.

CIU's main focus today is to protect the innocent from anyone that would do them harm.

Scrolling down farther, there were instructions on what to do if you encountered a Dis-con. She'd read it before, but maybe now that she'd met a couple of agents personally, she might notice something she hadn't previously.

It was laid out as a set of rules that Ella was pretty sure no one would follow if they knew a Dis-con personally, with their motto *Recognize, Run, and Reach out* at the top.

1. If you cast a spell on a person, and they have no reaction to it, call CIU immediately.

2. If you know of any Dis-con, they must be reported to CIU.

3. All Dis-cons must turn themselves into CIU.

4. If you suspect a person to be a Dis-con, contact CIU, and an agent will come out immediately to test the subject.

5. Reporting all Dis-cons directly to CIU is in the Dis-cons' best interests. Though CIU is actively pursuing all Trackers and their organization, they are still at large. The Tracker organization is a terrorist group and very dangerous.

Ella read number five over and over. In the past, she had only thought of it as a fear tactic to get Dis-cons to turn themselves in. But now? Maybe CIU really was trying to help or protect? If that man's story about his daughter was true, then they didn't kill her.

But what did they do?

And they caught her late, years after the Dis-con testing, so they knew she had cheated. Just like they'd know that Ella had cheated.

She guessed she'd find out if that was worse than coming clean at age twelve in the morning.

Closing her laptop, Ella decided that since she was wired anyway, she'd play *Hexsphere.* She pulled Veil out of her backpack, placed the headgear on, and turned on the device. She should probably delete Ash's avatar, but considering he didn't think she was a stalker, she figured what people didn't know wouldn't hurt them. Besides, it had taken hours upon hours and tons of in-game gold to create the perfect avatar of her crush, and she really didn't want to destroy all that hard work. Yeah, that was a great reason.

The holographic imagery quickly surrounded her, and she picked her favorite character, FearlessGirl22, again. Once she was standing outside her home base, she brought up the virtual keyboard and typed in *Buster44* to see if he was on. She didn't really feel like playing with any of her other game friends, and she felt bad for bailing on him without explanation last time. She needed him to know it wasn't personal.

Before she could finish typing, a message popped up on her screen: *Buster44 would like to join you. Do you accept?*

Ella didn't really want Buster44 at her home base house, so she entered a new game scenario in the Chicago cityscape, then clicked *Accept* to Buster44.

They both materialized in the middle of downtown Chicago at the same time.

It was deserted, no NPCs, only the two of them, which usually meant an ambush from Trackers.

Good. She wanted to take some Trackers down.

Buster44's thought bubble popped up by his head. *Ella, it's me, Ash.*

What?

Ella's mind raced. Could this be him? Her entire quantum spell-casting class had seen her avatar name in all its holographic glory. Ella wouldn't be surprised if the whole school knew by now. But Buster44? He was her friend, her fighting buddy. And now she realized he could be Rachel for all she knew.

But she decided to play it safe and typed, *What? Are you serious?*

Nice. Simple. Nothing embarrassing. Or did it come off as rude?

Hopefully her brain wouldn't short-circuit at just the possibility that she might be talking to Ash.

Buster44 responded, *I should have told you in the car today. I was going to, but I chickened out. I still feel so bad about yelling at you in class. It was like an out-of-body experience. I can't even comprehend that I did that.*

Okay. If this was a practical joke, it was certainly a nice one. The fact that he mentioned the car made Ella think it was indeed Ash. But anyone at school could have seen her get in his car. But if it wasn't Ash, the person behind it obviously wanted to make Ella feel better, which was nice. Probably because as Buster44 and Fearlessgirl22, they'd played so many games together. She wished there was some way of knowing for sure if it was actually him. Quickly, she racked her brain, going over their encounter after school second by second. There had to be something that she could ask him that only he would know. But after thinking about it, Ella didn't want to reveal to anyone the personal things Ash had said to her about his anxiety and about Rachel. If this wasn't him, they could use that information to hurt him, and Ella didn't want that, especially if she was never going to see him again.

She typed: *I pretty much had an out-of-body experience when*

Rachel showed my home base and the avatar I made of you. So I get it. I'm sorry about that too.

Buster44*: Don't be sorry. I don't even know why you'd want an avatar of me. I'm nothing special to look at.*

Ella choked on her spit as she swallowed, which almost knocked her visor off. Situating back in place, she wondered how someone as beautiful as Ash Torres couldn't see it. All he'd have to do is look in a mirror.

She typed: *I obviously disagree.*

Ella felt weirdly brave since she knew she was never going to see him again, and if it wasn't him, it wouldn't be a surprise that she found him adorable. Rachel had made sure of that.

The long pause caused her hands to shake.

Finally . . .

Buster44: *I think you're beautiful.*

Ella stopped breathing.

Yup.

Definitely not Ash.

She pulled off her visor and shut Veil off.

Why were people so cruel?

Placing Veil on her bedside table, Ella lay back in her bed and stared at the ceiling. With the thoughts of whoever had impersonated Ash and tomorrow's meeting with CIU, Ella was positive she wasn't going to get any sleep.

CHAPTER 22
WREN

Declarations of war were one thing, but at that moment, Moira sat on the stool as Wren stood in front of her, neither saying a word.

Wren was about to say something to break the silence when Moira carefully stood from the stool and did something Wren was not prepared for at all.

She hugged her.

It stopped Wren.

Her mind.

Her body.

Her soul.

She hadn't been hugged in four years.

It was such a foreign yet familiar feeling. She couldn't process it.

Wren's arms moved without her permission, and she returned Moira's embrace, tears forming in her eyes.

Wren wanted to both push Moira across the room and hold her tight, never letting go.

Finally, they both pulled away, neither one acknowledging how intense the hug had been.

Wren nodded toward the door that led downstairs. "My operation room is downstairs. I can show you what I've learned so far."

"Lead the way." Moira waved her hand toward the closed door.

Wren suddenly felt awkward as she walked toward the door, her feet clunky, her arms semi-useless at her sides. Should she swing them? Was that normal behavior? Certainly keeping them stick-straight at her sides wasn't natural. Wren wondered if she'd lose the ability to move at all if she didn't get her head together.

Breathe. Right foot. Left foot. Breathe. Right foot. Left foot.

Making it to the door felt like a triumph. Closing her hand over the knob, she turned it and hoped she wouldn't tumble down the stairs.

What was wrong with her?

Moira was wrong with her.

Moira.

A friend.

A truer friend that she could have ever imagined. She'd lost her twin sister like Wren had lost her mom. The information was short-circuiting her brain. It was as if she couldn't process not being alone anymore. Like if she breathed the wrong way, Moira would disappear and her mission would be her own again.

Just get down the stairs in one piece.

Wren opened the door and walked down first. Nothing said creepy more than if she had made Moira go first. This was a basement, after all. And she'd just admitted to casting the plague spell that took out the entire varsity basketball team. If it wasn't for their Dis-con families, Wren was sure Moira would have run screaming. Or worse, become a Tracker.

Once both feet were firmly on the basement floor, Wren's shoulders relaxed. After casting a quick spell to reveal her operation board and all the holographic components, Wren motioned Moira toward it.

Moira took in the room with a gasp, from the comfy couch and chair to the entire wall of floating images all connected together with three-dimensional strings. "This is intense." She looked back at Wren with a crook of a smile. "I thought I had thorough notes in my journal." Turning back to the board, she said, "Seeing this, I admit I know absolutely nothing."

She lightly touched the hologram of Madison. "How did you find out her real name?" Then she noticed Rachel's hologram with the name Sadie. "Sadie. Hmm. It fits her."

Wren wasn't ready to tell Moira about quantum phasing yet, so she told a half-truth, "I just found out. I used a spying spell on a squirrel since they both have quantum repellent gear on their temporal lobe."

Moira's head swung around to face Wren. "Quantum repellent gear? That's real?"

Wren walked up to stand next to Moira, focusing back on the board. Moira turned her head back around to join her. "Yeah, it's very real. I've tested out both of them, so I know which parts of the brain they have their gear on. I have a list of spells that will work on each effectively. Good spells."

"You mean Torment-hexes?" Moira raised an eyebrow.

"You have a problem with that?" Wren asked.

"Not in the least." Moira smiled. "I'm assuming they're illegal spells?"

"The less you know about where I find and get things, the better," Wren answered.

Moira's hands clasped Wren's, and she pulled her around until they were face-to-face. "Wren, you can tell me anything."

Wren believed her, but there was a tiny part of her that distrusted everyone. "I need some time. I've been working solo for a while, and you've been in direct contact with Trackers."

Moira pulled her hands away. "I didn't know they were Trackers."

Wren's heart ached when Moira pulled her hands away. She wanted to comfort her, make her feel better, anything. But she'd forgotten how. So she shrugged. "Maybe you should have." *That* wasn't comforting at all. Wren awaited the inevitable slap and storming out of the house she expected from Moira after what she'd said.

But instead, Moira paused, then slowly nodded. "I should have. You're right." Tears formed in her eyes. "I let too much time pass." She grabbed Wren's hands again, desperate. "Wren, I almost forgot her."

Wren squeezed Moira's hands back. "But you didn't. And as soon as you found out that Rachel—Sadie—was a Tracker, your instincts led you here. That can't be a coincidence."

Taking one hand away to wipe her tears on the sleeve of her shirt, Moira took a deep breath. "It's not. Us being friends. It means something." Moira gently cupped Wren's face with her free hand while still clasping her other hand. "Don't you think?"

Every cell in Wren's body tingled at Moira's touch. It must've been their connection because of her mom and Moira's sister. The longer they stood there, the more Wren wanted Moira to stay that way.

Eventually, Moira took her hand away from Wren's face, then let go of her other hand. "When you cast that memory spell to make everyone think you'd been here for three years, I thought it was just because you didn't want to be a loner. But then when you *did* want to be a loner, I had to know why. So I kind of pushed myself on you."

Wren smiled. "I'm kind of glad you did."

Moira smiled back. "Kind of?"

Wren didn't answer, but she was sure the flush in her face had and was happy to see a matching flush in Moira's cheeks.

Turning back to the holographic board, Moira asked, "So, do Madison and Sadie have last names?"

Wren tried to brush off the roiling emotions inside of her, but it was difficult. Mission. Breathe. "I was serious when I said I just found out—" Wren was about to say *right before you knocked* but stopped herself. She'd have to tell Moira eventually about quantum phasing if they were going to work together, but casually mentioning that she'd invented a spell that was scientifically impossible to the outside world wasn't something she was ready for.

"And if we don't have last names to start with, how will we search? Madison and Sadie are pretty common names," Moira grumbled in frustration.

"Someone was with them that we can search though. Madison's father," Wren said carefully.

"Do you have his whole name?" Moira perked up at the news.

"Verner Grant."

Moira's mouth dropped.

Literally.

"*Verner Grant? The* Verner Grant?"

"Yup." Wren was still processing it herself.

"Whoa."

"Yeah."

"So she's Madison *Grant*?" Moira asked hopefully.

"Maybe? I've researched Verner Grant extensively though. He only has two kids, Haley and Chase, and Haley is young. But he *is* one of the leaders of the Trackers." Wren pointed to a section of the holographic board on the far end where Verner Grant's face rotated next to seven other faces and three floating question marks all tied together with three-dimensional string connecting to the title *Order of Eleven*.

Moira's shook her head, awed. She mumbled the words, "Order of Eleven."

"You can see I've figured out who eight of them are, but the last three are hidden deep. And I mean deep." The fact that Wren had broken into twelve military vaults and still had no idea who the last three leaders were was significant. It was only a matter of time though.

Moira read each name, followed by a whistle for everyone. "Wren, these are some of the most powerful men in the world. You're telling me they run the Trackers? A terrorist group?"

"While they make the rest of the world think they're saints, they're secretly murdering innocent people," Wren confirmed.

"No one thinks Dis-cons are innocent. The only narrative ever told is that Dis-cons are assassins or super soldiers with blades or other such nonsense."

"It's not total nonsense. Most of those stories are true." Wren had seen a number of accounts written in diaries in the military vaults she'd broken into about some pretty gruesome deaths at the hands of Dis-cons. From using blades to their bare hands. Ironically, the same way Trackers killed Dis-cons. "But I'm sure those Dis-cons were the exception, not the rule. My mom, your sister—they weren't hurting anyone."

"They *couldn't* hurt anyone," Moira added. "Not with magic, anyway."

That wasn't true either, but Wren didn't correct her. Pushing against the quantum waves of a spell could be very dangerous. The little Wren's mother had experimented with it showed her that much. And Ella had this power too.

Moira reached over and clasped Wren's hand once more. The tingling sensation rose within her again at Moira's touch. She found that she liked it. It made her feel safe, connected.

"You're not doing this alone anymore, Wren. I'm here, and I'm here a trillion percent."

Wren wanted to believe Moira's words so badly.

Moira looked back at the sprawling holographic operation board. "Let's find out everything we can about Madison and Sadie."

Wren could get behind that. "My laptop is over there, and I have a few spells that'll help."

Moira smiled. "Let's do it." She tilted her head to the side in thought. "Wait a minute. I just realized something. How in the heck did you get past CIU that morning? They tested for spell signatures. I witnessed you passing!"

Um.

"Yeah, about that," Wren began. She guessed she'd have to tell Moira some things right now.

CHAPTER 23
ELLA

Upon waking up early, Ella's stomach roiled. She was shocked that she had slept at all with her pending appointment at CIU and Buster44 pretending to be Ash. *Beautiful?* A dead giveaway. Ella knew she and Ash had some kind of connection, but she seriously doubted Ash found her attractive, let alone beautiful.

It did seem like he was about to kiss her the other day though.

Stop.

She couldn't think the word *beautiful* without cringing. Plus, it almost upset her more that Buster44 was obviously a student at school. How else would they know her handle and that she drove home with Ash yesterday?

Unless it was Ash?

No. Not even a possibility. She needed to erase that from her brain.

Ella was grateful her parents had given her space after their ordeal with Rachel and the two basketball players. It made things easier for Ella this morning. Because if Ella talked to her mom at all, she knew she'd lose all her nerve and not go to CIU.

And she had to.

After quickly dressing, Ella carefully exited her room, headed down the stairs, and walked outside. She knew her parents would ask where she was going, so she jogged to the corner of her block where she could order a rideshare.

It took a few minutes for the rideshare to arrive, and she slid in the back seat.

"CIU office on Third, please," Ella informed the driver.

The driver raised his eyebrow in curiosity but didn't argue. He incanted a GPS spell with the correct address, and the 3D holographic map filled his front window. Ella always thought it'd be difficult to drive watching a 3D map, but the map perfectly lined up from the driver's perspective, with large turn arrows to make sure the driver stayed on route.

Ella wasn't allowed to learn to drive in the first place since her parents didn't want to risk any kind of testing that might show she was a Dis-con.

It didn't matter now anyway.

She kept her eyes on the scenery outside her window since, for Ella, the 3D map looked like a double jumble of images and outside streets.

Faster than she wanted, the driver pulled up to a large brick building that took up the entire corner of the block. A silver plaque was bolted on the wall next to a heavy wooden door that said: *Caster Intelligence Unit Office 423 Los Angeles.*

"All set," the driver said impatiently.

"Right. Thanks."

She needed to stop staring and start moving.

She unbuckled her seat belt and left the car, gently closing the door behind her.

Without another word, the driver sped off to pick up his next fare.

Standing in front of the building that might mean her death or, at the very least, her disappearance, Ella found that she couldn't move.

She didn't want to die.

She just didn't want to live the way she had been.

And there was the problem.

The cement beneath her feet was cold through her shoes in juxtaposition to the hot sun that beamed on her head.

Run, Ella's inner voice screamed at her.

Run and never come back.

"Ella? Is that you?" Malcolm's voice sounded a distance off.

The agent walked up the sidewalk toward her and the front door. He had a friendly smile as he approached, dressed in a white button-up shirt, no tie, and black slacks. A bit casual for a CIU agent, but it helped her feel more at ease.

"It's me," Ella answered lamely.

Malcolm took her hand and shook it. As he pulled away, he said, "You're here early. I wasn't sure if you'd come after last night."

"I wanted to come before school," she lied, though it was a believable one. "And thanks again, for scaring off the attackers."

"Of course. I'm glad you felt comfortable enough to call me. Unfortunately, I don't have good news on that front. My agents weren't able to catch them. Are you sure you didn't recognize anyone?"

"Yeah, I'm sure," Ella lied again. "And thanks for covering for me. I didn't want my parents knowing I was coming here. They'd freak out."

Malcolm nodded. "I understand. It's their job to be protective. And having your child meet with a world government agency can be a little daunting for any parent. But this shouldn't take long. Why don't we go inside?"

Ella was too nervous to answer verbally, so she simply followed Malcolm through the large wooden door and into the belly of CIU.

Too late now.

Ella was a little underwhelmed. It looked like any other office: cubicles, office chairs, dry-erase boards on the walls with scribbles of notes and case assignments, and a few spell stations (which she assumed were for interrogations, but they could've been for snacking—she had no idea). The room was almost empty, with only a few agents at their cubicles. She really was early. But better to get it over with than to worry about it all day. The longer Ella waited, the bigger chance she had of being caught by her parents as well. Not to mention the possibility that she'd have been too scared to come at all.

"There's a private testing room up here." It seemed like he said it more to break the silence than to actually tell her the information.

But it did calm her nerves a bit. At least when they found out she was a Dis-con, it would only be Malcolm and maybe one other agent. It wouldn't be like her nightmares, where a mob of CIU agents beat her to death since spells didn't work on her.

Oof.

Ella hoped that would never happen.

But a part of her wasn't sure.

The only people that knew what happened to discovered Dis-cons were captured Dis-cons.

Now Ella wished she had researched more about that guy's daughter that she'd read about last night.

CIU had to be better than Trackers though, didn't they? It was implied on their website at least, unless that was a trap. And if Dis-cons didn't pass the test at twelve, they didn't honestly murder kids, did they? She couldn't imagine Malcolm hurting anyone, let alone a child. But Ella didn't have enough experience interacting with people to really sense their intentions or character.

One thing she knew for certain was that Trackers were ruthless. Instant death. Snapped necks, crushed skulls, severed bodies. *That* Ella had seen in the news. The only deaths anyone had ever seen were by Trackers. They didn't exactly care who witnessed their murderous rages, especially since their glamour spells were so powerful all anyone ever saw was a blank smooth-skinned face slaughtering the innocent.

If CIU did kill Dis-cons, Ella imagined, with someone like Malcolm, it would be a sleeping/death pill or some other nice way to get rid of her. Or if they kept Dis-cons alive, maybe that was how they could erase memories? A nice easy pill. If her brain was about to be wiped, she'd much prefer a pill as opposed to being beaten by a bunch of agents.

Was this really happening?

The walk seemed longer and faster at the same time.

They passed the last line of cubicles. The entire back wall consisted of a row of doors that led to rooms with no windows. Not even the doors had windows.

Definitely private.

No one would notice or miss a girl from Tristan High.

Especially one that had never made any real-life friends.

Suddenly, Ella's parents' plan to not get close to anyone felt even more like a dumb one.

Moving to the last door on the right, Malcolm spelled it to open, and it swung gently inward. "After you." He held out his hand for her to enter.

She walked in and was not surprised to find it sparse and unwelcoming. Again, no windows, only the one door leading in and out, and a rectangular table with two foldout chairs placed across from each other under the table.

"It's not much, but the testing I'm going to do is all Skein level, so we don't need any equipment," Malcolm informed her.

A chill went down her spine, but she nodded. "Okay."

Every part of Ella wanted to run in that instant, but she sat instead.

Malcolm sat across from her, still friendly in his demeanor.

Wouldn't last long.

"I need to hold your hands. Is that all right?" he asked kindly.

Ella answered by giving him both her hands across the table.

Yup. Sweat glands had kicked in yet again. Her last parting gift to the CIU agent that discovered her.

Malcolm took her hands gently, not commenting on the embarrassing mutant sweat limbs. He closed his eyes.

Ella's heart pounded out of her chest, and she wondered if Malcolm could hear it. He surely knew she was nervous (waterfall hands), but he didn't *really* know why.

His incantation was a lower frequency at first, then it grew in volume and pitch.

Her heart immediately began fluttering. It was both jarring and uncomfortable.

She'd never heard a spell like that before, which only created more stupid sweat on her stupid hands. Ella silently prayed that the agent wouldn't politely ask to perform an anti-sweat spell. That alone would show him she was a Dis-con. But Malcolm continued to hold on to her slippery otter hands without complaint. His spell took a turn, and his voice grew higher pitched. Then he popped out ten staccato punches in a row, with Ella's heart missing a beat for every staccato.

Malcolm stopped casting.

His wrists and forearms were bright red from the spell blowback.

Opening his eyes, he withdrew his hands from hers.

Ella waited as her heart went back to its normal rhythm.

This was it.

Her sentence.

But after a quick healing spell to his arms, he smiled instead, albeit in a more contemplative way. "Thank you, Ella. I used a pretty powerful stripping spell to see anything you may have forgotten. Sometimes witnesses don't remember details that can help us immensely in our investigation."

Ella swallowed hard. "And . . . what did you see?"

Nothing! He should have seen nothing! No spell worked on her.

"Weirdly? Nothing," he answered. "I'd think you were a Dis-con, but your records show you passed the Dis-con test at twelve, I saw spell residue on you the day of the plague attack, and last night, you and your father had the same blister recovery."

Ella didn't know what to say.

She was frozen in shock.

The spell didn't work, and yet he didn't think she was a Dis-con.

She had her dad to thank for the blister recovery redness,

scraping his face like that with the alcohol wipe so they'd match.

But the retained residue was still a mystery. Was she *not* a Dis-con? Was she something else?

Did her strange ability to react with other spells and push against them mean something more?

But Ella's mom said that no spell they'd ever performed on her had left a residue.

She was so confused.

"Why wouldn't the spell work?" Why had that come out of her mouth? She should've smiled and left. And thanked him as she ran to school.

But Malcolm didn't seem fazed. He shrugged. "We've seen it before. It means the caster laid down some kind of spell suppressor. I'm shocked we were able to do a re-creation spell since the one cast on you is so solid. We're definitely looking for a Skein."

More bad information. More false evidence leading them in the wrong direction.

"Maybe it's just me? The attacker might not be a Skein." At this point, Ella kind of wanted to punch her own face with her own sweaty hand. *Stop talking!*

Raising an eyebrow as if thinking it through, Malcolm answered, "Maybe. But it's looking pretty clear that he or she is. The virus spell alone was incredibly complicated. This isn't the work of an amateur."

In a horribly strange way, that made her feel better.

"Oh, well, okay. If you're sure." Ella's mouth was officially diseased with stupidity.

Malcolm stood up and motioned for Ella to do the same. "You better get to school. I don't want you to be late. I'll have a car take you."

"Uh, thanks," she replied and stood up herself.

Ella nearly fell back into the seat her knees were shaking so hard. She quickly lied, "My foot got caught on the leg." She straightened herself out as she stood, trying to hide the shake in her entire body.

She was both relieved and terrified, and she couldn't differentiate between the two.

Her brain was on overload.

CIU had cast a spell on her. It didn't work. And they didn't accuse her of being a Dis-con.

Ella took a moment to let reality sink in.

She was alive.

She had been tested by CIU for the second time in her life.

And they were letting her go.

Malcolm led Ella out of the building, put her into a company car, and the driver drove her straight to school, no questions asked.

Exiting the car and walking with a crowd of students toward the front entrance, Ella reeled in shock.

Could she really be safe?

Could the combination of passing her Dis-con test as a kid and having spell residue on her from a psycho's plague spell now have saved her for the rest of her life?

A flood of happiness surged through Ella. The exhilaration was overwhelming. She couldn't wait to tell her parents, though they'd be furious that she'd gone to CIU.

But she didn't have to be afraid.

So why was she?

Oh right, because a vicious attacker was on the loose, a Tracker could still find out she was a Dis-con and kill her, and . . .

she was about to go to class with Ash.

No big.

Taking a large gulp of air and slightly choking on it, Ella walked to class even though she was a half hour early.

Lame.

CHAPTER 24
WREN

The sun barely crested the houses across the street, spilling light through the basement windows. It was early morning, and Wren and Moira wanted to have a game plan for the day before they went to school.

Moira had spent the night, and they stayed up to all hours talking, planning, bonding. They'd even cast some spells Wren hadn't tried yet from her safe. There was a language-learning spell Wren had stolen from Brazil's military vault, and now they both spoke perfect Portuguese.

But mostly, they talked about their losses. Moira losing her twin sister and Wren losing her mom bound them together in a way Wren had never thought possible. Moira was still in shock that Wren could change her spell signature, and Wren wondered how much more in shock Moira would've been if she knew she'd invented a spell for quantum phasing. Soon, but not now. It had become Wren's nature to hold things back, and it was a difficult habit to break.

At some point, Moira couldn't keep her eyes open, so Wren had cast a spell to hide the holographic spider diagram board so she could sleep as well. She didn't want her father coming home early and possibly bringing his memories back. The memory-restructuring spell would still be settling for a few days, so the less exposure to their past, the better.

But now that Wren was awake, she cast a quick spell to reveal the holographic board again. Standing in front of it, Wren examined each and every connection with all the notes they had made from the night's brainstorming session.

Madison was indeed Madison *Grant.* After they did a deep dive using hacking spells she'd stolen from Japan's military vault, the prodigal daughter had appeared. Verner had apparently kept her secret from the world so she could take over his spot on the Order of Eleven someday with complete anonymity. Wren wondered what it would be like to be raised as a tool to be used by her father. Her mother, Sheila Grant, seemed to be on board with the ruse since she only ever mentioned her other two children, Haley and Chase. And from digging deeper into the hospital DNA records themselves, Madison definitely was Sheila Grant's daughter. Wren had no sympathy for her mother's killer though. Madison enjoyed decapitating Wren's mom, and no amount of bad parenting could cause that. Madison was rotten to the core. Born that way. Madison's mother probably recognized the evil in her daughter and was glad she didn't have to pretend to love her.

That was how Wren saw it, anyway.

Sadie ended up being Sadie Kallum. As far as they could find, Sadie was twenty-five years old and had been recruited when she was fifteen. Apparently, her brother was a Dis-con, and she had killed him herself. There were no details of how he was killed, only a redacted file stating that his sister, Sadie, had murdered him in their house. He was ten years old.

Moira had almost puked when Wren discovered that piece of information. Wren only felt rage. Rage and justification for her mission: kill them all.

A shadow passed the basement window, distracting Wren.

"What was that?" Moira's voice cut the silence.

Wren glanced up at the window. "It's a car parking in front of my house."

Standing, Moira stood on her tiptoes and peered out the window. "You think it's a neighbor?"

"Or someone visiting? I don't think it's a big deal." But Wren's instincts were heightened too. Something didn't feel right.

"I woke up with the hairs on the back of my neck raised, and then that car pulled up." Moira craned her neck to get a better view.

"My windows have permanent glamour spells attached to them, so no one can see what I'm working on, and neither Madison nor Sadie have repellant gear on the occipital, but if another Tracker has repellent gear on the occipital?" Wren began to worry.

Wren incanted a quick spell to hide the operation board once again. The basement now looked like a regular old basement with two teenage girls staring out a window. Wren motioned for Moira to sit on the floor with her. She complied immediately but discreetly kept her side vision glued to the window. Wren did the same.

Feet and legs appeared against the window, then a familiar face leaned down and stared inside. Even from the corner of her eye, Wren recognized her.

Madison Grant, a.k.a. Lizzie Trent, a.k.a. Evil Incarnate.

There.

At her house.

Wren's hands shook, and Moira reached across to her, holding them in hers, attempting to calm her.

Wren could kill Madison now, end her misery and exact revenge before the first bell of school rang.

No.

Breathe.

Killing her now could possibly hurt Moira, and Wren knew with certainty that she'd never let that happen. Besides, murdering a Tracker would cause alarm in their ranks, and mostly likely, Rachel—Sadie Kallum—knew she was there, so they'd know exactly where she'd died. And since they knew who Wren was because of her mother's death, it wouldn't be difficult to figure out how and why she was killed.

No. They needed to make Madison think there was nothing of interest in there.

Why was Madison there? was the real question.

Why so bold, walking straight up to Wren's house?

The miniaturization spell.

When Wren shrunk that bottle, it had her spell signature, her residue.

"Did Sadie say anything to you about the water bottle I shrunk?" Wren whispered.

Moira's pale face said it all, but she whispered, "It was right before class, and she asked if I had done anything to the bottle, and I told her you miniaturized it for Hex Lab. She shrugged and moved on. I didn't think anything of it." Her eyebrows raised hopefully. "I thought you changed your spell signature though?"

"It was temporary, just to get past CIU and the signature-reveal spell. I can't change it permanently." Wren's hands stilled as she prepared for a battle. If Madison turned this into a fight, Wren was ready.

Moira seemed to sense this and straightened as well.

The only saving grace was that *Sadie* had spotted it and not Madison. But Madison was here now to check it out for herself. Madison would still have residue on her from the plague spell, so she was the best person to investigate if it was a match, and Wren's house was full of her spell signature, so it wouldn't take long. Plus, with her little confrontation with Madison the other day at Ella's, Madison was probably already suspicious of her.

This was all speculation, of course, but an educated guess.

Wren at least had an ounce of relief knowing that since Madison's occipital was free from repellent gear, she couldn't see through the windows because of the glamour spell Wren had set in place.

Wren needed to perform the spell she'd invented for changing her spell signature. There was no other way. It had worked with CIU. She just hoped it would work now. Spelling the entire house was a lot bigger than spelling herself though.

Wren whispered to Moira, "I'm going to try the signature-changing spell to cover the entire house."

Moira nodded solemnly, obviously knowing the enormity of what Wren was suggesting but understanding instantly. Having this connection with someone was something Wren could get used to.

Wren began incanting, weaving her words, transforming the very essence of who she was, then pushing it out of her and into the furniture, the stairs, the walls themselves. She could almost see the quantum waves twist and layer around her. Finally, when Wren could feel that the spell had touched the very tip of the roof, she stopped incanting.

Madison's head craned back and forth and around, searching inside the basement, staring at them, but her eyes showed no recognition, no sign that there was anything unusual happening. Standing back up, her legs moved past each sequential window, and she bent down one more time at the last one.

Then, standing up, Madison began to incant.

It was the same signature-reveal spell that CIU used, the most thorough one Wren knew of.

Wren held her breath.

If Madison recognized Wren's signature, she'd come in strong. She wouldn't hesitate. Her job was to snuff out enemies no matter the cost, no matter the attention it might cause. Trackers didn't care, and certainly the daughters of their leaders cared even less. If Wren's spell didn't work, Madison's spells would come hard and fast.

She looked briefly at Moira. Her eyes told her she was ready to fight, eager. They were more alike than Wren could have ever guessed.

Madison stopped incanting.

Wait for it.

Madison didn't move.

Wait for it.

What was she doing?

Wait for it.

Madison's voice was muffled through the window. She was on a holo-phone.

Moira cast a quick amplifying spell to both her and Wren, and suddenly, it was as if Madison were in the room next to them her voice was so loud. Of course, so were all the inside and outside noises as well. Who knew the refrigerator upstairs could be so loud?

"Nope. Different signature," Madison said.

Relief flooded through Wren.

Moira gave Wren a silent high five.

The voice on the other end of phone was Sadie's. "And same with Moira's?"

Moira's eyes widened at the mention of her name.

Wren's heart raced.

Madison answered, "Yeah, I went to her house first, and she wasn't there. I know she didn't say yes to joining us last night, but that doesn't mean she's against us. But no, neither signature matches the plague spell."

"And we're sure the plague spell was meant for you? Not just a prank on the basketball team?" Sadie asked.

"Yes, we've been through this. I'm sure. You saw for yourself that my injuries were hotter than the others. Plus, the attacker obviously knew where my repellent gear is attached so that it would work at all. It's the scattering that's throwing me off."

"That's probably on the caster. I know you and your dad still suspect Ella is a Dis-con, but I saw those blisters, and I saw her cast a levitation spell." She audibly sighed at Madison's obvious silence on the matter. "You should schedule a brain stem surgery so you can't get hit by those types of spells. It's by far the worst recovery time, but it's worth it, trust me," Sadie said.

"I'll think about it, but I'm not doing anything until we catch this rat."

"Well, we've been watching Moira and Wren since we got here, and so far, they've pretty much kept to themselves. The only reason we haven't tried to recruit Wren is because she knows her mother was killed by Trackers. We got lucky with Moira and her parents performing that memory spell on her. And we've seen surviving members of Dis-cons gravitate toward each other before. Larry and Riley were both pretty happy to not have to watch these two anymore. Moira and Wren have both grown very powerful," Sadie mused.

"Wombers usually do," Madison said.

Moira turned to Wren and mouthed, *"Wombers?"*

"I just hope Moira says yes." It almost sounded as if Sadie pouted.

"I'm sure she will. I'll speak with her today too. Maybe we can convince her together." Madison sounded like she was trying to be supportive.

Sadie sucked in a breath. "I'd like that, thanks. I'll keep a stricter eye on Wren, I guess, just in case."

"And definitely on Ella. I'm still not convinced she isn't a Dis-con." Madison drove in her suspicions.

"Don't you trust me?" Sadie sounded annoyed.

"I don't trust *her*. Something refracted that spell, and nothing happened to her when I touched her. I'm sorry, but that can't be a coincidence." Madison's voice was strong and overbearing.

"Fine. We'll take things up a notch today, then. Really do some testing," Sadie conceded.

"You know I'm in." The slight hitch in Madison's voice emphasized how thrilled she was at the prospect. She hung up the phone and walked back to her car.

"Wren. The spell you just did . . ." Moira's eyes widened again in awe. "You have to teach me."

"You're not freaked that they're going to try to recruit you again today?" Wren couldn't look her in the eye.

Moira leaned down until Wren's eyes met hers. "A little. But I can stall and avoid until we come up with a plan." Then she smiled. "But Wren. You changed your spell signature. Again. That's never happened in recorded history." She shook her head in amazement.

Moira was right. Wren had taken her spell to a whole new level *she* didn't even think was possible. Wren should be ecstatic.

But she couldn't seem to stop her internal organs from shaking with terror.

Moira tilted her head in thought. "Wombers. You think it's because your mom was a Dis-con and my twin was? Like we literally shared a womb with a Dis-con."

Wren nodded with a slight chuckle. "Leave it to Trackers to be on the nose."

"I mean, they named themselves Trackers." Moira shook her head, and they both shared a laugh at the Trackers' expense.

"How do the dumbest people end up in power?"

"It is interesting that our spell-casting skills are so strong. Better than anyone in our school, that's for sure. And the fact that you invented a spell that changes your spell signature? We should start an army of Wombers," Moira said in jest.

But Wren perked up. "It's not a bad idea, actually. We'd just need to find others like us." Another reason to break into the Tracker vault—a feat Wren had yet to accomplish. "I'm not sure how many twins there are like you and Luna, but there's gotta be a list of the surviving children of Dis-cons Trackers have killed." If they were going to do this, Wren would have to tell Moira soon about the vaults.

Moira breathed in deep. "Are we really doing this? Taking on the Trackers?"

"I've already been doing this, but you don't have to. I'd

understand if you wanted to back out now. Just politely tell Madison and Sadie no and walk away." Wren said it, but she was terrified Moira would take her up on it.

Moira's expression turned serious. "Never. I'm with you until the end."

The unsaid question between them: would that be sooner rather than later?

Moira continued, "We'll take shifts with Ella. Make sure she's out of their range. First period with Sadie will be difficult, but I have an idea for that." Her fists clenched with determination. "If they see she doesn't react to spells, it's done. They'll go after her, maybe even in class."

Wren noticed Moira hadn't questioned how Ella had been able to perform a levitation spell in class. It'd connect soon though, and she'd be asking. But Wren knew she was going to tell her the truth about Ella being able to push quantum waves and everything else.

No secrets.

As scared as Wren was for Ella, for herself, for Moira, her insides also burned with elation. Wren's chest felt lighter, even though it was weighed down with burden.

Sitting in front of Wren was Moira. In her house. Talking to her about Trackers and Dis-cons and her mission.

And for the first time in four years, she wasn't alone.

CHAPTER 25
ELLA

Ella floated on a cloud as she walked into quantum spell-casting. She still couldn't believe she had been let go by the CIU. A large part of her brain struggled with the fact that CIU thought they were dealing with a mastermind Skein spell-caster because they didn't know she was a Dis-con, but Malcolm had said that the plague spell itself was Skein level. And Ella had nothing to do with that. So the caster was a Skein or close to it.

Did that automatically eliminate students?

Looking at this classroom alone, Ella could name a couple of kids who were above and beyond in terms of skill level.

But could any of them actually hurt anyone?

Probably.

Ella would never have thought Ralph and Sarah from the basketball team would be capable of casting a Torment-hex on her and her father, but there they'd been with Rachel in her backyard, casting away. It just proved that Ella had to keep her mind open to anyone being the attacker, especially since she was the only one with all the information.

She quickly sat down in the seat farthest from everyone, at the very back of the very last row. Right where Ash had sat yesterday.

Ash.

She was going to see him again.

Any minute.

She hoped and prayed her hands wouldn't start sweating. For the moment, they seemed to be listening.

More students filed in as the minutes passed, but so far, no signs of Ash.

She kept an eye on each and every person though. Chances were high that Buster44 was in this class, which was fascinating on its own. Ella thought she knew that player pretty well, and pretending to be Ash or not, they were rather kind last night. Part of her wanted to meet them. And now that she'd been cleared by CIU and would be going to school again, her curiosity was piqued even more.

Ella tried not to stare when Rachel walked in, but it was difficult since Rachel couldn't seem to keep her eyes off of her. Oh man, was she going to attack her again? In class? Ella didn't have her mother's makeup kit to help her this time. From Rachel's narrowed eyes, it didn't appear that her anger for Ella had abated much. She still looked at Ella like she was enemy number one.

Distracted by Moira walking in with Wren, Ella was surprised when Wren nodded a hello to her. Even Moira smiled in greeting, which was a relief since she was the one pointing fingers at her in class yesterday. So far, only Rachel seemed to despise her. Ella just hoped none of the other basketball players wanted to exact revenge on her today. At least none of them were in this class.

Then it happened.

Ash walked in.

Should she look at him? Should she look away? Should she smile or wave or . . . Ella didn't know what to do, so she glanced up at him quickly to see if he was even remotely paying attention to her.

He was.

Ash smiled shyly, then sat down at the desk next to hers.

Ella didn't know what to do, what to say.

Luckily, she didn't have to decide as Mr. Tildon came to stand in front of the class right as the bell rang. "We're doing labs today again, so pair up," he announced out of nowhere.

Ella wasn't expecting that.

Labs on what?

She couldn't do labs.

They just did labs yesterday!

Ella knew it was a quantum *spell-casting* class, but still. They'd never had two lab days in a row.

But her question was quickly answered when Mr. Tildon said, "CIU has some things they want me to look over from the attack on the basketball team, so I'll be reviewing those at my desk. Work on your telekinesis spells from yesterday." And with that, he sat back down at his desk and began thumbing through a binder.

Ella wondered why CIU would have a high school teacher review paperwork. Were they looking for more spell signatures? Ones they obviously didn't detect when everyone left through the sealing-dome. Maybe someone in one of his classes? Ella's mind raced with the possibilities. So much so that she didn't notice when Ash stood in front of her desk. "You want to pair up?"

Gulp.

"Uh, sure." Ella really hoped her eyes weren't as bulged as she was sure they were.

Ash didn't seem to notice, or at least, he was pretending not to, which was a nice relief.

Ella followed him to the very back of the lab tables in the farthest corner next to the wall of windows.

On one hand, Ella loved the privacy; on the other hand, it meant they were alone. Really alone.

Double gulp.

He sat with his back to the rest of the class, and Ella sat on the stool across from him, which gave her a view of the entire room. No one seemed to be staring, so that was an improvement from yesterday.

Surprisingly, Rachel was paired up with Moira and not Will Locke, her normal go-to partner. Rachel seemed rather delighted by this. Maybe the two were becoming friends after bonding over Ella's apparent guilt. Rachel walked to the lab table next to Ella and Ash's, but Moira shook her head and said something to her. Ella wished she could have heard what Moira said, because Rachel looked downright pleased as she followed Moira to the lab table at the very front, as far from Ella and Ash as possible.

Happy coincidence, but she'd take it. Ella didn't want Rachel to cause another scene and remind everyone (especially Ash) that she had an avatar of him on her Veil.

The only couple close to them was Wren and Shara.

Shara, unlike Rachel, seemed annoyed by the partnering. Ella didn't like that Shara kept eyeing Ash like she wished she were sitting with him. Ella wondered why Wren and Moira hadn't partnered up since they seemed to be getting closer.

The same objects sat in front of them like yesterday, and Ella hoped Ash could perform at least one of the levitation spells so she could push against his and look like she'd succeeded again. But Ash stared at the objects with as much disdain as Ella felt.

"I'm a terrible spell-caster," Ash said shyly.

Not as bad as she was. "Me too."

Then his eyes flew up to meet Ella's, and he said, "I didn't mean to embarrass you last night. You signed off pretty quickly."

Um.

Uh.

Um.

What?

"It was really you? You're Buster44?" Ella sputtered.

Shock froze her in her seat.

Ash's head dipped. "I couldn't believe it either. When Rachel . . . you know, yesterday, and I saw your handle? I freaked. I tried to tell you about it yesterday in the car, but you took off pretty fast there too." He smiled shyly. "You thought Buster44 was pretending to be me?"

Holy.

Buster44 had been Ash the entire time. The games they'd played, the jokes they'd shared—he was a good friend. And it was Ash! No wonder Ella had felt a connection to him. She must have known on some level. It was probably the best thing she'd heard in a long time. Except for the fact that she had a raging crush on him and had no idea how to speak to him. Buster44 she could talk to, but Ash Torres?

"I can't believe it. So, we've been friends for two years?" Ella said it out loud and found she was actually smiling.

He smiled back. "Yeah." He ducked his head again. "And then I screamed at you."

"Total dick move. Buster44 would be very disappointed in you." Was Ella jokingly giving Ash Torres a hard time? She found that if she thought of him as his game persona, it was easier to talk to him.

Ash wore what Ella hoped was a teasing expression. His smile melted her brain completely. "He would be, actually. I'll never do it again. I promise." Ash reached out and brushed his hand against hers.

Brain, what brain?

"Why didn't you believe me last night though?" he asked.

Ella retrieved her brain and found that her nerves had come back full force. "I thought . . . after what Rachel did . . . that someone was setting me up. That you'd never actually say—or believe—I was beautiful," Ella admitted. "So I shut off my Veil."

Ash's eyes twinkled, and the side of his mouth pulled up into a shy smile. "You *are* beautiful."

Ella was pretty sure everything in her body had just short-circuited.

She had no words.

A complete shutdown of everything.

"*You're* beautiful," she muttered. *Why do I exist?*

Ash's smile grew into a full-blown grin, and he saved Ella from having to speak further on the matter as he slid the ruler closer to him. "I'll go first," he said.

With a sigh of relief, Ella nodded, though her head was giddy with excitement. It really was Ash last night. And he really did think she was beautiful. He was Buster44, one of her only friends for the last two years. It filled her chest with an elation she didn't think would ever go away. Even lab wasn't so scary anymore. Since he was going first, all she had to do was wait for him to levitate the ruler so she could do her trick. She hoped he could do it, because yesterday, it seemed like he was having trouble.

Ash was almost finished with the spell when Ella noticed he stuttered very slightly on the last word, so nothing happened.

Oh.

Speech impediment.

It was the only other thing that prevented people from casting spells besides being a Dis-con. Without the perfect incantation of sound, the quantum waves couldn't be activated.

It was also the one thing Dis-cons tried to teach themselves so they wouldn't be discovered.

Could Ash?

No.

Ella tried to shake the thought from her mind, her paranoia running rampant, attempting to remember a time when she'd witnessed Ash performing a spell successfully.

Apparently, Ash could tell by Ella's expression that his stutter had made her pause because he said, "I've been going to a speech therapist since I was five. I'm a lot better, but it makes casting almost impossible. I might as well be a Dis-con." He smiled.

It was the same joke Ella had used yesterday with Shara, but in her case, it was true. Was it true for him too?

Stop.

She smiled with him. "I was barely able to lift anything yesterday, and I don't even have an excuse." Except that she was a Dis-con.

Ella's heart fluttered.

And not from being this near to Ash.

No.

Someone was casting a spell.

On *her.*

Ella's eyes searched the room, looking for who it could be, when she saw Lizzie Trent through the window of the door, her mouth moving.

Ella had no idea what Lizzie was casting.

Looked like she was picking up where Rachel had left off last night and getting revenge for the plague spell.

Ella needed to do something. But before she could, the strangest thing happened.

Wren Martis followed Ella's gaze and stood up from her table and walked straight toward the door.

Ella had no idea if it was coincidence or not. But by simply striding toward the door, she'd made Lizzie leave.

Ella's heart beat normally again.

Ash stared at Ella, curious. "I feel like something just happened and I missed it." Then he reached out and touched the top of her right hand again, sending shivers down her back. "Are you all right?"

Uh.

Her brain was mush as she looked into his beautiful brown eyes.

"Yeah . . . I saw Lizzie Trent out there and wondered if she was okay," Ella lied.

Lizzie had been performing a spell on her.

It meant the basketball team wasn't going to stop. Last night wasn't enough punishment, apparently.

Ella needed to listen very carefully to everything that came out of their mouths. She was suddenly very grateful Moira had randomly picked Rachel as her partner, because she was making Rachel perform every spell twice, which kept her from performing any spells on Ella if she wanted to.

Ash nodded, responding to her lie, "That was pretty crazy what happened to the basketball team. I'm sorry you got blamed for it."

Her heart may not have been fluttering, but it was definitely squeezing.

The door swung open, and Ella's head craned to see if Lizzie had decided to come in after all. But, to her surprise, it was Agent Malcolm Gilroy, followed by his boss, Agent Rosia Alvarez.

All levitated objects dropped on cue from the shock of seeing CIU agents enter a classroom.

This classroom.

Ella pretended not to notice that all eyes kept bouncing back and forth between her and the agents. She would have thought Moira would've had her pitchfork out by now after her accusations in class the other day, but weirdly, her eyes were completely on Rachel.

Malcolm and Rosia quietly made their way up to Mr. Tildon, not making eye contact with anyone in the room. Ella secretly wished Malcolm would give her a wink or a smile to give her some kind of comfort, because at that moment, Ella was thinking he'd changed his mind and was coming to take her away for being a Dis-con.

But after a few words with Mr. Tildon, their teacher stood in front of the class, clearing his throat. "CIU is going to need to interview the following people: Rachel Fen, Shara Ralter, Wren Martis and Ella Buckley. Please go with the agents now."

Interview?

Didn't she just have an interview?

Maybe this was for show? But for . . . who? Why would CIU care what a bunch of high schoolers thought? And why Wren and

Shara? Neither one of them was at the scene as far as Ella knew. Rachel made sense. She and Ella were both there in the thick of it, Rachel trying to get to Lizzie and Ella stopping her.

From the expression of relief on Ash's face, Ella could tell he was grateful his name hadn't been called, but then his eyes turned to hers with sympathy. "See you when you get back," he said quietly.

Ella stood with Wren, Rachel, and Shara, then followed Malcolm and Rosia out of the room.

Rachel walked behind Ella, and she could feel her staring into the back of her head. Rachel and Lizzie really had it out for Ella, and she didn't know what to do about it.

Wren was next to Ella, and Shara walked almost parallel with Malcolm and Rosia like she knew them. Ella wished she had her kind of confidence.

Tugging on Ella's sleeve, Wren motioned for her to slow down. Since she'd rather not have Rachel behind her, Ella followed Wren's lead. As they fell behind, Rachel threw the both of them dagger eyes as she was forced to walk ahead of them.

Wren's pace slowed enough that they were very far from the group, at least thirty feet and well out of earshot, but luckily, no one seemed to notice. "You're in danger." Wren's voice was almost too quiet to hear, but Ella did, and it sent shivers down her spine.

"I know," was all Ella could utter. "Rachel attacked me last night at my house, and Lizzie just tried to cast a spell at me. They still think I cast that plague spell."

"No, that's not why."

"Then why?" Ella asked.

"Because they're Trackers."

What?

What?

What?

Ella stopped walking.

Wren pushed her forward with a warning glance and nodded toward the distant group. They continued moving, but Ella's legs shook uncontrollably.

"My mom was a Dis-con like you. I know what to look for. They suspect you, but they don't know for sure yet. Whatever trick you pulled last night wasn't good enough. They're going to be casting spells on you today to see how you react. I can help." Wren whispered to the point that Ella had to strain to hear, but she was grateful, because she didn't want anyone to hear what was happening.

And speaking of: what *was* happening?

Wren's mom was a Dis-con? *Was?* Had her mother been killed by Trackers?

Ella's heart dropped. Tears instantly formed in her eyes, blinding her.

But Wren kept her hand on Ella's arm, guiding her forward.

"I wanted to cast a hearing-block spell, but Rachel is immune to temporal lobe spells, so we have to keep our voices down to almost nothing, even at this distance," Wren warned. "I performed a glamour spell on myself though, since her occipital lobe is clean, so they all think I'm right behind them. It only looks like you're lagging behind, at least. Hopefully it'll be enough for Rachel not to strain to hear anything since she'll think you're alone."

"Oh. Okay, thanks," Ella whispered, but she was more confused than ever.

Immune?

How could Rachel be immune if she was a Tracker? Ella had thought only Dis-cons were immune, and she thought Trackers killed Dis-cons *because* they were immune.

Ella was really regretting not spending time with Wren earlier. She had obviously wanted to talk to her about this that day she tried to walk home with her, and now, the conversation was almost impossible.

"Did Trackers kill your mom?" Ella asked. She needed to know.

Wren's eyes met hers, and she nodded once.

A bond sealed them together like nothing else ever could.

Wren knew what she was. Her mother was murdered for it. And she wanted to help.

"I'm going to stay next to you all day. I'll be able to recognize their spells and tell you how to react. Okay?" Wren's eyes pierced Ella's. Wren looked worried, scared, and hopeful all at once.

Ella grabbed Wren's hand and squeezed it. "Yes. Thank you. I . . ." She had no words to express how she was feeling, but Wren seemed to understand, because she squeezed her hand back.

"Moira can help too. Her sister was also killed by Trackers."

Ella's heart raced. Two people knew? Two people who had lost people they loved simply because they were Dis-cons. For the first time, Ella felt protected. Her parents had tried, but all they ever made her feel was scared, ashamed, and lonely. Not on purpose. Ella knew they loved her. But the reality was, the only way her parents knew how to protect Ella was to hide her from existence.

Up ahead, the others came to a halt at a doorway leading to the faculty lounge area.

Ella heard Wren cast a spell under her breath to break the glamour spell on herself as they arrived at the door.

Malcolm looked Ella in the eyes and smiled a small greeting.

After smiling back, Ella turned to Wren.

With a slight nod, Wren's message was clear: they'd talk later.

Ella nodded in agreement, and their small group entered the lounge.

Now for the interviews.

CHAPTER 26
WREN

Wren did it.

She told Ella.

Wren was still reeling, but she knew it had been the right thing to do. Ella was so entrenched in her life of shutting people out that Wren couldn't risk Ella ignoring her. She needed help, and Wren and Moira were the only people who could give it to her.

The lounge was set up with a few round tables surrounded by hard metal chairs. Two couches lined the back and side wall, with four recliners scattered throughout. There was very little decoration on the walls, only a small framed painting of a pirate boat in rough waters above the couch and a large photograph of a rose close-up above the other couch.

As they stood there waiting for instructions, Sadie eyed Wren and Ella. Wren would have to tell Ella the Trackers' real names, but for now, she didn't want to confuse her.

Wren could tell Sadie hadn't heard a word they'd said outside in the hallway. Wren had made sure they were far enough behind everyone that their voices wouldn't carry. There had definitely been a possibility of exposure, but Wren couldn't risk Sadie performing a spell on Ella on their way back to class and Ella not responding. Wren didn't think Sadie would try anything in the interview room, as she wouldn't want to hazard being discovered by CIU, but in the hallways, all bets were off.

Wren's worry for Ella had overshadowed her worry for herself, because . . . why else was she there?

Before Wren had cast the glamour spell, she had incanted the spell that changed her spell signature yet again because her instincts told her that was what they were checking for.

Shara was there for backup, though no one knew that but Wren.

Ella's eyes kept shifting toward Wren, her expressions switching through an array of emotions: fear, relief, happiness, leeriness, then back to fear. Wren could only imagine what Ella was thinking.

How could Wren cast a listening spell without CIU or Sadie noticing? Because Wren needed to hear what CIU said to Sadie and Ella.

"Wren Martis, you'll be first," Agent Malcolm Gilroy said.

Agent Alvarez nodded to the rest of the group. "Go sit on the couches over there. We'll go one at a time."

Rosia and Malcolm sat next to each other at one of the tables, arranging it so only one person could sit across from them at a time.

Wren sat down, projecting as much confidence as she could.

Rosia motioned to Wren's hand. "May I?" she asked.

Reaching across the table, Agent Alvarez gently took her hand, casting a spell. Wren recognized it immediately. It was a signature-reveal spell like the one at the sealing-dome.

Sweat beaded at her temple.

Breathe.

It worked at the sealing-dome. It worked at her house with Madison. It would work here.

Time seemed to stretch into an eternity as Agent Alvarez cast the spell a second time.

This could only mean she doubted her first reading. But did she doubt it because she was sure Wren's signature would match? Or because Wren's spell was throwing her off, as if she sensed it?

After another long pause, Rosia finally released Wren's hand. Her lips pressed into a line. She didn't look happy at all. "Where were you the morning of the attack?"

"In the hallway, getting ready for school," Wren lied.

"You weren't anywhere near the gym?" Rosia tilted her head, eyes penetrating Wren's.

What did they know? Or what did they *think* they knew?

"Not that I can remember." Wren mimicked as if she were trying to think. "I mean, I may have walked by it to get to the hallway. It's on the way from the west entrance." Which was true, and those were definitely the doors Wren had used. Maybe being close to the truth would help her cause. They were fishing, which might've meant there was a witness that had named Wren.

Rosia and Malcolm exchanged glances, then Malcolm shrugged.

Sighing heavily, almost disappointed it seemed, Agent Alvarez nodded toward the couch. "Take a seat and send Rachel Fen over here."

Wren did her best to appear as clueless-teenager-y as possible as she stood up and walked over to the couch, plopping down next to Ella. Wren's eyes met Sadie's, and she motioned toward CIU with her head. "They want to talk to you now."

Sadie barely acknowledged Wren as she stood and walked over to the table and sat down. Wren seriously hoped they'd cast a temporal lobe spell on her and think she was a Dis-con or figure out what she really was—a Tracker. Not that CIU could doing anything about Trackers. Sure, they'd haul her in, but the organization was so tied into the world's infrastructure, Sadie would be out within the hour. There were little to no consequences for Trackers (not for lack of trying by the CIU). It was almost a joke watching CIU trying to take them down. But the desire to destroy Trackers was at least one thing Wren had in common with the organization.

Turning to Ella, Wren made sure only she could see her. Shara was feigning disinterest. Wren turned her back to her.

Wren mouthed to Ella, *"Talk so I can cast."*

Picking up immediately on what Wren intended, Ella began rambling about how she wondered what they wanted and why the four of them were the only ones brought in. It was enough to keep Shara disinterested.

Casting the listening spell didn't take long. Wren focused it on Malcolm since Sadie's repellent gear would've rendered it useless. Wren's back was to the table too, so she had to side-eye Malcolm to make contact. So far, he didn't seem to notice any spell had been cast on him as he spoke to Sadie.

"You were one of the first people to arrive on the scene. Is that correct?" Malcolm asked.

Ella continued to talk to Wren, even though she knew Wren wasn't listening. Ella reminded Wren so much of her mother that it almost threw off her concentration. Her mom would seamlessly be able to pretend things were "normal" in public situations. This was obviously old hat for Ella. Her expression didn't appear worried at all, though Wren knew she must've been in full-blown shock by now.

Wren's focus shifted back to eavesdropping as Sadie answered, "That's correct." She must have indicated Ella in some way, because she continued, "Just in time to prevent her from finishing the job."

Rosia interjected, "Ella Buckley did not cast the plague spell."

"So you say." Sadie huffed. "How do you know for sure?"

The girl was good. Redirecting the conversation so she didn't have to answer any questions about herself.

But Rosia was no fool. "We're asking the questions, Miss Fen."

"You can't touch me." Sadie put on an air of defense. "I know my rights."

Rosia must have reached across the table to perform a signature-reveal spell as she had done with Wren, and Sadie was obviously afraid that Rosia would cast a spell that her quantum repellent gear would render neutral. It made Wren wonder how Trackers got out of situations like this one. It couldn't be the first time an undercover Tracker was interviewed by CIU.

Wren pretended to be paying attention to Ella as she listened as carefully as possible to what was happening behind her.

Malcolm's voice was calm and commanding as he said, "If you know your rights, then you know as one of the first witnesses to a scene, CIU has legal precedent to test you for residue and signature."

Wren had been right. That was all they were testing for.

A thought hit her that she wasn't prepared for.

Wren had been so worried about them checking for her signature, she hadn't thought of what would happen if they checked for residue on Ella!

Signature-reveal spells were fine for Dis-cons because if you came up blank, it meant you were innocent, but residue? Ella wouldn't have any since she was a Dis-con.

Wren had to do something.

She had to get Ella out of there.

They'd only need to stall a few more days. Residue rarely lasted longer than that.

Wren wanted to scream at herself for not thinking of this. Frankly, she was shocked they hadn't tested Ella the morning of the attack when the residue would have been at its strongest. But if Wren had known this was coming today, she could have cast some of her test spells that she had planned to use on her mom to throw off Trackers and CIU tests.

Then Wren remembered.

She *had* added that to her plague spell. Though she had been sure that Madison's brain stem was clean, Wren had added the extra precaution just in case Madison had quantum repellent gear there.

Of course, so far, Wren had no proof it would actually work on a Tracker with gear, or even on a Dis-con, but she had figured it couldn't hurt.

If a smidge of her spell residue had rubbed off on Ella, she'd be safe. Or safe-ish, anyway. Safe enough to survive this interview. But Wren couldn't be sure. She couldn't rely on the hope that one of her experiments was not only successful, but would have lasted longer than a few hours.

Sweat beads formed on the back of Wren's neck as she tried to keep it together.

Think.

Think.

Think.

"Ella Buckley?" Malcolm's voice cut through Wren's panic.

She hadn't realized that Sadie had finished and sat across from them next to Shara.

Ella gave Wren a small forced-relaxed smile and walked over to Agents Alvarez and Gilroy.

Do something!

Cast something!

Save her!

Wren's listening spell still ran on Malcolm as she sat frozen on the couch staring at the wall.

If they tried anything, she was going to destroy them. Skeins or not, with some of the arsenal Wren had collected from military vaults, she was sure she could take them.

Because one thing Wren knew with absolute certainty.

She would never let Ella get hurt.

Never.

Wren shifted her position on the couch so she could have a better view of Ella and the agents, her side-eye now on Sadie, who appeared to be on her phone, probably texting Madison.

As Ella sat down, instead of Rosia reaching forward to perform both the signature-reveal and residue spell, it was Malcolm. Wren was surprised when he gave her a supportive smile, as if to say to her that she was . . . safe?

Wren wondered if she was misreading that. Or was she seeing things she wanted to?

But no, his eyes, the slight tilt to his head, the kindness that radiated off of him was how a big brother looked at his younger sister.

Wren held her breath.

Waiting.

He performed the spell.

Despite his kind face, Wren had three spells ready to cast that would immobilize everyone in that room aside from Ella.

But he pulled his hands away and smiled again. Even Rosia smiled in thanks.

Malcolm said, "Thank you, Miss Buckley."

Then Rosia and Malcolm stood with Ella. Addressing the rest of them, Rosia said, "Rachel, Wren, and Ella, you may go back to class." Her eyes met Shara's. "Miss Ralter, you're next."

Shara put on a show of nerves, shaking hands, shifting eyes, but Wren knew it was fake. They obviously wanted to talk to their lackey alone.

Wren's knees wobbled as she stood. She had been ready to take on three CIU agents and a Tracker only seconds ago; now she was going back to class.

Breathe.

Calm.

Breathe.

Calm.

Wren kept her listening spell active as Ella approached her and they headed toward the exit. Sadie lagged behind them as they entered the hallway heading back to class.

No.

Sadie wanted to cast something on Ella.

Wren slowed down, causing Ella to slow as well. She was following her lead as if they'd been friends for life. A strange trust brewed between them, though they'd barely spoken.

Sadie sneered. "I'm not walking with you two."

Stopping in the hallway, Wren made sure they were face-to-face when she said, "Well, we're not letting you walk behind us either. I can see the way your bratty little eyes look at Ella. You plan on casting some nasty spell to make her fall? Choke? Or maybe another spell like you cast on her last night?"

Sadie reared her head back slightly. Wren wasn't sure anyone in that school or otherwise had ever given Sadie attitude before, because she looked downright shocked. She recovered quickly though and shoved Wren back. "You're disgusting." Then she stormed off ahead of them.

No longer a threat.

Wren and Ella stood in the hallway, watching Sadie until she entered the classroom and closed the door behind her.

They were alone.

"How did you know she was at my house last night?" Ella's expression was dumbfounded.

"We have to talk, but not here." Wren made sure they made eye contact. "You go on to class. I'm going to listen in on their conversation with Shara."

"You think Shara has anything to do with this?" Ella asked, her eyebrows scrunched together.

"She's undercover CIU—a Dis-con scout, to be precise—and she was testing you yesterday." It felt good to be so honest.

Ella nearly fell as she took a step back.

Wren placed a steadying hand on Ella's arm. "We'll talk after school. Wait for me, and we'll walk home together." Forcing eye contact so that Ella really listened, Wren said, "Moira and I will be sticking by you today. Lizzie and Rachel will be testing you, and you'll need us both to help." Wren used the Trackers' aliases so Ella would know who she was talking about.

Wren's body stiffened with shock when Ella embraced her. "Thank you," Ella whispered in her ear.

And before Wren could hug her back, Ella raced down the hallway toward the classroom.

Wren leaned up against the nearby lockers, trying to be inconspicuous as she listened in on the CIU agents. She'd already missed the first chunk of the conversation, but she couldn't worry about that now.

Shara's voice was the most prominent as she said with an annoyed edge, "I'm telling you, I saw Ella perform the telekinesis spells. She was terrible, but she levitated the objects just fine."

Malcolm's huff was evident from where Wren stood. "None of the spells we've cast on her have had any effect. How can you explain that?"

Rosia cut in, "Malcolm, Ella had spell residue all over her body. Dis-cons are incapable of carrying residue. You know this."

Wren's heart nearly stopped.

Spell residue.

Her spell residue.

It worked!

The fact that there was residue on Ella? A Dis-con? Obviously the spell hadn't actually worked on her, so it wasn't a total success, but residue was a start. A huge start. Wren would have to talk to Moira about this. Maybe she could help Wren figure out a way to tweak it so it would actually work on Trackers. But Wren's biggest hope? That she could find a way for it to work on Dis-cons. If her protection spell had worked that day, her mom would still be alive. And though it technically hadn't worked on Ella, it still saved her from being hauled in by CIU. A small comfort for her guilt, but a comfort nonetheless.

Malcolm responded, "I'm telling you, I tried five different spells on her in the office this morning, and none of them affected her. I think she could be different. A Dis-con, but with limited spell capabilities."

Shara laughed. "That's absurd. You sound like a Tracker zealot. You going to be spouting conspiracy theories now?" Wren could hear the sarcasm dripping from Shara's voice.

Rosia interceded, "That will be enough, Agent Gordon." Agent *Gordon*—Shara's *real* last name, good to know. A pause. "Agent Gilroy, you will find a way to pull Ms. Buckley aside to perform more tests. Agent Gordon, you'll continue to keep an eye on the Torres boy."

"I'm pretty sure it's just a stutter," Shara answered.

"We have to make sure," Rosia said in a matter-of-fact way that only a CIU cold-hearted snake could pull off. "And there's something about Rachel Fen that rubs me wrong. Make sure she's not a Tracker."

The sound of chairs shuffling was Wren's cue to hurry back to class.

Her heart raced as everything they'd discussed washed over her.

Ella had retained spell residue; they suspected Rachel might be a Tracker; but more importantly . . .

Ash Torres might be a Dis-con.

CHAPTER 27
ELLA

Ella sat across from Ash quietly, her mind going a mile a minute.

Too much information to process.

Too much emotion.

Ash stared at her with his eyebrows crinkled, and genuine concern radiated from his deep brown eyes. "Are you okay?" he asked. "What did they tell you?"

Ella couldn't answer.

She glanced over at Moira, who was trying very hard not to look like she was keeping an eye on Ella. It was then that Ella realized Moira had picked Rachel as a partner to protect her from Rachel's spells. When Lizzie had been at the door trying to spell her, Wren had stopped her. They were like Ella's guardian angels.

Moira.

Moira who had practically accused Ella of the plague spell the other day.

Moira who was at least a Skein, maybe even higher, though there was no classification for that.

Her sister was a Dis-con.

Dead.

Wren.

Her mother was a Dis-con.

Dead.

Dead.

Dead.

Wren. Wren. Wren. She knew. Moira knew.

And they wanted to help her.

Ella cleared her throat because it was the only thing she could do to yank back the tears beginning to form.

Ash reached across the lab table and touched Ella's hand again.

It was enough to jolt her out of her spiraling.

Ella pulled her hand away, though her heart ached at Ash's downcast eyes as she did.

"It's fine. Really. Just some follow-up questions. I guess it brought up the day of the plague spell all over again for me again." Ella smiled, hoping it was enough to placate him. The impulse to run out of that room and never stop was so strong, Ella had to place both her hands on her legs to stop herself.

Wren walked into the room and sat at her lab table, which remained empty across from her since Shara was still with the CIU agents. Ella corrected herself: Shara was a CIU agent.

Her hands turned to fists on her legs now, the fingernails digging in, giving Ella some kind of stability. Because she was about to fall apart. It was like she had carefully crafted this facade her entire life and each lie, each new place, added another piece to a puzzle she was creating, but now, it was as if someone was rapidly flicking out puzzle pieces one at time until it would all become a pile of chaos.

Mr. Tildon didn't seem to notice any of their returns, as whatever CIU had given to him to examine took his full attention. Wren took advantage of this and slid off her stool, arriving at Ella and Ash's table a second later. "Hey, Ash. Hey, Ella." She focused on Ella. "You okay? That was pretty weird."

Wren was giving Ella an excuse, a breather, a way to explain why she must've looked like a caged animal. "Yeah," Ella answered. "They were kind of freaking me out a bit." They didn't, but everything Wren had told her was.

"Same," she responded.

Gently, Wren touched one of Ella's clenched hands that at this point had probably left bruises on her legs. It was enough to make Ella release her grip. Circulation rushed through her thighs. Ella hadn't realized how tightly she was squeezing them.

But Wren had.

And she'd come over to help her.

Tears of gratefulness came unbidden to Ella's eyes.

"Ella," Ash reacted to her tears. But the way he said Ella's name made her want to cry more. So much worry, so much concern. She was overwhelmed again.

Ella breathed in a couple of deep breaths until she could think clearly.

Wren did the same.

All the terrors of these last three days tried to creep in and overtake her thoughts again, but she pushed them away each time they reared their ugly heads.

"Better?" Wren asked with a small smile.

"Better." Ella nodded, wiping her cheeks of the tears, but at least there were no new ones to replace them.

Ash's shoulders relaxed as he looked at her, but his eyebrows were still furrowed with concern. "I'm such a jerk for yesterday."

"Let's not even think about it." Ella really didn't need another stressful thought poking its anxiety-inducing head into her brain.

"You both seem to be friends now at least?" Wren offered.

Ash smiled at that and nodded. "I hope so. Actually, we just found out we've been friends for a couple of years now; we just didn't know it."

Wren eyed the both of them with curiosity.

Ash continued, "We both play *Hexsphere*, and we've apparently been playing together."

Why was he the cutest?

"That's amazing. I'm happy for you guys," Wren said and gave Ella a little squeeze of comfort on her arm.

Ella tried to enjoy the moment. These past few days had been filled with more interaction with people than she'd had in her entire life. That alone would be overwhelming, but add Trackers and CIU agents?

She'd be taking deep breaths all day.

Wren ended up sitting with them for the rest of the period as Shara never returned to class. It was nice having a buffer with Ash. Ella's brain still couldn't comprehend that they were actually talking to each other and that he was Buster44. And Wren made sure they kept the conversation light, never mentioning the last couple of days or anything that would trigger Ella. The kinder she was, the more Ella wanted to leave school and really talk to her. She wanted to know about her mom. She wanted to know everything.

The bell rang.

Focus.

Trackers.

Rachel and Lizzie.

With a slight nod from Wren, Ella stood and they waited for all the other students to file out of the room. Ash stood with them, obviously thinking they didn't want to go with the other students for other reasons.

Not the I'm-about-to-be-attacked-by-Trackers reason.

"You want me to walk you to your next class?" Ash asked so sweetly, Ella's heart jumped.

But Wren saved her again. "Oh, no. I mean . . . of course, you should totally walk with Ash. We can go over our English assignment another time. I can get Moira to help me." She shuffled nervously, tilting her head down in mock disappointment.

Ash shook his head apologetically. "It's okay . . . I'm sorry. I didn't realize you guys already had plans. Maybe later?" he asked.

Ella's body couldn't take all the yanking of nerves from every source imaginable. "Yes. Of course. I'd like that."

Ash's grin was contagious as he nodded, then walked out of the room.

Approaching from the left, Moira walked up to them, eyes expectant. They were the only three students left in class. Mr. Tildon was far enough away at his desk to not hear what they were saying, though she wasn't sure it would matter anyway as he was still engrossed in whatever CIU had handed him.

"Wren told me—" Ella had been about to say *Everything*, but she knew that wasn't true, which made her want to talk to them even more.

Moira nodded. "Sorry about yesterday. If I had known . . ." She shook her head. "If I had known, I'd have handled myself a lot differently. Putting the spotlight on you like that was so dangerous. I really am sorry." She seemed to be holding her breath, waiting for Ella to respond.

"I totally get it. I would have thought the same thing." Ella weirdly wished people would stop apologizing to her. It was uncomfortable. Like whenever she got a compliment. Her face went all red, and she had no idea what to say.

Wren motioned with her head for them to exit. "We'll have to split up. I'll stay with Ella at all times, and you stay with Lizzie and Rachel. I'm going to cast a two-way listening spell on us." Casting the spell didn't take long, and the two of them tested it out briefly. "Perfect. Now when they cast a spell on Ella, tell me what spell it is, and I can tell her how she should react."

"What if they split up? They both have repellent gear on the temporal lobe," Moira pointed out.

Ella turned to Wren. "You said that before. What does it mean?"

"I can't explain it fully here." She nodded toward the distant Mr. Tildon. Plus, they were about to enter into the busy hallways. "But Trackers get brain surgery to block spells being cast on them. The temporal lobe is a big one because it has the auditory cortex, which means no listening spells."

As Wren reached for the door handle, Moira's eyebrows raised, an idea seeming to pop in her head. "If they do split up, I can cast a listening spell on whoever is next to the one I'm not with."

Wren opened the door. "Good." The noise from the hallway hit them with a wave of chatter. "You guys ready?"

Ella nodded, but she was absolutely not ready at all.

Moira mock saluted, and upon seeing Rachel and Lizzie huddled by Rachel's locker, she headed their way.

"Well, at least they're together." Wren's lopsided smile put Ella slightly at ease, but not much. "Let's make you a target."

Not words Ella liked hearing, but this had to happen.

Obviously, last night's theatrics weren't enough for Rachel. She needed to be sure. If her parents had known Rachel was a Tracker, they'd have already been halfway to Kansas by now.

Ella hoped Rachel wouldn't cast the same plague spell. There was no makeup or prosthetics to help her here. But Ella was sure that if Rachel and Lizzie cast spells on her today and they worked, they'd be convinced she wasn't a Dis-con.

And they wouldn't kill her.

Ella took a deep steadying breath while Wren guided her right past Rachel and Lizzie, making sure they were visible.

It worked.

Like sharks, Rachel shut her locker and the two started to follow them.

The halls were crowded, but they still had room to move about. Ella and Wren didn't speak. They just waited.

Were they going to cast anything?

At least Ella's next class was on the second floor. It gave Rachel and Lizzie plenty of time to cast something on her.

The longer Ella and Wren walked, the more Ella's heart pounded.

Trackers were hunting her.

Breathe.

Not hunting. Testing. Testing like last night. And testing today, and Wren was going to help her.

Ella and Wren reached the stairs at the end of the hall and took each step of the incline slowly.

Oof.

Ella almost tripped from the giant flutter in her heart. Wren caught her before she could fall, and Ella whispered, "They're casting something."

Wren cocked her head to the side, probably surprised Ella would know that, but then she shifted slightly as if hearing something. Her eyes focused on Ella's as she grimaced in sympathy. "You're right. Moira says it's a leg-locking spell. Now."

Gratefully, Ella had that one down. The leg-locking spell was a staple of bullies everywhere, so Ella had the reaction memorized.

She seized up her knee and crashed down on the stairs.

Ow.

Laughter, some concern, and stares on Ella, but mostly, students just walked around her paralyzed body to get to class. Bullying pranks weren't exactly new in that school. A leg-locking spell was technically considered a Torment-hex, but Ella had never seen anyone punished for casting one.

Wren bent down next to Ella dramatically, loudly reciting a counter spell for everyone to hear.

Ella acted as if her legs could move again, then let Wren help her up.

She whispered in Ella's ear, "Moira says they're going to try one more. But you did great. Interestingly though, Moira says that only Lizzie was shocked. Rachel must already think you're not a Dis-con from whatever you did to fool her last night."

Ella still wondered how Wren knew about that, but she obviously didn't know the details on how her mother had applied makeup. She wanted to laugh and celebrate this small victory, but she knew more was coming and hoped she could fake it.

They safely made it up the stairs and headed toward Ella's next class.

What was it going to be?

The anticipation was almost worse than faking the spell itself.

Flutters.

Here it came.

Wren's voice sounded pained as she said, "Oh man. Moira says it's a puking spell."

Puking?

How was Ella supposed to puke on cue?

But this was her life.

If she didn't puke, she'd literally die.

Ella gagged loudly, coughing more than anything, then focused on everything that had been happening to her: the plague spell, the boiling puss, the smell, Ash yelling at her, Ash being Buster44, Ash saying she was beautiful, Ash touching her hand, Rachel attacking her last night, going to CIU, finding out Trackers suspected her and were there in the school. Ella's very survival rode on her throwing up.

Right now.

Vomit flew everywhere.

Screams from the surrounding students, especially the ones Ella hit.

Joy flooded through her as she puked yet again. She'd never been so happy to throw up in her entire life.

She did it!

Ella was now covered in her own vomit and standing in a puddle of this morning's lame Pop-Tart she'd snagged from the vending machine. Look, sprinkles. But she'd done it.

Ella could tell Wren was trying to act disgusted like she was, but her eyes said it all. She was thrilled. She was happy. She was proud.

Rachel and Lizzie walked by laughing. "Got a little bit of food poisoning, did we?"

The rest of the students veered clear of Ella's puke puddle as her English lit teacher, Mr. Peake, ran out of his classroom, instantly by her side. "Ella. Oh my goodness. What happened?"

Wren wiped a chunk of Pop-Tart off her T-shirt. "Rachel Fen and Lizzie Trent thought it would be funny to cast a vomit spell on Ella."

Mr. Peake shook his head. "Are you sure? We can't accuse them based on feelings."

Moira stepped up beside them, careful not to step in Ella's puddle. "I heard them, Mr. Peake. I know that spell, and they cast it on Ella."

Shaking his head, Mr. Peake said, "Those girls have always been menaces. I'll have a word with Ms. Busby about the use of Torment-hexes in school." He eyed Ella sympathetically. "Go on to the nurse. She'll clean you up. You too, Wren. You look just as bad."

"Yes, Mr. Peake. Thank you." Ella wasn't sure why she thanked him, but it was enough for him to turn around and go back to class.

The gawkers still gawked, so they couldn't really talk, but Moira smiled and whispered, "You're in the clear. Lizzie was utterly shocked, and you sold it." She glanced down at the vomit and shook her head in amazement. "I don't know how you did that, but I'm impressed."

The smell reached Ella's nose, and she suddenly felt like it might happen again.

"Let's get you to the nurse," Wren said.

The three of them exchanged smiles, and for the first time in her life, Ella felt what it was like to have real-life friends.

CHAPTER 23
WREN

Wren couldn't believe Ella had puked.

She was so proud of Ella and she barely knew her.

In the nurse's office, the nurse twittered and grumbled at seeing Ella covered in vomit.

"Who did this to you?" The nurse placed both her hands on her hips, eyes glowering with empathetic rage.

"Lizzie Trent and Rachel Fen," Wren said, figuring that the more adults she told, the more of an eye they'd keep on the two of them. She had almost slipped and called them by their real names, but caught herself. Madison had gone from *Evil Incarnate* to Lizzie Trent to Madison freaking Grant. Still reeling over that one.

The nurse shook her head, furious. "Those two," she practically spat. She eyed Ella in sympathy. "I'll cast a cleaning spell on you two real quick."

As calm and cool as could be, Ella said, "Actually, could I just take everything off for you to spell and take a quick shower?"

"Of course, dear," the nurse cooed. "The shower is through that door."

Wren was impressed at how deftly Ella managed to avoid the nurse's attempt to cast a cleaning spell on her, but like her mother, a situation like this was probably old hat to her.

Once Ella was behind closed doors, the nurse cast a quick cleaning spell on Wren until she was good as new.

After Ella walked out of the shower a few minutes later and dodged another spell from the nurse (she wanted to dry Ella's hair), Wren and Ella left the nurse's office and headed to their next class.

Wren was a little late to Hex Lab since she walked Ella to calculus.

Mr. Finley waved her in with a smile. "Come on in, Miss Martis. Miss Kurt has told us all of your unfortunate predicament. Is Miss Buckley doing better?"

"I think so. She went to class, anyway. And the janitor seems to have already cast a cleaning spell, because the vomit is all gone." Wren was silently grateful he hadn't been there when it happened, as the puke would have disappeared everywhere but on Ella.

"Good." He addressed the class. "But this brings up a topic we need to discuss more, and that's Torment-hexes. They are forbidden at this school and can cause real damage to a person. Forcing someone to throw up or leg-locking them to fall down the stairs—these are not funny. They are dangerous." Tuning out as Mr. Finley began to preach about Torment-hexes, Wren planned the rest of her day to revolve around following Ella. At least to her classes.

The hour passed, and the bell rang.

Moira was instantly by Wren's side as they walked out of class and headed toward Ella's. Moira didn't question it. It was like they had the same brain.

"I'll keep checking in with Madison and Sadie today, though I'm pretty sure they're not going to try anything on Ella again," Moira said.

"You think that was enough for them?" Wren asked.

"I honestly don't know. When they saw me near them, I pretended to be catching up to them. I asked them if they still thought Ella was a Dis-con, then really played up how gross the puke had been. Sadie was definitely on my side. She brought up the attack on Ella and her dad last night to prove the point to Madison, but she still seems to be on the fence. From what I gathered, Madison grabbed Ella's arm when she was in the throes of the plague spell, and she could see that it didn't affect her at all."

"That would definitely flag a Tracker. Hopefully whatever Ella's parents did last night and today's display will keep them off Ella's trail for a little while anyway." Wren desperately wanted to break into the Tracker vault now more than ever. She just knew the answers to taking Trackers down would be in there. If only she could! Every time she had tried, she failed miserably. "So they still think you're considering being a Tracker?"

"Oh yeah. I'm stringing them along as best I can, though all I want to do is cast some horrible Torment-hex on them," Moira grumbled.

"You'll get to. I promise."

Moira seemed pleased by this, then asked, "So, I'm coming over tonight? Try to come up with a plan?"

"Yes. Definitely. I'll order the pizza."

With a slight pep her to step, Moira grinned at her. "I'll see you tonight, then."

Madison and Sadie walked down the hallway, talking quietly to one another.

Moira nodded in their direction. "My duty awaits." Then she headed off toward them, flagging them down and chatting like they were friends.

Wren's stomach turned at the sight. If it was bad for her, it was probably ten times worse for Moira. Wren couldn't imagine pretending to be friends with her mother's killer. But it was to protect Ella and other Dis-cons, so Moira was doing her duty.

The rest of the day was surprisingly calm. After the turmoil of CIU interviews and Ella faking it for Trackers, school felt downright mundane.

As Wren waited at the corner of the school where she and Ella had agreed to meet, Wren found herself wondering exactly what she was going to tell Ella. Everything, she guessed, though part of her wondered if she should leave her out of it. Her and Moira could keep Ella safe for the time being, but their protection needed to extend to Ash too if he ended up being a Dis-con. And especially if Madison and Sadie ever started to suspect him.

Potentially, two Dis-cons in one school.

What were the odds?

Or were Dis-cons more common that anyone knew?

Wren didn't have answers, but it certainly seemed to be that way. No one ever talked about it. Not the families of the Dis-cons who were killed and certainly not the Dis-cons who were alive and hiding in plain sight. Wren and Moira had family members who were murdered by Trackers for being Dis-cons, but how many other people had the same story? Wren's gut told her a lot more than she thought.

"Hey." Ella's voice came from behind.

Wren turned and smiled shyly. "Hey."

"Thank you for today. I'm pretty sure I'd be dead without you and Moira." There was a slight catch in her throat.

Wren didn't know what to do when other people cried.

It froze her.

Wren began to walk toward the crosswalk, and Ella followed.

Ella's tone was calm now, as if she had pulled herself together. "How did you know Rachel and Lizzie were Trackers?"

They crossed the street side by side and strolled down the sidewalk. "Lizzie is the Tracker who killed my mom. I saw her do it. She doesn't know I countered her glamour spell." She referred to Madison's alias to avoid confusion.

Ella's hand flew to her mouth. "I'm so sorry."

Wren continued, "With other Trackers like Rachel, I usually cast a spell I created that sniffs out memory spells. Trackers use them to make the people around them think they've been there longer than they have. I use them as well. We've only been living here since a little bit after Lizzie and Rachel got here. I tracked her to our school. But my neighbors and people at school think we've been here for three years. Rachel and Lizzie have made everyone think they've lived here half their lives."

"But . . ." Ella's face scrunched in confusion. "It makes sense with them because, yeah, I knew they've only been here five months or so, and Shara too. But you? I thought you'd been here the whole time. You weren't new to me. As a Dis-con, that shouldn't be the case, right?"

Whoa.

The same spellwork Wren had used in the plague spell that left residue on Ella she had used in the memory spell. But to work entirely on Ella? Wren would've celebrated completely if it wasn't for the fact that the plague spell had bypassed Ella. But the memory spell had not. It had worked on a Dis-con! Wren still needed to research exactly why the memory spell had worked so thoroughly on a Dis-con, whereas the plague spell had only left residue. She couldn't tell Ella yet though because she had no idea Wren was responsible for the attack on the basketball team. With a giant sigh, Wren knew it was a conversation they had to have.

"I'll explain everything, but let me cover a few things first. Even knowing Rachel had cast a memory spell on herself and about her obvious closeness to Lizzie, it still wasn't enough to condemn her, so I had to make certain when I first got here. To do that, I cast a couple of preliminary spells on her to see if she had any quantum repellent gear attached to her brain." Wren explained how the surgery worked and watched as Ella's eyes grew rounder and rounder.

"That's insane."

"Yeah."

"Do you think someone attacked the basketball team because Lizzie is a Tracker?" Ella asked innocently.

It was time. Ella might run, and Wren wouldn't blame her. But Wren was on a mission, and that mission meant taking down all Trackers and most definitely killing Madison Grant. That was nonnegotiable.

"I cast that spell," Wren admitted. "It was only meant for Lizzie, but because you're a Dis-con and you stood right in front of the quantum waves, it dispersed."

Ella stopped in her tracks.

Wren was pretty sure she'd overloaded her.

And she was pretty sure Ella was about to throw something at her.

But after a deep breath, she said, "So me being a Dis-con hurt all the innocent basketball players?"

Of course she'd find some way to blame herself. Oh, Ella.

"No. None of it was your fault. It's all on me. I cast the spell."

After another moment or two of Ella looking at Wren and Wren wanting to sink into the cement, Ella finally asked, "Were you trying to kill her?"

"Not then, but yes. That is what I plan to do." Wren was trusting Ella because Ella trusted Wren. To be a Dis-con was the biggest secret one could have on this planet, and the fact that Ella hadn't denied it or used the skill she had of pushing back on quantum waves to prove her wrong showed Wren that Ella wanted to trust her. So Wren had to be honest with her no matter what.

"I don't know if I'm okay with that," she said quietly, almost as if she was ashamed.

"You don't have to be." Wren didn't mean to sound harsh, so she continued, "I mean, you don't have to be involved. I can keep you safe without involving you in my plans."

"No." Ella's face was unreadable. After a moment of silence, she said, "I want to be a part of taking down the Trackers more than anything I've ever wanted in my entire existence. I just . . . I can't hurt anyone. Or, I don't *want* to hurt anyone." Her eyes searched Wren's. "But I do understand why you want revenge."

Another silence between them.

Finally, with no outside cue, they both started to walk again.

Wren wasn't sure what to say. Ella wanted to help take down the Trackers, but she didn't want to hurt anyone? It was just not possible. Not when dealing with an organization that killed for what they perceived as righteousness, but more than that, what Wren had seen in Madison Grant's smiling eyes as she decapitated her mother was pure evil. Madison didn't deserve to live and Wren's mother had. It was that simple to her. Her mother was a better human being, a person who wouldn't kill a spider she'd found in the house, a person like . . . Ella.

Wren's chest tightened, and she was finding it difficult to breathe.

She broke the silence. "You don't have to hurt anyone. Leave that to me." Wren made sure they had eye contact when she said, "But if I'm going to destroy the Tracker empire, that means death and probably a lot of it." Wren stopped them again and reached out to hold Ella's hand, which was a foreign gesture to her after years of isolation but somehow felt right in that moment. Ella clasped back as if she also wasn't used to contact but craved it. "Ella, Lizzie and Rachel won't think twice about killing you. They *want* to kill you. They need it. They were disappointed when you responded to their spells. Disappointed because more than anything, they love to hunt down Dis-cons and slaughter them. It's fun for them." Wren could hear her voice cracking as she continued, but she did so anyway. "I watched as Lizzie decapitated my mother. Decapitated. Then she laughed like she had orgasmed or something." Wren pulled her hand away to wipe the unbidden tears on her cheeks. The only other person she'd told about her mother was Moira, but their mutual pain from losing family to the Trackers had ignited rage and determination at the time. But standing in front of Ella, a Dis-con, and knowing that if a Tracker found out, she'd be brutally murdered just like Wren's mother—it brought out emotion she usually tried to shove down and bury so she could focus on her mission.

Ella reached out and grabbed her hand again. "I'm so sorry." There was a slight shake to hers, and it was wet and clammy to the touch. She was terrified. And she had probably been that way ever since she found out she was a Dis-con.

And Wren was the genius who had shared that her mother was decapitated with glee.

Wren's stomach twisted in agony.

"Don't be sorry. I'm the one who's sorry. I can't believe I told you that. I make everything worse."

"The fact that you're still holding my hand despite the fact that I'm practically giving you a shower with it speaks volumes for you." Ella smiled weakly, trying to break the heavy moment between them.

Wren's guilt still hung heavy, but she understood that Ella needed to abate her fear after how close to death she had come today with Madison and Sadie.

Wren smiled back and said, "I don't mind. Must make it hard to flirt with Ash though. You don't want to blind him when you talk with your hands."

Ella laughed, and Wren laughed with her.

Her chest lightened for a second, and she was eternally grateful. Wren didn't get many moments like that.

They began to walk again.

Ella took her hand away, her expression thoughtful. "I really have no chance with Ash, do I? I can't get him involved in all this."

Wren was tempted to tell her CIU's suspicions, but he hadn't been on Wren's radar for a Dis-con, so she decided to investigate herself first before she told Ella anything. "I don't know. I'd say enjoy his company while you can. He definitely likes you."

"You think?" Ella asked, her eyes radiating with hope.

"Oh, definitely." It was completely obvious. "I'm glad he came to his senses though after his fit yesterday. He definitely doesn't like attention." Because he might be a Dis-con.

"If Shara is a Dis-con scout, why does she seem interested in Ash romantically? Do you think . . . ?" It seemed Ella's brain was already piecing things together, but then just as suddenly, she switched the subject. "If the plague spell was yours, do you have any idea why there was spell residue on me? I went into CIU this morning, and that seemed to be the reason they let me go."

Wren knew about the spell residue from eavesdropping, but . . . "Wait a minute. You went to CIU? On purpose?"

Ella nodded. "I was tired of everything. Tired of hiding. Tired of only having internet friends. Of course, now that I know one of them was actually Ash, I probably would have reconsidered. I was just tired of not living." She said the last part very quietly. "But Malcolm let me go. He said I had spell residue. That must have confirmed I wasn't a Dis-con to him."

"I'd been trying for years to tweak my spells to protect my mom and other Dis-cons, but when I confirmed that Trackers had repellent gear, I shifted my focus on breaking through that, but I had no way to test it," Wren confessed. "But Ella, it may have only given you residue for the plague spell, but it *did* work on you with the memory spell. I actually got a spell to work on a Dis-con, which means if I perfect it, I can keep you safe. I can cast a protection spell on you."

"The memory spell *did* work on me . . ." Ella's dazed expression worried Wren for a moment, but then Ella shook her head as if in awe. "You made a spell work on a Dis-con."

Wren decided to let Ella ponder that one on her own. Wren had her own feelings about it as well. She couldn't wait to tell Moira.

"You should know, Malcolm does suspect you're a Dis-con, but Shara and Rosia seem pretty convinced you aren't. And just so you know Shara's real last name is Gordon, not Ralter." Wren breathed in deep and pushed forward. "And Ella, when I said you were like my mom, I meant you are *exactly* like her. She could push on quantum waves as well. I saw what you did with Shara's spells in lab the other day."

Ella stopped in her tracks again, and Wren was pretty sure this was the longest it had ever taken to walk home, but she understood Ella's surprise.

"I'm doing what now?" Ella wasn't upset. Her eyes were round with curiosity. "I knew I was doing something, but I had no idea what I was actually doing."

"Quantum waves. You can't connect or utilize them because you're disconnected from them, but you have the ability to push against them and essentially create a magic of your own. My mom didn't really experiment much with it, except to do what you do to hide the fact that she was a Dis-con."

Another deep breath and Wren hoped she wouldn't terrify her even more. "But Ella, the Trackers know about Dis-cons like you. I've only found bits and pieces in military vaults about it. I still haven't cracked the Tracker vault yet. But from what I've gathered, when they discovered my mom, there was a vote within their leadership. They're called the Order of Eleven, and not all of them wanted her dead. Some of them wanted to experiment on her. Obviously, the vote came down to thinking she was more dangerous alive. But if they ever find out about you?"

Ella lifted her head, eyes to the sky, as if she were contemplating her existence. And she was. Finally, Ella leveled her head to Wren's and said, "I'm in."

CHAPTER 29
ELLA

As if Ella didn't have enough questions racing around in her head, Wren kept hitting her with new and alarming information. Wren knew more about Ella than Ella. But she was in. This was the answer to her freedom. And now that Ella had a taste of what it was like to have friends and talk to a boy she liked in person, not just in-game, she couldn't go back to her old life.

Wren's face had lit up at Ella's declaration, and then she'd simply nodded her head in what Ella hoped was approval.

They approached Wren's house, and Ella found that she didn't want to leave. She wanted to pick Wren's brain all night and probably for the rest of eternity. Ella had never realized how little she knew because she was never taught to try to figure things out. She was taught to hide no matter what, which essentially equated to *ignore* no matter what.

Wren's smile was small and a bit shy. She'd been through so

much and not even for being a Dis-con, but for simply being the daughter of one.

But Ella couldn't ignore the fact that Wren had cast the plague spell. The plague spell that Ella had been blamed for. But now knowing why and who her real target had been, could Ella really blame her?

Her mind twisted with so many conflicting thoughts.

But one thing she knew for certain: the Trackers had to be stopped.

Maybe Ella could influence Wren not to hurt anyone. She knew Trackers couldn't care less about killing innocents, and Wren was just trying to stay in their mindset to defeat them, but it was *their* mindset. Ella could tell by spending twenty minutes with Wren that she didn't used to be this way. Trackers had turned her into this, and Ella would be damned if she was going to let them turn her into them completely.

Ella wasn't going to say anything now though. Wren might shut her out, and Ella wanted to be a part of this.

They stopped in front of Wren's house.

"This is my stop," Wren said with a small smile.

"Meet here tomorrow morning? Walk to school?" Ella asked.

"Sounds good," she responded. "Moira is coming over later, and we're going come up with some ideas." Wren's entire body language changed when mentioning Moira. She looked downright dreamy.

"Oooo, someone is crushing."

Furrowed brows and a crinkled forehead was Wren's answer. "Moira is just a friend."

Ella internally cringed. She'd overstepped. She realized in that moment that they didn't know each other well enough for her to talk about Wren's love life. It was none of her business anyway.

"Sorry. You lit up when you talked about seeing her. Like I do when thinking about Ash."

But Wren didn't seem angry, just surprised. "Huh," was all she said.

Ella took that as her cue to leave before she really messed things up. She waved to Wren with a small smile. They'd been through a lot that day, and Ella's gut was screaming at her that there was a lot more to come. "See you tomorrow."

Waving back, Wren walked toward her front door, and Ella could tell she had opened a can of worms.

Ella tried to organize her thoughts as she walked the rest of the way home, but it was difficult as she'd been thrown so many things at once. Where did she start? Did she tell her parents about the fact that she was apparently pushing quantum waves? It made instant sense when Wren had said it. That was exactly what it felt like, like pushing up against some invisible barrier. Ella was surprised she hadn't thought of that theory at least. Again with the ignorance. She vowed to change that. To question everything. To figure things out on her own. It was a complete rewiring of the brain.

The desire to meet and know Wren's mom made Ella's chest ache. She was like her. Not just a Dis-con, but one that could manipulate energy, in a sense. Why did Trackers hate them so much? Why did they think they shouldn't exist? And why did they get freaking brain surgery to become like them? Absolute crazies. And now it made so much more sense why everyone acted as if Rachel and Lizzie had been in school forever. Of course their memory spell wouldn't work on a Dis-con. But Wren's? It worked. On *her*! Weirdly, Ella wanted Wren to make her a lab rat. What if Wren really could protect her?

Ella's thoughts buzzed around her brain until she could no longer differentiate any of them.

"Hi." The familiar voice jolted Ella out of her insanity.

Ash's voice.

For a moment, Ella thought she was hallucinating, but no, about thirty feet from Ella's house and standing right in front of her was Ash.

Ash!

Why was he here?

And why was that the first question she thought of?

But of course, Ella's mouth betrayed her anyway. "Why are you here?"

He lowered his head, embarrassed. "Now you're going to think I'm the stalker." Ash lifted his eyes to meet hers. "I really wanted to see you."

"Oh." Ella didn't know how to respond to the most amazing thing she'd ever heard in her life. Was this actually happening to her?

"Sorry, I didn't mean to freak you out." Ash glanced back at Ella's house. "And I didn't want to disturb your parents, so I waited here like an idiot."

In that moment, Ella realized that Ash was her respite. He was the only person that made her forget she was a Dis-con and fighting for her life every day she existed, which was ironic considering he might be a Dis-con himself. But standing there with him on the sidewalk near her house, Ella was normal, she was happy, she was alive. And it was the same when they played together in-game. Ella could forget everything and just play. She still couldn't quite wrap her head around the fact that she'd been playing with Ash the entire time, but the more it sank in, the more she wanted to be near him in person.

"You didn't freak me out. I'm happy you're here," Ella admitted.

"I'm happy too," he said.

There went his sparkly eyes again.

Ella couldn't invite him in; her parents would pack their bags on the spot. Ella was grateful Ash had parked far enough away that her parents wouldn't be able to see him from the window.

"My parents won't let me have boys inside. They'd probably freak out if they knew I was talking to you." It wasn't really a lie. They *would* freak out, and they absolutely would not let her have a boy inside. They wouldn't let her have anyone inside. It had almost given them a heart attack when Wren had shown up the other day and then Lizzie right after. Plus, after last night's attack, it wasn't like Ella could blame them.

"I get that." Ash nodded.

His sweet smile sent lightning bolts through Ella.

She could no longer speak.

Ash stepped closer to her so that their faces were only inches apart. Her heart thudded in her chest. He brushed his hand against Ella's cheek, and she was pretty sure her knees were going to collapse. "There's something between us, isn't there?"

Ella still didn't believe she wasn't hallucinating.

But she nodded all the same.

Yup. Still staring.

Couldn't seem to move. Or talk. Or breathe.

Ash took his hand away, and his eyes darted away too, unsure.

Ella quickly reached out and grabbed his hand, hoping to all that was holy that she wouldn't start sweating. Instantly, he intertwined his fingers in hers, and every nerve in her body tingled from the rush.

"Ash?" Good. A word. His name, even.

Ella could no longer feel her fingers.

"Yeah?" he answered, his voice husky.

"What are we doing?" Ella hadn't meant for it to come out like that, but it did.

But Ash smiled again, and it radiated through every feature in his face. "I don't know, but I don't want it to end." The way he said it was exactly the way Ella felt. She'd never been allowed to think of anyone like this, to be with anyone like this. It had only been a fantasy, hence the avatar she'd created in her game.

Maybe it was the same for him too?

"I don't want it to end either," Ella admitted, and the rush of rebellion it gave her almost drowned her. Her parents were only thirty feet away. She knew they couldn't see them, but if they could?

And suddenly, Ella didn't care.

Ash saw it too.

Their eyes met, and he leaned down to kiss her.

When their lips touched, it was like an explosion erupted in her head. She'd never felt anything like it. Ella had thought holding hands was intense, but this? It was like an overload of sensation that her mind didn't know what to do with, but somehow, her body did. Their hands untangled, and Ash pulled her closer to him as they kissed more passionately, more intensely. Ella reached up and wrapped her arms around his body, feeling his chest against hers, their lips moving in perfect sync. Ella wanted him more and wanted him to stop all at once; the kiss was so overwhelming.

Finally, Ella yanked herself away. She gasped for breath, and so did Ash.

But when their eyes met, they were both smiling.

"We should probably stop," Ella said but didn't mean it in the slightest.

"That was intense," Ash agreed, though he couldn't stop smiling, and neither could she.

Ella knew she should end it right then before it went any further, but she didn't want to.

"I guess I'll go," Ash said, lowering his head down, bashful.

No.

But he should.

They couldn't stand out there all night.

Ella's parents were probably already wondering why she wasn't home already.

"I guess," she finally uttered to her own disappointment. "Meet in-game later?"

He took both her hands in his. "Yes, definitely." His expression turned thoughtful then, his eyebrows crinkled in concern. "I heard about what happened today. I'm really sorry. Rachel and Lizzie are the worst."

"It's okay. It's not the first time I've been spelled to puke." Yes it was, but he couldn't know that.

"I don't get why everyone is so loyal to them when they just moved here." Ash shrugged. "I guess if you come in with enough attitude, people fall in line." He leaned down and kissed her forehead. "Maybe if we stick together, they'll leave you alone."

Did he just say Rachel and Lizzie were new?

Ella barely breathed as he kissed her one more time, then waved in an aw-shucks kind of way as he slid into his car. "See you tonight. We can take down some Trackers in the Chicago level this time."

"Uh, yeah. I'll meet you there," Ella said, trying to hide the shock on her face after hearing Ash confirm he was immune to Rachel and Lizzie's memory spell.

Ash smiled, shut his door, and drove away.

Certainty destroyed any doubts she may have had: Ash yelling at Ella to leave him alone, not wanting attention, Shara's interest in him, their connection, him not being affected by the memory spell.

Ella swallowed hard.

It was undeniable now.

Ash was a Dis-con.

CHAPTER 30
WREN

Moira sat across from Wren.

Wren couldn't shake what Ella had implied out of her head. Did she like Moira? Of course she liked Moira, but could it be more? Was that electricity Wren felt when she was around her because she viewed Moira as more than a friend? Should she ask her?

Wren didn't want to lose her, not now when she had finally found someone who could help her.

She had never considered how she felt about women or men. Wren honestly had thought neither were for her.

But the flutters in her tummy when she'd seen Moira come up the walkway? Wren didn't know if that was excitement for a new friend and partner on the mission or because she may have been developing feelings for her.

Enough.

She couldn't afford to be distracted by this.

Not now.

Too many people were involved now.

Moira was in the middle of gushing about the fact that Wren's memory spell had worked on a Dis-con while they sat on a few cushions downstairs with the holographic map of all Wren's findings slowly rotating above them.

"Are you even listening to me?" Moira asked with a smile.

Wren shook her head. "Yes, of course. I got distracted for a second."

"Well, all I was saying is that what you did is legendary. Trackers would be shaking in their boots if they knew. If it works on Dis-cons, it's only a matter of time before it works on Trackers. We should start doing tests on Madison and Sadie. I really do hate them. And I hate having to fake being nice to them." Moira rolled her shoulders back to stretch out her back. "Have you told Ella their real names yet?"

Wren shrugged. "Not yet. I didn't want to overwhelm her any more than I already have."

"Yeah, good call. We can tell her tomorrow or whenever you think she's ready. But we should tell her," Moira added.

Wren nodded. "We'll see how she is, but yeah, she needs to know." Wren shifted herself to get more comfortable. It was time to tell Moira everything. "We need to break into the Tracker vault."

Moira chuckled as if Wren had told a joke. "Right? That would be amazing."

"I'm serious," Wren answered. "I've broken into twelve military vaults already. That's what the countries stand for on my board. It's how I have all those powerful spells I showed you."

She pointed to the holographic images of each of the countries, rotating on display.

"You what?" Moira's mouth stayed open after she spoke; she was obviously in shock. Sensing the seriousness, Moira bit her lower lip. "What are we talking about here? Some kind of body takeover spell of a guard?"

Wren shook her head, not sure how she was going to respond. "I figured out a spell to quantum phase."

Moira's eyes widened even more. "Are you serious?" she asked. "No one has ever come close to making that work or had enough evidence that it's possible. We're talking theoretical science here."

"Well, it works. And I used it to get into the military vaults. I think that's why I've been able to break in so easily. There are no defenses against it." It sent a thrill through her, seeing how impressed Moira was with her mouth still open.

"I just . . . I can't fathom." She reached over and took Wren's hands, squeezing them as she stared at her. "I'm speechless. You're . . . amazing. That's not even an appropriate word. I . . ."

Wren didn't want to end the moment, but she had to confess, "Except, it doesn't seem to work on the Tracker vault."

Shifting closer so their knees were touching, Moira said, "You think they've come up with a quantum phasing spell too and know how to block it?"

"Honestly, I don't know. It's very weird. My phase-self gets to the vault and . . ." Wren lowered her eyes, embarrassed, not wanting to continue in front of Moira.

Moira's grip tightened. "What is it? You can tell me."

She lifted her eyes to Moira once more; the connection between them was almost tangible. Wren needed to tell her. So she continued, "Whenever I get there, I get locked in place somehow, and I'm lulled into a sense of calm and don't want to leave. I've never felt more comfortable or more at home in my life. It's like they have a spell that hypnotizes me so that my phase-self will be stuck there forever and my body back here will just be in a coma or something." Now for the difficult admission. "So I break the spell and jump out, though I don't really want to, and when I get back here, I'm crying, as in full-blown bawling." Wren despised admitting that, but Moira needed to know. "Really strange, right?"

Moira's eyebrows furrowed as she looked at Wren. "Some kind of emotion spell? Tricking your consciousness into staying until a Skein can get there and destroy the phased consciousness?"

"Could be." Wren really didn't know.

Sighing heavily, Moira shook her head. "This is so beyond my skill level. I don't know if I'd know the first thing about how to help you. I may be a liability to you."

Her hands began to loosen, and a jolt of panic rushed through Wren. She firmed her grip on Moira's hands. "You are way more powerful than you think." Wren was afraid of losing her. "Moira, I need you. I can't do this without you." Her pulse raced. Moira was definitely going to leave now, and Wren found that the thought took her breath away.

But Moira stared at Wren in a way that Wren could no longer feel her toes. Moira's hands held on tighter to hers. "I said I would do this, and I meant it." One deep breath and one nod of her head later, she said, "I'm ready."

Keeping a tighter grip on Moira's hands, Wren said, "We need to stay connected. I'm going to cast a binding spell so we can't be broken apart."

"Ow." Moira laughed.

"Sorry." What was Wren's problem? "I just don't want us to

break contact. Some of these spells I'm using to break into vaults are volatile, and I'm only used to risking myself." Which was true. "Binding spell first," Wren said.

Moira's nods were quick now, and there was a slight shake to her hands. She was nervous.

Knowing the spells by heart, Wren cast the binding spell. Like an invisible rope Wren could sense more than see, it tied them together. First cementing their hands, then traveling up the arms, through the chest, and all the way down to their toes. Wren fully connected to Moira. It was as if they were one being.

Wren hoped Moira could break past whatever this protection spell was surrounding the Tracker vault or come up with a spell Wren hadn't thought of. And maybe by having Moira with her, she wouldn't end up crying afterward. Or at the very least, they both would, and then Wren wouldn't feel crazy. Because that was how the vault made her feel: crazy.

But first things first: Wren cast the rest of the quantum phasing spell, and the familiar sensation of phasing out of her body flowed through her.

"Whoa. Those are our bodies down there." Moira's voice sounded as if it were right next to her, but Wren knew it was coming from inside her own head.

Being in this form, they couldn't see each other, but they could hear each other because of the binding spell. No one else would be able to though. Essentially, they were speaking to each other in their minds.

Their bodies were exactly as they'd left them, hands clasped together, eyes closed, as if they were in some kind of meditative state, which to a large degree, they were.

"We're bound by the spell, but try to picture our hands

together if you can," Wren advised.

She had to get into the vault. There had to be something in there that would help her take the Trackers down, whether it be a spell or some kind of evidence that would destroy them. At the very least, there should be a list of every Dis-con they'd killed and the family they left behind. Wren was taking Moira's offhanded suggestion of building an army of Wombers seriously.

Wren wanted all Trackers to die, and she'd need more than Moira to do that. An army would do nicely.

"That's easy enough to do." And Wren could picture Moira smile as she said it.

It threw Wren off so much that she had to struggle to recall exactly what she had said to Moira to figure out what she was referring to. Oh. Keeping their hands together. Though Wren was in incorporeal form, she could almost feel her chest squeeze at the thought that Moira might view her in the same way.

Stop.

What if she could hear her?

Wren waited for a response.

After several moments of silence, it was safe to assume they couldn't read each other minds. Wren certainly couldn't read Moira's, which she was both happy about and disappointed by.

"Get ready to fly," Wren said and led them out of the basement and through the walls of the house until they were outside in the night air. They couldn't feel it, of course, but it was an odd sensation floating in a form they couldn't see and soaring in the sky. The closest thing Wren could compare it to was a flying dream—no body, just gliding amongst the clouds without a care in the world. Wren hadn't had one of those dreams in a while. Now, hers were usually filled with blood and her mother's head rolling away from her body.

"This is incredible." Moira's voice resonated awe as they flew over the city on their way to the Trackers' headquarters.

Wren appreciated Moira's excitement, but she needed to concentrate on their path. Getting through the building was kind of a maze. It had taken Wren years to find the building itself; then to find the vault on top of that was an entirely different sort of challenge. The building was hiding in plain sight, of course. Wren should have known better. In the center of downtown Los Angeles under a generic spell-tech sky rise called Hex Solutions. The building was owned by a shell company that was owned by another shell company that was owned by yet another shell company. The only reason Wren was able to track the real owner down was because of a document she'd found in France's military vault that made reference to Hex Solutions and owing Verner Grant money.

Verner freaking Grant.

Madison's dad.

This building, this vault, it took on a whole new meaning now that Wren knew that particular connection.

At the *ooohs* and *aaaahs* of Moira, Wren wished she could see her face, even if it was some kind of ghost-phase-face. She imagined her beautiful brown eyes wide and open in shock and awe and her dazzling smile to match.

Seriously?

Stop.

Wren hadn't been sure how she felt about her only days ago, then finding out that Sadie was trying to recruit her as a Tracker? And now she was full-on mooning over the girl? Wren reminded herself that Moira was a soldier in her very small army and that was it. She needed to get it together before she made a mistake that could hurt them both.

Having no body or bodily sensations, it was surprisingly easy for Wren to calm herself down. Physical bodies could be such a hindrance, especially when dealing with things like feelings and emotions. Wren really wished she didn't have those sometimes.

It didn't take long to reach the Hex Solutions building. The moon reflected on the glass windows that seemingly stretched all the way up into the night sky. It was one of the tallest in the Los Angeles skyline and almost smack-dab in the middle. Funnily enough, it actually was a business building that dealt with spell technology.

Underneath it was the key.

Veering forward, they passed through the wall of the first floor, then directly down into the flooring itself. Deeper and deeper, they traveled easily through the levels of cement and dirt. Moira was quiet now, these sights no longer awe-inspiring and probably more terrifying, but she didn't complain. Wren was amazed at how well Moira had been taking everything, but having a twin who had been killed by these monsters . . . it hardened a person. And vengeance could help soothe a lot of fears.

Finally, they reached the floors of the Tracker facility. Wren had never explored the place as her mind had only been focused on the vault, but from the little she'd seen, it was a lot of offices and rooms divided by hallways. Very simple. Almost like an actual business. A secret underground business, but still. They passed through five levels until they arrived on the floor with the vault.

It was empty as usual. No Trackers or guards anywhere in sight. Just a long hallway that seemingly went on forever in both directions and a large red metal door that extended from floor to ceiling at the end of it, which was at least ten feet high.

Most vaults were like that because they were spelled with so many defense spells that anyone that came near the vault would either be blown up or incinerated. But to get to this level, one would have to break through actual soldiers and guards. And Trackers with repellent gear were no joke. Only Dis-cons would be immune, but they'd have to get there first.

And Wren.

With her theoretical spell that wasn't so theoretical anymore.

"The vault is behind that door." Wren positioned them so they were facing the red metal door of the Tracker vault.

And there it was.

Comfort.

It enwrapped Wren like an old friend, embracing her, loving her, like someone had injected her with a kind of euphoric serum.

"You feel that?" Wren asked Moira.

"I feel the same, though a little dizzy from all the flying and quite possibly from quantum phasing." Her voice was excited after doing what she had thought was impossible.

Wren was dizzy too, but from the sensation she currently felt and nothing else. How could it only be affecting her? If they weren't completely alone in that hallway, Wren would've thought she was being hugged. One giant hug that made her want to stay there forever.

"We have to go. I can't move again," Wren managed to sputter out. Because she couldn't. Couldn't move. Didn't want to. She just wanted to feel *this*.

"I can move. Whatever it is, it's not affecting me. Maybe because we're bound and it only affects the caster?"

"Maybe." Wren said the word, but her mind floated. Peace. She was at peace. Why would Wren want to be anywhere else?

This was the moment when, in the past, she had forced herself back into her body. The Trackers would probably be there any moment to trap her phase-self—their phase-selves—there forever. Wren couldn't do that to Moira. No matter how good it felt.

"We have to go back," Wren managed to say, but her heart didn't mean it. She never wanted to lose that feeling.

"Let me peek in. We came all this way." Moira pulled Wren forward, and they phased into the red door.

And then they were inside.

The vault.

The comforting sensation threatened to swallow Wren's brain, and all she wanted to do was sleep. "Moira," Wren uttered.

Wren wouldn't have her mind much longer; she could feel it. She was ready to succumb to the peace. To the tranquility. To the pure unadulterated love.

She couldn't.

Lose.

Herself.

Wren incanted the words that broke the quantum phasing spell.

Her eyes flew open as did Moira's, and they slammed back into their bodies.

It was gone.

That feeling of love and comfort.

Wren was empty again.

Lost.

And it happened again.

Wren began to sob.

Moira de-cast the binding spell, and now even *she* had separated from her.

Wren was truly alone.

Moira's arms instantly wrapped around Wren, pulling her

toward her and against her shoulder. Wren clung desperately to Moira, her lifeline. Moira kissed the side of Wren's head, repeating the words that she'd be okay.

But Wren was not okay.

And she didn't think she ever would be.

CHAPTER 31
ELLA

Ella climbed from her bed and got dressed for school. Her parents had grilled her about her day yesterday when she had come home from school, but she'd deflected and kept most of the day's events hidden from them. Once Ella was relatively convinced she had placated their fears enough to not move on the spot, she went to her room and played *Hexsphere* with Ash. It was better than any other time they'd played because they knew who was on the other end of Buster44 and FearlessGirl22. Ella couldn't stop thinking about their kiss and the fact that Ash was a Dis-con, but working together to kill Trackers in the game helped distract her and made her realize that this game was how they coped with being Dis-cons. Having some measure of control over Trackers was comforting. She wanted to confront him about it, but not in-game. Who knew who might've been listening? Ella even typed in the command to push back on spells to gauge what Ash's reaction would be. But he simply asked what she'd done so he could do it too. He didn't recognize it. He might've been a Dis-con, but he wasn't like her and Wren's mom.

Tying the last shoelace of her Chuck Taylors, Ella's mind wandered to the fact that Ash was a Dis-con again. The proof was there, but there was a tiny part of her that didn't want to accept it. A Dis-con. Like her. It explained Ella's obsession with him before she'd met him in person. In-game, she'd gravitated toward Buster44 and continued to play with him over the last two years. And in person? Well, his perfect broody looks didn't hurt, but still. Something had pulled her to him—something strong. Maybe that was how it was with Dis-cons. She didn't know because she'd never met another one before.

Should she have Wren test him today? To be sure? Was that horrible? Was she a horrible person?

It really felt like the answer to that question was yes, but Ella had to know definitively. Because if she was right about Ash, then they needed to stick together, especially with two Trackers lurking about.

Ella resigned herself to telling Wren about it.

Gray clouds in the sky and a slight whistle of the wind—it was a safe bet that it was cold outside, even for Los Angeles, so she threw on her a cardigan for good measure. She hurried downstairs, hoping not to have a run-in with the parental units. Ella didn't know if she could continue to hold back everything that had happened to her yesterday for much longer. Her parents had a way of extracting information from her.

Hushed talking in the kitchen led Ella to believe they were having a conversation about moving, so she snuck out the front door before they could rope her into that one. Because Ella didn't want to move.

She had three friends, and her head was giddy from it.

Sure, she had two Trackers and a CIU agent that suspected her of being a Dis-con, but weirdly, the three friends thing was the most dominant force of emotion for her right then.

As Ella walked toward Wren's house, she was grateful for the sweater when a gust of cold air hit her from the side. It didn't take long to get there, and as she was about to knock on the front door, it opened. Ella was surprised and also not surprised to see Moira next to Wren.

"Hi, guys," Ella said brightly.

"You're in a good mood." Wren smiled as she shut the door behind them, and then they walked to the sidewalk.

"I've got you two now. I'm weirdly happy," Ella admitted. "And Ash kissed me last night." She threw that in there.

"What?" Moira exclaimed, mouth opened and smiling in shock. "When? How? What? I thought you and Wren walked home together."

Wren smiled at Ella, and Ella noticed she seemed a bit brighter too.

"We did, but Ash was waiting for me when I got home. And it just happened." Did she tell them her suspicion about him being a Dis-con? Ella wasn't used to having friends. Did friends tell each other everything?

"Wow," Moira said, shaking her head in amusement, then she pulled her lips to the side in thought. "I hate to be the jerk in this situation, but are you putting him in danger by entertaining the thought of dating him?" From the furrowed eyebrows and concerned eyes, Ella could tell she really hadn't wanted to say that, but it seemed like the perfect segue, to be honest.

"I'm pretty sure he's a Dis-con too," Ella said quietly.

"CIU thinks that as well," Wren admitted.

Um. What?

Maybe that idea that friends told each other everything wasn't real.

"You knew and didn't say anything?" The crack in Ella's voice betrayed her.

"I didn't know anything. I overheard Shara saying she suspected. I didn't want to say anything until we knew for sure. I thought I'd test him a bit today." Wren stopped walking to look directly at Ella. "I was going to tell you. I promise. I wanted to make sure first."

Ella paused, staring back at Wren, seeing the sincerity in her expression. Finally, Ella nodded for them to keep moving. "Okay. But no more withholding information. If we're really going to do this and take down the Trackers, we have to be completely honest with each other."

"Agreed," Wren said. "How did you figure it out?"

"He thinks Rachel and Lizzie just moved here. Their memory spell didn't work on him," Ella confessed.

"I wonder if mine did. Like it worked on you?" Wren mused.

"We'll have to confront him, I guess, to find out." Moira didn't look happy about saying that aloud.

Wren agreed and told Ella everything she and Moira had done the night before, almost breaking into the Tracker vault.

Quantum phasing?

Breaking into vaults?

This was happening.

Really happening.

And Verner Grant? The business guy? She'd seen him on TV but never thought anything of him. It made sense though since he had so much money. The Trackers went so much further and deeper than Ella had ever dreamed.

"Also," Wren began. "We know Lizzie's and Rachel's true identities." She paused, then pushed forward. "Rachel's name is Sadie Kallum, and Lizzie is Madison *Grant*. As in Verner Grant's daughter."

"Uh, what?" Ella could barely conceive of Verner Grant being a leader of the Trackers, but Lizzie being his daughter?

"Yeah." Wren sighed.

Ella's mind came up with a million more questions to add to the already waiting million questions. Things were moving fast. But hopefully, after yesterday's performance, Ella would have at least a couple days to relax somewhat and maybe come up with a plan.

The high school loomed before them, and Ella found that she was actually excited to go today. She was walking with her two new friends, and she was about to meet Ash.

With a giant sigh of happiness and satisfaction, she crossed the street and headed toward the east entrance. As if her day couldn't get any better, Ash jogged up to them with a shy goofy smile that made Ella's heart squeeze. To her utter shock, his hand reached for hers, and their fingers entangled once more.

Moira grinned and discreetly winked at Ella.

"Good morning," Ash greeted them all.

"Good morning." Ella basked in the glow of her day so far.

Thinking of Dis-cons and Trackers could come later. Honestly, Ella just wanted to go to quantum spell-casting and stare at Ash's face for the entire first period.

Ella's heart fluttered.

As in: the beats could barely thump in rhythm.

Rachel and Lizzie stepped out from the parking lot, eyes

focused on Ella and Ella only. She knew those weren't their real names, but the terror that pumped through her veins caused her to forget.

Lizzie's car levitated in the air and flew directly toward her and Ash.

It was so shocking, Ella and Ash froze in place, almost waiting to be smashed by the small sedan.

Move! Ella's mind screamed at her.

And it listened.

She yanked Ash with her by their entwined hands, flying to the ground, the car smashing next to them.

Wren yelled over the crunching sound of metal as the car screeched to its final resting place. "Ella! Are you okay?!"

"I'm fine! We're both fine!" Ella yelled back.

Chills raced down Ella's spine as Wren and Moira walked toward Rachel and Lizzie, heads pushed forward, eyes glaring, mouths moving, casting.

Two more cars rose from the parking lot, but this time, they flew toward Rachel and Lizzie. The pair split up and ran in opposite directions, the cars smashing on the cement where they had just stood. Screams from nearby students filled the air, and Ella saw some of them race inside the school for protection.

Wren's voice carried over to Ella as she said to Moira, "Madison's brain stem, occipital, and hypothalamus are clean, and Sadie's occipital, cerebellum, and hypothalamus are clean."

Moira responded, "Got it. I'll take Sadie. You take Madison."

Hearing Moira and Wren calling the Trackers by their true identities helped cement their names in Ella's head. She didn't want to think of them as aliases anymore. She needed to see them for who they truly were: Sadie and Madison. Trackers. *Killers.*

But hearing Moira and Wren spout off parts of the brain, Ella had no idea what part did what, so she had no idea what kind of attack to expect. But she did know she needed to get Ash and herself to safety.

Their hands were still bound, but Ella realized she hadn't seen his face. Looking at him, she saw his eyes were round, but also, there were tears streaking his face. "I'm so sorry, Ella. You have to get away from me. They're here to kill me."

Ash pulled his hand away from Ella's and scrambled to his feet, but she grabbed his arm. "No, Ash. They're here for *me*."

That stopped him.

Confusion, then understanding. "You're . . ."

"I am."

Before Ella could say more, Sadie stomped toward them, mouth moving. She knew she couldn't hurt Ella with spells, so Ella immediately searched everywhere she could for flying objects. Ella's heart was fluttering like mad, so she knew something was coming. Ella saw it before it hit: a boulder from the rockery against the parking lot wall.

Ash embraced Ella in his arms and rolled the both of them across the lawn. Ella's foot burned as the giant rock scraped across her ankle, then smashed into a thousand pieces as it was crushed against the side of the school.

At this point, the screams became a sickening backdrop to the battle that was happening in front of them. Out of the corner of Ella's eye, she saw more students run inside the building, trying to escape the continuing onslaught of flying cars and boulders.

Sadie kept thundering closer to them, holding a Tracker blade in her hand.

Ella had never wished she could cast spells more than she did in that moment.

Out of nowhere, Moira stepped in front of Ella and Ash, blocking a physical attack from Sadie, voice booming in spell.

Crack!

Sadie's bone snapped out of her right upper thigh with a sickening crunch, blood bursting everywhere. She howled in aguish, nostrils flaring as she grabbed the broken bone in her hand. "You should have joined us!" Sadie yelled at Moira.

"You people murdered my twin! What did you expect?" Moira cast another spell.

Crack!

Bone burst out of Sadie's left leg this time.

Sadie didn't answer Moira, obviously in too much pain. With another scream, Sadie shoved her bones back into her legs and cast a spell. The legs knitted themselves back together until it was as if nothing happened.

But her focus was now on Moira.

Sadie grunted. "I know the Tracker that killed your sister, and Luna died slowly and painfully."

Ella was amazed that Moira could keep her focus with Sadie's vicious words, but strangely Sadie's face showed no signs of pleasure when she said them.

Moira cast a spell at the exact same time as Sadie, and the two spells hit each other midair.

Boom!

The two spells cracked against each other and dissipated so that neither Moira nor Sadie were affected.

Ella gasped for breath, heart fluttering uncontrollably. She couldn't take much more of this.

But Ella took advantage of the moment and led Ash away and toward the parking lot. Hiding behind cars seemed like the only option at that point. They needed barriers to protect them from anything thrown at them.

As if agreeing with Ella's thought process, another boulder smashed next to Ella and Ash, destroying some poor student's car.

Ella peered over her shoulder; that one had come from Madison.

But Wren, full of fury and wrath, cast a spell so strong that Ella's flutters sped up too fast, and her heart nearly stopped. Ella dropped to her knees.

Ash's arms surrounded her. "What's happening?"

"My heart." Ella gasped. "The fluttering. It doesn't happen to you?" she barely managed to croak out.

He shook his head, his face racked with concern and terror. "No. I don't feel anything."

Just Ella, then.

Shocker.

Wren's spell had done its job though. Boils and puss burst off of Madison's body, much worse than it had been from Wren's first attack on the basketball team. But Ella had been the one to lessen the results on Madison that morning. According to Wren, Ella had scattered the spell so it hit all the players and not just Madison. The full effects of the spell were terrifying to witness, but there was a serene, almost calm expression on Wren's face as each blister bubbled and exploded in an avalanche of puss and blood. Madison dropped to the ground in silent agony, just as she had in the gym.

Wren's hands and arms were covered in blisters of her own from the blowback, but she quickly cast a healing spell, erasing them completely.

As she did that, Sadie's voice reverberated in Ella's ears as her heart barely chugged along at this point. It was another healing spell, directed at Madison.

And Madison's sores and blisters healed within seconds. It took her a moment or two to stand. But Sadie and Madison were wary now, obviously not expecting to have this intense of a fight with two high school students.

Ella ducked and pushed her and Ash's heads down as Sadie's eyes searched for her. They were crouched behind a black sedan, and Ella was really hoping it didn't suddenly fly up, then crush down on them.

All they could do was run from car to car, but with the way her heart was functioning, she could barely stay conscious.

The squealing of car brakes caused Ella and Ash to lift their heads to see what had happened.

A CIU car screeched to a halt, and Agents Malcolm Gilroy and Shara *Gordon* raced out of the car, mouths moving, Ella's heart skipping every other beat.

Things were about to get crazy.

CHAPTER 32
WREN

"CIU!" Wren yelled at Moira, giving her a heads-up.

Not sure if they'd attack her and Moira, Wren rushed behind a parked car, then signaled Shara with a wave. "Trackers! Lizzie and Rachel!" She referred to Madison and Sadie by their aliases to avoid confusion.

A rush of relief washed through Wren as Shara nodded and directed her spell at Sadie.

Madison and Sadie had split up again, and instead of running like any sane person would, they'd spread out within the parking lot, casting their own spells.

One of which hit Wren full force: strangulation spell.

Wren grabbed her throat, trying to cast through coughs of air, but couldn't get the right words out. Hence why this spell was genius for an attack and why a lot of Trackers had the quantum repellent gear attached to their brain stem.

Malcolm was by Wren's side and incanting until she could breathe again.

"Where's Ella?" he asked.

"Hiding. With Ash." Wren let that sink in.

Malcolm eyed Wren with a new kind of interest, then Wren continued, "Moira and I have been holding them off, but they're determined." Wren figured Malcolm might not know the details of how much she knew, but he could logically guess at some of it.

"You guys get out of here and try to take Ella and Ash with you. CIU's got this." Malcolm nudged Wren behind him.

Oh, Malcolm.

"Two against two isn't a fair fight, and you don't know which parts of the brain they have gear on." Wren might've been revealing too much, but she needed Madison and Sadie to die. Because now that they knew for sure Ella was a Dis-con, they were never going to stop until Ella was dead.

Malcom reared his head back despite the raging battle happening in front of them. (Moira had just cast a body-locking spell on Sadie, and she went down hard and fast, but before Shara or Moira could reach her, Sadie cast the counter spell, hitting Shara with a bone-separating hex. Shara screamed as her skin became loose from the bones inside her body tearing apart.) Malcolm's voice was steady but urgent when he asked, "And you do?"

"Sadie's—I mean, *Rachel's* occipital, cerebellum, and hypothalamus are clean, and Lizzie's occipital, brain stem, and hypothalamus are clean," Wren said, then cast a blinding spell on Madison, hoping Malcolm wouldn't notice her slipup calling Rachel Sadie.

Malcolm cocked his head to the side. "You know both their true identities?"

Guess he noticed.

"I'll tell you after. We're kind of in a battle here, if you hadn't noticed," Wren deflected.

Meanwhile, the spell Wren had just cast turned Madison's eyes ice-white, but like a soldier, she leapt behind a car and cast the counter before her blindness could be any more of a hindrance.

At this point, everyone except Malcolm had red and inflamed arms, necks, and legs from the blowback of so much casting.

Shara's bones were back in place, but she was huffing.

"You better help your girl." Wren nodded toward Shara. "And tell her their weaknesses. Moira and I got your back, and we're getting Ella and Ash out of her before you can take them."

Malcolm didn't seem offended or defensive. He nodded. "Keep them safe."

A moment passed between them, then Wren nodded. "I will." He wanted them safe. That was interesting information. From the worry in Malcolm's expression, Wren could tell that whatever CIU did with Dis-cons, it wasn't deadly—maybe not even bad.

Madison leapt from car to car, searching everywhere for Ella. It didn't really matter that Madison and Sadie didn't know Ash was a Dis-con too, because they'd kill him for just being near Ella. Doing their job without ever knowing it.

But it was time.

Madison Grant was dying today.

And Wren was going to be the one who did it.

Wren had been saving a spell since the moment she hunted Evil Incarnate down to Tristan High.

It was from the Argentinian military vault. Only used once. To blow up their president.

The spell would boil her blood, create hydrogen gas inside her body, and then when Madison took in a breath of air, the last part of the spell would create a spark of fire inside of her and boom! Evil Incarnate parts showering all over the parking lot, and Wren could finally have revenge for her mother's death.

Wren focused only on Madison.

And she started to incant the spell.

It was strong. It was loud.

And unfortunately, it drew the attention of Moira, Sadie, Shara, and Malcolm.

But Wren didn't care.

She had to get it out before anyone could stop her.

Sweat instantly poured down Madison's face and body as Wren raised the temperature of her blood. She dropped to her knees on the roof of a car.

Almost there.

Wren began the second part of the spell, building the hydrogen gas inside Madison's system.

Wren's hands blistered and burned the spell was so powerful.

It could kill her.

She didn't care.

Wren's skin bubbled at this point, blood bursting from pustules, but Madison's terrified grimace made it all worth it. Now to finish the spell by creating the spark of fire that would end her enemy forever . . .

Thwack!

Moira tackled Wren to the ground from her side, terror in her eyes. "Wren! Stop!"

"Get off me!" Wren shoved her aside.

Yanking Wren back down, Moira gasped. "Wren, you were going to die! What were you thinking?"

"I wasn't going to die!" Wren yelled back. But she didn't know that. Then Wren saw what she had done to herself. Blood dripped heavily down her arms, and more of it seeped through her jeans from her legs. Wren touched her face, and more blood came away on her hands. From what she could see of her body, she looked as bad, if not worse, than Madison. The spell might cause a gruesome death, but it seemed to do the same to the caster.

Grabbing Wren's hand, Moira cast a healing spell on her, and the pain Wren hadn't noticed was there because of her pounding adrenaline dissipated. Her blisters healed, and the blood dried on her skin. "She's not worth dying over." Tears streamed down Moira's cheeks.

Yes. She is, Wren wanted to say, but Moira suddenly clutched her throat, desperately trying to breathe in air.

Sadie.

Wren cast a counter spell, and Moira gasped for air, able to breathe once more.

Sadie leapt past them to heal Madison.

Choking out her words, Moira said, "No more spells like that. CIU will take her in."

"No," Wren said with steely composure. "She needs to die."

"Ella and Ash need our help. They are the priority," Moira said with just as much steel.

Wren's insides began to shake, but not from a spell, from guilt.

Moira was right.

If her mom were there, she'd have been risking her life to save Ella and Ash, not trying to murder someone.

Priorities.

Wren would deal with Madison later.

Madison wasn't doing so well, which made Wren a little more

than happy, her spell having lasting effects despite Sadie's healing. But she was still mobile, searching.

Both Trackers had split up again.

Wren wished she knew where Ella and Ash had gone so she could lead Madison away. Wren had no idea if Madison was close or nowhere near them.

Malcolm and Shara were busy with Sadie. She'd managed to cast a body-locking spell on Shara and a mouth-sealing spell on Malcolm. Wren should've probably helped them out, but Ella and Ash were more important.

Moira stuck by Wren's side now. Her crinkled brows and worried eyes indicated she didn't trust Wren to not try to kill Madison again. Wren turned to her. "Do you know where Ella and Ash are?"

Shaking her head, Moira said, "Last I saw them, they were in the parking lot using the cars as cover. They could be anywhere."

"We have to get to high ground." Like Madison was doing.

Climbing on top of the car closest to them, Wren popped up on the roof.

Madison was thirty feet away, frantically searching, but she looked like she was dragging her own body. Wren couldn't help the warmth of glee at seeing Madison suffer. It soothed the memory of her mother's death, but only a little.

When she cast a quick throat-closing spell on Madison, the Tracker dropped to her knees, not able to handle another blow. Wren and Moira used Madison's momentary choking to leap from car to car, trying to find Ella and Ash.

Where were they?

Part of Wren was happy she couldn't find them because it meant they were hiding well, but the other part of her needed to protect them. Maybe simply weakening Madison would save them.

Wren's legs locked, and she dropped from the roof of a car to the hood, smacking her chin on the metal. As Madison was still distracted with finding Ella, Wren could only assume the attack had come from Sadie. It had obviously come from a distance too, because Wren couldn't see Sadie from where she was.

Moira unlocked Wren with a few words and helped her back to her feet. "I see them over there." Moira nodded discreetly to their right so as not to alert Madison, who annoyingly seemed to be gaining her strength and composure back.

Wren and Moira were closer.

"Keep pretending like we're looking," Wren said as they started leaping from car to car once again. They meandered to Ella and Ash rather than booked it, all the while keeping themselves as a shield from Madison.

Four cars away.

Sadie was back in view.

Malcolm hit her with a balance spell as she jumped up on car to join the search. It hit her legs first, and she didn't make it to the hood, tumbling off and smashing her face on the pavement.

Shara entered the search, running up a car like it was a ramp and jumping from roof to roof.

Three cars away.

Sadie gained her bearings and cast a lesser version of the plague spell on Malcolm, who had almost reached her.

Two cars away.

Madison turned in Wren's direction and must have seen something on her face or she spotted Ella herself, because she picked up her speed, leaping on the cars as if they were the ground itself.

One car.

Wren's eyes met Ella's. She and Ash huddled together behind a large black SUV. "We gotta run."

"Every time we try, they throw something at us." Ella grimaced in frustration.

"You've got us. We'll divert anything they cast to throw at you." Wren hoped she wasn't lying. "We gotta do it now though."

Madison leapt the final car to theirs and tackled Wren off the car and to the ground.

Too late.

"Run!" Wren screamed at Ella and Ash.

Madison shoved Wren's head into the pavement with one hand and grabbed Ella's ankle with the other, screaming to Sadie: "She's over here!"

The only sound was thuds of metal as Sadie and Shara jumped onto cars, following Madison's voice and last location.

Moira yanked Madison up by the hair and punched her face with the heel of her hand, right on the nose. Blood sprayed out everywhere, hitting Wren in the face, but she couldn't be prouder. Madison lost her grip on Ella's foot, and Ella was free.

Malcom arrived first on foot. He cast a choking spell on Madison, causing her to keel over, coughing uncontrollably.

"You two get out of here!" Malcolm pleaded with Ella and Ash, and they listened.

Ella and Ash took off but couldn't run full speed because of all the parked cars surrounding them. Their hiding place might have kept them hidden for most of the battle, but it also sandwiched them in a sea of cars they now had to traverse.

Madison's cough stopped as Sadie arrived above them on the SUV.

This wasn't a battle Wren could win.

It was a battle they needed to run from.

To protect Ella and Ash.

To protect Dis-cons.

Grabbing Moira's hand, Wren chased after Ella and Ash, catching up to them quickly. "We'll keep our backs to you and make sure they don't cast anything to throw at you."

It was slower, but safer.

Ella didn't argue. They kept moving through the cars. Only five rows until they were in open ground and running freely.

They could do this.

Wren's eyes were peeled for any levitated objects Madison and Sadie might conjure as their prey slipped through their fingers, but nothing came.

Two-on-two, Malcolm and Shara versus Madison and Sadie, each hurling spells with such speed Wren couldn't keep up. She quickly glanced at Ella and Ash, making sure they were okay. They both seemed scared, but prepared. As Dis-cons, this confrontation was something they had both anticipated their entire lives, but no one could fully prepare for a Tracker attack. And it usually ended with the Tracker winning.

Rage flowed through Wren.

Not this time.

"They're down, they're down!" Moira screamed.

Wren whirled her head around. Malcolm and Shara doubled over, arms and legs broken, gasping for breath.

Madison and Sadie leapt to the top of the SUV and held hands, their lips moving in unison.

Some kind of joint spell.

Even from here, Wren could feel the power of the spell,

radiating a kind of energy that only illegal spells did.

Whatever this was, it was big.

Something they obviously thought would take Wren and Moira out and leave Ella vulnerable to a physical attack.

Ella stopped with Ash and turned to Wren and Moira. "Get behind me!"

"Ella, no! Just run, please!" Wren begged.

Wren couldn't lose her.

Not like her mom.

The spell released. Wren could almost see the quantum wave gushing toward them.

"I'm not letting you die," Ella said with determination. "I said get behind me!"

CHAPTER 33
ELLA

Wren and Moira clambered behind Ella. Ash positioned himself next to Ella as another shield, but she shook her head. "You too! Get behind me!"

"But I can protect them too!" Ash said over the noise.

"No! Rachel and Lizzie don't know you're a Dis-con, but if they see their spell does nothing to you, they'll know right away." She nodded to Wren and Moira. "Cover them as best you can, but I'm the only shield here."

The spell was almost there.

"Now!" Ella screamed.

Ash did as he was told and squatted with Wren and Moira so Ella could cover them with her body.

She braced herself for impact.

Ella's heart fluttered like crazy, but she was weirdly growing used to it, like it was a new beat, a beat Ella needed to embrace and accept. She turned her body at the last second so that the spell would hit her back instead of her chest. Ella draped her arms over Wren and Moira while Ash threw as much of his crouched body as he could over them as well, creating a dome of protection.

Swoosh!

It hit hard.

Like a gale wind.

Pushing against her.

Ella dug her feet farther into the ground to keep some kind of purchase, but the strength of the wind from the spell moved the small group inch by inch. If the spell was just wind, a blow to throw them against a car or truck, then slice their unconscious throats, Ella thought they could survive it.

But no.

This was different.

It was more.

If Ella's erratic heartbeat was her only indicator, it appeared to beat differently for different types of spells.

And this felt like Wren's plague spell.

Sure enough, even through Ella and Ash, parts of the spell seeped into any exposed parts of Wren and Moira, ripping pieces of their skin right off. They screamed in pain as bits of their flesh tore off their bodies and flew away in the fury of the wind.

No.

They were going to die.

No.

Because of her.

No.

Ella's parents were right.

She should have listened.

Friends were dangerous.

But not for her.

For *them*.

Now Ella couldn't save the two people who'd risked their lives for her.

No!

Ella closed her eyes.

She felt it then.

The spell.

The force of it.

The shape of it.

Push it back.

Push it away.

Save her friends.

Boom!

Boom!

Boom!

A roar of sound, almost deafening, shook the ground beneath them.

Crunching metal and skids across pavement.

Then nothing.

Total silence.

Opening her eyes, Ella saw Wren and Moira first, hurt but otherwise okay. Then her gaze met Ash's, his mouth agape as he stared at what was behind her.

All three of them followed his gaze.

Oh, she'd pushed the spell all right.

There were only empty parking spots in front of them. Every parked car was now crunched and demolished, plastered to the back wall of the lot.

And every person in view lay still on the ground.

Malcolm, Shara, Sadie, and Madison, even inside the school. Ella could see through the glass doors, bodies, unmoving.

What had she done?

Wren, despite her open wounds, rushed to Malcolm's body, feeling for a pulse. Then she did the same for Shara. She rushed back. "They're fine. Whatever you did knocked them out but didn't kill them." Wren took in the wrecked scene once more and shook her head. "Such power . . ." Her expression was far-off and dazed.

Moira took Wren's hand to jolt her out of her reverie, then turned to Ella and Ash. "Lose the holo-phones and let's go."

At first, Ella wasn't sure why she wanted them to abandon their only connection to the outside world, but then it dawned on her that holo-phones could be traced. Ella pulled it out of her pocket and threw it on the ground with everyone else's.

A few of the unconscious students began to stir behind the glass doors, which sent a thrill of relief through Ella. But also dread. They didn't have much time, and they needed to leave. Moira cast quick and dirty healing spells on Wren and herself.

This time, the path was clear. No spells, no Trackers, and no CIU. They ran. Ella wasn't paying attention to where they were headed; they just needed distance. Ella followed Wren and Moira since they'd taken the lead. Ash wasn't saying a word either as they all ran across the street and raced down the sidewalk.

Finally, Wren yelled as Ella kept pace behind her: "My house is the first place they'll look. I have to get my spells out of the safe, then I can take us to a place to hide."

She was right. When Sadie and Madison woke up, they'd be coming for them, and Wren's house was the most obvious choice.

But then they'd go to Ella's.

Her parents.

She had to warn them.

Ash's mind seemed to be in sync with hers as he shouted, "Ella and I have to warn our parents."

Wren answered as they arrived at her house, out of breath. "We will, I promise, but Ash, the Trackers don't know you're a Dis-con. They only know about Ella. And CIU wanted you guys to run. I don't think they hurt Dis-cons." She said it as if it were a revelation for her as well. "CIU will protect your parents."

With no time to talk, the four of them hurried through the door, heading downstairs as soon as they were inside, but Ella's mind raced. Ella had felt that about Malcolm. She was pretty sure it was why she'd agreed to go into CIU headquarters in the first place. Ella had never felt he meant her any harm. Of course, she assumed that was because he didn't know she was a Dis-con. But Wren had confirmed that he suspected she was one, and yet he'd still treated her like she was human, even let her go back to school. No kidnapping. No killing. Ella still had no idea what CIU did when they took Dis-cons, but her gut told her she'd be safe.

Wren opened her vault and stuffed piles of papers and notebooks into a duffel. "I've got what I need from the safe, but I have to destroy the rest."

She turned to Moira, eyes asking for her help, and Moira nodded. Together, they incanted a spell that first revealed the place to be like something out of spy movie—holographic spider diagrams on the wall, papers with notes strewn on side tables. Ella was even on the diagram with the label *Dis-con* underneath. Years of work. Then the second part of the spell shattered and shredded every piece of Wren's research into a million pieces. As Ella watched

Ash's holo picture being dissipated into nothing recognizable, a weight lifted. Hopefully, Sadie and Madison would never find out about him. It was the best way to keep him safe.

She sounded like her parents.

Her brilliant amazing parents who really were just trying to keep her alive.

And now their worst nightmare was here.

Ella was on the run and being hunted by Trackers.

After every tidbit of evidence was destroyed, Wren chucked the duffel over her shoulder and headed for the stairs. "Let's go."

No one argued as they started their next run.

Wren said she had a place to hide, and this didn't surprise Ella. Wren had been hunting down Trackers since her mother's death, so she probably had a lot of contingency plans. They cut through neighbors' lawns to steer clear of sidewalks and roads. Moira's and Wren's skin was still red and raw from all their spell-casting and the nasty spell Sadie and Madison had cast, but otherwise, they seemed okay.

It was not lost on Ella that they'd suffered because they were protecting her and Ash.

It brought unbidden tears to Ella's eyes, and she had to wipe them away quickly so she didn't trip on anything as they ran. The gesture alerted Ash though as he gently guided Ella's elbow, helping her keep her balance.

"Feels like we're Buster44 and FearlessGirl22," Ash said through panting.

"I think my character . . . is in better shape . . . than me though." Ella gulped between breaths.

"Same," Ash admitted, breathing heavily.

Ella's adrenaline had gotten her this far, but it was starting to wear off. Barely able to breathe, Ella slowed down. "I need a breather," she gasped out.

Wren and Moira slowed until they all stopped near a clump of pine trees in someone's backyard. Wren was panting a bit too, but not as bad as Ella. "We'll take a few to rest."

"Thanks," Ella said, still not able to catch her breath. "Man, I'm out of shape."

Ash puffed out a heavy breath. "I think running after everything we just went through would take the breath out of anyone. In shape or not."

"Can they track us?" Ella asked, not knowing how tracking spells worked.

"They can track our signature. I already cast a spell on myself and Moira that altered our signatures, and Ash is totally untraceable. But you? You definitely left a signature with that blast, and I don't think my spell will work on you, even with my tweaks. I'm pretty sure you're the only one they can trace, so we have to get to this hideout quickly. I've spelled it to hide anything. Even you, hopefully." Wren tried to make Ella feel better.

But it didn't.

Ella was the one that put them all in danger.

Again.

Wren stepped forward, placing a hand on Ella's arm. "Don't you dare think about running away from us. We're all in this together. I can't let my mom down."

Moira placed her hand on Ella's other arm so they both faced her. "And I'm not letting Luna down." Looking back and forth between Ella and Ash, she continued, "We never felt more helpless in our lives than when we lost our family. We're not letting that happen again. Ever."

Ash finally caught his breath, and he nodded to Moira and Wren, his expression humbled. "Thank you." He walked over and stood behind Ella, hands on her shoulders. They were a group, a family, bound together by tragedy, but bound all the same.

Wren let go of Ella first and situated her duffel for comfort. "It's not far from here. But we are going to be crossing a couple roads. We can mainly stick to alleys though."

Taking the lead, Wren walked through the last of the trees, and they all followed.

They'd left the suburbs and had entered a more urban part of town with shops, businesses, and worst of all: people.

Since Ella and Ash had stayed hidden most of the battle, their clothes and skin were relatively clean, but Moira and Wren? They were speckled with dried (and some not-so-dried) blood on their skin, clothes, and hair.

Wren obviously seemed to notice this as well, as Ella heard her incant a spell until both their skin and clothes were clean—a bit ratty, but clean. No one paid them any mind as they traveled, but they also didn't see very many people either. Like Wren had said, they stuck to mainly alleys and the back parking lots of stores. No more running at least since it would've only drawn attention to them, but they did walk like they had an appointment they were late for.

After about an hour of walking, they hadn't run into any trouble. Ella wanted to sigh in relief, but she knew that wasn't smart, so she kept her guard up.

Wren broke the silence. "It's down here."

They headed into another alley and arrived at a cement stairwell that led down eight steps to a metal door. It was at the base of a five-story brick building that, if Ella had read correctly from the sign they passed, was some kind of business complex. Wren pulled out a set of keys from her pants pocket and found the correct one.

After climbing down the stairs and unlocking the door, she held it open for them all to enter.

Inside was one large room with a kitchenette (more like a hot plate, mini fridge, and sink) and a door with a three-drawer dresser right next to it. The door itself, Ella assumed, led to a bathroom, or at least she hoped it did, because she knew they'd all need that at some point. A small couch leaned against one wall with an end table on each side and a couple of framed pictures on their surfaces. In front of the couch was a coffee table surrounded by one recliner and two high-back wooden chairs that looked as if they used to belong to an old dinette set from decades ago.

"Make yourselves comfortable. There's a sandwich place in this building, so I can grab us some food." Wren motioned to all the seating available.

Ella plopped down on the couch, and Ash sat next to her. She knew it was from extreme fatigue, but Ella had never felt more comfortable in her life. The couch might've been old and dingy, but its plushy cushions surrounded her like clouds. And as Ella sat, leaning her head against the fluff of the heavenly couch, her eyes were drawn to the two framed photos on the side table nearest her. She reached over and pulled one to her.

"Who's this?" Ella asked.

The picture was of a stunning woman with curly black hair, large brown eyes, and a dazzling smile that added a twinkle to her eyes.

"That's my mom," Wren said quietly. "This is the only place I have pictures of her. My dad won't let me have anything in the house that reminds him of her, so I keep the photos here."

Ella could tell Wren didn't want to elaborate from her hunched shoulders and darting eyes.

"She's beautiful," Ella said, placing the picture back down on the end table, not wanting to upset Wren further. A deep throb of pain filled her chest at the thought of Wren having to witness her mother's murder. And to make it worse, Wren not being able to have mementos of her mom in her own house. She had to rent a place like this just to spend time with what she had left of her.

Moira had picked up another framed photo from the other end table, admiring it as well. "You look so much like her."

Wren's expression softened a bit more with Moira's comment, as if hearing Moira say it gave her some comfort. But Wren still didn't elaborate.

As Ella watched Moira and Wren, exhaustion hit her hard, and her eyes began to droop. Ella shook her head. She needed to stay up. She needed to know what had happened to her back at the school. Wren probably had a theory. Ella was about to ask her what that might be when her eyelids won.

Ella fell back onto the couch.

Maybe just a little nap.

CHAPTER 34
WREN

Walking back into the little apartment, Wren carried a bag of deli sandwiches. She had bought four but wasn't sure what everyone liked, so she'd picked out a good spectrum, from all veggie to all meat. Wren was starving, so she'd be fine with anything. She could have just spelled some food, but Barry's Deli was one of her favorites, and they all needed some comfort at the moment.

Wren quietly walked over to the coffee table and placed the bag of sandwiches on top.

Moira came out of the bathroom in fresh clothing, towel drying her wet hair. Glancing first at Ella's sleeping figure, she turned to Wren and whispered, "I hope you don't mind. I raided your dresser and took a shower. Spelling myself clean wasn't going to cut it."

"Of course," Wren whispered back, self-consciously looking down at her clothes and body she had spelled clean. Had she missed a spot? They actually looked okay, but what did her hair look like? Why did she even care about this? "I might do that too after we eat."

Moira sat on one of the wooden chairs, while Wren sat on the recliner.

Ella was fully out cold on the couch across from Wren, so she couldn't appreciate that Ash was letting her rest in the nook of his arm. Wren wanted to ask Ash what he thought about everything that had happened, but she wasn't sure if he was ready to share. He carefully pulled himself away from Ella and grabbed one of the veggie options.

"Thanks," he said in almost a whisper, obviously trying not to wake up Ella.

But the crinkle of the bags and the unwrapping of paper around the sandwiches caused Ella's eyes to slowly open. "Oh." She eyed the food greedily. "I'm starving." She reached forward and grabbed the first sandwich she touched—definitely not picky. "Thank you so much."

Moira leaned forward, taking one herself, and Wren chose from what was left. It ended up being a faux meat salami, which was actually quite good as she took her first bite.

Between bites, Wren nodded toward the bathroom door. "There's a shower in there and fresh towels if you two want to clean up."

After eating half the sandwich, Ella relaxed and sat back on the couch. "What are we going to do? We can't hide forever, can we? And are you sure our parents are okay?"

Ash's eyes searched Wren's for the answer to that one as well, as if she were some kind of expert on everything that was happening. But she answered all the same. "Yes. I'm sure. It's standard CIU protocol. They came to our house right after my mother died to protect us. Not that we needed it. Trackers don't like to kill the families. Their main objective is the Dis-con. The only time a family member is killed is if they are collateral damage. But regardless, CIU put us in protective custody for about three weeks. They do that until they're sure the family is safe."

Moira backed Wren up: "Yeah, once my sister was dead, CIU guarded us for a few weeks, but the Trackers as a whole never paid attention to us again, aside from their little spies they assign to us to make sure we don't try anything." Throwing the wrapper into the now empty plastic bag, she added, "Like what we did today."

Ash shook his head. "You two were amazing. I've never seen spell-casting like that." Then he eyed Ella with curiosity. "And what you did . . . you protected us all. How can you do that and be a Dis-con?"

"My mother was like Ella," Wren said so Ella didn't feel like she was on the spot. "She can push on the quantum waves of a spell. Dis-cons repel spells—it's why they don't affect you—but Ella and my mother somehow found a way to push back on that force."

Ella shrugged as she took her last bite and placed the paper wrapper in the plastic bag as well. "It's helped me hide, but obviously not enough." Her eyes met Wren's. "I thought I fooled them yesterday and the night before with Sadie."

"I thought so too," Wren agreed. "But maybe they heard Moira relaying the spell? Or me telling you the spell? Or you not reacting fast enough. It could've been anything. They're relentless, especially Madison."

"Wait, who is Madison?" Ash asked, brows furrowed in confusion.

Wren and Moira filled him in.

"Verner Grant." Ash shook his head. "And Madison's his daughter." He didn't phrase it as a question. It was as if he were convincing himself it was real.

Ella sighed. "If Madison killed your mom, how did she not recognize you? Or even you, Moira? Didn't their 'spies' as you called them, keep tabs on you?"

Wren nodded. "They do know us. We overheard them after my plague attack trying to match my spell signature to the spell, but the spell I invented to change my signature worked, so I thought they didn't suspect me anymore. As far as I know, Madison had no idea I saw through her blank-face glamour when she murdered my mother. She must now though."

"And with me, they were trying to recruit me to the Trackers. My parents used a memory spell on me to make me forget Luna and what happened her, but I invented a counter spell, so it didn't work. Sadie and Madison were at Tristan High for me. It makes me sick thinking they might have successfully recruited me if that memory spell had worked." Moira cast her eyes down as if she'd been thinking a lot about the topic.

"You'd never." Wren needed Moira to know she believed in her.

Ash shook his head, looking impressed. "I know they didn't expect to get their butts handed to them by you."

Moira focused on Ella. "We might not have made it out of there without you."

Ella shifted uncomfortably on the couch, then sat up. "I really don't know what I did, and I'm not sure I could do it again. I'm just glad it gave us enough time to get away." Her eyes met Wren's again. "And I'm very grateful you actually had a place for us to hide. How do you rent this place as a teenager?"

"That's what glamour spells are for. The people that rented me the place think I'm a forty-year-old guy. And it helps to have a dad who was in a walking coma. He always knew what I was doing, though, since I used his money. He just never reacted to it. But I know he'd be happy I used it to protect you two." Before anyone could question Wren about her dad, she continued, "I'm not sure who will get to him first, CIU or Madison and Sadie, but my house will be everyone's first stop. I hope my dad's memory spell doesn't crack."

Moira knew what Wren had done to her dad, but Ella and Ash didn't.

They were smart though, and Wren could see the lightbulbs go off over both their heads.

Ella nodded. "It was too hard on him? Losing his wife?"

"Losing her by decapitation and having her head and body dragged away didn't help." Wren didn't want to talk about it. "I figured at least one of us could be happy."

Ash rubbed his neck, as if imagining the same fate as Wren's mother. "Trackers are evil."

Moira answered, "Beyond evil. And we're taking down the whole organization."

Ash took in a quick breath. Wren couldn't blame him. It would've sounded like a bold—even crazy—statement to anyone who didn't know how much work Wren had already put into her cause.

Ash sat forward, hands clenched. "I guess this should go without saying, but I'm with you. I know they didn't know I was a Dis-con when we got there, but they're going to figure it out if they haven't already." He turned to Ella. "I wish I could do what you can."

Ella pressed her hands down on her pants, and it reminded

Wren of something they hadn't discussed at length.

"We know some of my spells have worked on you. We could experiment on something small? Like maybe if your hands happen to be sweating?" Wren didn't want to embarrass her in front of Ash, so she tried to sound as casual as possible. "My hands are sweating like crazy after what we went through." They weren't, but it would help Ella feel less conspicuous.

After looking down at her hands plastered to her legs, Ella eyed Wren gratefully. "Yeah, they are a little sweaty. I'd like that."

"Perfect," Wren said and grabbed her duffel that was at the foot of the coffee table, pulling out a standard quantum spell-casting textbook. "There's an anti-sweat spell in here that will do nicely. Combined with my tweak, let's see what happens." Checking the table of contents and flipping to the correct page, Wren was ready.

Wren could tell Ella was trying to avoid Ash's gaze, as she was obviously self-conscious about her hands. Wren reached over and took Ella's hands in hers to perform the spell. And dang, they were like wet logs. Wren pretended not to notice though and incanted the anti-sweat spell first, followed by the addition she'd invented that had at least affected Ella's memory in the temporal lobe, but she had no idea if it would affect the hypothalamus, which regulated emotion, body temperature, and physiological cycles. Added to the fact that the hypothalamus was so well protected in the center of the brain, Wren's spell might not be strong enough.

Pushing doubts aside, Wren incanted her self-made addition to the spell.

Moira and Ash watched intently. Both of them had stakes in this working: Ash because he was a Dis-con and Moira because she wanted more spells in her arsenal that could hurt Trackers.

As the last of the words left Wren's mouth, the sweat on Ella's hands completely dried up.

Pulling her hands away gently, Ella examined them with wide awed eyes. "That's amazing."

"A spell worked on you." Ash couldn't stop staring at Ella's hands either. "I can't believe it." He turned to Wren. "Can you try something on me? Maybe it works on her because of her quantum wave-pushing thing."

"Sure. Of course." Wren didn't want them to feel like living experiments, but she was curious about that as well, and he was volunteering. "What do you want to test?" Wren gave him the option.

"What about that language spell you used on us?" Moira suggested. She turned to Ella and Ash with a smile. "I speak perfect Portuguese now."

"A language spell?" Ella exclaimed in amazement. "I've never heard of something like that."

Wren nodded. "It's from a military vault. I've broken into a few," she admitted.

"Dang," Ash responded with a nervous laugh. "You are way more powerful than a Skein."

Wren shrugged, hoping she wasn't scaring him too badly. She rummaged through the duffel and pulled out the language spell Moira had referred to. Adding her own words to the spell, she incanted it flawlessly.

When finished, they all stared at Ash.

Moira asked him in Portuguese if the spell had worked.

"I understood that," Ash said with rounded eyes. "You asked if it worked!"

Wren had never seen Ash so animated, and she had to admit,

it was pretty cute. "Try saying something back," Wren prodded.

Ash paused, thought for a moment, then shook his head. "It's weird. I understand it, but I can't seem to speak it. The words aren't coming to me."

"Let me try something." After grabbing a pen from her bag, Wren pulled out some of the paper that the sandwiches had been wrapped in and scribbled on its surface. She wrote a few sentences in Portuguese, then handed it to Ash. "Try reading it."

Ash carefully examined the paper, then read it out in perfect Portuguese. "I can read it, but I didn't know what it meant until I said it out loud."

Wren and Moira exchanged glances. It hadn't worked perfectly, but it did work to some degree. Wren turned to Ash. "It looks like we got your visual and auditory, but not your ability to speak it on your own. But it is a start."

Ash leaned back on the couch with the largest grin Wren had ever seen on him. "Are you kidding? It's more than a start. It's incredible! Even with it kind of working, it's a miracle." He leaned forward now with an awed expression. "You may just change the world, Wren Martis."

His sentiment filled her with an indescribable rush she couldn't explain. Wren had been fighting for vengeance for so long, she'd never stopped to think about the fact that what she was doing could actually flip the entire planet on its axis. Spells that worked on Dis-cons? Ash was right. It changed everything.

Boom!

The front door flew inside the apartment with terrifying speed. It slammed into Moira's body, pushing her and the chair until the door's flat surface pinned her to the wall.

"Moira!" Wren yelled, as if that would somehow help her.

But Moira's still form was all that answered her. She was either out cold or dead. Wren prayed she was just unconscious, or she'd never forgive herself.

Wren immediately began to incant, but her throat closed from a spell being cast on her. She watched through blurred eyes as Ella pushed back on the quantum waves of the spell, throwing the now visible Sadie through the open doorway and against the stone steps.

Wren choked out a counter spell, and air flooded her lungs in relief.

Sadie, fully recovered, ran inside, charging toward her.

Wren cast a body-locking spell she had stolen from the Argentinian vault that turned every joint in the body into metal. Sadie's scream was loud but short as every joint solidified until the spell reached her jaw and locked it into place.

Madison couldn't be too far behind.

Ella and Ash peeled the door from Moira's body, and Ella pressed her ear to Moira's chest. "She's breathing, and her heart is beating."

Wren's knees almost gave way the relief hit her so hard.

Sadie began to move again. Madison must have cast a counter spell for the metal joints. Good information, as that meant she had some background with that stolen spell. Either the Trackers had a deal with Argentina, or they'd been busting into military vaults as well.

But where *was* Madison?

She was keeping out of view, which was the strategy they should have used at the school. Wren couldn't cast a spell at someone she couldn't see.

Wren began to incant a protection bubble for any unforeseen spells.

The recliner smashed into her back from Sadie's levitation spell, knocking Wren on her knees so she couldn't finish her protective shield spell. "Get out of here!" Wren yelled at Ella and Ash.

Ella, ignoring her, pushed on the tail end of Sadie's spell, causing Sadie to hit the wall, but not full force like the last one.

Ash grabbed the lamp off the side table and threw it at Sadie's face. He grabbed Ella's hand. "Wren's right. We gotta get out of here."

"Not without Wren and Moira! We can't leave them!" Ella's voice was tinged with desperation.

Pain seared through Wren's spine from the impact of the chair, but she scrambled to her feet, readying another paralysis spell.

Smash!

The entire couch lifted from the floor and hit Wren's head full force, then landed heavily on her chest.

Ella pushed back harder on that one, and Sadie went flying through the air and back out the doorway.

"Wren!" Ella screamed. "We'll get you out!"

Wren's head swam, and black spots swarmed her vision.

She couldn't move.

She could barely breathe.

She was losing consciousness.

Ella and Ash grabbed the two ends of the couch, ready to pull it up.

Wren tried to help them by incanting a levitation spell, but she choked up blood instead.

Madison took advantage of Ella and Ash lifting the couch off of Wren. She and Sadie hurried inside the apartment, barely acknowledging Wren's existence, faces forward, on a mission.

Thwack!

Thwack!

The couch landed with another thud on Wren's chest as both Ella and Ash were rendered unconscious from the discarded lamp Sadie used to smash them into sleep.

"We'll take the boy as well. We can use him as leverage," Madison said.

Sadie already had Ella's unconscious body secured, hands tied behind her back, hood covering her face.

Madison did the same with Ash's still form.

"Ella," Wren choked out.

But Ella was unconscious, preventing her from hearing or responding, and Madison and Sadie had already spelled gurneys that floated in from outside, then lowered them to the floor. After lifting Ella and Ash and rolling them onto the gurneys, the Trackers cast the gurneys to float again and exited the apartment with the two floating Dis-cons without another glance in Wren's direction.

Wren tried one more time to cast a levitation spell, but somewhere in the middle, her mind went blank, and everything went black.

CHAPTER 35
ELLA

Ella's body jolted, and she came to.

The hood obscured her vision entirely, but from the loud hum of the engine, she recognized that she was in a car. And with a slight screeching of brakes, they had come to a halt as far as she could tell.

Ella didn't know what fabric the hood was made of, but it was itchy and difficult to breathe through. It was the only thing she could focus on that didn't send her into a massive panic attack though. The stupid, scratchy, annoying hood.

She had no idea where she was as she was hauled out of the car and led forward. Through the bottom of the hood, she caught a glimpse of cement as they walked, which then led to marble flooring, followed by an elevator ride down—*way* down—then back to marble. Ella wasn't sure which Tracker held her arm, leading her forward. At the sound of other people shuffling behind her, Ella could only hope it was Ash.

Wren and Moira.

Ella's heart sank.

She had been knocked out before she knew if they were okay. It had all happened so fast.

Neither Sadie nor Madison cast any more spells as they trudged forward—proof they weren't taking any chances with her abilities.

The real question was: did they know Ash was a Dis-con too?

Finally, they reached their intended destination with a jangling of keys, clicking of a lock, then a push of a door.

Ella fumbled over her feet as she was thrown inside a room, but she managed to somehow keep her balance. Another body nearly knocked her over as they were shoved inside as well, and Ella's heart raced with relief as she recognized Ash's voice.

"Ella?" he asked.

Sadie yanked off Ella's hood, her sneering face there to greet hers.

Madison pulled off Ash's hood, then cut the ties that held their hands with her knife. After they were free, she stood back in the doorway with Sadie next to her.

"Try not to get too comfortable. We'll be testing out that power of yours soon enough." Sadie's eyes were only on Ella. Then she nodded toward Ash. "And he's here to keep you in line. You seem to get all wobbly-kneed when you're around him." Her demeanor was matter-of-fact, not what Ella was used to. She had expected some kind of gloating or taunting, but Sadie wasn't putting on an act anymore. She was probably just being herself. "I don't think you'd like it if we cast an acid spell on his skin."

She and Madison left, shutting the door and locking it behind them. Their hushed voices echoed outside in the hallway as they walked away.

"I guess they still don't know I'm—" Ash started.

But Ella cut him off with a quick shake of her head, pointing around the room. She was willing to bet Trackers would have some kind of listening device placed in the room. She would've.

"They'll find out soon enough," Ella whispered. She tried to think of how to word things without giving too much away. "What is this place?" she asked, examining the room they were in.

It was a box, no more than a hundred square feet. The walls were metal with no windows and only the one door, basically a prison cell. Her face flushed with embarrassment at the fact that there was no bathroom. What if they didn't let her relieve herself? And now she had to go because she was thinking of it. How long was she going to have to hold it? Was she going to pee her pants in front of Ash? Should these even be her worries at the moment? Why was her brain like this?

Ash craned his head in all directions as if he could find something they'd both missed, then he answered her question. "I didn't think Trackers had prison cells. I thought they killed all Dis-cons on sight."

"Yeah, me too," Ella agreed.

"It's because of what you did. They're going to try to make you do it again, but in a space they can control." Ash stared at her, appearing full of sympathy.

And terror.

Because the unspoken fear between them was that when they found out Ash was a Dis-con, they'd kill him immediately.

"I don't know if I can repeat it," she confessed. "I did it to pass my Dis-con test when I was twelve and really only on small spells in class, just to divert any attention away from me."

A clank of the lock being turned, then the door swung open.

Sadie and Madison walked in, their expressions unreadable.

That was quick. What? Did they walk to the end of the hallway, then double back? Ella hadn't moved from the spot she was in when they left. Noticing their new attire, Ella realized they had simply left to change clothes.

They were dressed like proper Trackers now—armored bodysuits, utility belts strapped with Tracker blades, and heavy boots. This was what the public knew as Trackers, not high school student mean girls. Though that look suited them well too. Ella kept expecting them to have smug evil villain looks on their faces, but instead, from the careful way they moved to their quick darting eyes, they were still being cautious.

Because Ella scared them.

She wished it was warranted.

Sadie spoke first. "What age were you when you realized you could push quantum waves?" Her voice was calm but firm.

Ella decided to answer truthfully. "I was ten. I didn't know that was what I was doing until Wren told me. I thought I was more of a magnet, repelling spells rather than anything . . . well, like what I did in the parking lot." Taking advantage of their calmer demeanor, Ella begged, "Please, let Ash go. I'll cooperate any way you want me to. I'll answer all your questions, take any tests you want. He's innocent in all this. Perform a memory-erasing spell on him and please let him go. You don't need leverage." Ash was a Dis-con, so he'd be used to faking reactions to spells, like Ella was.

Madison shook her head. "No. We're not going to do that. You can say you're telling us the truth, but there's no way for us to actually know if that's true. We can't exactly cast a truth-telling spell on you, now can we?" Then an outright evil smile curved the tips of her mouth. "But we can cast one on Ash and see what he knows."

Oh no.

Turning to Ash, Madison cast what Ella could only assume was a spell that would force him to tell the truth.

Ash sighed and slumped his shoulders. His eyes met Ella's just as he made them glaze over. Exactly how she would have done it. Truth spells always made the recipient appear slack-jawed and almost comatose.

But instead of asking him questions, Sadie and Madison looked at each other, mouths slightly open, eyes wider than normal.

Then Sadie cast something on Ash—sharp, staccato, an attack spell.

Ella didn't know the spell, and Ash obviously didn't either, so he just stood there, eyes darting.

"A Dis-con," Madison hissed. She pulled out the Tracker blade from her utility belt and placed it against Ash's neck.

She was going to kill him!

"Stop! Please! Don't kill him!" Ella screamed. She wanted to leap forward and jump on Madison, but she was afraid that would only make her kill him faster.

Sadie seemed to suspect Ella's intentions, grabbing her arms, holding her in place. Ella struggled against her, but she was too strong.

But Ash didn't fight. He simply closed his eyes.

Ready to die.

Ella's heart dropped.

He'd been waiting for that moment since the day he found out he was a Dis-con. She knew because she'd been doing the same. No matter what they did, their fates would always lead them to a

Tracker who would kill them for what they were.

But Madison didn't move the blade; she kept it there like a threat. "Are you like Ella? Is that why that blast was so powerful? Because it was the two of you?"

"Yes!" Ella yelled. "He is like me. That's how we found each other," she lied. Anything to save Ash.

"We'll have to test him away from her." Sadie's voice was cold and calculating.

"Agreed." Madison placed her blade back into the belt and pulled out hand ties, then secured Ash's hands behind his back yet again. "Let's go."

Ash's terrified eyes met Ella's as he was led through the doorway by Madison.

Sadie pushed Ella away from her, and Ella stumbled from the force. She whirled around to face Sadie, but she was already headed toward the door. Before Sadie left, her strangely calm demeanor a counterpoint to her crazed behavior at school, she tilted her head to the side. "It's nothing personal, you know. Dis-cons aren't meant to exist. We're just setting the balance to the way it's supposed to be."

Okay.

Trackers really were deranged.

"Then why keep me and Ash alive?" Ella asked.

Sighing, Sadie shrugged her shoulders. "We've only found one other Dis-con like you and possibly Ash. You have your uses."

"Obviously not that useful since *Madison* decapitated Wren's mom, *Sadie*," Ella said, including their true names.

Sadie reared back slightly, but she quickly hid her shock. "Wren. She's more clever than we gave her credit for."

Without another reaction, Sadie simply closed the door

behind her, leaving Ella completely alone. Ella slumped down to the ground, leaning the back of her head against the cold metal wall.

Oh, Ash.

They'd find out soon enough that he was an ordinary Dis-con, and then they'd kill him.

Ella was never going to see him again.

Tears of pain, rage, and helplessness poured down her cheeks, and Ella couldn't stop sobbing. She knew they could hear her, probably reveling in the fact that they'd broken her. Because they had.

There was no way out of this.

She sat there crying for what felt like hours, but she had no sense of time anymore. This cold metal box only had one source of overhead lighting, and that was it. A small oval of light that her eyes kept staring at because she didn't know what else to do.

Clunk.

A square of the smooth metal floor suddenly rose up from the surface, and attached underneath it was a toilet. A toilet with a roof. Ella didn't know whether to laugh or cry at the sight, but she really had to go, so she sucked up her pride and walked over to it and did her business.

Ella's earlier fear of Ash seeing her go to the bathroom now seemed like a dream. Who cared if he saw? He was probably dead.

After relieving herself, she started to cry again. Ella couldn't seem to stop. Curling into a ball in one of the corners of the room, Ella waited for it to all be over.

A wave of comfort suddenly flowed through her.

It startled her so much, Ella instantly stood up as if she'd been attacked.

Attacked by a hug?

Because that was exactly what it felt like.

The warmth enwrapped Ella further, and her tears turned from aching sadness to pure love. She'd never felt anything like it. The closest thing she could compare it to was when her dad gave her great big bear hugs. Feeling his arms wrapped around her made her feel invincible, like nothing could ever happen to her.

What *was* this?

The sensation was so comforting, it drew Ella out of her spiral of panic and depression. She was herself again. She could think clearly.

Ella was a fighter.

She'd never give up.

As soon as Ella felt steady again, the sensation left her as suddenly as it had arrived.

But whatever it was, it had done its job.

Ella's head was clear again and she needed to think of plan to get out of there. If Ash was still alive, she had to find him and save him.

She could do this.

Ella needed to provoke the next Tracker who entered her cell so they'd perform a spell and then push it so hard they wouldn't know what hit them.

Yes.

A plan.

To keep herself alert and ready, Ella paced back and forth in her tiny cell, shaking out her arms and hands and breathing in deep.

The locks clanked at the door and her heart raced as it opened. She was ready.

Ash's unconscious body was thrown inside the room first, slamming into Ella, and they both tumbled to the floor. Sadie and Madison followed, their expressions flat and uncaring.

While still encompassing Ash in her arms, Ella moved him slightly away so she could examine him.

He was breathing.

He was alive.

Ella found it hard to swallow properly the relief hit her so hard, but at the amount of bruises and cuts on his body, her relief quickly turned to fear. They might not have killed him, but he couldn't survive much more of this. He might not survive his current wounds at all.

"Ash," Ella said gently. "Ash, wake up."

"We tested him thoroughly. He's not like you." Madison's voice cut the silence. "He's just a regular old Dis-con."

"Please, don't kill him." Ella's tears were back, but she readied herself for them to cast anything she could grab hold of.

Madison's calm demeanor changed in a millisecond as she kicked Ash's body away from Ella's, sending him flying against the wall with a loud thud.

Ash's body started to seize, his limbs jerking in unnatural ways and his teeth clenching down as if he were being electrocuted.

"Do something!" Ella screamed as she raced to his side. He showed no sign of stopping. Foam mixed with blood creeped out of the corners of his mouth.

"You see? This. This is the natural order of things. He can't be fixed because no spell works on him. He can't be healed," Madison said with a small glimmer of glee in her eyes.

Sadie landed on the other side of Ash.

Ella was surprised to see Sadie's eyebrows furrowed together in concern. Ella couldn't tell if it was a trick or not though. She said, "He's a Dis-con. Like she said, we can't cast any healing spells on him. It won't work."

The life of a Dis-con.

No help.

No solutions.

No way to save him.

A flash of blue light hovered over Ash.

Ella blinked, and it was gone.

It flashed again, this time like a grid of blue lines, pushing into Ash.

Like a spell.

It disappeared again.

But Ella suddenly knew what to do.

"Cast one anyway! I'm going to push it into him!" Ella had no idea if it would work, but she had to try something, and it seemed like this was what the blue lines had shown her.

Ash's body jerked harder, and Ella knew they didn't have much time.

"Now!" Ella screamed.

Sadie nodded and cast a healing spell at Ash.

Ella could physically feel it being repelled by his body and from her own, but she concentrated as hard as she could and pushed against the wave, forcing it into Ash's body. His seizing was less, and some of his cuts began to close. "Again!" Ella yelled.

Sadie cast the spell again, and Ella repeated what she'd done before, shoving the healing spell's waves directly into Ash's body. Her arms and legs shook from the exertion of it, but it was all worth it when Ash's eyes flew open and he sat up coughing. His body was no longer seizing, and there wasn't a scratch on him.

She did it.

He was okay.

Whatever those blue lines were, they'd shown her how to save him.

Ella's arms wrapped around Ash, and she could feel his wrap around her.

"Ella, you saved me," he said, his voice shaky.

"Very nice." A man's voice sounded from behind them.

Ella and Ash, still holding each other, both turned to see who had entered the room.

An older man in his early fifties with gray hair and a lined face stared at the two of them with a large grin. "Hello, Ella Buckley. I'm Verner Grant, and it is my pleasure to meet you."

Verner Grant. Just like Wren had told her. One of the leaders of the Trackers. But seeing him in front of her, examining her like she was some kind of prized toy, it really hit home the kind of power and money that was behind the organization.

Ella suddenly wondered if they were in the Hex Solutions building. The one where Wren said the vault was. If that was the case, then maybe there was a chance Wren could find them. Ella needed time. Time to keep both herself and Ash alive until she could figure out how to escape.

Ella positioned herself so that she was in front of Ash, her old plan still in place. She would push anything they cast at her right back at them.

"Don't worry. I don't plan on killing you . . . yet," Verner continued as he smiled, seeming amused. "You almost had us fooled, you know, faking your reactions to spells. That makeup trick with your parents was brilliant." Verner chuckled. "It was your insistence on playing *Hexsphere* that brought you down.

Hex Solutions makes the game. *We* make the game. We put the command to push on spells into *Hexsphere*, then released it into the press. It was an easy way to track players. And since we can also track search history in your internet browser, we knew that you typed in the command first, *then* searched for it after the fact. Imagine my surprise when this morning my head technician alerted me to your account. Everything fell into place."

Oh man.

Ella had walked into that trap.

And now it made sense why Sadie and Madison had been waiting for her in the school parking lot. All ruses gone. They'd known for sure what she was.

Ella thought back to every in-game battle, every fight, every command, every conversation she could remember. Trackers had heard and seen it all! They probably knew her better than her own parents at this point. And the fact that so many people played the game! Millions! The information they'd gathered over the years must've been astronomical. And with the players' permission! What people will sign away for a bit of fun . . . Ella had been no different. And even knowing now that Trackers had made the game, she still loved it. It had given her freedom, friends, confidence. So basically, the lesson to be learned was that Trackers ruined everything.

Why had she thought using that command after she discovered it was a good thing? The fact that it existed was a glaring red flag. And how did she not make the connection that Hex Solutions made the game? When Wren told her Verner Grant was a leader of the Trackers and owned the Hex Solutions building, she should have put it together. Ella had just gotten too wrapped up in actually having friends that it hadn't occurred to her.

Yet again, her parents' warning to not make friends was the right one. Even virtual friends.

Verner continued, "The Order of Eleven has voted to kill the likes of you like the last time we encountered one of your kind, despite my arguments against it." He nodded to Madison. "Bring her to me."

"Yes, Dad," Madison said and reached down, grabbing Ella's arm, yanking her away from Ash. She tugged Ella into place so that she was eye to eye with Verner.

"I'm not going to kill your little boyfriend either. But I will if you don't cooperate. Do we understand each other?" he asked.

"I understand." Every second of more time equated to hope that they could escape.

Verner smiled, and Ella recognized the family resemblance. "Good." Nodding at Sadie, he said, "Leave the boy alone and tell the others to do the same."

Sadie bowed her head in acquiesce, but Ella caught a glimpse of the horror in her eyes. She was terrified of Verner Grant. And if Sadie was terrified of someone, Ella knew he was really bad.

Verner turned to his daughter and Ella. "After you." He waved his hand for Madison to lead Ella out of the room.

As the four of them entered the empty metal hallway beyond and walked toward whatever experimental torture room they had in mind, Ella really wished that strange hug-force would find her again.

CHAPTER 36
WREN

"Wren? Wren, wake up. Please wake up."

Moira's voice called to Wren from the darkness.

Slowly opening her eyes, then immediately having to shut them from the intense brightness, Wren groaned.

"Wren, it's okay. We're safe . . . ish," Moira pleaded.

Ish?

Her stomach sank.

Wren knew what that meant.

CIU.

She opened her eyes once more and was greeted with the bright lights of a small room that had been set up as a medical recovery station. Most of the decor was white: floors, walls, ceiling, bed, furniture, except for the bright blue painting on the wall in front of her, nothing on it, just a canvas of deep ocean blue. Wren was sure it was supposed to calm her, and it weirdly did, but CIU was the last place she wanted to be.

She and Moira needed to get out and find Ella and Ash.

If it wasn't too late already.

Anger boiled Wren's blood, and she wanted to crush something.

But Moira's hand reached over, touching Wren's, and her rage quelled. "We're at the Caster Intelligence Unit headquarters. I woke up first after they healed me, and I think we can trust them."

"I figured we were here." Wren sat up in the bed, tossing the blanket aside, relieved that she was still wearing her own clothes and not some kind of hospital gown. They had obviously cast a cleaning spell on her as well, as there wasn't a speck of dried blood or dirt on her. "We gotta get out of here."

"Wren, seriously. We need backup. We only made it out of that parking lot because of Ella. Madison and Sadie took us down quickly and efficiently at your apartment. And we both know there are hundreds more where they came from." Moira leaned forward in her chair for emphasis.

Sighing deep, she let Moira's logic slowly seep in. "Well"—Wren motioned around the room with her head—"where are they, then?"

"Just waiting for you to wake up." Moira smiled.

Wren was about to jump off the bed to get this confrontation over with when Agent Malcolm Gilroy beat her to it by walking in the room. "We need to talk," he said.

"Oh, hi, yeah. We were just about to find you," Wren acknowledged, not sure exactly what to say.

Malcolm's eyes met Wren's, and he sighed. "We know you're the one who cast the plague spell."

Wren froze.

Was she under arrest?

Was she going to have to fight her way out of CIU headquarters?

"I only meant for it to hit the girl you know as Lizzie Trent. I didn't know Ella would be there," Wren spilled out, not bothering to deny it.

Malcolm paused for moment, then leaned his head to the side. "The girl we know as Lizzie Trent, huh? And are you going to tell us her real name?"

"Probably. Depends on whether you're going to arrest me or not." Wren shrugged.

"So you cast the spell at *Lizzie*, and Ella being a Dis-con changed the spell?" Malcolm surmised.

Wren's shoulders relaxed. She could tell by the way his curious eyes looked at her that he was trying to figure out what happened the day she cast the plague spell and not there to punish her. She relaxed further when she realized that if she had been under arrest, she would have been strapped down and muzzled to prevent spell-casting.

So she decided to answer Malcolm truthfully. "Ella refracted it. When my spell hit her first, it scattered and took out the whole team." Wren lowered her head at the thought of the innocent players writhing in pain. "I only wanted to hurt *Lizzie*."

Malcolm stood at the doorway, then slowly nodded his head. "Come with me. I need you to talk to the team."

Team?

If they were willing to help Wren and Moira, great, but if they expected them to take the sidelines, they were in for a fight.

"I see that look," Malcolm said. "No spell-casting. We're not cutting you out of the rescue mission. After seeing the both of you and your skills against those Trackers, we need you. Come on."

With that, Malcolm led them out of the room and down a corridor of CIU headquarters.

Wren stayed close to Moira, her presence calming Wren's nerves in a way she couldn't describe.

It was much more colorful in the hallway, though more on the beige side, but there were some pops of green from large potted plants with lots of small leaves situated every twenty feet or so. Along with the random framed paintings in between doors, the hallway was downright comfy compared to the sterile box they had just been in. Wren wasn't seeing any windows though, only doors.

"Are we underground?" Wren asked as they made their way down another corridor.

"Yes. It's better to keep our headquarters inaccessible to the public," Malcolm answered. "Up here."

"Why is there nobody here?" Moira asked.

With Wren's mind being frazzled from waking up in a strange place, she hadn't noticed, but yeah, they were the only people walking through these hallways.

Malcolm answered, "We cleared the floor. We didn't know what we were going to be dealing with when you two woke up. We've never seen fighting like you displayed, and frankly, we wanted to be able to contain you if needed."

"Why didn't you just muzzle us?" Wren asked, genuinely wondering.

"I'm still hoping we can work together on this. I didn't think muzzling you two would garner much trust."

Fair.

They still might have to escape though.

Wren moved closer to Moira so that their arms were touching.

The corner of their eyes briefly met and an unsaid agreement passed between them.

They'd take down all of CIU if they had to. They were not abandoning Ella and Ash.

They reached a large oak door at the end of the fifth hallway. "In here." Malcolm pushed the heavy door inward and held his arm out for them to enter first.

"You go first," Wren said.

Malcolm nodded and entered.

Wren and Moira had to move apart from each other as they walked through the doorway. A large dome-shaped room greeted them, with beautiful arched dark wooden beams framing the walls and ceiling, stretching to the same dark wood beneath their feet. Wrapping around half the circumference of the space was a U-shaped glass conference table that bent in perfect unison with the rounded walls. At least twenty metal chairs rested behind the table, but only two of them were taken, and Wren recognized the both of them: Agents Rosia Alvarez and Shara Gordon. From all the research Wren had done on the CIU, she knew of five other agents that were probably listening to whatever they said in that room, Director Wyatt Jayson being at the top of that list. The man who ran all of CIU.

"Wren Martis and Moira Kurt." Agent Alvarez announced their names like she was taking attendance.

Following Malcolm, Wren and Moira stood in front of Shara and Rosia. The two agents stood themselves, shaking their hands.

Rosia spoke first. "I've met you, Miss Martis, but pleased to meet you, Miss Kurt. I'm Agent Rosia Alvarez, and you probably already know Agent Shara Gordon as a fellow high school student."

This was weird.

Wren's first thought was that they really *should* be arrested.

And maybe they still would be.

A thought hit her. Maybe they already had been and this was their way of fooling them.

How did she get out of this place again?

Having a glass conference table between them was awkward because it kept them at a distance, which, Wren figured, was probably on purpose.

Rosia continued, "How did you know what quantum repellent gear each Tracker had?"

Wren was pleasantly surprised Rosia hadn't asked the obvious, which was how Wren knew repellent gear was real, so out of respect, she went for honesty again. "I've been testing both the Trackers you know as Lizzie and Rachel over time at school. I wasn't sure about all of Rachel's gear until recently, but Lizzie I tested as soon as I found her at Tristan High. I've been tracking her ever since she decapitated my mother."

Wren analyzed their faces and body language to gauge how much they knew about her. From the lack of any real reaction, she concluded that they knew about her mom already.

Obviously the boss and the person in charge of this conversation, Rosia continued, "We'll get to the Trackers' real identities in a minute, but let me be clear: we knew about your mom and Moira's sister. The Trackers did too, but you managed to keep them off guard. How?"

"I was young when they killed my mom. Lizzie didn't know I managed to break through her glamour spell and saw her face. Trackers may keep track of the families they've destroyed, but they're too arrogant to think their blank-face spells might be hacked." Wren cleared her throat. "Before I left Portland, I tricked my current Tracker spy into thinking I didn't want to move, that my dad had to for work. Once I started at Tristan, Lizzie and Rachel took over his job as my watchers. Basically, their inflated ego was how I kept them off guard. They'd never consider that anyone would hunt *them* down." Wren indicated Moira with her head. "Moira never planned to help me take down the Trackers, but when Rachel approached her and tried to recruit her to be a Tracker, she knew she had to do something. And when she found out Ella was a Dis-con and then Ash, it was a no-brainer." Wren thought she sounded like a soldier, breaking down her mission, but she didn't know how else to answer a high-ranking member of the Caster Intelligence Unit.

"Why would the Trackers ever think you'd join them, Miss Kurt?" Rosia asked.

"They knew my parents cast a memory-erasing spell on me to make me forget ever having a twin sister, so they thought it was safe to recruit me. I developed a counter spell though, so my parents' spell didn't work." Moira's voice was soft from nerves.

Wren's patience grew thin. "We're running out of time. Ella and Ash may already be dead. We have to get them back."

Rosia ignored Wren as she continued, "That plague spell was like nothing we've ever seen. And some of the spells you cast in the confrontation at Tristan High I know for a fact are classified." Her eyes pierced Wren when she said, "You were also able to change your spell signature, and your spell left residue on a Dis-con. We need to know how you did this. Full details."

Ah.

The real reason she stood there before them.

She'd befuddled the CIU.

"I'm smart." Was that too snarky? Yeah, probably a little too snarky. It got a chuckle out of Malcolm and Moira anyway.

Rosia didn't look impressed. "You'll tell us, or I'll have you muzzled and put in a cell, and no one will ever find you."

"I'd like to see you try," Wren said before she could stop herself.

"Talk about arrogant," Shara accused.

Malcolm placed his hands up in a placating manner, eyeing both Wren and Rosia. "We're here to work together, not turn on each other."

Moira finally spoke. "Agent Alvarez, my sister, Luna, was murdered in front of me and my parents. *My twin*. Lizzie and Rachel took both Ella and Ash. They're probably already dead, but I saw the way they looked at Ella when she pushed their spell back on them. They may have kept both of them alive for experimentation."

Rosia shook her head. "Ella can't perform magic, so that must have come from one of you."

Okay.

They didn't believe or understand what Ella was.

Wren didn't have time for this.

Wren's temper flowed through her like lifeblood. It was familiar; it had been her home for the last four years. "Look," she said with impatience, "I don't have time to stand here and give you lessons on what you don't know, but Ella is a Dis-con, and she can push on quantum waves when someone casts a spell. My mother was the same, and they decapitated her because they were so afraid of her power. They even took her head and body with them, so my father and I were never able to bury her. Moira and I are not going to stand here and listen to you and all your questions when Ella's and Ash's lives are at stake. Either help us or show us the door so we can get out of here."

Rosia touched her ear as if it were bothering her, but Wren knew it was because she had an earpiece in and her little revelations had obviously stirred up a thunderstorm of questions.

Malcolm's mouth had slightly dropped. "Ella can push quantum waves? This is insane."

"Not insane. True. But Ash doesn't have that power, so the Trackers are going to want to kill first and ask questions later. Our only hope is the fact that they said they wanted to use him as leverage before I was knocked out, so he still might be alive." Wren prayed that was true.

After a tense silence, Rosia finally nodded. "We want the same things." Shaking her head, she sighed. "We obviously have a lot of questions, but they can wait until after this mission. Tell us what you need."

"I have a way of finding Ella, but you're going to freak out again," Wren said.

Rosia's jaw tensed as if she almost didn't want to hear any more, but she replied, "Like I said, whatever you need. How do you propose we find her?"

"Quantum phasing."

Both Shara and Rosia froze and stared at Wren with wide eyes, and this time, she could actually hear the screaming in Rosia's earpiece.

Malcolm's raised eyebrows showed his genuine surprise as well. He grinned.

Time to blow some minds.

CHAPTER 37
ELLA

Ella wasn't sure why Sadie was strapping her down to this table since she had the arm strength of a toddler, but she seemed to think Ella would suddenly develop superhuman strength and escape.

Sadie was right about the escaping part, but it wouldn't come from Ella's arms or legs.

The Tracker also wouldn't make eye contact with her. She put on a good show of being evil at school, but deep down, Ella suspected Sadie was terrified of Dis-cons, or at least a Dis-con who could push back on spells. Why else would Madison decapitate Wren's mom?

From the way Sadie's eyes darted as she averted them from Ella's, her mean-girl act at school was exactly that: an act. Her showing an ounce of fear alone showed Ella she was a completely different person. The Sadie Ella knew would have had at least five snarky comments to put her in her place. But this Sadie was quiet, seemingly scared of Ella's abilities, but also of Verner Grant. It almost made Sadie appear human. Almost.

Madison, on the other hand, was much calmer and more "normal" here in her little Tracker lair. And from the way her eyes surveyed the room and each situation: calculating. Even now, she stood behind a glass observation window staring at Ella with an expression Ella couldn't read. It was infuriating. A mean-girl-basketball-player-popular-girl Ella could handle, but an intelligent strategic evil fighter? Ella was way out of her depth.

She guessed she always had been.

Observing the room more carefully, Ella wasn't sure what to think. In her mind, she had imagined some kind of torture chamber with spikes or needles or some kind of brain-sucking machine. But this? It was actually quite pleasant, aside from currently being strapped to a bed and all.

The room itself was a box, though three times the size of the prison Ash was still in. There were three twin beds like the one she was strapped into, with metal frames to hold the mattresses in and a pedestal leg each for support. From the placement of the joints and bolts of the legs themselves, Ella was reasonably sure the beds were adjustable, as if each metal frame and pedestal leg were an arm holding a shield.

Currently, she was lying on the middle bed, putting her in perfect view of the observation window, which took up an entire wall itself. The two walls that met at the window were filled with cabinets, white in color, very hospital-like. And the wall behind Ella's head was where they'd come in, one door, a counter with a sink, and more cabinets. The ceiling appeared to be made of light as it gave off a white glow, but it had six metal arms bolted to its surface with lights attached to their ends, two for each bed. If Ella wasn't so sure she was about to be tortured, she'd have thought she was in some kind of dentistry school.

Madison and Verner stared at Ella through the window of the observation room. Two women in lab coats stood next to them, eyeing Ella with interest.

From the way the other Trackers (they'd run into a few on their way to the lab) deferred to Verner Grant, he was definitely the leader of this particular facility as far as Ella could tell. Wren would be happy that he'd outright admitted to there being a Tracker order. And he had voted against killing Wren's mom. That was something at least. Honestly, Ella was probably alive because of it.

When Sadie secured the last leather strap over her left ankle, Ella was officially pinned down.

Sadie stood beside Ella as another woman in a lab coat entered the room. Her eyes were cold and distant as she examined Ella. "The subject appears secure," she announced.

Subject.

"We will begin simple tests on it first, then move up to more advance experiments," she told the crew watching them.

"Thank you, Dr. Nort," Verner said calmly, his voice projecting into the room through some kind of intercom speaker or spell. It could've been either, Ella guessed.

Ella had gone from *subject* to *it.* This woman obviously didn't view Ella as a human being. The sheer stupidity of the entire situation astounded her. Just because she was immune to spells, she was no longer *human* in their eyes? She should be obliterated?

"We'll start with electricity first."

Um, what?

Dr. Nort pressed a button somewhere on the metal frame of Ella's bed.

Ella's body and brain seized as an unimaginable pain hit her all at once, and her jaw snapped shut, teeth grinding. Then the rattling started, her hands, feet, arms, legs, neck all shook uncontrollably as the searing pain coursed through her like fire in her blood.

All at once, it stopped.

She gasped for breath, not realizing she'd been holding it.

Dr. Nort eased one of the lights into Ella's face, examining her closely, looking at her eyes but not into them. "Two hundred volts and a thousand milliamperes of direct current was used on the subject. No dilation and only slight foaming of the mouth."

Foaming of the mouth?

Oh yeah. She could taste it.

And a thousand sounded like a lot.

What was electrocuting her going to prove? Ella couldn't cast spells, so it wasn't like she could save herself from the pain or the shocks. Did they think because she could push back on spells, that she'd be able to push back any attack? Ella wasn't invincible.

Or did they even care?

She was only a thing for them to play with and see what happened when they poked her.

Ella struggled against the straps that held her down, knowing how useless of an act it was.

"Note that the subject is now trying to break out of her restraints after only one session," Dr. Nort said matter-of-factly.

Ella stopped struggling and looked at the observers through the glass window. Verner watched with little to no interest, along with the two women in lab coats, but Madison's eyes met Ella's, and she wasn't sure what she was reading from her. Madison definitely wasn't looking at Ella like a thing, but she wasn't exactly showing signs of caring either. But there was something there. Ella had no idea if it meant anything but—

"Again," Dr. Nort interrupted Ella's thoughts.

Like tiny knives all stabbing her at the same time, Ella's body tightened at the onslaught of electricity. She didn't go into a seizure this time, so that was progress, and Ella remembered not to clamp down on her jaw as well. It didn't hurt as badly as the first round, so her assumption was that Dr. Nort had chosen a lower setting.

The pain stopped again as she released Ella from the bolts of electricity. "Note: we doubled the volts and direct current. The subject handled the shock much better the second round even though it was twice as much voltage." Still no eye contact from the good ol' doc, but the slight curve of her lips indicated she seemed pleased.

How could doubling the amount of electricity they were attacking her with be easier to take?

Every muscle in Ella's body twitched and ached, and her fingers tingled uncontrollably.

"Also note that the subject isn't speaking," Dr. Nort observed.

Ella opened her mouth to retort and found that she couldn't form words—a bit of croaking and wheezing and that was it.

A flush of panic seized Ella but not before another jolt interrupted any worries she might have had. All the twitches in her body firmed up and trembled, then her feet and hands went completely numb.

As Ella was about to shut her eyes to block out the pain, she saw the blue lines again, like the ones that had shown her how to help Ash. They were clearer now, probably from the amount of amperage being thrown into her body—distinct blue lines like threads crisscrossing through everything, from the people, to the machinery, to the floor, to the electric waves entering her body.

The electricity still flowed through Ella's veins, and the warmth she had felt before when she was in her cell suddenly washed over her again. The comfort of that energy was stronger than the amperage destroying her body, and her head began to clear.

And that was when Ella knew . . . that energy was a *person*.

Someone. Here. Who had found a way to travel outside their body.

It was hard to describe, but Ella could sense their intelligence, their voice, and that they were trying desperately to communicate with her again.

"Show me," Ella croaked out loud.

This stopped the shock torture, and Dr. Nort's face appeared in front of Ella's, her eyes searching for something. "Show you what?" the doctor asked.

"I wasn't talking to you." Ella coughed. She was relieved she could speak again, but her vocal cords sounded like they'd been grated on glass.

"Who were you talking to?" Dr. Nort's eyebrows furrowed as she watched Ella intently.

Ella ignored her and focused back on the strings of light. They were fainter now, no longer lit up from the amount of amps thundering through her body. But they were there, and she still felt the presence of whoever this person was. Ella knew instinctively that she could trust them, though no words had been spoken. She sensed that this person couldn't speak; they could only make Ella feel their emotion or their comfort. Maybe they were a prisoner like Ella and Ash. Someone else they'd done this to? Ella didn't know, but she knew they wanted to help.

"Show me," Ella said again.

And they did.

The blue lights that connected everything doubled so that there were two layers of the lines.

Her eyes felt as if they were being forced to see a single thread that connected Dr. Nort's brain to her heart, and then the doubled line ripped.

It was instructions.

Whoever this spirt or person was, they wanted Ella to rip that single line.

Sweat dripped down her forehead as she wondered what would happen if she tore this thread. Would Dr. Nort die? Ella couldn't do that.

The comforting sensation overwhelmed her instantly, and Ella knew without words that she was telling Ella that Dr. Nort would be fine.

She.

Yes, this entity was a she.

Ella trusted her.

She concentrated on the string the entity had shown her and found that her mind could touch it, move it, do anything she wanted with it.

No more double lines now, only the single strong originals. The doubles had simply been a map.

Taking hold of the string with her thoughts, Ella snapped it in two.

Dr. Nort fell to the ground, unconscious but breathing.

As the doctor hit the ground, the string Ella broke repaired itself. It had been just enough to knock out Dr. Nort.

Screams and knocking jolted Ella out of her fascination with what she had done.

Verner pounded his fist on the window, yelling at Sadie to do something.

The blue lines disappeared, and Ella's vision was sharply brought back into focus so she could see more clearly the horrified faces of the people behind the glass.

Oh.

They're not happy.

Nice.

Sadie's widened terrified eyes were the last thing Ella saw before the Tracker slammed her fist into Ella's face and everything went black.

CHAPTER 38
WREN

"Quantum phasing is impossible," Shara said in disbelief.

"Not anymore," Wren retorted and felt the seconds they could be helping Ella slip by.

Moira stepped in. "We don't have time to stand here and convince you. I was shocked too when she told me, but she did it, and she took me with her. It's possible."

The voices in Rosia's earpiece had quieted, and she shook her head. "You are full of impossibles it seems." Nodding to Malcolm, she said, "Make sure we recruit these two after this is done."

Wren wasn't sure how she felt about that, so she veered the group back on target. "I have a suspicion that Ella and Ash are being held in the Hex Solutions building downtown. That's Tracker headquarters for Los Angeles. On paper, it's owned by three different shell companies, but I found proof that the true owner is Verner Grant. He's one of the leaders of the Tracker's Order of Eleven."

That grabbed Rosia's attention, her stare more penetrating. "We obviously need to share notes after this is over." She shook her head. "We know about Verner and four other members of the Order, but the rest are a mystery."

"I know of eight, but can't pinpoint the other three. Maybe we can put together a list of the whole Order," Wren suggested, though she could pretty much bet the four they knew about were a part of the eight she did. "And now's a good time to tell you, Lizzie is Verner Grant's daughter. Her name is Madison. Rachel's true identity is Sadie Kallum."

There went that earpiece.

Rosia tugged it out of her ear. "I can't think straight with them yapping at me." She nodded to Wren. "We obviously have a lot to go over, but let's save your friends first. I know the public doesn't know it, but you may: we don't kill Dis-cons; we recruit them."

Oh, wow.

"I figured I should say that right away so you know we have no intention of harming your friends if we can return them safely. I can't go into details, but again, you probably already know this." Rosia's jaw tensed, and her eyes never left Wren's.

She was telling the truth.

And Wren *didn't* know that. She had suspected because she'd never seen any evidence in any vault she'd broken into about CIU harming Dis-cons. She'd only seen or read about them taking them into custody, but after that, they disappeared.

Recruited.

Interesting.

"I didn't know that, but thank you for telling me," Wren responded.

"We better get started." Moira brought them back to their focus.

"Who's coming with?" Wren asked.

The three CIU agents looked momentarily startled as they obviously hadn't expected Wren to let them come along. Or probably more accurately, they had no idea how her spell worked, so they didn't know it was a possibility.

Malcolm raised his hand. "I'm down."

Shara tentatively raised hers as well. "I'm coming too."

Rosia shook her head. "I'm staying here." She motioned to the earpiece on the table. "They're going to want an outside observer for this."

Wren nodded and motioned Malcolm, Shara, and Moira to the center of the room. Shara walked around the U-shaped glass table to join them in the middle.

Wren didn't want to show them her quantum phasing spell. She'd already cast it with Moira and had figured she'd be the only one Wren would ever tell. But Ella was in trouble, and Wren was stuck there with CIU, so she was desperate. Wren had to cast it to find Ella, to see if she and Ash were still alive. There was no other way.

Her chest had lightened a bit since confessing some of what she knew to CIU. Wren seriously doubted they wanted to kill every Tracker like she did, but she did know they wanted to take the organization down, and that was enough of a connection for her to be on board. And maybe shutting them down would be enough for Wren. It wasn't as if she'd ever killed anyone before. Her rage told her she could do it with no problem, and even in the parking lot, she had almost killed Madison and herself in the process. But she had never taken a life. Wren's mind was muddled. She had gone from having no one to having friends and—she wasn't sure what she'd call CIU—co-workers?

Wren sat cross-legged in the middle of the strange domed room, and the others followed her lead. Shara Gordon sat on her left, Moira on her right, and Malcolm Gilroy straight across from her. She motioned for them all to hold hands, and Moira's touch sent goose bumps up her arm, whereas Shara's was cold and clammy. The CIU agent was obviously nervous. Wren didn't blame her. If someone she barely knew told her they were going to cast a spell to quantum phase her body, Wren would've run for the hills. With a gentle squeeze from Moira, Wren was reminded that Moira had barely known her, and yet she had jumped in with two feet when Wren cast the spell before.

"I have to bind us first," Wren said and quickly cast the binding spell at their small nods of approval.

In the corner of Wren's eye, Rosia sat behind the glass table and watched them carefully, no doubt getting an earful from her earpiece.

Wren sensed the invisible ties of the spell bind them together.

Now for quantum phasing.

Shara's hand shook lightly in hers, but Wren kept her focus. She couldn't worry about Shara's fears. Wren had to recite this perfectly. She'd done it so many times, it was like second nature to her.

When she finished casting, her second-self phased out of her physical body. From the binding spell, she knew the others had phased as well, though they couldn't see one another.

"The binding spell allows us to speak, but we're doing it inside our heads. If you think it at us, we'll all hear it." Wren thought she sounded like an expert, but she really had no idea if that was true. It had been true with Moira, but now there were four of them. She didn't even know if this was safe.

"Flying time," Wren warned them, then pulled up and out of the dome.

"Holy!" Shara exclaimed.

"Try to relax as much as you can. I've never done this with more than one person, so we have to be careful," Wren confessed.

"Careful of what?" Shara's voice caught.

Malcolm answered before Wren could. "We're quantum phasing, and Wren cast a binding spell. There's a large possibility our consciousnesses could swap when we go back to our bodies."

Wren hadn't thought of that, but he was actually right. Theoretically, that could happen.

"Try to picture your own body and your mind being in it. Moira and I have done this already, and we're fine," Wren said as calmly as possible.

Shara stopped talking, and Wren didn't know if it was because they were currently in the sky floating above CIU headquarters at night or because she was concentrating so hard on not phasing into one of them.

The building below them was a doll-making factory. Interesting that CIU felt the need to have hidden bases, just like Trackers, but now knowing they recruited Dis-cons, Wren guessed it wasn't that surprising. It took Wren a moment to gain her bearings since they were in a warehouse district she didn't recognize.

Wren asked for help. "Where is downtown from here?"

"Can I steer us?" Malcolm asked.

"I think so. Imagine yourself pushing forward. That's how I do it." Wren had to shake out the weirdness she felt at instructing people how to move while phasing.

They were moving.

Soaring over warehouses, then suburbia, and finally the

sparkling lights of the Los Angeles skyline appeared in the distance.

"I can take it from here," Wren said and pushed the invisible group toward Hex Solutions. They approached the tall windowed building, and Wren dove the group in and down through the bowels underneath.

Her instinct was to go straight to the vault, but she couldn't show CIU her secrets, not about breaking into vaults anyway. They were working with her because they'd seen her casting abilities and were impressed, and Wren was sure the only reason she hadn't been arrested for that plague spell lay solely in the fact that Madison was a Tracker. But if they knew she had broken into twelve military vaults? Wren was pretty sure their hands would be tied and they'd have to arrest her for diplomatic reasons alone.

No.

She wasn't going to tell them about the Tracker vault or any other vault.

Since Wren was always so laser-focused on the vault and had never really gotten a good look at the place, they started with the first floor, flying up and down the corridors and through the walls of the rooms facing each other.

Nothing but offices and bigger spaces full of cubicles.

They had at least five levels to go through, so after searching the first floor, they phased down into the second floor: more of the same. Just like Wren had always seen through flashes. Nothing had ever stood out to her as nefarious. But she'd never gone behind the closed doors on each level, and maybe there was a level underneath where the vault was. Wren's tunnel vision on the vault had kept her from caring to explore the rest of the Tracker facilities.

Floor three: offices.

Floor four: more offices.

Floor five.

Though Wren was not in her body, her fear and nerves were at an all-time high. They were about to enter the vault floor. And so far, she had been swallowed by what equated to a giant hug that left her sobbing. It didn't happen to Moira, so chances were high that it wouldn't happen to Malcolm or Shara either, but what about Wren? She couldn't be rendered useless when Ella needed her.

If she was even there.

Wren steered them to the west side of the floor, knowing full well that the vault was on the opposite end, to give herself some time. Upon flying through into first room, her heart stopped.

A man was strapped to a table on a pedestal arm and screamed while another man in a lab coat watched with interest, scribbling down notes. Tears streamed down the captured man's face. His screams turned to loud coughs, and he spat up blood and foam.

"We have to help him!" Moira yelled.

"We can't do anything in this form," Wren said, though she completely agreed with her.

Malcolm's voice cut through her thoughts. "He's a Dis-con."

"They're torturing them!" Moira choked.

"Worse. They're experimenting," Wren answered. It all made sense to her now. How they knew exactly where to place the quantum repellent gear. Years and years of experimenting on Dis-cons.

She couldn't watch this.

Wren pushed them through to the next room.

Three more Dis-cons were strapped to the pedestal tables, two unconscious with drool dripping in large heaps down their cheeks and the other awake but staring at the ceiling, moaning. No lab coats in there. They'd left them to suffer while they what? Took a break? Had a snack? Chatted about how the Dis-cons reacted to their torture?

Wren was suddenly glad she wasn't in her body, because she knew she wouldn't be able to breathe if she were.

It wasn't just Ella and Ash they needed to save; it was all of them.

Wren had been so wrapped up in breaking into the vault that she never even looked in those rooms! She had assumed because the upper floors were offices that floor five would be the same. She could have tried to save these people ages ago. Instead, she had let them suffer. She'd never forgive herself.

And one thing became crystal clear.

Not a single doubt in her mind anymore.

Wren would destroy them.

She didn't want to go into the next room, knowing they'd find more of the same, but she did it anyway. Ella and Ash were there. She knew it now.

They soared into the next room.

Malcolm stopped them. "It's Verner Grant."

He was right. Verner towered over Madison and Sadie, his face beet red from what looked like anger. "She's tapped into our security somehow!"

"Somehow? You *know* how." Madison shook her head, obviously frazzled.

"She? You think he means Ella?" Moira asked.

"God, I hope so," Wren said, hoping Ella had used her ability to somehow gain the upper hand over them.

Verner slammed his hand onto the wall. "Madison! I don't want to hear it! You know that's impossible. There's no way that girl could connect to our ley lines! The subject is dead. We only used her synapses for the rest!"

"Well, she figured out a way, because she dropped Dr. Nort pretty easily." Madison placed her hands on her hips.

Sadie stayed silent, and from the tenseness of her jaw and the squeezing of her hands, she was scared. Really scared.

"Do you have any idea what Verner is talking about?" Malcolm asked.

Wren didn't.

Ley lines and the synapses of a corpse? But she took a stab: "It sounds like they've built a security system out of a dead Dis-con, if I'm guessing."

"We have to kill Ella. She's too much of a threat. Her boy at least," Madison grumbled.

Verner reached down and grabbed Madison's shirt, bringing her face to his. "You need to get your killing urges under control. You hear me? You won't touch the girl or the boy yet." He released his daughter, then shrugged. "Don't worry, they'll both be dead soon enough, but I have to find out if she connected to the system."

"I think it's obvious—"

Madison's voice cut off from Wren's ears.

No.

The warmth encased Wren like it always did, finding her all the way down on this end of the floor.

It had to be the security system they were talking about.

It filled Wren with such love and comfort, her brain couldn't comprehend the feeling. It was too much. She wanted to stay there forever.

No.

Must stop.

They'd find the four of them floating above them.

This was a trap.

With all the strength Wren had, she yanked them back to their bodies.

All their eyes opened at the same time, and Wren cast the spell that unbound them and kept them from phasing again.

"What happened? Why did we leave?" Malcolm asked, confused.

But Wren couldn't answer because all she could do was sob.

CHAPTER 39
ELLA

Ow.

Ella woke, and her entire body ached, but mostly her forehead.

"Someone hit you hard." Ash's voice came from next to her.

Wait.

Ella looked more closely. Her head was in his lap, and she was staring up at his beautiful face as he gently brushed the hair from her cheek. Her heart raced at his touch, and she was grateful her hands couldn't sweat anymore. (Still not sure if that was the best idea health-wise.)

They were both on the floor of their strange cell, Ash leaning his back against the wall, letting Ella use him as a pillow. She tried to move, but her muscles were so tight it felt like she had a cement block on top of her.

"What did they do to you?" Ash asked, concern in his eyes.

She must've looked horrible.

Considering how badly her head hurt from Sadie's punch to her forehead, Ella could only imagine.

"Sadie punched me out when I . . ."

The blue lines, the snapping of Dr. Nort's string, the panic in Verner's face, Sadie's terrified expression as she hit Ella—it all came back to her in a giant flood. She sat up from the force of it despite her pains.

"There's a person—a Dis-con, I think—that's in here with us? I don't know. It's a she for sure, and she showed me things . . . strings or lines . . . They all connect, Ash. Everything down here connects . . . and I can connect with it, like her. I broke a string on a doctor that was electrocuting me, and it knocked it her out cold. She knew exactly where to attack so that I wouldn't hurt anyone." Ella shook her head, and it hurt. "I know I sound crazy, and maybe I am. Dr. Nort had fried me a couple times before then. But Verner and Madison were so panicked and scared when I took out the doctor." Ella's mind raced. "But why couldn't this entity do it herself? She knew exactly where to attack. All she could show me was where—"

Ash reached over and brushed his hand against her cheek. "Slow down. We'll figure it out." Then he motioned up to the ceiling and mouthed, *"Ears, remember?"*

Ella grabbed his hand and held on to it like it was her lifeline. "Ash?" Her eyes met his. "It doesn't matter that they can hear us. I don't think we have time."

His jaw set, and his hand squeezed hers back. "Right. What are you thinking? Can this person help? Do you see these blue lines anymore?"

Ella hadn't thought of that.

She pulled her hand away and stood, searching the room, the air, the space around them.

Nothing.

"No, I don't see them anymore." Ella's chest deflated, knowing that if Verner was listening to her, he was feeling relief at her words. "Maybe it was the whack to the head by Sadie. Let me see if I can make contact with whoever this woman is." Ella closed her eyes and concentrated as hard as she could on . . . what? She didn't know what to fixate on first. She didn't even know who or what the entity was. Was she like her? In a prison cell, but had somehow found a way to cast a spell of communication either as a Dis-con or with a Dis-con? Ella would say this was a trap set by Sadie and Madison, but the fear in Sadie's eyes had been real. Ella knew Sadie was a Tracker and they were trained to pretend to be someone else, but Ella didn't think anyone could fake that kind of terror. Sadie had known exactly what Ella had done, even though Ella wasn't quite sure herself.

After another few moments of trying, Ella breathed in deep. "We have to get out of here."

Ash stood and walked over to the door. "I've been looking for a way out ever since they took you. There are vents and that weird elevator toilet."

Ella glanced in the corner where the toilet had been before, only to find it had slunked back into the floor.

Feet clanged down the hall.

"They're coming." Ella searched the room for anything that could help them.

Ash said what they were both thinking: "They don't want you to make contact with whoever this woman is."

The footsteps grew louder, closer.

Almost there.

Ella turned to Ash, shaking her head. "What do we do?"

Too late.

The door burst open, almost hitting them with the impact.

Sadie and Madison strode in alone, holding Tracker blades in their hands.

No Verner.

But he must've been watching.

Whack!

Sadie hit Ash across the face with the handle of the blade. His body flew across the small room, slamming against the wall, slumping to the floor.

Madison shoved her arm holding the blade against Ella's neck, pinning her to the wall, instantly blocking the air from her throat. She couldn't even cough the pressure was so tight. Ella pressed her hands up against Madison's arm, desperately trying to push it off, but Madison was too strong.

This was it.

They'd come to kill them.

They'd heard everything she had said and knew she was powerless, so there was no reason to keep them alive. But they couldn't kill them with spells because they were Dis-cons, and they knew Ella could use it against them.

Madison pressed her lips against Ella's ear, then growled, "Thanks for the admission of tapping into our security system. That's a green light to kill you now."

Sadie reached up and swung the blade at Ash's chest. He jumped to his feet and kicked her in the stomach with enough force to knock off her balance before she could make contact.

Go, Ash.

Ella had seen that move before by Buster44.

Maybe they could use the skills they'd learned in-game and apply them here.

Ash went in for another kick while Sadie tried to steady herself, this time causing her to hit the ground hard.

Madison turned her head, and Ella took advantage. She remembered a move she'd made in-game and put it to the test. Ella scraped her nails down Madison's forearm.

Madison grunted in pain and loosened her grip.

Taking a much-needed gulp of air, Ella jerked her knee up, connecting with Madison's crotch.

The door was open.

They might make it out.

But Madison's evil smile indicated that Ella's kick hadn't affected her at all. She renewed her push on Ella's throat with her arm. This time, Ella's hands were there at least, one layer of protection between Madison completely crushing Ella's windpipe.

Why not use the blade though?

Sadie swung her blade at Ash, but he ducked and rolled in time.

Ash they were trying to kill.

Ella they were trying to knock out.

Ella wasn't going to let them hurt Ash. They could do this.

Blue lines formed everywhere all at once.

A surge of warmth and power flowed through Ella.

The entity was there.

Doubling the lines for Ella to study, the entity showed her the same string as Dr. Nort's on both Madison and Sadie.

Without further thought, Ella concentrated on Madison's string and yanked it in two.

She dropped to the floor.

In mid-swing, Sadie dropped as well.

Ella's eyes met Ash's, and he stood there catching his breath, eyes wide. "I saw the lines," he said. "She doubled them just like you said, and I cut Sadie's in two."

They stood there staring at one another, Sadie and Madison at their feet.

Ash could do it too.

Did that mean he could do what Ella could do?

Could every Dis-con?

The questions whirled around in her head, but she had no way of finding any of the answers.

"Do you see that?" Ash asked her.

"The blue lines? Yes, I still see them. It's what I was describing to you before."

Ash shook his head, then walked over to Ella, gently holding her arms. "No. The other lines. The white ones."

"White ones?" Ella turned her head every which way, but the blue lines were the only ones visible to her, like a grid of everything living in front of her.

"You can't see this one, between us?" Ash pointed from the top of his head to hers.

As he traced what he saw in front of him, it was as if he were drawing it on air, instantly revealing a strong white glowing string that tied Ella and Ash together from head to head.

"I see it now," Ella said.

"And the others?" he asked. His gaze darted from one place to the next.

As he said it, the white lines appeared in front of Ella. Bright white strings. But instead of the strong connection she and Ash had, these white lines were flailing, weak where they almost touched them, but stronger where they met the wall.

"She wants us to connect to the white strings by bringing them to our chests," Ash said. "You don't see it? She's showing me now."

Ella couldn't see it. She could only see the white strings. Instant doubt washed through her. "I don't see that, Ash," she said, her gut screaming at her that it wasn't the entity showing Ash these lines, that it was something else entirely. The more Ella concentrated, the more the strings of white light didn't feel like the entity at all. They felt like . . . other entities? Yes. That was it. Other beings. Maybe hijacking the woman's method of showing them they existed? Her stomach twisted with indecision.

Sadie and Madison began to stir, and sounds of feet hitting the hallway floor echoed outside their room.

The door was still open.

They needed to get out.

They were running out of time. Shoving aside her instinct to keep the lights disconnected, Ella knew they had to do something or they'd end up locked in another cell or worse. "We better do it quick," Ella said.

Ash nodded, taking her hands.

"I'm still not seeing what to do. The lights just want us to connect to them?" Ella asked, operating blind on this one.

Ash cocked his head to the side. "You really don't see what she wants us to do?"

"I don't think it's the entity that's showing you what to do, Ash. If it were her, I'd be seeing it too."

The running footsteps were almost there.

Ash tightened his grip on Ella's hands. "Pull all the lights into your chest. As simple as when we snapped the blue lines that knocked out Sadie and Madison."

Ella nodded her head in agreement

"On three. One . . . two . . . three . . ."

They used their minds and pulled every single tail end of light into their bodies.

Boom!

Every blue line of light in the grid combined with the new strong white strings, almost blinding Ella with their intensity.

Ash squinted his eyes. “I can’t see much, can you?”

“It’s too bright. I can only see the blue lines and those new white ones,” Ella answered, which solidified for her that she was dealing with two different beings. Blue was the entity she trusted, white she wasn’t so sure about. “Let’s just get out of here.”

Ella led since she seemed to be the only one able to see through the brightness to the hallway beyond. She felt like she was trying to look through the sun though, which made it difficult to determine which way to go.

Outside on their left, Ella could make out a dozen or so silhouettes charging toward them.

Right it was.

They ran, lines of the blue grid moving with them as they went.

The white strings stayed connected to them but seemed to have a life of their own as they pulled away until Ella and Ash were only connected to them by the thinnest of strands. The distance freed up her vision at least, the blue grid not hindering her view as much.

She turned, following the white lines with her eyes. They sped straight for the charging Trackers like a blazing glow-train.

Ella and Ash ran down the seemingly endless hallway, but Ella kept checking over her shoulder to observe what the white strings were doing, though it was difficult from that distance. It was almost impossible to differentiate each string. They looked like a traveling ball of lightning. All Ella knew was that she couldn't control the white lines, only the blue ones.

"Ella!" Ash whispered harshly.

Ella looked up at him. His gaze pointed behind them.

Following his line of sight, Ella gasped.

The white lines.

Their glow had filtered down enough that she could witness what they were doing.

They entered into each Tracker in pursuit . . .

And snapped every single blue string inside of their bodies.

At once, every Tracker dropped to the ground.

Ella and Ash stopped running.

Shock raced through her, and she couldn't think straight. The white lights traveled farther away from them, searching for more prey.

"They're dead." Ash's voice cut through her racing thoughts.

"Ash," was all Ella could say.

"We helped them do that." Ash's voice shook.

"Maybe they're not dead. Maybe it just knocked them out." The words came out of her mouth, but she knew it was a lie.

Those Trackers were dead.

The white strings had severed their life force.

And they were hunting for more.

Maybe she should let them.

Ella shook the thought from her head.

No.

She knew that was Wren's goal, but it wasn't hers. Punishment, yes. Death? Murder? It made her just like them.

She wasn't like that.

She'd never be like that.

And as Ella's eyes searched Ash's face and he stared down at her with utter hopelessness, she knew he felt the same.

"You were right. It wasn't her. These lights are something else. We have to stop them," he said.

"Them?" she asked.

But he was right.

Each line, each bright white string, was a person, and by connecting them, they just created an army.

"You feel it too?" His face crinkled with worry.

"I do."

Without having to say another word, they tightened their grip on each other's hands and ran back in the other direction, following the white strings in front of them.

"Should we try to disconnect them? We connected them; you'd think all we'd have to do is reverse that," Ash suggested.

"Worth a shot," Ella said as they maneuvered their way through the strewn bodies of dead Trackers.

They kept moving forward. Ella concentrated as hard as she could, envisioning disconnecting from the strings, severing the strings, jolting them loose somehow.

But they were as strong as ever.

As they headed down another hallway, Ash looked down at her, shaking his head.

"We'll keep trying. Let's just catch up to them. Maybe we need to be closer," Ella suggested.

He nodded. More dead Trackers and now a few doctors littered the floor as they hurried toward the brighter thicker lines of white light.

Finally, the lines congregated into one large area ahead of them, some kind of room.

Ella reached for the door, and they entered.

"Oh god," Ash said, his voice stunned.

Through the blue grid of lines, the most horrific sight imaginable surrounded them. A cylinder-shaped room at least a couple hundred feet in diameter stretched up five stories and was lined with glass-covered pods. Every single one had a person inside, standing in hospital gowns, hooked up to life support and IVs, eyes closed.

And the strings of white light connected to a single body each.

The lines of light belonged to these people.

"They're all Dis-cons. In comas, of course." Verner Grant's voice echoed around them. "We're not always killers, you see. Unlike your kind."

Out of another door he walked through, followed by Madison, Sadie, and about three dozen Trackers armed with Tracker blades.

The white strings of the Dis-con prisoners pushed forward and down, racing to kill everyone in the room.

Ash's hand tightened in hers.

Ella focused every ounce of concentration on the lights. Ash's light weaved with hers, and they melded into one. Together, they pushed against the white lines, holding them back. But it was temporary. She could feel the white lines forcing their way forward.

Ella grunted. "Knock them out, like before."

Ash nodded, sweat beading down his face from the exertion.

Ella concentrated on the inside of the Trackers' bodies, the small blue lines they'd used before to render them unconscious.

Verner lifted a small square device up in front of him, the smirk on his face indicating he had no clue how close he was to death as Ella and Ash held back the white lines pushing in to murder him. He pressed a button on its surface.

The blue grid disappeared, as did the white strings.

Ella and Ash were suddenly connected to nothing.

The woman entity was gone.

The comatose Dis-cons in the room were forced back into their bodies.

Madison sneered. "Can't knock us out now."

The swarm of Trackers raced toward them.

Uh-oh.

Smash! Smash! Smash!

Glass broke everywhere at once, falling down on all of them like shards of sharp rain.

Verner might have turned off the security system that had allowed Ella and Ash to connect to the blue grid and the strings of light, but those lights had returned home.

And they were awake.

Body after body smashed through the glass of their prison and dropped to the floor. Instead of Ella and Ash against an army of Trackers, their numbers grew by the second.

This was going to be one heck of a fight.

CHAPTER 40
WREN

"Whoa, did you feel that?" Wren asked Moira as they jostled forward in the back seat of the SUV taking them to Hex Solutions. The building was in sight and only a block away.

"No, what is it?" she asked.

"I don't know. Something big," was all Wren could answer. "A force of some kind. I just felt it."

Malcom drove, and Shara sat in the passenger seat, monitoring the building through CIU cameras and sensors.

Shara turned her head toward Wren. "I don't know what you felt, but something definitely happened in the building. The lower floors we searched are no longer hidden by spells. Security has lifted entirely. We can set our plan in motion now and not have to improvise like we thought we'd have to."

Wren glanced behind her at the caravan of vehicles all holding CIU Skeins ready for a fight. Buses, SUVs, squad cars lined up like a civilized army, though Wren had no plans of being civilized. She'd given their army its best shot by telling Rosia, Malcolm, and Shara in Varian the spell she'd used to break through Dis-cons and possibly quantum repellent gear. Still fully untested, but today would be the day for it.

Malcolm pulled over and parked right on the curb of the building. "Can we gain access to the stairs? Because trying to get a hundred Skeins down an elevator in shifts doesn't seem like the best option."

Examining her tablet more closely, Shara nodded. "There are two staircases and five elevators. We can raid the lower levels pretty efficiently."

"Good," Malcolm responded and exited the SUV.

Wren opened her door, and she and Moira slid out on Wren's side.

Here they were.

The place Wren had visited so many times, though never in person. The thought of being paralyzed with emotion by their security system made her heart beat faster. If it was able to do that to Wren when she was in phase form, how much harder would be in physical form?

Shaking aside her fear, Wren took a deep calming breath.

This was it.

She was going to battle.

She was going to kill them all.

Wren, Moira, Malcolm, and Shara led the way as the rest of the CIU Skeins parked on the sidewalks all the way down three or four blocks and began to exit their vehicles. They headed into the lobby. It was an enormous room and empty except for one man, who sat behind a lone security desk. Wren's shoes squeaked on the marble flooring as they walked toward what was a seemingly solid wall on the east side, ignoring the line of elevators and exit doors leading to the main staircases of the building straight in front of them.

Shara incanted a spell that erased the illusion over the wall, revealing five elevator doors and exit doors on either side.

More and more CIU Skeins piled into the lobby and situated themselves behind them, ready for orders. Out of the corner of her eye, Wren noticed the lone security guard quietly getting up from his desk and discreetly leaving the building.

Smart.

Malcolm motioned to three Skeins, then nodded toward the elevators. "See if you can use a couple of mechanical spells to get those elevators locked up. I'll give you the order when we're down there to unlock them again when we need them."

The Skeins began incanting. The elevator cables ground on the brakes as the wheels screeched to a halt.

Their large group was split into three separate teams. Wren's third headed toward the left exit, while another third went to the right, and the last third stayed behind for Trackers attempting to flee.

Malcolm led their group of thirty down the steps and into the bowels of Tracker headquarters.

Clanking and footsteps echoed through the stairwell from deep below.

Something was happening.

Wren's heart continued to race. Maybe Ella had found a way to escape? Could it be that easy that they'd run into each other somewhere in the middle?

Malcolm and Shara seemed to think the same thing as they

hurried their pace down the steps. Moira stayed close by Wren's side, not saying much, but her presence was enough to calm her somewhat.

The footsteps grew closer, pounding on each stair, racing to toward them.

Definitely an escape.

Wren's and Moira's eyes met, then focused back on the stairs ahead of them, expecting Ella and Ash to fly around the corner.

"Get ready," Malcolm said.

Though her heart wanted it to be Ella, Malcolm was right; they needed to prepare themselves for anything. Malcolm held them all back with a hand signal, and everyone paused on the steps.

Ten figures came into view as they flew up the stairs, eyes bulged, mouths open and gasping for air.

No Ella.

Other Dis-cons?

When the first one—a man of medium build and height—laid eyes on them, he glanced at Malcolm, Shara, and the crowd behind them, who all wore CIU uniforms. The man cast an air displacement spell that knocked Wren and the first five rows of CIU agents down onto the steps.

Ow.

Trackers.

But Wren and the others were up in seconds, a cacophony of CIU casters incanting spells to bind the ten Trackers coming straight for them. The Trackers kept looking over their shoulders, back toward the bowels of their facility and not to the battle in front of them. And Wren knew then: they weren't scared of them. Of thirty CIU Skeins! What would make them more afraid than that?

The binding spell worked on five, dropping them on the stairs at uncomfortable angles, but the other five must have had repellent gear on their cerebellums, because they were still moving, albeit slowly, crawling up each step. Wren's spell addition might not have worked entirely, but it seemed to work enough to throw them off. Good to know.

Finally, their first attacker whose legs and arms were locked solid said in a desperate tone, "We promise not to attack, just arrest us. Don't make us go down there!" His eyes darted, and his breathing was hard and fast.

Malcolm took the two steps to reach him and yanked him to his feet. "What's down there?" he asked.

He gasped. "Dis-cons. They're killing us all."

The public's worst fear. Dis-cons, supposedly the most dangerous beings on the planet, taking down Trackers? The second most dangerous? What was happening down there?

Malcolm motioned to two of the closest Skeins. "Unlock their legs and get them muzzled, then take them upstairs. But send the rest of the CIU team down here ASAP." His voice had a slight quaver.

It sent shivers down Wren's spine.

Agent Malcolm Gilroy was scared.

If Wren hadn't grown up with a mother who was a Dis-con with powers, she might have been scared too, but all she wanted to do was race down there and help them destroy every last Tracker. She didn't wait for CIU, and neither did Moira. They pushed past the remaining Trackers writhing on the steps and hurried down the stairs.

Wren barely heard Malcolm screaming at them to stop.

Wren didn't want to stop.

It was bad enough that she couldn't take out the Trackers up there, but there was no way she could with thirty Skeins at her back. But the ones downstairs? They were fair game. Malcolm would try to make her save them, arrest them, keep them alive.

But that wasn't her mission.

"We have to hurry if we want to give ourselves a good lead over CIU," Moira whispered next to Wren. She knew. She wanted the same thing.

Level after level, they flew down the steps, and the noises of battle grew louder as they went.

Then she felt it.

That same comforting sensation Wren always felt when quantum phasing there.

Tracker security.

But this was different somehow, not stronger like she had thought it might be. No. It was calmer, more focused.

And familiar.

Wren couldn't explain it. It was as if she knew the feeling intimately, as if it were somehow a part of her. She had no idea what to make of it. "Can you feel it? That comfort feeling?" she asked Moira as they continued to race down the stairs.

She shook her head. "It's all you again. You must have some kind of connection with their security system, probably from all the times you've come here in phase mode."

"Yeah," Wren agreed, but she was still confused. The last thing she needed right then was to break down into a sob.

Slam!

Something or someone smacked hard against the metal exit door.

They'd reached their floor.

Noises of Malcolm, Shara, and the rest of the CIU Skeins thundered above them. They didn't have much time.

"Ready?" Moira asked as she placed her hand on the metal lever of the door.

Wren nodded. Her targets were Trackers only. She didn't want to hurt any innocents by accident. Being that she'd never killed anyone before, her heart was out of control at this point, thudding in her chest, but her mind felt ready. It was time. Trackers had no problem murdering innocent people, so Wren wouldn't have a problem murdering them.

Moira turned the lever and kicked the door open with her foot.

Mayhem and chaos greeted them.

And blood.

So much blood.

Pushing through the doorway, they entered into a cluster of bodies all fighting each other for as far as she could observe in both directions armed with Tracker blades. Each side had them. Necks were being sliced open, chests being impaled—it was a living nightmare, and Wren couldn't tell the good guys from the bad guys.

No one noticed Wren or Moira as each person concentrated on trying to end the attacker in front of them with their blades. Wren heard Trackers incanting all around them, though she knew most of the spells would be useless for both sides. Dis-cons were immune but also unable to cast.

Boom!

Wren was knocked to her feet as a push of air slammed into her. Moira and the eight people next to them fell as well.

Another air displacement spell.

“Their uniforms!” Moira said to Wren.

Wren nodded. She could tell the Dis-cons from the Trackers now. Trackers in their tight-fitting gear.

And to Wren’s delight, it was the Dis-cons that smiled in triumph while chasing the Trackers, who skuttled toward the exit.

No.

Not escaping.

They’d earned their punishment, and it was time they got it.

Wren cast a body-seizing spell on the four Trackers closest to the exit and added her extra spell that would potentially push past their repellent gear. It worked on three with perfection. Each body dropped to the ground, writhing in pain, eyes bulging. The fourth, however, fell to the ground, as it had affected his legs, but the top half of his body still worked. He pulled himself closer to the exit with his arms, frantic to get away from the attack.

The ones Wren recognized as Dis-cons gave her and Moira a nod of respect, almost as if they recognized them. Instead of using their blades, the Dis-cons dragged all four bodies back to the hallway, kicking the Trackers’ prone bodies with every ounce of force they could muster. The sounds of snapping ribs and broken bones followed by blood spurting out of mouths and injuries should have filled Wren with glee.

But it didn’t.

Bile rose in her throat.

Why didn’t watching this feel good?

Why was she disgusted and a bit sympathetic to these creatures that had tortured innocents and murdered her mother?

That familiar wave of comfort hit Wren again.

It was the security system somehow giving her sympathy for the enemy. It was the only thing that made sense.

More Dis-cons and Trackers poured in from all sides, the fight ongoing, blades flying everywhere and bodies pushing into Wren and Moira.

Wren's and Moira's eyes met. They couldn't be trapped there. They didn't even have blades, not that she knew how to use one. Tightness in her throat. Every muscle tensed. Claustrophobia threatened to overwhelm her.

That comfort feeling washed over her, stronger this time.

"I know where to go," Wren said, and it was like an invisible path opened before her.

Hundreds of Dis-cons and Trackers shoved their way against each other, blades slicing, fists pounding, hair pulling, arms breaking, but Wren threw them aside like they were inanimate objects, Moira following close behind. She came with her, no questions, no talking, only trust.

Pushing their way down another hallway of chaos, Wren finally reached the door she was destined to open.

She felt it.

Whatever was behind the door had been calling to Wren for months now. The security system she must destroy. It had too much power over her, and she had no idea why.

After giving one last look to Moira, Wren opened the door and entered, then shut it behind them. The room's walls were lined with computer screens, gears, buttons, and more electronics she couldn't possibly identify.

Wren was right.

State-of-the-art security system.

"Wren." Moira's voice broke as she spoke her name.

Wren looked at her face. Moira's lips trembled, and her hands shook as she stared ahead.

Wren couldn't imagine how computer parts and a security system could cause Moira to be so terrified. "What is it?" Wren asked. Maybe Moira was seeing something on one of the screens that her eyes had missed?

She turned to see what Moira was looking at.

Her entire body seized in pain, and her breath stopped.

In front of her was a cylinder tube filled with clear gel and a severed head with curly black hair like hers floating inside, its brain connected to hundreds of wires and tubes that flowed into the computers surrounding them.

"Mom?" Wren croaked.

CHAPTER 41
ELLA

A momentary panic hit Ella as she turned and Ash was gone.

But when she craned her neck farther, he was close behind.

It was insane down there, getting lost in the hallways, pushing through fighting bodies, stumbling over bloody corpses, avoiding Tracker blades, sensing spells here and there, but not a lot they could do against Dis-cons.

Ella had almost puked several times, the gruesome spectacle too much for her.

A familiar voice rang out in the next hallway.

Agent Malcolm Gilroy.

"It's Malcolm!" Ella said to Ash as he came up beside her by elbowing a Tracker that had almost managed to punch her face. "Thanks."

Ella and Ash had barely escaped the cylinder room of Dis-Con craziness with their lives. Verner Grant had been the first to bail once his "experiments" woke up and came down for blood.

And there was a lot of blood.

It wasn't like she could blame them; Ella only had one electrocution session, and she wanted payback. Who knew how long some of these people had been there? Days, weeks, months, years of torture and experimentation with doctors like Dr. Nort hovering over their heads, treating them like nonexistent things.

No, the chaos around them was well deserved.

Her plan had been to escape, find Malcolm, and get them down there to save the prisoners. But it seemed once Ella and Ash had been taken, CIU had found a way to find them. Ella was sure Wren had something to do with it. She could've really used Wren's and Moira's special sets of skills about now.

Pushing her way down another corridor, Ella made out the top of Malcolm's head.

Ash moved ahead of her in a protective stance, which was adorable but really didn't help as there were too many bodies shoving against them. In some ways, it was lucky that it was so crowded, because hardly anyone seemed to be able to get purchase on their blades. So it was more of a fist brawl than anything else. Ella appreciated it, anyway. Severed body parts and bloody bodies wasn't something Ella ever wanted to see again.

Malcolm spotted them over the crowd, and now she made out Shara as well as they fought their way toward Ella and Ash.

Another elbow miss.

A Tracker, pinned by two Dis-cons against the wall, blade abandoned on the floor, cast a spell in desperation, knowing full well it wouldn't work on his attackers. Ella felt the wave of the spell and pushed against it. The force of her pushback hit the Tracker in the head, smashing the back of it against the wall. He slumped to the floor, unconscious.

The two Dis-cons turned to Ella, somehow knowing it was her who'd done that, and nodded their thanks. One of them picked up the fallen blade on the ground as three Trackers tackled the two Dis-cons from the side before the blade could be used.

Ella and Ash maneuvered past that burgeoning fight.

Finally, like a surreal eye in the storm, Ella and Ash met Malcolm and Shara.

Ow. A fist to the back of Ella's head.

Not quite the eye of the storm.

"Where's Wren?" Ella asked. "Did she come too?"

Malcolm shoved a Tracker who got too close to their little circle. "She raced ahead of us. I thought for sure we'd get down here and all the Trackers would be dead. Granted, a lot of them are, but it's from this . . ." He motioned to the melee of blades and fists surrounding them. "Not Wren."

He was right. Wren's mission was to kill every Tracker alive.

Ella shuddered.

Maybe she'd seen the Dis-cons slicing and dicing Trackers and wanted to let them get their own revenge? Or maybe the sight of all this blood and carnage had finally made her see reason? Or maybe when confronted with taking another human being's life, Wren realized she couldn't actually do it? Ella hoped so. Trackers were evil, but they were people. Besides, Ella would rather they lived and be locked up for the rest of their lives and be stuck with themselves and their thoughts. Death was too easy for murderers.

Malcolm continued, "She told us in Varian the added spellwork that breaks through Dis-cons and now it looks like Trackers—a little, anyway. So far, it's worked at about fifty percent capacity? Better than nothing though," he said, his tone laced with a hint of awe.

Wren had obviously impressed him.

The entity flowed through Ella suddenly. It was a joy she couldn't describe. Her knees buckled from the intensity of it. Ash caught her elbow as they both were shoved up against Malcolm and Shara by a Tracker-Dis-con fistfight.

"What is it?" Malcolm asked once they'd gained their balance while trying to avoid blades and flailing arms.

"It's some kind of person or entity. I'm pretty sure it's their security system. I don't know if you guys know this, but Verner Grant is a leader of the Trackers, and this is his facility," Ella informed them.

But she could tell from the looks on their faces that they already knew that. Malcolm nodded. "We're here to take him in. This may only be one faction of the Tracker organization, but we plan on taking it down any way we can."

"Good luck with that!" Sadie's shouting voice was close, then Ella saw her ten feet away at the other end of the sea of fighting.

Ella motioned with her head where Sadie stood, and now all four of them stared at her. Madison was next to her, lips curled into a sneer. She wanted blood.

Probably Ella's.

Sadie yelled above the noise to the other Trackers: "Focus on CIU! Torment-hexes!"

All around them, Trackers began casting, focusing on the suddenly very clear and obvious CIU agents in uniform. They must have been so distracted by their attacking prisoners, they hadn't noticed the officers.

Time to organize.

"Dis-cons, to me!" Malcolm yelled as he began to back up toward the end of the hallway.

Four CIU agents dropped to the floor, writhing in anguish.

But finally, the chaos seemed to become more coordinated, Trackers moving to one side of the hallway, CIU and Dis-cons moving to the other.

Ella was impressed that most of the Trackers no longer carried their blades because the Dis-cons had confiscated them. The Dis-cons' only weapon.

Incantations from both Trackers and CIU became the loudest noise in the hallway, and more and more Trackers and Dis-cons started to arrive from all the other hallways in the building. It was as if a message to come to this spot had been sent out and everyone had received it in their heads.

Bodies dropped on both sides, CIU and Trackers alike. Only the Dis-cons weren't affected. Dis-cons were crouched, blades in hand, ready to pounce again.

The sensation was back.

Even with the switch turned off, this entity still was connected to Ella, to this place.

A sudden flash of lights formed when she blinked.

It disappeared when she tried to focus on it, but it was there when she blinked again.

White lines like before.

But even though they were white and not blue, Ella was sure that the entity was showing them to her.

The light of each and every Dis-con.

And it was strong where she stood.

More Trackers joined Sadie and Madison and began to

outnumber CIU two to one.

Ella's heart fluttered like crazy from all the spells being cast around her.

Energy.

Strings of light.

The quantum waves smashed against her like the ocean breaking against a wall.

Blink.

Lights connecting.

Blink.

Pushing against that force.

Blink.

Ella knew what she had to do.

Ella grabbed Ash's hand, then with her other hand, a Dis-con next to her. She nodded for both of them to do the same with the other Dis-cons. No words were spoken. They all understood. Dropping the blades they held, they replaced them with the hand of their neighbor.

As each hand clasped together, Ella could feel the connection growing stronger. They were becoming one, united.

Open.

It wasn't only her.

She wasn't special.

All Dis-cons repelled quantum waves; Ella had just happened to stumble across how to do it.

Now, with the help of this entity, Ella was about to teach every single Dis-con in that facility how to gain their power back.

Ash's eyes met hers. "I can feel the spells pushing against us."

"We all can," Ella said.

And she swung her head around to look at every Dis-con

near her. Their bright expressive eyes said it all. In her peripheral vision, Madison's eyes grew round, obviously suspecting what was about to happen. She turned to leave.

"Now!" Ella screamed with complete faith that the Dis-cons knew what she was asking.

They did.

A push stronger than any she'd ever experienced flew out of their bodies, enwrapping the quantum waves of spell-casting all around them.

As one, they slammed the force into the Trackers' bodies.

Every single one of them dropped to the ground, unmoving.

Ella's eyes searched for Madison and Sadie. Sadie was on the ground motionless, but Madison was nowhere to be found.

Malcolm whirled around to Ella, shock and terror in his eyes. "You didn't . . ."

"Kill them?" she finished his accusation. "No. They're just unconscious like at the high school. But Madison got away. I don't see her here."

Shara's quick check of a few pulses proved Ella right. "She's right. They're all knocked out cold, like they were at Tristan High."

All the Dis-cons let their hands separate, breaking the connection.

Ella looked up at Malcolm. "I'd get them all out of here and to safety."

"Safety? I feel like we could use their help down here." Malcolm shook his head in wonder. "Did you do this to them? Or can they do it on their own?"

"All I know is we did it together but that the entity helped. I have to find it. I'm pretty sure it's a person. A woman. I have a feeling that's where Wren is."

CIU agents cast healing spells on their fallen numbers, bringing them all out of the Torment-hexes. They healed the Trackers with stab wounds as well, but moved past the Dis-cons who were bleeding to death.

"You can fix them," Ella said, distracted by the CIU agents not helping the wounded Dis-cons.

"Spells don't work on them." Shara shook her head, genuine sympathy in her expression.

Ella motioned to a few of the Dis-cons near her. "You can help the CIU agents save your friends."

The Dis-cons nodded, their submissive body language showing Ella a kind of reverence. "Show us," one of them said.

Ella kneeled down next to a Dis-con whose arm had been severed at the elbow. He was weak, having already lost so much blood, but he held on to his arm as if he could stop the bleeding by squeezing it shut. She motioned to Shara, and the agent sat down next to Ella and the injured Dis-con.

"Perform the healing spell you'd use for this kind of injury," Ella instructed.

Shara's eyes couldn't hide her skepticism, but she incanted the spell all the same.

Ella pushed the spell into the Dis-con as she had with Ash when he'd been injured. The arm began to cauterize around the edges.

"Again," Ella said.

Shara cast the same spell.

Ella pushed it into the arm until it cauterized fully.

Everyone except Ash and Ella stared at the healed Dis-con with complete and utter shock.

Ella made sure both CIU and Dis-cons focused on her. "It may take a few times, but do what we just did. Cast and push, cast and push. Got it?"

A group of nodding heads answered her, and CIU and Dis-cons got to work healing the Dis-cons around them.

Malcolm stood with his mouth slightly agape. "This is . . . This changes everything."

"Malcolm, I have to go find this entity and Wren." Ella didn't have time to indulge him.

Malcolm shook his head to snap out of his awed stupor. "Yes, of course. You go. I'll assign some agents to take these people to safety." Then he looked at the hundred or so unconscious Trackers. "We'll get them muzzled and cuffed, and then we'll get some gurneys down here so we can levitate them up the stairs."

Ella grabbed Ash's hand, ready to leave.

Gently touching her arm, Malcolm said, "Be careful. If Madison and Verner Grant are still down here, they'll be dangerous. I want to take them both in alive so we can show the Trackers we can take down their leaders too."

Ella nodded as she pulled away from him, leading Ash toward where she felt the entity pulsing. That was what the entity felt like at this point—a solid pulse, like a beacon. Ella was determined to save her and get her out of this place. She already knew the entity could teach her so much. Ella needed that. She loved her mom, but her mother had always taught Ella to hide who she was. This woman—whoever she was—could show Ella how to use her power for good, like she did healing Ash and those Dis-cons. Ella's heart sped up at the thought. A real mentor. She'd never dreamed it was possible.

Shoving the thoughts down so as not to get ahead of herself,

Ella followed the pulses until they reached a smaller, empty hallway.

She was there.

Ella could feel it.

They arrived at a closed door, and she stared up at Ash before she opened it.

His eyes were round with wonder. "I feel her too."

A rush of blood traveled to her cheeks.

Finally, Ella could meet the woman who'd saved them.

And Ella was hoping to return the favor.

Ella and Ash separated their hands as she pulled the lever of the door and they entered.

Wren and Moira stood there, unmoving, and for a moment, Ella thought they'd been paralyzed by a spell.

"Wren?" Ella asked, wondering where on earth the entity was as the room was only full of electronics and screens.

Wren turned to Ella, her eyes filled with tears. "Ella," she choked. "You found us."

Ella nodded. "I was following some kind of entity. I thought I'd find a woman in here. I'm pretty sure they're using a Dis-con as their security system."

Wren choked a sob, and Ella had no idea what was going on. "You were right." Wren turned her head back and motioned to something resting on top of one of the shelves. "It's my mom."

Ella saw it now.

The cylinder.

The head.

The wires.

Ella gasped. "Oh, Wren."

Wren fell into her, sobbing. Ella clung to her like they were each other's salvation. Wren's mom. Here. Decapitated. Used for the same power Ella had discovered in herself. Half-alive, half-dead. Her chest nearly burst from tightness, realization hitting her hard.

Ella couldn't save her.

The blue lines appeared in front of Ella again, right over Wren's mom's head. A single blue string, the brightest of them all, connected the floating head to the computers around her. The lines doubled like before and showed Ella where to cut: right down the middle of the brightest light.

Ella's heart crushed knowing what had to be done.

She knew now why Wren's mom had lured her here.

She wanted to die.

CHAPTER 42
WREN

Wren couldn't.

She just couldn't.

How?

Why?

How?

I . . .

Ella's arms were all Wren could feel around her, stabilizing her in some tiny way.

Right foot.

Left foot.

Right foot.

Left foot.

She wasn't moving though.

What was happening?

"Wren? Your mom is showing me how to shut it down." Ella's

voice was warped and echoed against Wren's ears.

Shut what down?

"She needs you to let her go," Ella choked through tears.

No. No. No. No. No.

Wren pushed away from Ella, darting to the wall where her mother's head was to stand in front of her. "Don't you dare come near her!" Wren screamed. "I'm taking her with me! I can fix her!" What was she saying? What was she doing? Wren's base instincts had kicked in, and she had to protect her mom because she wasn't able to protect her then.

Wren fell to her knees, covered her hands over her face, and sobbed, her body racked with each gasping choke of air.

"She's been here the whole time!" Wren screamed. They'd know she was a monster now, leaving her mother in this place to become some kind of security experiment. Wren may not have known, but she *should have.*

"It's not your fault." Moira pulled Wren's hands away from her face, kneeling in front of her now, tears streaming down her own cheeks. "God, Wren, no one could have known this. No one."

"I should have! I should have! I should have!" Wren couldn't stop yelling it. She couldn't stop thinking it.

Wren leapt to her feet and plastered her forehead against the wall of the cylinder, staring into the dead eyes of her mother. "Mom!" Wren screamed at the unmoving head. "Mom!" Wren placed her hand on the glass, palm out. "I'm so sorry," she cried. "Mom, I'm so sorry." It was barely a whisper.

Suddenly, a wave of comfort and love washed through Wren, just as it always had when she'd try to break into the vault.

It was her mother the whole time.

She was still in the preserved head somewhere.

Wren's mom was still there.

No wonder Wren was the only one to feel the sensation of comfort and love when coming there through phasing. Her mother had been trying to communicate with her. Trying to let Wren know she was there. Screaming for help and Wren was too stupid to understand it.

Ella walked up beside Wren, placing her hand on her shoulder. "You feel it too?"

Wren peeled her forehead and hand away from the glass to look at Ella.

Ella continued, "Like a comforting hug."

Another choke of tears hit her hard, but Wren nodded. "She gave the best hugs." Her voice was hoarse and cracked from the screaming and crying.

Ella's arms were around her again, and she embraced her back. Ella could feel her mom too. Her mother must've trusted Ella and cared about her to do that.

No.

No!

Wren pushed Ella back. "How could you want to murder her when you know she's still alive in there?"

Tears flowed down Ella's cheeks. "I don't want to, Wren. But she's showing me how. She protected me when they were torturing me down here. She showed me how to stop them then, and she's showing me how to let her go now. She can't live like this anymore. She wants to move on. She doesn't want to be this." Ella motioned to the cylinder.

"I have to try," Wren pleaded. "I have to!" She shook her head, not wanting to hear Ella's reasoning or the fact that it was her mother's wish to die. "I let them take her! I could have saved her!"

Ella reached out and grabbed Wren's hand, squeezing it tightly. "Wren, she was decapitated. They animated what was left, and yes, a part of her is still alive in there, but she's gone. Let her be at peace."

"I can't," Wren whispered. "I just can't."

Ella turned Wren to her, forcing eye contact. "Wren. It's what she wants. She brought you here to say good-bye."

The warmth hit Wren again, so overpowering that her body collapsed to the floor. She fully felt her mother's embrace now, knowing exactly what it was and why it had always left her in tears.

Wren looked up at the cylinder. "But I love you."

The warmth intensified, and Wren could almost hear her mother saying that she loved her too.

Ella kneeled down next Wren. "She's ready, Wren."

Wren stared at Ella, terrified. "I'm not."

"I know," Ella said. "But it's time." She brushed her hand over Wren's cheek.

Wren's insides squeezed in ways she'd never felt before.

But Ella was right.

She couldn't let her mother live like this.

Not when she could do something about it.

Wren nodded her head.

Ella stared up at the cylinder.

Snap.

Wren's body shuddered.

The feeling of comfort disappeared.

Destroyed.

The aching absence of it crippled her.

Her mother was gone.

Truly gone.

Madison appeared in the doorway, holding a small device in her hand. "I came to finish the job." She pressed the button.

Boom!

Wren's entire body jumped at the sound.

The cylinder.

Wren's head turned.

Tiny bits of flesh in a thousand pieces floated to the top of the gel in the cylinder, the wires drifting uselessly with nothing to connect with.

"You . . ." Wren could barely form words.

Madison smiled as she surveyed the four teenagers in front of her. "My father can't have the most powerful Skein he's ever seen on top of her game, now can he?" She pointed at Wren like a jealous sibling. "My father thinks what you did with that add-on spell is genius. He thinks it might be able to fully penetrate repellent gear in the future, though I seriously doubt it. And like the coward he is, he left for a secure position as soon as the freaks got loose."

Madison's words floated around Wren, but she couldn't comprehend any of them.

Wren was broken.

She was finally broken.

To lose her mother a second time . . . The last shred of sanity left her entirely.

Wren was vaguely aware of Moira casting a spell next to her. Madison cast at the same time, and the two spells hit each other midair, dispelling in a giant boom.

Madison laughed. "You're fast, but not fast enough." Madison cast a short staccato spell, and Moira hit the ground, body seizing.

Moira's eyes rolled back in her head, and she choked up spittle from the corner of her mouth.

Moira.

Ella and Ash kneeled at Moira's side, desperately trying to prop her head up, to help her while she coughed. Ash screamed something at Madison, angry, fierce.

Ella yelled at Wren to cast a healing spell.

Moira was going to die.

Wren's heart pounded in her chest, beating so loud it awakened every cell in her body.

Moira was going to die.

Blood pumped wildly in Wren's veins.

No.

She wasn't.

Words flew out of Wren's mouth, words she'd never spoken before, but only thought of.

She was no longer sad.

She was furious.

Rage burned through her like oxygen, feeding her, nurturing her.

Finally, Wren was able to face her mother's killer.

And finally, she could tear her to pieces.

Wren finished her incantation, and the spell hit Madison's entire body like a blast of lightning. Madison slammed against the wall of the room, short-circuiting half the monitors and computers in a fireworks display of sparks and broken glass.

Madison's eyes were round with terror.

"You took everything from me!" Wren screamed and incanted the same spell, this time with more precision in her tone.

Crash!

Plaster and cement smashed into pieces as Madison's body blew a hole straight through the wall. The sound of her bones breaking as she landed on the floor of the hallway beyond was music to Wren's ears. Madison's cerebellum had quantum repellent gear, so she couldn't break her bones with a spell, so she'd broken them with the building instead.

Through the newly made hole, Wren watched her try to crawl her way to standing, though her right shin bone protruded out as a jagged shard of white against the gushing red of her blood.

Wren stepped through the hole as Madison quickly cast a healing spell on her leg, the bone pushing back and her skin knitting closed. Madison scrambled to her feet, incanting another healing spell to her ribs.

No.

Wren cast a bone-breaking spell anyway but combined it with her experimental spell to push past the quantum repellent gear, a flash of rage and inspiration giving it a slight tweak.

It worked.

Every bone in Madison's body snapped loudly, echoing in the empty hallway. She screamed and fell to the ground once more. Madison started to cast another healing spell, but Wren countered it with a mouth and throat muscle-locking spell so she couldn't speak.

Wren walked over to her writhing body and stood over her head. "You turned me into this. I saw you laugh when you decapitated her! Then you brought her here and tortured what was left of her?"

The words flew out Wren's mouth. She was going to kill her mother's murderer. She was finally going to destroy the woman who'd destroyed everything Wren had ever loved.

Before the final words left Wren's mouth, Ella hit Madison on the head with a fallen piece of wood from the hole in the wall, knocking her broken and destroyed body unconscious.

Wren stopped incanting, whirling on Ella in anger.

Ella said, "Don't become her, Wren. Your mom wouldn't want that."

"You don't know what my mom would want! And no one will *ever* know what my mom would want!" Wren screamed, then turned back to Madison's still body. She could still kill her. Wren began to incant the spell again.

Ella tried to yell above Wren's voice. "Actually, I do know what she would want, because whatever was left of her could have killed every last one of the Trackers with a single thought but chose not to."

Wren stopped casting but pushed Ella aside, not wanting to hear what she was saying. "I'm not her. They need to die, Ella."

Reaching forward, Ella touched Wren's arm. "Are you going to let Moira die, then? For your vengeance? She's still seizing in there while you stand over this monster trying to kill her. Ash and I can't save her. Who are you, Wren Martis? Decide now," Ella said with authority.

Moira.

Wren raced to the security room, all thoughts of killing gone. Madison had hit Moira hard with a spell, and Wren had just left her there! Ella was right. This couldn't be her. Moira was all she had left.

Wren cast the healing spell, and Moira's seizures stopped, her body limp. "Moira!" Wren yelled.

Was she too late? Did her need for vengeance destroy the only person she loved?

Because Wren did love Moira.

With everything that she had.

"Moira, please don't die. Please." Wren cradled her in her arms, casting another healing spell, but Moira's eyes were still closed. "Please wake up," Wren cried into her ear.

Moira coughed awake, eyes opening, arms quickly embracing Wren. "Leave a girl hanging, why don't you?" She smiled weakly.

"Oh, Moira." Wren sighed in relief, hugging her as tightly as she could.

Moira's grin was stronger now. "A little air here."

Wren smiled as she gave Moira a chance to breathe.

"Sorry to break this up, but we have to get out of here." Malcolm poked his head through the gaping hole in the wall. "I don't want to know how this happened, though I'm sure it has something to do with Madison Grant's unconscious bloody body out here."

"She's lucky I went easy on her," Wren said it and meant it. If it hadn't been for Ella, there was no doubt in Wren's mind that Madison Grant would be dead. "You can thank Ella for that."

All Wren wanted to do was sit there with Moira and not have to think about what had happened. Malcolm didn't even know about her mother and what Verner Grant had done to her. Wren wondered if Ella would tell him.

Boom!

The ground shook, and plaster dust drifted from the ceiling.

"Like I said, we gotta get out of here. Most everyone is evacuated, but I came to find you four. And an unconscious Madison is a bonus." Malcolm motioned to someone in the hallway. "Heal that monster and secure her. We're taking her in."

That was all Madison Grant had coming to her? She was being arrested? With her father's money, she'd be out by morning. Maybe killing her wasn't off the table yet. Wren would wait though. See what happened first.

Through the hole, Shara and another CIU Skein escorted a now conscious but muzzled and handcuffed Madison down the hall. Her bulging eyes glanced into the room to meet Wren's. Even from there, Wren saw Madison's body trembling. She was terrified.

Good.

Wren hoped she'd inspired the same fear in Madison that the Trackers had caused in every Dis-con to ever live.

Malcom noticed the look, then nodded toward Wren in appreciation. "Never thought I'd see a Tracker like Madison scared of anything." Then he smiled. A genuine smile. "Good job."

It caught Wren off guard, and she wasn't sure if she smiled back, but at least she wasn't snarling.

Boom!

Glass rattled, then shattered from the windows in the nearby rooms.

"Right." Malcolm motioned for the four of them to come outside again. This time, Wren and the others complied. "We gotta take the stairs. The elevators are already demolished."

"What is happening?" Ella asked.

Malcolm led the way down the empty hallway as the ground shook from a third boom and the door next to them popped out of its frame from the jolt. "Some of the Dis-cons didn't trust that we'd shut down this lab, so they're blowing it up," he informed them. "I can't say that I blame them. Shara spelled through some of the files, and these people have been through more torture than I could ever imagine. They want to make sure it never happens again."

A soft vibration buzzed in Wren's jeans pocket. She pulled out her phone. There was a text: *Don't panic. I'll meet you all at the stairs.*

It was from Moira.

Wren whirled around, and Moira was gone. How? When? Where? Too many questions. But she didn't want to alert Malcolm either. Whatever Moira was doing, she obviously felt it was important enough to risk escaping before the Dis-cons destroyed the building.

Wren wondered why Moira wouldn't have wanted her to go with her.

Her heart pounded in panic.

Because Moira knew Wren could cover for her. She needed to cover for her. Breathe. Calm. Right foot. Left foot.

From the tenseness of Malcolm's shoulders, Wren could tell he was too focused on getting them all out safely to notice Moira's absence.

Boom!

They all struggled to stay upright as the floor cracked in front of them. Another door exploded outward.

"How are they doing this?" Wren asked, trying to keep Malcolm focused ahead and not behind. Wren examined the damage around them. It looked like some kind of earthquake spell. But they were Dis-cons.

Malcolm answered, "All the Dis-cons we found here are like Ella and your mother now, Wren. Ella somehow showed them how to trigger their power. It looks like Ella and your mom stumbled across their gifts by accident. The Dis-cons are outside on the sidewalk pulling from every spell around them and pushing the quantum waves back into this place."

That almost stopped Wren in her tracks, but as the track she was walking on just opened up into a giant crack, she kept walking. Ella's eyes met hers, and she looked spooked by the news.

Texting Moira on her phone, she typed: *We're almost to the stairs. Whatever you're doing, finish it and get back here.*

As if responding to the text directly, Moira was suddenly by Wren's side, as if she had never left.

Wren mouthed, "*Where did you go?*"

Moira shook her head with a look that said she'd tell Wren everything later.

"I've got twenty Skeins protecting the staircases upstairs, but we have to hurry. We gotta run up five flights. You ready?" Malcolm said as they raced the rest of the way to the door leading to the stairs.

Boom!

The wall collapsed on top of them.

Wren spelled the debris off their bodies.

"Is anyone hurt?" Wren asked.

Grunts answered her, and heads shook in the negative.

Malcolm swung the door open. "Now!" he yelled.

They all scrambled to their feet and leapt through the doorway. As the door clanged shut behind Malcolm, the hallway floor that they had just stood on collapsed into an abyss.

Time to run.

CHAPTER 43
ELLA

Malcolm slammed open the exit door to the lobby, and Ella and the others spilled out like the staircase was on fire. The lobby was empty, everyone outside looking in. Large cracks opened the marble flooring in front of them as the Dis-cons outside pushed the quantum waves of every spell around them into the ground and the five floors of hell below.

One thing Ella was sure the Dis-cons didn't realize or, more likely, didn't care about: when the foundation of the building was destroyed, the whole thing would collapse.

Racing outside, they joined the growing crowd. The majority of the CIU Skeins pushed cuffed and muzzled Trackers into the surrounding vehicles, ready to drive them to prison.

Ella suddenly noticed that her heart wasn't fluttering.

With the amount of spells the Dis-cons were gathering, she should've barely been able to walk. But somehow, pushing back against spells seemed to steady her heart.

A CIU Skein ran up to Malcolm. "We can't budge the Discons' grip on the quantum waves. We managed to get everyone out of the building, but we need to evacuate this area in case the building falls."

Malcolm shook his head. "Evacuation won't save everyone. We need to keep the structure in one piece when the bottom floors collapse. I need a Skein at every corner to spell the building to stay together so it'll sink down. We can't have this thing break apart."

The agent nodded and hurried off, grabbing a handful of Skeins and barking orders.

Turning to Ella, Ash, Wren, and Moira, Malcolm said, "You four get into one of those vehicles and get as far away from here as possible." He didn't wait to see what they'd do as he ran off to help the other Skeins with keeping the building in one piece.

Ash motioned to one of the CIU buses with his head. "Let's go."

Ella's eyes met Wren's.

Wren wasn't coming.

Confirming Ella's suspicions, Wren said, "We're going somewhere they can't find us." She bit her lower lip as she glanced at Moira.

But to no one's surprise, Moira nodded. "You guys should come with us."

The building slammed down as if a hammer had smashed it into a hole. From Ella's count, over twenty Skeins cast at the walls, windows, and steel frame, keeping the monstrosity together so it didn't collapse, but the cracks and fissures were deep and irreparable. There wasn't much hope for the building, but at least because of the Skein spellwork, no one would get hurt.

The Dis-cons were finished with their task.

And they ran.

It was such a shocking move that a part of Ella wanted to join them. Did they know something she didn't?

No.

Ella trusted Malcolm.

Maybe she shouldn't have, but she did.

Flutters were back.

Dis-cons left, and now with the massive amount of spells being cast, her heart couldn't catch its rhythm. Definitely connected. Who would she even talk to about this?

Ash grabbed his chest. "Uh."

"Heart skipping beats?" Ella asked.

He nodded, looking at her for answers.

She shook her head. "It must be connected to our abilities. I just don't know."

"It's horrible," he said, rubbing his chest.

"Welcome to my life," Ella said.

The ground beneath them shook from the impact of the settling building, and the CIU vehicles began to pull out and peel away from the scene in case it broke apart.

The rumbling grew less and less though.

Wren touched Ella's arm. "Please, come with us. CIU won't kill you, but now that the world knows that Dis-cons did this . . ." She looked over at the considerably shorter building hanging on by a thread. "Things won't get easier. They'll get harder. The public may have hid their heads in the sand before, but they won't now. They'll side with the Trackers."

"She's right," Moira agreed. "We can protect you."

"I can't," Ella said, surprising herself. She turned to Ash. "But you should go with them. I don't want to be responsible if I'm wrong about Malcolm. But I trust him. I can't explain it, but I do."

"Then I trust him too." Ash stared at Ella, eyes intense. "And if you think I'd ever leave you, you're insane."

Ella's cheeks burned.

Another jolt from the building as it shifted yet again, but this time with finality.

The rumbling stopped.

The Skeins continued to cast, knitting up cracks and crevices, making the mess of a building stronger and more solid.

Ella turned to say good-bye to Wren and Moira, but they were gone.

Her chest tightened, but she knew they couldn't stay.

Wren's mission was to take down the Trackers, and this was only one facility. Ella hoped Wren no longer wanted to kill them, but after what Wren had just witnessed with her mother's head? She wasn't so sure. Ella's whole being ached at what Wren was going through.

"They'll be okay," Ash said as he nodded toward the CIU bus.

"Yeah," Ella agreed, but she worried.

They walked onto the bus and sat on the front bench behind the driver's seat. Except for a few empty benches in the front, all the other benches were full, mostly with CIU Skeins, but there were a few bound and muzzled Trackers as well.

As the hinged door was about to accordion shut, Malcolm slid in and sat on the bench across the aisle from them. "We'll have a team out here to take the building apart piece by piece and see what we can eventually excavate from the Tracker facility. Maybe some of their spells from the vault will have survived." He spoke as if they were fellow CIU agents. "From the files Shara found, it looks like Verner Grant was acting without the permission of the Order of Eleven. They won't be happy with him."

The bus door closed, and it drove away from the building.

Malcolm searched the bus. "Where are Wren and Moira?"

"They don't trust anyone," Ella said, tightening her grip on Ash's hand.

Sighing, Malcolm nodded. "I guess I should have figured."

A low murmur of voices mixed with the loud roar of the bus's engine caused Ella to have to raise her voice for Malcolm to hear her. "Are you going to hunt them?"

Ella hoped she hadn't made a huge mistake getting on the bus.

Malcolm reared his head back. "Hunt? No. We may try to find them, but we're not Trackers."

Ella was nearest the aisle, so Ash leaned forward, still holding her hand. "What are you going to with us?"

Taking another deep breath, Malcolm said, "I want to recruit you to the CIU."

What?

"Like agents? We're only seventeen," Ella said before she could process what Malcom had offered.

"Yes, you two are young, but that's what the CIU does when we find Dis-cons. We recruit them. If you two hadn't tried to fool the Dis-con test when you were twelve, you would have figured out that we're not only here to protect you, but to give you purpose. To help people and other Dis-cons. Our Dis-con units make up a very elite branch of the CIU and have helped this planet in so many ways no one even knows about." Malcolm shifted to sit on the edge of his bench so now his whole body faced them. "It's a lot to process, but we've never seen anything like you. We would love you on our team, but we also need to keep you safe."

"What about the other Dis-cons? The ones that destroyed the building and ran away?" Ash asked.

"And why did you guys let them do that? They could have hurt a lot of people." Even though Ella understood the Dis-cons needed to destroy their prison, it was irresponsible and dangerous.

"My people up on the surface tried, but they were too powerful. All we could do was keep the building contained. Either way, we just sent a huge message to the rest of the Tracker organization. Their days are numbered." Malcolm leaned his shoulder against the back of his bench. "As for the Dis-cons' powers? I'm going to need you to help me help them. Years of torture may make them do things like what they just did with the building. We're going to have to find them and assess their threat level. Will you guys help?" Malcolm's eyebrows furrowed with hope.

Ella wasn't sure how to respond.

Was he asking them to track down other Dis-cons and capture them? And if he was, was she okay with that?

"I know it sounds bad," he said after their apparent silence, but then added, "Let me put it this way: if we don't find them, the Trackers will, and they will kill them on sight. No more experiments."

He was right about that.

And if Ella and Ash were involved, then Ella could make sure to keep them safe.

Because she knew her power now.

And she'd use it to protect others like her.

Ella looked up at Ash, and he nodded his agreement.

Turning back to Malcolm, Ella took a deep breath. "We're in."

CHAPTER 44
WREN

"Do you see her?" Wren asked Moira as they hid behind a parked car in an alley overlooking the building and the mayhem surrounding it.

"No. Maybe Madison is already at CIU headquarters. I used a listening spell on Shara when she reported everything that had happened at the facility, and she said Verner Grant escaped. They couldn't find him anywhere," Moira said.

Wren nodded. "He's at the top of our list of people to hunt down. We'll have to find out for sure where they took Madison though."

They kept their position in the alley behind the parked car, and Wren hoped the owner didn't come rushing back to take away their hiding spot.

"We can't stay here long. CIU will be looking for us," Moira said, as if reading Wren's thoughts.

"You think we might be able to work with them? Ella seems pretty convinced they're the good guys." Part of Wren wished she had yanked Ella away and taken her by force for her own safety. But Ella had to make her own decisions. And at least she had Ash.

"She might be right, but we can't be certain. Better to observe from a distance," Moira answered.

"Yeah," Wren agreed. "But we can trust her and Ash, at least."

"And they'll give us eyes and ears directly into CIU."

Wren thought they sounded like soldiers. And she guessed they were. She thought back to first arriving at Tristan High and not knowing what to make of Moira Kurt—an overachiever, Skein-level teenager who wanted to talk to her for some reason.

"We can't go back to our houses. You know that, right?" Wren said.

"I know. Our families are safer that way."

Wren squeezed her hand. "I'm going to leave the memory spell in place on my dad. I hope me leaving won't be enough to untangle the spell, but he's better off without me."

Moira blushed slightly. "No one is better off without you."

Wren blushed as well, a small smile tugging at her lips.

A sudden flash of a thought hit her.

She turned to face Moira. "Um," was all she could get out.

Moira tilted her head to the side. "What is it? You look like you saw a ghost."

"I'm not sure if I should say," Wren admitted.

Moira took her hand, and together they squatted down behind the car so they were completely out of view, facing each other. "You cannot leave me hanging like that."

"The thought of getting your hopes up and then crushing them if it's not true? I shouldn't have said anything." Why did she even bring it up? Wren should have kept the thought to herself until she could research more.

Moira squeezed Wren's hand. "Tell me. I can handle it. You're seriously freaking me out right now."

She was right.

There couldn't be anything between them. Not if they were going to take down the Trackers together.

"Your sister," Wren said, hoping Moira would connect the dots.

She did.

Moira's eyes widened. "But the Dis-cons down there had been taken, not killed like Luna, right?"

Wren shrugged her shoulders, shaking her head. "We just don't know." Wren held her hand tighter. "I mean, you said Luna died from a blow to the head, right? You saw the facilities down there. If they could make my mom's severed head alive in some way, a hit to the head would be nothing to fix." Wren's entire body cringed when mentioning her mother, but the thought that Moira's sister could potentially be alive helped ease the ache inside her chest.

"There was so much blood though." Moira's eyes were distant now.

Wren tried to bring her back to the present. "This could be a good thing, Moira."

Moira plopped down the rest of the way to the ground. "Oh my god, Wren. I don't want to get my hopes up."

Wren sat down cross-legged, still holding Moira's hand. "We won't. We'll find a safe place where we can phase, and we'll search. There's got to be some kind of record of who was down there and who escaped. If not that, then we'll get access to the cameras and search for her. See if we can spot her."

Moira's breaths were short and choppy, and her hands began to tremble. Forcing her eyes to meet hers, Wren took Moira's other hand as well, trying to steady her. "We will get through this together, no matter what happens, okay?"

Tiny nods of her head, then finally, big deep breaths. "Together." Moira leaned in and hugged Wren tightly. When she pulled away, she was calmer, focused, determined. Moira on a mission. "I have just the spells that will help us," Moira said as she pulled her hands away and reached into her jacket.

"You brought spells with you?" Wren asked.

Shaking her head, she smiled. "Remember when I disappeared down there for a little bit?"

"Yeah?"

Moira pulled out a stack of sealed envelopes. "I may have made a little trip to the vault."

The world's most insane organization and their hidden spells.

And Wren's best friend had stolen them.

"Moira, I love you," Wren exclaimed.

"You better." She grinned. "Now let's get out of here."

Books by Becca C. Smith

The Riser Saga:

Riser

Reaper

Ripper

The Atlas Series:

Atlas

Grigori Returned

The Underworld

Riser Saga/Atlas Series Finale:

Atlas Rising

The Dream Diaries:

The Dream Diaries

The Dream Diaries: Blood Ties

Alexis Tappendorf Series:

Alexis Tappendorf and the Search for Beale's Treasure

Alexis Tappendorf and the Search for Atlantis

Stand alone:

Anna & Bronwyn: Priestesses of Avalon (with Marni L.B. Troop)

Jeraline's Alley

Love & Dark Series (with Hina McCord):

Vessel

First Born

Gutian Code

BIOGRAPHY

Becca fell in love with storytelling at an early age. The first book she read was The Lion, The Witch and The Wardrobe and she's been looking for the door to Narnia ever since! Becca is a passionate reader, consuming anything sci-fi or fantasy. Mix it in with YA and she is a fan for life. So it's no surprise that she writes in these genres as well. When Becca isn't writing, she loves to sew. From Mortal Instruments rune pillows, to elaborate Firefly/ Serenity bags, Becca loves to create!